S.R. Fraser

Elected:
The Book of
Daniel

Printed in the United Kingdom

First Printing, 2018

ISBN-13: 978-1985749276
ISBN-10: 1985749270

Cover design by Louise Darnley

First and foremost, I dedicate this book to my beautiful family: Mum, Dad, Peter, Kayleigh, Nicholas, Arleanna, Callum & Caitlin. I am nothing without your unconditional love and support. I love you forever.

To the girls: Elle, Jenni, Dawn, Lisa, Isabel and Zoe. Thank you for your never-ending encouragement and support. I promise that the sequel is on its way!

To my Fairy Godmother, Ela, who taught me that dreams do come true! There are no words to express how honoured and privileged I am to have you in my life.

To the one who stole my heart…until our paths meet again.

Contents

Prologue

Although Lucas had stood in the chamber countless times, the stench of decay and death always made him nauseous. The ceiling and chamber walls boasted hundreds of engraved religious images and symbols, most covered over by the roots of the trees and plants that had pushed their way through from the earth above. The coldness in the cavern was knife sharp and had tinged his skin a corpse blue. But it was not the air that caused the goose pimples to run up and down his skin like armies of snow white spiders; responsibility lay with the creature sitting before him upon a throne of death.

The throne was perched in isolation upon a platform of grey rock in the middle of the chamber. Lucas began the dreadful walk across the delicately carved ivory bridge that linked the lonely platform to the entrance way landing. Beneath his feet, a monstrous black hole lay in wait to consume those unfortunate enough to fall into its menacing jaws. The bridge creaked and swayed softly from side to side as he walked with impossible grace. Soon he was kneeling with his head bowed, ready to report to his master.

"She's dead." Lucas' voice was strong, and his words laced the air with a thick cloud of icy breath.

"Her husband?"

Baal's voice cut through Lucas, and he felt a million frosty needles pierce his heart and soul. How he did not go blind by setting his gaze upon such a foul and wicked beast he would never know. The words Baal had spoken bounced around the vast chamber and rattled off the stony, plant ridden ceiling. Calmly, Lucas cleared his throat.

"Dead," came his reply, as he took in Baal's demonic appearance.

The demon's face was as white as a blanket of freshly fallen snow, yet it was not bestowed with the same smoothness. Instead of the skin being untouched, it was laden with deep rooted scars from wounds received over millennia of battling his oldest and deadliest enemies. Baal's eyes were his most striking feature, made even more so by his alabaster skin. They were simply blacker than black, like polished onyx, with only a fleck of red in the centre of each eyeball.

The expression of satisfaction on Baal's face was chilling. He'd always taken great delight in death, but this particular occasion was different. The fact that two of his greatest adversaries had fallen made this victory all the more pleasing. He grinned manically and exposed a set of flawlessly twisted teeth complete with vampire like fangs.

"Oh, how the mighty have fallen," Baal said at last, the coldness in his voice snuffing out any warmth left in Lucas. "It's mine…mine at last. After all this time…but then, what is time if not an eternally burning candle?" The demon was about to speak again when a flutter of wings resonated overhead.

In the most delicate fashion, Baal manoeuvred his head and peered up at the ceiling. A large black crow suspended itself in the air, floating against a backdrop of engraved religious imagery.

"Izeel! Oh my dearest Izeel! You have returned," he exclaimed, clapping his hands together in an act more suited to a small child. The crow swept down and landed majestically onto Baal's cloaked shoulder. His eyes closed immediately as the bird brought its beak to his ear and clacked away for a full five minutes. When it was finished, it nibbled his ear affectionately before taking off once more.

"Izeel brings news from London," Baal announced. The soulless eyes opened, and a terrifying grin crept over the demonic face.

"Master?"

Lucas was genuinely curious about any news from the human world. It was important to keep up with the affairs of men as their numbers were growing far too quickly, and their thirst for knowledge and power had bred a dangerous new kind of intellect. On the mainland in which Lucas currently resided on, there had been a lot of unrest between two neighbouring countries for an exceptionally long time. Invasions and wars had become common practice, but the distraction they provided was useful for the demon world. Perhaps Izeel had come with news that it was all over. Lucas prayed that Longshanks had lost.

"It appears the champion of this country, Wallace, has fallen at his enemy's hands. He was executed three months ago in London; hung, drawn and quartered I believe. I do love a public execution. It's a pity I couldn't have been there. No matter, I'm sure I'll forget all about it in the very near future." Baal's grin grew colder and even wider. "Izeel's news is most welcome, but yours, Lucas, is supremely delicious."

Lucas watched as Baal stood up from his throne, the muscles on his perfectly formed forearms rippling as they helped the demon to his feet. The throne itself glowered through black, empty eyes. It was a menagerie of dusty, cracked and chipped skulls, each one claimed by Baal after its owner died fighting valiantly against him.

Baal took a step forward, his usually stony, lifeless eyes suddenly ablaze with the reflected light offered by the candles that lit the chamber. "So, my dearest, you have done well. You were always my favourite, Lucas." Baal's words were unmistakably woven with venom. "Where is it? Where is my Power?"

Lucas felt the tension rising within, but his centuries of training had prepared him for such situations. His angelic features remained passive and neutral, although he suspected that Baal knew of his treachery. A violent wave of fear was threatening to engulf him completely, but his resolve was not washed away. "The Power wasn't with them, and we have no idea where it is."

Lucas didn't see Baal whip his hand through the air, caught no sight of movement as the hand shot backwards with snake like speed before angrily striking forward. He recoiled as his face erupted in pain, the stench of burnt flesh permeating the air. A blazing, angry red mark spread from the corner of his eye down to his chin, the visible result of Baal's outburst.

"Oh, Lucas!" Baal looked shocked and regretful. His expression softened as he reached out to Lucas with skeletal hands that wore dark crimson veins. "Lucas, forgive me." Baal said softly, carefully caressing the fresh wound on Lucas' face. "I must have misheard what you said. I thought you came here without the Power." Baal's voice was almost humane. Almost.

"Master, you heard correctly. The Power has eluded capture." Lucas bowed his head slightly and clenched his teeth.

Baal moved slower this time, and Lucas glimpsed him raising his hand. Even with the impending pain and torture he was about to feel, Lucas still marvelled at the fluidity and grace of Baal's movements. This time, he saw the energy forming in the demon's hand, twisting like a brilliant flaming red viper. Making the same lashing movement as before, Baal brought the newly formed energy screaming through the air like a whip. It cracked off Lucas' face once more and disappeared in a shower of ruby red sparks that crackled and fizzled into thin air.

"FOOL!" Baal screamed, his face now contorted in rage, his body trembling in his terrible fury. The stone walls quaked, and even the darkness quivered at the sound. "IMBECILE! How could you let it escape you? You killed its protectors! How difficult is it to take something which is

8

unprotected?" With every word he bellowed, Baal's vocal cords seemed to tear in protest.

Lucas stood stone still, never daring to clutch at the wound on his face even though it ached and stung painfully. "Metatron. We...I heard he interfered and aided the Elect." Although he stood like a marbled statue, Lucas' mind was frantically trying to find a way to escape, and he hoped this information would buy him enough time.

"The Elect?" Baal hissed, his face now inches from Lucas'. "The Elect, apart from *him*, are no more! I destroyed them all myself. I crushed each and every one of their beating hearts between my hands! Look!" he commanded, gesturing furiously towards his throne of death. "Look at how I sit upon their worthless bones. It must be found!"

"But master, it's true! Three other Elect members survived your persecution and were hidden by Metatron and Uriel. They also escaped our most recent attack and have gone into hiding. Motaris and Natalya have scoured the entire country, but there are no traces of them. They've even evaded the Templars."

"IDIOT!" Baal conjured the familiar scarlet whip and swung it in Lucas' direction. The demon's face contained mild surprise mixed with amusement as the whip bounced off a magnificent blue blade. The surrounding air ignited with colourful confetti like sparks as the two energies collided together. In the following silence, Baal could sense the fear radiating from Lucas.

"I wondered when we would get to this point," Baal finally said, eyeing up the samurai style sword that Lucas had summoned to his defence. "I've long suspected that you were plotting against me, a disgusting spy amongst my legions, but I gave you the benefit of my doubts."

"You should have listened to your instincts," Lucas fired back.

Baal chuckled and began to circle his prey. A black forked tongue flickered out from his mouth and moistened his lips. "Young Lucas, how foolish you have been. Before I kill you, I wonder if you could do me the smallest of favours?"

Lucas didn't respond and tried to pierce Baal with a stare of pure hatred.

Baal continued. "Answer me this—just how much is your betrayal costing Him? What did He offer you? What was your price?"

Lucas drew himself up to his full height, his blond hair cascading down to his shoulder blades, his eyes alive with a blazing blue fire. "He gave me the freedom to return home."

The demon stopped. He stared in pure disbelief, and then gave the tiniest little shudder as an unearthly giggle escaped his mouth. The giggle turned into a chuckle which in turn became hysterical laughter. Baal's unpleasant merriment echoed through the black cavernous surroundings as he succumbed to the hilarity of Lucas' statement.

Having eventually composed himself, Baal looked once more at the fallen angel with an expression that almost resembled pity. "He lied to you," he sneered. "Once cast out of heaven, you can never return. You were used, you poor fool, like so many. He knows as well as I do that a traitor, any kind of traitor, belongs to *our* God."

"He promised me!" Lucas snapped, never before despising a creature as much as the twisted and foul being in front of him.

"He also promised the angels that we'd be made and valued a little higher than the plague of humanity, but look how He favours them, and how He has forsaken you to die at my hands!" Baal crowed, thoroughly enjoying berating Lucas. "His promises mean nothing, little one, and you'll be remembered in history as the hapless fool who died because of a false promise. You don't get the rainbow at the end of your story."

"His promise has been kept!" Lucas bellowed, the white tunic covering his torso tearing completely as a pair of lavishly white feathered wings exploded from his back. "He keeps his promises, Baal, son of evil, and now it is time for you to return to the abyss that spawned you!"

"Traitor!" Baal screeched, sprouting his own wings and reducing his black cloak to tatters. Apart from being bigger and black like the night, the demon's wings were identical in every way to Lucas' angelic ones. Baal spread his wings wide and pulled an enormous blade out of thin air. "Are you sure you're ready to die?" he asked.

Lucas responded by leaping forward and swinging his sword ferociously. The clanging of metal rattled through the air as the blades clashed together repeatedly, the scraping of steel on steel singing loudly as the angel and demon danced in a battle to the death. Although Lucas fought valiantly, it was not long until he made his first, and last, mistake. He appeared to have bested Baal and knocked the claymore like blade from the demon's hand, but as he leapt through the air to land the final blow, he realised to his horror that he'd been lured into a trap.

The scarlet whip of demonic energy was around his neck before he could reach his target, and Lucas found himself pulled to the floor. He landed harshly and dropped his sword. "Ba...al!" he croaked, his eyes pleading with his former master.

Baal's lips were pulled back in an evil grin, and a laughter like sound rasped from his mouth. "It hurts, doesn't it?" he goaded before yanking the energy whip towards himself. Lucas spiralled through the air and crashed against the stone floor while Baal cackled mercilessly. "Have you forgotten what happens to traitors?" he asked softly, watching his victim writhe in pain. As an answer to his own question, Baal rained down countless lashings upon the angel.

Lucas lay face down on the ground at the feet of the demon, fearing he was going to die. He screamed out when Baal's foot crashed down onto his back and pinned him to the stone floor. He shuddered when ice cold hands lovingly stroked his brand new wings.

"They are beautiful, Lucas. They really are something." Baal caressed the wings, appreciating them as if they were something priceless and precious. "It would be such a shame, seeing as they are so new, if something truly awful were to happen to them."

There was no mistaking the intention in Baal's voice, and as he took a vice like grip on Lucas' wings, the angel thrashed and bucked, but it was all in vain.

Lucas heard the ripping of flesh and bone as one of his wings was torn from his back. Of all the wounds he'd ever received, and of all the pains he'd ever endured in the countless centuries of battling in a never ending war, this wound and pain was by far the most excruciating that he'd ever been inflicted with. It felt like his shoulder blade had been scorched by the very flames of hell.

Lucas' cries of anguish filled Baal with a euphoria he only ever felt when torturing another being. The demon shuddered ecstatically as the second wing suffered the same fate. He watched Lucas press his trembling hands into the ground and push himself up onto all fours as blood pumped from the wounds. Baal chuckled when the angel retched and coughed up dark red liquid.

"You make me angry, Lucas. You were my favourite. For millennia I've looked at you and seen nothing but loyalty. Now? Now you stink of betrayal." Baal delivered a swift but powerful kick into Lucas' ribs and shivered in pleasure when he heard a cracking sound. "I will find what the Elect have stolen from me, make no mistake about that. They can't hide that kind of power forever no matter how cleverly concealed. Sooner or later, someone will slip up, and when they do, my sons and daughters will be ready."

Baal paused to let his words sink in before setting his gaze upon the wings he held in his hands. "These will look simply divine on my throne, don't you think?" he said, his tone suddenly warm and friendly. He turned from his victim and carried the wings over to his chair of bones. On either side of the chair, he attached a wing by jamming it into the spaces he found between the skulls. Once both were securely in place, he stepped back, admiring his new addition. "Yes, I think it gives it a touch of elegance. Thank you."

Lucas shook his head from side to side in an attempt to shake off the pain that was making him slip into a state of semi-consciousness. Coming to his senses, he turned his head to find that Baal was busy adorning his throne. With one hand, he reached for his sword which lay close by. He couldn't quite reach it without moving, so he gritted his teeth and dragged himself across the cold stone.

As Lucas gripped the handle weakly, he started to pray. Streams of vapour licked the air as he murmured an incantation at great speed. Speed was essential; he could already feel the effects of losing his angelic wings taking hold. The veins in his hand were already beginning to darken. The sword glowed a light blue as he chanted, and the building energy radiated and warmed his marred face. The unmistakable sound of a steel blade scraping off the stone floor filled Lucas' ears, and he knew that his enemy was now armed again. Footsteps sounded and gradually grew louder as he lay there like a trapped fly crippled in a web, helpless and pathetic as the predator stalked forward. Baal's icy voice filled the cavern, bearing a likeness to the cry of a thousand tormented souls.

"I'm going to show you mercy," the demon began, running the tip of his blade over the fresh wounds on the fallen angel's back. "I'm going to end it all for you so you won't have to suffer. I know you've suffered, Lucas. I've known for a very long time that you were working against me. I have to say I didn't believe it at first, but when the overwhelming evidence was brought to my attention, I couldn't deny the truth any longer." Baal jabbed the sword into one of the wounds causing Lucas to scream out in agony, bringing yet another smile to the demon's lips.

"Your suffering will continue after I end your existence on this plane because you are a traitor. As I've already explained, traitors belong to Lucifer, and he is just dying to see you again. Before you die, you simply must see how your wings give my throne that extra special touch." Baal reached down, grabbed Lucas by the head, and yanked him up.

The demon's taunting had incensed Lucas, enabling him to reach deep inside of himself and find the strength to fight back. He moved with lightning speed and drove his enchanted samurai blade through the demon's chest, the hilt grinding to a halt at the bone. The unexpected turn of events caused Baal to stagger backwards and slump to his knees. A river of black blood ran down his torso.

Seizing his opportunity, Lucas viciously kicked the demon in the face and sent him crashing to the ground before stumbling towards the ivory bridge, while all the time trying to block out the agonising pain that coursed through his body. As he ran, blood poured down his back, soaking and tainting his golden hair. The bridge swung dangerously as he tried to manoeuvre quickly and carefully across it.

When he was half way across, he looked back to see Baal wrenching the blade out of his chest, releasing a fresh fountain of inky blood that spurted in all directions. Lucas tore his eyes away and concentrated on crossing the bridge.

Meanwhile, on the lonely platform, the bleeding from Baal's chest had subsided, and the wound began to heal. It happened slowly at first, but then accelerated until it had closed completely. Roaring like the ferocious beast he was, he opened his wings to their full span and leapt into the air, shooting straight towards Lucas who was almost at the other end of the bridge.

Lucas knew that if Baal caught him, there was no chance of survival. He kept his eyes locked firmly ahead, focusing on the small opening in the chamber that would lead him to safety. As he approached the end of the swinging ivory, he heard the thrashing of wings behind him, and a brand new surge of fear and adrenaline spurned him on faster. His feet hit stone, and he knew he was off the bridge. Every muscle in his body screamed in protest, but they powered through, carrying him closer to the exit. He could practically feel Baal's breath on his neck which prompted him to thunder on. Yards away from safety, Lucas suddenly dropped to the floor.

In his blind rage at being stabbed and kicked, Baal had been flying at full speed to ensure that he would catch Lucas and cause him unspeakable suffering for daring to impale him with his angelic blade. Just as he was about to snatch the wingless angel in mid-flight, his talons hit nothing but cool cavern air. In the following confusion, Baal went hurtling into the cave wall just above the exit and crashed to the floor in a crumpled heap of black feathered wings.

If Lucas hadn't been in mortal danger, he would have laughed at the demon's stupidity, but he knew better than to stall. He jumped to his feet, despite the objections from every cell in his body, and leapt over Baal.

He dived through the threshold and into the alcove where he proceeded to stagger up the spiral staircase that would lead him out of hell. Baal's roars of fury chased after him like demented spirits as he took the steps two at a time while clinging to the slimy cave walls for support.

After an eternity of roughly wooden hewn stairs, he reached a rotting wooden door at the top and burst through it into a large church. The church was in complete darkness, but Lucas was so familiar with the building he knew exactly where to go. He fumbled about in the dark, holding onto the backs of the benches so he didn't trip or fall. The thought of Baal's minions coming after him encouraged him to keep moving as fast as he possibly could in his current state.

Lucas saw moonlight peeking through the cracks in a sturdy double door, and he knew he'd reached the entrance to the church: his salvation. He bolted towards them and pointed his palms at the beam of wood which acted as the doors' locking mechanism. Two orbs of dazzling white energy erupted from his hands and shot off to fulfil their mission. The holy orbs collided with the beam and reduced it to kindling. Using the remainder of his strength, he pushed against the doors and stumbled out into the courtyard which was bathed in exquisite silver moonlight.

Moving through the courtyard, a thick carpet of snow crunched beneath his feet. A slight breeze ruffled the snow speckled trees and bushes that decorated the church grounds and soothed the burning pain of his wounds. It was under the moon's watchful eye that he finally collapsed under the weight of the horrific damage done to his earthly body. He lay, soaked in his own blood, looking up at the millions of stars that sprinkled the black canvas above him.

"Help...me."

The faintest of whispers escaped his lips before the stars became blurry. He'd failed his mission, and *He* had forsaken him like Baal said He would.

As he lay in the snowy courtyard, he knew that all was lost. Baal's minions would find him soon, and he'd be dragged back down into the demon's filthy lair where he would be forced to spill the shocking secrets of the Elect, ending their noble quest to avert the second fall of humanity and the following apocalypse. Baal would find the weapon he needed to reign on Earth for all eternity, and there was nobody left who had the power to stop him. Tears spilled from Lucas' eyes as defeat gripped him. Each tear witnessed the twinkling lights of heaven before falling from his face and disappearing into the red stained pillow of snow that lay beneath his angelic head.

CHAPTER 1
LEO

"Okay guys, have a great weekend, and I'll see you all on Monday."

Leo dismissed the class after the high pitched shrilling of the school bell came to a halt.

An army of twenty nine children made for the classroom door, erupting in chatter about the upcoming weekend. Leo stood by the open door and waved the students goodbye as they marched towards freedom.

"Oh, and remember your maths homework for first thing Monday morning. Especially you, Joe! Your homework has yet to come in on time. Tuesday is not Monday."

"Uh huh. Mine will be the first one on your desk, Mr Alexander!" Joe called back, a beaming grin plastered on his face.

"I'll hold you to that, Mr Saunders!" Leo said with a hearty chuckle, knowing full well there would be more chance of hell freezing over.

Some of the other teachers in the school would have lynched him by now without asking questions. In fact, most of the teachers who had taught the child in previous years had done nothing but run him down, warning him about the terror that was Joe Saunders. Like always, Leo had taken the dire warnings with a pinch of salt, reserving judgement until he'd gotten to know Joe.

It turned out that Joe was from an extremely deprived background with abusive parents. Those other teachers didn't care enough to ask Joe where the bruises had come from, or how he'd broken his arm, or how the cigarette burns kept appearing, but Leo did. Joe had instantly trusted Leo, or as the children called him, Mr Alexander, and shared the horrifying secrets of his family life with his teacher. It didn't take long for Leo to alert social services. Joe was now living with a thrilled foster family who treated him as one of their own and, aside from handing homework in, was thriving in all areas of his life.

After the last of the students had filtered out of the class, Leo turned his attention to his desk which was usually overflowing with jotters, textbooks, piles of pencils and precisely three large mugs at the end of each teaching day.

He sighed in relief when greeted by an immaculately tidy desk. His laptop was placed exactly where he liked it: the edges parallel to the sides of the desk and in line with his chair. The laptop was flanked by a desk tidy where all the pens and pencils stood the same way up, the rubbers were all together in the proper compartment, and each sharpener was placed with precision into their designated spaces. Perfect. In many areas of his life he allowed chaos to reign, however, when it came to certain things such as his desk at the end of the week, he was compulsive.

He pulled out the chair from under the desk and got himself comfortable, stretching out the stresses of the working week. He reached over to open the laptop when he noticed a luminous green post-it note stuck in the centre. A grin spread across his face as he read it. *'Another bomb exploded on your desk, so I tidied it. Have a great weekend! Daniel.'*

He crumpled the note and threw it towards the bin, rolling his eyes after watching it hit the rim and fall to the floor. He'd get it later. After making a mental note to thank Daniel on Monday, he started up the laptop and drummed his fingers gently on the desk, humming a Kylie song as he waited. His mind wandered while waiting for the programs to load, and he found himself thinking about how lucky he was to have a job he truly loved.

He was in his fifth year of teaching and had already built up an excellent reputation as a firm but fair teacher despite being only twenty six years old. He'd moved away from Inverness to study in Aberdeen for four years but returned after graduating. His heart lay in his hometown, and he wasn't ashamed to admit it. He'd completed his first two years in a small country school before landing a job at a much bigger establishment. Wherever he went, the children seemed to adore him, and he had no problems maintaining a positive and effective learning environment. It was true, he was strict when he was teaching but always made room for laughter. The children respected the boundaries and rules that were set in place, and his current class practically skipped to school, as did he.

He would never admit it out loud for fear of being labelled unprofessional, but he loved his job and always grew to love the kids he taught, treating each and every one of them equally. Each year, however, there seemed to always be a child in his class that brought out paternal feelings in him; this year was no different.

Pushing all of these happy thoughts to the back of his mind, he typed in his log-in details and password before running a hand through his short brown hair and letting out a big yawn.

"Tired, Mr A?"

Leo jumped up and cursed when he battered both knees off his desk. "Jeez, Wendy. Don't sneak up on me like that. You almost gave me a heart attack." He rubbed his knees to dull the ache and let his expression of pain turn into one of adoration. "What can I do for you, my lovely lady?"

Wendy laughed. "I'm sorry. I did knock, but you were obviously too engrossed. Here, these were in your mail box." She threw down a small pile of envelopes and perched on the edge of the desk. "Plans for the weekend?"

Leo picked up the envelopes, arranged them in size order from biggest to smallest, and placed them neatly back on the desk before looking up at Wendy.

At five foot six inches, she was the same height as him but looked younger than he did despite being four years older. She was slightly pale with perfectly smooth skin and long brown shimmering hair that cascaded down to her shoulder blades. It was usually straight, but today she'd worn it in long curls. The lavish curls rested on a casual white blouse which she had teamed with a plain black pencil skirt and black Jimmy Choos.

He greeted her question with a smug smirk. "Well, Miss Westwater, seeing as I have managed to mark all of my kids work during lunch break, *and* seeing as I will have finished planning my lessons for Monday within the next hour, I shall be as free as a bird."

Wendy's bright blue eyes twinkled. "Saturday will be a fabulous mix of shopping, lunch, more shopping, home, dinner, beautify ourselves, drinks, drinks and more drinks."

"I am *loving* that plan of action," Leo grinned. "Dinner tonight? Highland Stag Inn? Four thirty?"

"Plan in motion," Wendy said, hopping off the desk and kissing him swiftly on the cheek. "Highland Stag sounds awesome. See you soon." She headed for the door, her stiletto heels clicking as she walked. "By the way, Golden Boy did a good job." She stopped and turned around with a knowing look on her face, her eyes roaming Leo's immaculately tidy desk.

"Golden Boy?" The look of pure innocence that was etched on his face wouldn't fool her, but he liked to play the part.

"Golden Boy," she repeated, lightly waving a hand in the direction of his desk.

"Wendy, my sweet, you know as well as I do that I don't have favourites amongst my students, and that includes Daniel."

Wendy's expression was one of pure triumph. "I didn't say it was Daniel, did I?" She winked. "See you at four thirty." The clicking of her heels grew fainter as she disappeared up the corridor until all that could be heard was the droning of the cleaner's vacuum.

He shook his head gently from side to side and laughed before turning his attentions back to the whirring machine lying in front of him. "Oh, come on," he said to the laptop which was still trying to log him in.

He resumed drumming his fingers on the desk, looking down when they came into contact with the letters that Wendy had delivered. He picked the pile up.

"Crap...crap...crap..." he muttered to himself as he sifted through them. From the printed labels and HC stamp he could tell they were from the Highland Council. He assumed they were all to do with the current pay cuts, pension cuts, resource cuts, and every other cut the council were trying to justify in order to defeat the recession. Of course, the big directors of the council wouldn't be taking any cuts at all and had the best of everything in their cosy offices where they had people employed with the sole purpose of running around making them cups of tea.

He threw the letters back down in disgust but then noticed he'd missed one. It was the smallest letter in the pile and had somehow managed to lodge itself between the desk and the laptop. He pulled it out.

Like the others, it was in a plain white envelope, but the name and address were hand written in red ink. The style of handwriting was unusual yet beautiful. It was the kind of writing, he thought, that looked like it was from Victorian times or an even older period. He sat up a little straighter, took a deep breath, turned the envelope around, and began to unseal it.

The envelope contained a small, neatly folded piece of paper which he freed and unfolded carefully. He hadn't realised he'd been holding his breath until his reflexes kicked in, forcing him to exhale. There was something about the unknown that made him uneasy. Every time his mobile phone rang with an unknown or withheld number, he would get the same feeling. It was as if a withheld phone number or an unknown letter was going to provide him with unpleasant news of some sort which was never the case. He read the note through twice, turned it over repeatedly, and examined it to make sure there was nothing else written on it.

The note wasn't threatening. The note didn't contain any unpleasantness. The note didn't contain anything to get nervous about. All it contained was a few words written in the same beautiful handwriting as the name and address. It read, *'Meet me at 7:30pm, Canal Gates. Come alone.'* Did it mean seven thirty tonight? There was no day or date to indicate exactly when the meeting was to take place.

He picked up the envelope again and looked at the place where the postage stamp was meant to be. There was no postage stamp which meant the envelope had been hand delivered to the school. Suddenly, it all made sense to him. The janitor sorted out the mail. He and the janitor had an ongoing battle of playing practical jokes on each other. This had Rob the janitor written all over it. As he tucked the note back inside the envelope, he amused himself with the thought that Rob would be expecting him to be waiting in the freezing cold of early January for ages. In reality, he'd thwarted the janitor's feeble attempt at a practical joke. He made a mental note to begin plotting revenge at his earliest convenience.

"Finally!" he grumbled as the computer programs finally launched.

An hour later, he had completed the weekly plan for next week's lessons, organised all of his teaching resources for Monday, and even looked out a gas mask and some rationing coupons. A quick sweep around the classroom revealed that Shae, Alfie and Will had forgotten to check under their tables for dropped pencils, but other than those three usual suspects, the room was tidied to the high standard that Mr Alexander had come to expect from his students.

Once satisfied that all was as it should be in the classroom, he walked to the door, removed the door stop and glanced down the corridor to make sure that nobody was about. He closed the door and stepped back into the middle of the room where he shut his eyes and took a deep breath. Once he was completely relaxed, he held out his left hand with the palm facing upwards. There wasn't a sound in the room except for the faint whispered chants coming from his mouth. He chanted like this for a few minutes, and with each passing word, the tiniest orb of light appeared out of nowhere about an inch above his palm. The light was tiny at first, perhaps the size of a fly, and it was pale green in colour. As the chanting progressed, the tiny orb began to grow until it was the size of an apple.

The speed of Leo's chanting increased until the words seemed to merge into one long ramble. He was growing hot now, and beads of sweat had formed on his forehead as the pale green orb turned a dazzling emerald colour.

He stopped chanting abruptly. His eyes flew open. The soft green irises that usually lived there were gone, and the whites of his eyes were non-existent. Instead, each eye seemed to be a blazing emerald flame that matched the colour of the orb.

"Cleanse."

On speaking the word, he lifted the orb high above his head where it erupted into rays of brilliant green light that bounced off every wall, every window, and every structure it could reach. He watched as they engulfed all the unseen energies in the room, strengthening the positive and burning away the negative. Once they had completed their task, the rays were slowly sucked back into the orb.

Dropping his hand to where it had started originally, he watched the orb shrink as its light faded like the dying embers of a fire. He could tell his eyes were reverting back to their natural state; he could feel it.

Soon, it was like nothing out of the ordinary had happened. Nobody would have been able to tell that a moment ago he'd summoned mystical energies. He, however, could feel the powerful effects of the spell he carried out routinely every Friday. The air was clearer, and there was a feeling of calmness and tranquillity permeating the room. Inwardly, he thanked the Divine for the love and protection he received daily and for blessing all who entered this room.

Teaching was his passion; he lived for his job. But he had also fallen in love with something else: magic. Witchcraft was the other passion in his life, and one he kept ruthlessly hidden, even from Wendy. It was a taboo subject to most people, and he knew of those who had flirted with it, bought a published book of spells, and called themselves a witch. This label lasted until being a druid was 'in' and being a witch was 'last season'. These were the people who tried a few incantations and gave up when met with failure. For him, it had been very different. He could actually make magic work. It'd been a terrifying experience when, at sixteen, he'd conjured his first energy sphere and couldn't get rid of it for over an hour. Ten years later, he was far more adept and spent his free time conjuring the elements, summoning fire, earth, air and water whenever he required them. It was like having handy tools. When he found himself without a lighter for his cigarette, he simply summoned the element of fire and was on his merry way. Magic was his own escape from reality, and he dearly cherished the gift from the Divine. As far as he was aware, nobody he knew could utilise magic like him, so he felt that there was no need to share his mystical talents with anyone else. Besides, a lot of the residents in Inverness were staunchly Christian. Any whisper of the occult or magic and it was Satan's work, an abomination. Suddenly, he could picture mobs armed with pitchforks and blazing torches.

After pulling on his black duffle coat and wrapping his dark green woollen scarf tightly around his neck, he checked to ensure he had his wallet and car keys before leaving the sanctuary of his classroom. It was time to celebrate the weekend. As usual, he popped his head in to the other three teachers who worked in the upper school department and bid them a good night.

He walked out of the upper school corridor and into the tunnel that joined the infant and upper departments together, pulling his jacket tighter around himself as an invisible and freezing mist enveloped him. He could see his breath coming out in a thick cloud as he hurried through the glass tunnel.

Reaching the reception area of the school, he found Wendy sitting on one of the chairs, flicking through a magazine. She too was wrapped up tightly, except she wore a luxurious purple coat that reached down to her knees. Her slender frame was highlighted by a belted waist.

"Hope you haven't been waiting long for me, love," Leo said as he approached her.

Wendy stood up and closed the magazine, her thumb tucked into the page that she'd been reading. "I just got here. As usual, your timing is perfect. It's like you're psychic or something. Let's hurry, I'm bloody starving!" She smiled and looped her arm through his, and together they walked out into the wintery darkness of January.

A few flakes of snow danced through the air like tiny fairies while they walked to the car. Wendy told him that she was getting her hair done tomorrow and showed him a picture from her magazine of the style she'd decided on. As he climbed into the driver's seat, he agreed the style would suit her. When they were both in and buckled up, he pulled out of the car park and began the drive to the restaurant.

"Did you have a good day?" he asked, his eyes vigilantly fixed on the road and scanning for potential hazards. The snow was falling faster now, and the snowflake fairies danced more erratically.

"It was fine. The kids were great, but I'm exhausted. I don't know what's wrong with me. I seem to be fine in the morning, but by the afternoon, I just want to send the kids home and fall asleep on my desk." She yawned as if to prove her point.

Leo grinned. "That fiancé of yours keeping you up at night?"

Wendy smiled knowingly and blushed at the same time. "Something like that," she replied, reaching over to turn on the radio and indicating that particular subject was closed.

A comfortable silence emerged between them, and for a lengthy time, the pair were lost in their own thoughts while the radio hummed along quietly.

Leo excited himself with thoughts about Saturday night. He thoroughly enjoyed the clubbing scene, especially with Wendy. They were both as bad as each other and laughed and danced their way through the night. Most Saturdays they could be found in The Den with a drink in one hand, a cigarette in the other, and engaging in some hilarious gossip that caused tears of hysteric laughter to run down their faces.

"Have you heard from Tyler yet?"

Wendy's question pulled him out of his weekend reverie. It was only a matter of time before the Tyler subject would be brought up. After all, the weekend was upon them.

"No, I haven't," he replied, "and I don't expect to until tomorrow afternoon."

"Yeah, the standard text to see if you're going out which means he'll get laid."

He didn't miss the venom in his friend's voice. She was fiercely protective of him, and heaven help anyone who upset Leo Alexander in her presence.

"It's all good, Wends. Don't get yourself worked up about it."

Wendy couldn't contain herself. "But how can you let him use you like that? It's been eight months now, and the only time he contacts you is to get his rocks off. You're way better than that."

Leo took his time to respond. He felt the first stirrings of anger and hurt building, and he had to be careful that he didn't direct these feelings at Wendy. It wasn't her fault he was allowing himself to be used by Tyler. It wasn't her fault that Tyler only contacted him on a Saturday night in the hope he'd get a leg over. It wasn't her fault he'd never had a boyfriend and was secretly hoping that Tyler would develop feelings for him. It wasn't her fault he'd sit at home all week, diving for his phone every single time a text message came through only to feel the sting of disappointment on discovering the message wasn't from Tyler. They were *never* from Tyler. Leo knew he was angry and hurt because of the situation, but it was rare that any man showed interest in him. Having Tyler was better than having nothing at all. He cleared his throat.

"I'm cool about it, honestly. He's tall, dark and handsome, and an awesome kisser. What more do I need?"

"How about someone who actually respects you enough not to use you for sex? Or how about a guy who cares about you and will treat you the way you deserve to be treated?"

"Well…" He could see her winning smile as he faltered. "On nights out he pays for all of our drinks and the taxi home. And last week, after the club, he bought me a McDonald's before we went back to my place. I mean, he is a nice guy."

A laugh exploded from Wendy's mouth. "Jesus Christ! I've heard it all now. The way to Leo's heart and into his pants is a McDonald's!"

He had to join in with Wendy's laughter; it was infectious. "You know all it takes to get me into bed is a Big Mac meal and a caramel sundae," he quipped, resuming the laughter.

Wendy eventually calmed down long enough to continue the conversation, and she reached over and placed her hand over his. "You know I'm just looking out for you, right?"

"I know you are," he assured her, giving her a warm smile.

"I just feel you're selling yourself short with Tyler. He isn't even out of the closet yet for crying out loud. But, if that's what you want to do, then I'll not interfere." The Tyler topic of conversation was brought to a close, and the topic of Wendy's Valentine's Day wedding was opened.

"What do you still need to do?" Leo asked as he pulled into the car park of the Highland Stag Inn.

Leo killed the engine and stepped out onto a crunchy layer of snow. He locked the car after Wendy had evacuated herself. They walked towards the restaurant as the snow fell heavily, and he listened as his friend listed the final tasks still left to do for her big day.

"I don't know what flowers to have yet. I have the florist on Sunday at eleven. That'll be fun with a hangover—not! The final dress fittings are on Monday after school so I'll just take my own car to work that day as I need to leave straight after the bell. The last thing on my list is for Alex to get his kilt. Then in five weeks, I'll be getting married!"

Leo felt her squeeze his arm excitedly, and he allowed her to snuggle into him as they walked. It was then he noticed that she was shivering. "That's brilliant. I can't believe how quickly it's come around. It feels like it was only yesterday that he proposed to you," he said, wrapping an arm around her shoulders.

He found it odd that she was so cold seeing as she was dressed for winter. Perhaps, he thought, she was feeling the cold more because she was tired from working all day. There was also the fact that she hadn't been feeling her best for a couple of days, and with all the wedding hype, she was bound to be feeling run down.

"I know. Time flies when you're having fun, and Alex and I…well, we have our fun." When they reached the restaurant door, Wendy pushed it open. "Ladies first," she teased.

28

Leo bowed his head. "Thank you so much." He laughed lightly as he stepped through the door and began unravelling his scarf. As he was removing his scarf, a tall woman with a massive smile and an even bigger bust greeted them.

"Hi there, welcome to the Highland Stag. My name is Rhonda, and I'm the restaurant manager for the evening."

Rhonda was a blonde, vivacious woman with curves in all the right places. She was dressed in a black skirt and a white blouse and wore her hair in a perfectly woven pleat. Leo noted that there was not one single hair out of place.

"Table for two?" Rhonda asked brightly.

Before either of them had a chance to respond, Rhonda had grabbed two menus and was off towards an empty table situated by a window. They were guided through the busy restaurant as waiters and waitresses bustled around carrying platefuls of food, taking orders, and clearing tables. Every single one of them was focused on earning as many tips as they possibly could. Rhonda seated them, handed out the menus, told them the specials, took a drinks order, and was on the move once more. Another waiter appeared moments later with two glasses of coke.

"Rhonda will be back very shortly to take your order," he said before taking off towards the bar.

Leo sipped from his glass and took a moment to scan the other diners in the restaurant. One thing he loved to do was people watch. People fascinated him, and he always invented little stories to go with each person. Rhonda returned at that moment and took their orders, encouraging them to take the extra side of onion rings.

"Be a devil. It's Friday night!" she chuckled, and then promptly left again to help the drinks waiter who had just sent a tray of cocktails crashing to the floor.

Leo had scanned the room several times before he noticed that Wendy was watching him. "What?" he asked, knowing fine she was going to pull him up on the game he was playing.

"You're doing it again, aren't you?" She rolled her eyes when he flashed her a toothy grin. "Go on then," she said, turning her head nonchalantly so she could pick a target.

It was all part of the game. She'd pick somebody and he would give her their 'story' or what he *thought* their story was. Her eyes examined the unsuspecting diners for a few moments. "Cute blond over by the buffet bar, sitting alone," she said, picking up the cocktail menu and trying not to look too conspicuous.

Leo let his napkin fall to ground. He shuffled his chair backwards and leant down to pick it up, stealing a glance at the guy in question. Once he rescued the napkin, he pulled his seat back into place. "Aw, he's reading his menu now. I can't see his face. Choose someone else."

"I don't think you'd want me to choose someone else. Wait for him to put down the menu. Trust me, you'll fall in love." Wendy began to giggle.

"I can't keep up a prolonged stare. Stalker much?" he protested with a giggle. "Besides, they have to be incredibly gorgeous before I fall in love and get slapped with a restraining order. You know how high my standards are, and how I—"

Leo stopped talking, and it wasn't through choice. His breath caught in his throat, and he was pretty sure his heart had stopped beating.

The menu was gone, replaced by a breath taking view of ocean blue eyes, cropped blond hair, high cheekbones, perfectly formed lips and a strong chiselled jaw. He guessed the Adonis, who was currently running his finger down the side of a glass of water, was in his late twenties or very early thirties. Suddenly, the ocean blue eyes met with his.

Leo quickly looked away and reached out to his drink. The glass was closer than he realised, and his hand collided with it, spilling coke all over the table. "Shit!" he cursed, jumping up quickly. He threw his napkin over the spillage and tried to minimise the damage.

A few diners looked over; some chuckled, some looked sympathetic, and some wore expressions of distaste, probably because of the language he'd used. He noted the blond guy didn't seem to be paying any attention to the chaos and was apparently checking out the dessert stands. On closer inspection, Leo could swear there was a hint of a smile forming on the blondie's face.

"I'm so embarrassed!" he hissed at Wendy, who was laughing while at the same time trying to help clean up the mess with her own napkin.

Rhonda was over in a flash with a large cloth in hand and a tray containing a fresh glass of coke and two starters. She had also brought her smile.

"It's okay, Sir. Don't worry about it. It happens more often than not."

She had the puddle under control in no time, and soon there was no evidence of the coke carnage that had happened moments before. Leo apologised numerous times to the Duty Manager as she placed the starters on the table.

"Enjoy your starters," she said with sincerity and departed to seat new guests.

Wendy began her inquisition. "What was all that about? You totally freaked out."

"I did not 'freak' out, thank you very much," Leo responded indignantly. "I just got caught. He made eye contact, and I wasn't expecting it. He's beautiful!"

Wendy let out another infectious giggle which lightened his mood. "What's his story then?" she asked, stuffing a piece of haggis into her mouth.

He swallowed a mouthful of peppers before responding. "Well, if I was going to guess," he began, while stealing another look at the guy who was now cutting into what looked like a piece of chocolate fudge cake, "I'd say this dude is an accountant. Working late at the office tonight, popped in here for a quick bite to eat. Wife and four kids. A girl, twin boys and another girl." Leo glanced over once more and noticed the Adonis had raised an eyebrow as if he had somehow heard what was being said.

Wendy scoffed. "Oh please! You can do better than that. Look at him for Christ's sake. He's like an Abercrombie and Fitch model!"

Leo chuckled. "Okay." He thought for a minute, and then it came to him. "He's an angel. He's been sent to Earth by God because he went rogue and now has to make it up by living a human existence. We'll meet again as fate dictates it. He'll fall in love with me, and I'll get lost forever in those beautiful, oceanic eyes. He'll find redemption on Earth, and he'll be welcomed back into heaven. Except…"

"Except what?" Wendy prodded, finishing the last of her haggis starter.

"Except," he continued, really getting into his stride, "he spurns his chance to enter heaven again, for the time being, because he's so in love with me that he couldn't bear to leave me, even for a few decades. We grow old and die together, then leave this mortal coil and live eternally in the paradise we call heaven. They'll write stories about us, like David and Jonathon." He grinned before stealing another glance.

To his utter amazement, Adonis was wearing a huge grin. Once again, Leo had this ridiculous feeling that the handsome man was somehow listening in to their conversation, however, the relentlessly noisy restaurant between their tables made this feeling null and void.

"That's more like it, Mr Alexander," Wendy beamed. "So much more entertaining than some boring accountant! Do one more."

"Sure," Leo agreed, pushing his empty plate away and waiting while Wendy did her usual search.

She took a few seconds to explore before turning around. Leo opened his mouth to say something, but both the expression and colour on his friend's face stopped him. She'd gone from the picture of health to looking like death warmed up in mere seconds. "Oh my god, are you alright, honey?" he asked, his face etched with concern.

"I don't feel so-" she began to explain before being interrupted by a convulsion that rocked her entire body. Her hand shot straight to her mouth. "I think I'm gonna hurl!" She took off from the table and dashed through the restaurant, disappearing into the toilets.

Leo found that he didn't quite know what to do with himself. He knew he couldn't just walk into the female toilets, but he wanted to make sure Wendy was okay. Five minutes later, a smiling Rhonda came over to clear the table, and his friend still hadn't returned.

"Excuse me, Rhonda. My friend wasn't feeling well, and she had to go the bathroom. I know you're extremely busy, but she's been gone for almost five minutes now and — Wendy!"

Wendy made her return to the table and sat down as Rhonda took away the empty plates. Her hands were shaking, and her face was an unpleasant shade of grey.

"I think we should get you home. No offense, Wends, but you look horrendous."

She gave a weak smile. Beads of sweat had formed on her forehead, she was flushed, and she had strands of hair sticking to parts of her face. "Cheers for being honest, friend. I think you're right though. I'm sorry for bailing, but I feel like I've been run over by a truck. Maybe it was the haggis?" While still seated in her chair, she pulled on her coat before picking up her scarf. "No, it couldn't have been the haggis. I didn't feel right when we left work. I was so cold before, but now it's like I'm burning up—oh god!"

With impressive speed, the scarf was flung onto the table, and she was up and dodging the waiting staff in an attempt to get to the toilet again.

By the time she'd returned from the second round of vomiting, Leo had explained to a very understanding and concerned Rhonda about Wendy's situation, paid for the little food and drink they'd already consumed and was waiting patiently, holding her scarf and hand bag in his arms.

"Let's get you home," he said sympathetically while rubbing her back.

As they made their way to the exit, he stole a final glance at Adonis. Leo's eyes met with the piercing azure blue of his, and his mind went completely blank, lost in the depths of two endless oceans. His heart leapt up into his throat when Adonis winked at him before turning to speak with one of the waitresses who was fawning over him like a lovesick teenager.

Leo averted his eyes immediately, flushed furiously, and concentrated on walking and breathing. It wasn't until he and Wendy were stepping onto crunching snow that he trusted himself to walk and breathe without having to focus consciously on doing so.

"If I need to throw up again, I'll give you plenty of notice," Wendy assured him as she clambered into the car. "Jeez, is it just me or is it like a million degrees?"

She strapped herself into the seat and leant her head back. By the time Leo had gotten into the driver's seat, her eyes were closed, and her face was resting against the cold glass window. He inserted the key into the ignition and turned it.

Wendy was out of it for the twenty minute journey which suited Leo fine because he was lost in the memory of blue eyes and blond hair. He was annoyed with himself for reacting to the Adonis' wink the way he had. Why couldn't he have mustered up a witty chat up line like he would usually do, or winked back at the very least? He continued scolding himself until he reached Wendy's house.

"Okay, 'not so beautiful at the present time due to vomiting a lot', you're home." He went to unclip his seat belt but was stopped when Wendy put her hand on top of his. He gave her a puzzled look. "You don't want to go home?"

"You don't have to walk me to the door. Although it feels like a million degrees to me, it's freezing out there. I'll be fine, sweetie. Thank you for driving me home and paying for dinner." She made a move to kiss him on the cheek but stopped herself. "I better not. I might pass it on to you."

He rolled his eyes. "Oh, don't be daft! You've probably breathed out nasty sickness spores and infected me with your nasty little bug already. It's inevitable that I'll be ill." He kissed her on the cheek, and when he pulled away he gave her a look of total horror. "Oh no! What if I'm sick tomorrow and can't go out?" he joked.

It was Wendy's turn to roll her eyes. "Then you'll not give in to that little leech, Tyler, and I'll have done you a favour. Night, sweetie. I think I'm out of it for this weekend. I'll call you on Sunday night." She opened the car door and stepped outside.

"Okay, Wends. Make sure Alex looks after you." The car door closed, and he watched his friend make her way up to the front entrance.

As she approached the house, the security light went on, and the front door opened. Leo caught the concerned expression that washed over Alex's face as Wendy bolted past him, presumably to the bathroom. Alex waved before closing the door. She was in good hands. With that comforting thought, he started the drive back to his own home.

A few minutes into the drive, he checked the clock on the dashboard. It was twenty eight minutes past seven, and Rob's little note popped into his mind. He grinned to himself at the thought and continued to motor onwards through the city.

His flat was located in the middle of Inverness city centre where the buildings were a spectacular blend of old and new. The newer buildings ranged from modern blocks of flats and offices to fast food chains, while the more historic structures included a castle which was situated on a grass covered hill overlooking the River Ness. On the other side of the river, and down a little from the castle, lay a gothic looking cathedral. The city had always had a very strong Christian following, and several churches were scattered along both sides of the river, but the Cathedral was the most impressive.

The river itself meandered right through the heart of the city like a massive artery and was flanked on both sides by beautiful beech trees that were lit up with twinkling lights at night. Six bridges, each one unique in its design, lay at convenient points along the River Ness. Three of them were for vehicles, and the other three were for pedestrians.

Leo often walked along the river at night to admire the beauty that lay right on his doorstep. From his flat, he'd marvel at the lights and the moon reflecting on the river and count his blessings.

"Inverness, you might be small, but you are the most beautiful city ever," he told himself as he drove alongside the river. He noticed the snow had stopped falling, and the sky was now a black canvas speckled with millions of stars.

The sky disappeared when he drove into the car park that lay underneath his block of flats. He couldn't wait to get inside and was looking forward to snuggling up on the couch with his duvet and Friends box set. The thought that he didn't have anybody to watch them with crept into his mind, and he let out a heartfelt sigh.

He knew it shouldn't bother him, but the fact he'd never been on a proper date and had never been in a relationship really got to him. Wendy and his other friends from work always told him what a catch he was, that he was a good looking guy who had everything going for him. If this was true, he thought bitterly, why was he always watching box sets alone? He banished the unpleasant thoughts to the back of his mind and focused on parking.

Once he'd parked into his allocated space, he stepped out of the car, locked it, and began walking through the dimly lit car park towards the elevator. As he walked, he began to feel like he was being watched. He'd done this walk every night for the last year and a half of his life and had never felt as if someone was lurking in the shadows. Tonight was different.

His eyes searched for any signs that suggested he wasn't alone, but there was nothing to indicate another presence apart from his own intuition. His finger hit the 'call' button when he finally reached the elevator. His heart began to beat faster as he watched the dial above the elevator door.

'This,' he told himself, 'is the part in the movie where the killer comes stalking towards the helpless victim and stabs them to death.'

The dial was displaying a gleaming red '2'. He risked a glance behind, half expecting to see an axe murderer coming towards him, but there were only a few parked cars in an otherwise empty car park. The pinging sound of the elevator made him turn around.

The doors opened, and he wasted no time getting into the elevator and pressing button number four repeatedly. His whole body sagged with relief when the doors closed, and he leaned against the back of the elevator, cursing his overactive imagination. It was absolutely absurd to get into such a state for no reason.

'God help me if something scary actually does happen!' he thought with amusement.

The elevator ascended to the top floor which he shared with four other flats. His one was the furthest away from the elevator, but he had the best view as far as he was concerned, so it didn't bother him in the slightest.

He made his way down the hall which was decorated as plainly as could be: mahogany doors, royal blue carpets, and white walls. That was it. The interior décor of the flats themselves made up for the plainness offered by the hall. He reached the door to his flat and unlocked it.

After stepping inside, the door closed with a satisfying clunk behind him, and he quickly locked it before putting the keys into his coat pocket. The flat lay in darkness, and the feeling of unease that he'd felt in the car park began to creep back into his stomach. Fumbling for the light switch, he clicked it on, and the hallway lit up. Empty.

"See, Leo! No psychopath waiting to murder you," he mumbled to himself and walked down the small hallway. He pulled his scarf and coat off as he entered the living room and tossed them over the back of a black leather couch.

The living room was shrouded in darkness except from the beams of moonlight that shone through the large balcony window. The silver beams illuminated the pristinely kept fireplace, which was directly opposite the door, and reflected off the poker stand. He walked to the window and admired the Cathedral which stood like a big stone mountain on the other side of the majestically moonlit river. Everything about the scene was exquisite and peaceful. He took in the beauty of it all for a few moments and allowed the calmness and tranquillity to envelope him.

Soon, he was completely at peace. After taking a few moments to enjoy the calmness, he moved to the lamp that sat a few feet away from the window on a beautiful wooden table. He bent over the table and rummaged around for the switch.

"Come on!" he muttered to himself, resorting to getting on his hands and knees.

"Hurry up with that light. You never know who's lurking around in the shadows."

The male voice that slithered out of the shadows caused Leo's whole body to freeze. He felt the cold, paralysing, undiluted fear touch his soul, rendering him powerless. Footsteps hit the hard wood floor in the hallway and grew louder as they came stalking into the living room. As his cognitive processes caught up with him, he bolted up from the floor and spun around to confront whoever was in his flat.

Suddenly, the room was far too bright, and he was temporarily blinded. When his eyes had adjusted to the light, they settled on the intruder who was standing by the main light switch. The fear he'd been feeling subsided slightly as recognition set in.

"What the hell are you doing in my flat?" Leo demanded, staring into a pair of breathtakingly beautiful, crystal blue eyes.

Chapter 2
The Messenger

"That's not the politest way to greet a guest, Mr Alexander."

Adonis from the restaurant stood before Leo, his long black leather coat hanging open to expose a white t-shirt and dark blue denims.

Leo stepped back against the wall. "Guests are invited. You weren't, so leave." His voice was strong and confident; inside he was terrified.

As Adonis' expression changed into one of mock hurt, his thick American accent filled the room. "Aw, that's not very nice." He crossed his arms over his chest, and his 'hurt' expression reverted back to one of smug confidence. "Nice apartment you have here," he said, looking around and nodding appreciatively. "Must have cost you a small fortune." He slouched casually against the doorframe.

"Thanks. It did. Get out." Leo's voice turned even more hostile. As the intruder's cerulean eyes scanned the room, he slowly slid his hand down the wall behind him and grasped the fire poker firmly. He stepped forward and stood to his full height. Adonis did the same, which was much more impressive given he was almost a foot taller.

Leo's heart was beating rapidly. Fear and adrenaline coursed through his veins like a deadly cocktail as Adonis removed his leather coat and draped it over a muscled forearm.

"Didn't anyone teach you to be hospitable towards guests?" Adonis said, turning his head to take in the moonlit scene offered by the window. "Wow, stunning view."

The distraction was all that Leo needed. He swung his arm in an arc, driving the poker through the air towards the intruder's head. In a heartbeat, the poker was torn from Leo's grasp and dropped unceremoniously back into its stand with a clang.

"Like I said, you should really learn how to treat guests. I'm not leaving any time soon. Get me a drink, sit down, shut up, and listen to what I have to say."

Adonis wandered over to the couch and tossed his coat over the back of it before easing himself down. He proceeded to pick up a magazine from the coffee table and started flicking through it. After a few moments of reading, he looked up at Leo and leant forward, cocking his head to the side. "Uh hello, drink please!" he demanded. "Then we can talk."

Leo's mouth fell open as his unwanted guest settled into the couch and continued to read. Who the hell did this guy think he was barging in here and making himself at home? "Listen, Yankee Doodle," Leo said curtly, "I'm going to ask you once more to leave my flat. If you don't, then I'll have to make you."

Adonis, apart from wearing a patronising grin, remained seated and had the cheek to put his feet up on the coffee table.

Leo laughed in sheer disbelief at the display of arrogance. "Fine. You can't say I didn't warn you."

"Just get the drinks, and then I'll explain why I'm here," Adonis said without looking up.

Leo closed his eyes and started to attune himself to the element of fire. He'd yet to perform this particular spell but had studied it in a book he'd bought years ago. It was going to be the most powerful spell he'd ever used, and he wasn't entirely sure if his mystical energy was up to it. In this particular moment, he didn't care.

His body began to grow warm as he visualised his whole being becoming fire. He felt the flames of the element licking the air around him and radiating glorious heat. When he opened his eyes, orange and red coloured energy sizzled and ignited the air around him like miniature fireworks.

"I'll ask you once more," he warned, seeing that he had Adonis' attention at last. "Leave."

Adonis closed the magazine and placed it onto his lap before leaning back and spreading his arms horizontally over the back of the couch. "Do your worst," he goaded.

"Fine!" Leo snapped, turning his eyes to the magazine sitting on the intruder's lap. The magazine burst into flames, and it was Leo's turn to be smug as Adonis leapt off the couch, threw the magazine to the floor, and stamped the fire out.

"Right, okay, so you don't have a sense of humour. I get it." Adonis held up his hands. "Enough games, let me tell you why I'm—hey! Holy fuck! That's my good coat!"

Leo watched in amusement as fire ate the leather coat resting on the back of the couch. "I warned you. Get out of my home before I set *you* on fire!"

Adonis wasn't listening now. He was busy trying to rescue his burning coat. "That...was uncalled for," he said, his voice dangerously low.

"Uncalled for?" Leo shot back, even though Adonis' menacing tone had sent shivers through him. "You've broken into my home, moron!" The fire energy was still lingering around him, building up and waiting to be used, and he was not going to disperse it just yet.

"You'd better calm down, boy, or you'll get to see what I can do. Believe me, it's a lot more impressive than your pyrotechnics," Adonis seethed, tossing his burnt coat over the couch once more. "Now, get the drinks, and then I'll tell you why you're in serious danger," he growled.

"Danger?" Leo repeated, his eyes like emerald fire. "I don't think I'm the one in serious danger here." He hadn't felt this powerful in his entire life, and he was convinced it had something to do with the energy he was channelling. By invoking this higher level of magic, it was as if he'd awoken something deep inside his soul. "Are you going to leave now, or do I have to cremate you?"

Adonis sighed, and his anger seemed to fade as quickly as it had appeared. "Have you always been this annoying, or did you have to work at it?" There was a short silence before Adonis rolled his eyes. "For the last time, get us some drinks. Believe me, you'll need one by the time I've finished telling you about the danger you and Daniel are in."

"You're not getting a drink until you tell me what you— what? What did you say?" With astonishing abruptness, the fire element died, and all of the magical energy evaporated into the ether. Leo's eyes were back to their natural state, but there was nothing natural about the concern and worry on his face at the mention of Daniel's name. "How do you know Daniel? What danger is he in?"

"The danger you're both in," Adonis said regretfully. He looked very remorseful, and as he spoke, his voice grew softer. "Listen, I'm just the messenger. Go and get the drinks, and then I'll explain everything to you about Daniel and who he really is. We don't have much time. Once you've heard what I have to say, then you can throw me out. My job is to deliver the message and leave."

He should have been very suspicious of the incredibly beautiful guy standing before him, but there was something inside of him telling him that this was important. Intuition? Stupidity, perhaps? Either way, it was clear this man wouldn't be standing in his living room if there wasn't a good reason. He knew only one Daniel, and that was the boy who he currently taught; the Daniel who made him long for a child of his own.

Slowly and awkwardly, Leo moved towards the kitchen. "I...I'll just get the drinks," he stammered, completely thrown by the intruder's warning. "Is vodka okay?"

"Perfect. On the rocks, please," Adonis replied, returning to the couch and sitting on it casually once more.

"I'll be right back," Leo said, making his way to the door. When he got to the door, he stopped and turned around. "Um...sorry about your coat."

Adonis chuckled. "Don't worry about it. I don't need it. I just think they look good on me." He winked and gave a smile that stopped Leo's heart.

Leo promptly left the room, bumping into the door frame as he did so. When he reached the kitchen, he realised he was shaking uncontrollably. He placed his arms on the breakfast bar and lowered his head, trying to get his thoughts in order. Here he was, on his own, with a complete stranger who'd told him that he and a student of his were in danger. Not a typical Friday night by any means.

'*Daniel... who he really is.*'

The words swam around in his head, and a bad feeling gripped his insides. The fact the stranger knew personal information about him and Daniel should have been ringing alarm bells, however, there was something about the handsome man that he trusted. There was a part of him screaming to call the police. The other part, a bigger part, was extremely interested to find out what the stranger had to say.

"Get it together," he whispered to himself before pushing off the counter. He grabbed the vodka and poured a healthy measure into two glass tumblers. He placed ice in both drinks, filled one with coke, and then carried the glasses through the living room along with the vodka and coke bottles.

Upon entering, he wasn't prepared for the beauty that greeted him. In the short time he'd been in the kitchen, he'd forgotten just how beautiful Adonis was. He noticed the living room was much dimmer; the main light was now off and had been replaced by the softer glow of two small lamps.

Adonis turned his head and smiled as Leo approached. The gentle light from the nearest lamp caught the left side of his face, illuminating it in all its stunning magnificence. Leo had never before seen such a chiselled jaw and such flawless golden skin.

"Here you go," he said, handing over the vodka and ice. His hand brushed against the bare skin of Adonis' hand. For a split second, a bolt of energy surged through his fingers and rocketed through every part of him. His face flushed crimson as blood rushed to his cheeks, and his heart tried to burst through his chest.

Adonis took a sip and grinned. "Thanks. That's better." He placed the tumbler on the coffee table. "Sit," he said, patting the cushion that lay to his left as if he were inviting a close friend to sit next to him.

Leo raised an eyebrow. "No, I'm good here, thanks."

Adonis smirked. "Oh, come on, I don't bite. Well, only if you ask. Just come and sit down. You'll need to, trust me."

He may have inspired feelings of trust in Leo, but that didn't mean he had to like the guy. "Fine, I'll sit," he said rather huffily, which appeared to amuse Adonis even more. He sat down and took a big gulp from his glass before beginning his inquisition. "Who are you? What danger is Daniel in? How do you know my name?" The questions came out in a flurry, his brain having to work extra hard due to the effect that this man was having on him.

Adonis chuckled and reached for his tumbler. "Wow, you do like to get straight to the point, don't you?" He took another sip before carefully replacing the glass onto the coffee table. "My name is Lucas. I know who you are because I was sent here to find you—"

"By who?" It was out before Leo could stop himself.

Lucas rolled his eyes once more. "Are you planning on interrupting me all the way through this? Tell me if you are so I can leave you another note."

"The note, at my work? That was you?" Leo exclaimed.

Lucas nodded. "Yup. Thanks for turning up by the way. Do you know how many dog walkers think there's now a total pervert lurking by the canal?" The smile that flickered on his face let Leo know he was joking. "So, are you able to listen to the whole story without interrupting?"

"Yeah, I will," Leo promised.

"Good. Like I said, I was sent here to find you by the High Council of the Elect. The Elect are the last remaining guardians of the Power. They were almost wiped out hundreds of years ago when they were betrayed, but a few survived to continue their legacy."

Leo reached over to the coffee table and picked up a packet of cigarettes and a lighter. "Do you smoke?" he asked, placing a cigarette between his lips and lighting it. When Lucas nodded, he tossed one across to him followed by the lighter. He watched as the story teller expertly sparked up and took a long drag before exhaling with a moan of pleasure.

"It's always the good things that are bad for you, isn't it?" Lucas said, looking visibly relaxed and at complete ease, a direct contrast to how Leo was feeling. "As I was saying, the Elect's legacy is to protect the Power.

"It's had many names, many guises. You'll probably know it best as the Holy Grail. All the legends and stories they've woven were lies created to deceive mankind. I think my favourite was when they said the Grail *was* The Magdalene. Even Mary herself had a laugh at that." Lucas flashed a heart melting grin and displayed a mouthful of perfect teeth.

Leo was itching to ask a hundred questions but knew that silence was golden. All he had to do was listen…and drink. The vodka was going down too easy.

"You see," Lucas continued, "ninety five percent of humans are deeply stupid. Don't be offended, it's true. Most humans believe everything they read and then spout it off to their children who go on to pollute the minds of their own children and so on and so on. You end up with generations and generations believing the same old nonsense. The Grail lore that is widely believed and written about is bullshit. It was conceived a long time ago to throw mankind off the scent so no one would ever know its true power."

"A deception...but why?" Leo asked.

"There was a time, a long time before humans were created, where all was...what?"

"You just said everything that was written was bullshit. I'm assuming you're referring to all religious texts. The Holy Bible said we were created, and the Bible is a religious text. Are you telling me the creation story in Genesis is true?"

Lucas smiled. "Remember when I said that ninety five percent of humans were stupid? How stupid does one have to be to think that we're all here by chance? The Big Bang Theory? Evolution? Quite frankly, it's insulting to the Divine, but humanity has always been desperate to play God, to *be* God. It goes right back to the Pharaohs and Roman Emperors, and it all comes down to power. You humans, always believing that something mightier than yourselves can't possibly exist," Lucas chuckled. "Sorry, I've digressed. The creation story in the Bible is actually the closest to the truth, but it's been tampered with. After all, when can mankind be trusted to tell the entire truth?"

Lucas laughed properly for the first time, and the sound sent ripples of pleasure through Leo, causing goose bumps to form over his arms and neck.

"Tell me about this Power," Leo said, taking a sip from his nearly empty glass and trying to ignore the tingling sensation running through his body. He'd never heard such a melodic and beautiful laugh before; the sound was enchanting, hypnotic even.

"The Power has remained a closely guarded secret due to the fact that the best lies are those containing half-truths. Before humans were even considered, there was a time when everything was…perfect." Lucas' eyes misted over. "Nothing but pure happiness existed. Everywhere was heaven. The angels' songs rang through the very fabric of time and space. Everything was pure love. The angels loved each other, and they loved the Father, or the Divine, or whatever you want to call God. That is why the angels hold Him in such high esteem. He gave them immortality, beauty and power. That period has many names; Paradise, Nirvana, Utopia."

It was clear to Leo that this was an issue close to Lucas' heart by the wave of emotion that emanated from him as he recounted the story, but he couldn't figure out why. Feelings of deep longing, loss, regret and sorrow permeated the room. "And then what happened?" he asked gently.

Lucas' angelic face darkened, and the mood of the story changed. "What do you know about Lucifer?" he asked, stubbing out his cigarette into the ashtray.

Leo couldn't help but notice the room growing colder at the mention of the Devil's name. He thought about the question while he drained the last of his drink and set his empty tumbler back down. "According to Christianity, he's the epitome of evil. He was the most beautiful angel ever, and he knew it. He wanted to be like God, so he started a rebellion. He was then cast out by God after he and his angels lost the Great War in heaven. Now lives in hell, right?"

"I'm impressed. You clearly know your stuff." Lucas raised his glass, toasting the fact. "But once again, that version has only a few elements of actual events."

Leo's interest was positively peaked. "Enlighten me."

"Lucifer was indeed the most beautiful angel heaven had ever seen. To gaze upon him was almost like gazing upon God Himself. The truth is, he didn't start the war. Well, not on his own anyway. There were others who were also responsible, but Lucifer was held accountable for the entire fiasco." Lucas sighed, sounding as if the war in heaven was simply a mere misunderstanding, a minor event in history. "Lucifer never wanted to be like God, that's a common misconception. It was something else entirely that ruffled his wings. The fall of Lucifer came from the fact he was insanely jealous."

Leo snorted. "Jealous!? Are you kidding me with this? What did the most beautiful angel that ever existed have to be jealous about?"

A wide grin spread across Lucas' face. "Genesis 1:27. So God created human beings in his own image. In the image of God He created them; male and female He created them."

"Humans?" Leo's mouth fell open in incredulous awe. "He was jealous of humans?"

"Ridiculous, isn't it? Don't get me started on that one or we'd be here all night, but yes, he was simply jealous of the fact that God had created human beings and had given them the Earth and the ability to love each other. He grew to despise them, as you know, but he wasn't the only one. You see, angels might have been created a little higher up in the divinity chain than humans, but the two are more alike than you might think, especially when it comes to God. We all want him to love our own kind the most, don't we? Pathetic really."

"What did Lucifer do?" Leo asked, while refilling both tumblers.

"His growing jealousy slowly drove him to the brink of insanity and created a wickedness like no other. Likeminded angels were attracted to the fiery darkness that burned inside of Lucifer, and they ended up joining him. With their help, Lucifer almost succeeded in overthrowing God and destroying mankind forever. This is where the Power comes in.

"The Power is the very heart of God's creativity, and to touch it is to touch the entire universe itself. This creative force exists separately from God, but it wasn't always this way. After God finished His creation, the Power detached itself from His being. Nobody really knows why He allowed for it to happen, but we just accept that He must have had his reasons." Lucas gave a little shrug as if the mere fact God parted with this incredible life force was no big deal.

Leo shrugged too. "He's the boss, I suppose."

"The Power remained in a glorious chamber in heaven and was closely guarded by the Archangels. Only they knew of its existence and vowed to keep it a secret forever."

"Wait a minute," Leo interrupted. "Wasn't Lucifer an Archangel?"

Lucas nodded grimly. "He shared the secret of the Power with a particularly vindictive angel called Baal. Baal's hatred of humanity rivals that of Lucifer's, and it was he who masterminded the entire rebellion. He convinced Lucifer to begin a war in heaven so terrible that heaven itself would never be the same. Baal, being an exceptionally cunning being, carried out a cloak and dagger operation, recruiting other like-minded angels into destroying the plague of humanity. With the distraction of a raging war, Lucifer and Baal would be able to steal the Power for themselves.

"The war erupted as planned, and legions of angels fought against each other. Amidst the chaos and hysteria, Lucifer and Baal made their way to the Power's chamber where they were unexpectedly confronted by an Archangel. You see, the other Archangels didn't fully trust Lucifer, and they had heard whispers of a rebellion. Michael, in his infinite wisdom, didn't want to leave the Power unguarded, so he chose Raphael to watch over it while he and Gabriel joined the fight."

Leo was so absorbed in the story that he'd barely remembered to breathe. "Did they hurt Raphael?" he asked, horrified.

"I should tell you at this point that every angel was blessed with one unique gift. Baal's angelic gift allows him to open portals to any place in the entire universe. Angels, as you know, are not omnipotent and can only be in one place at one time. During the fight, Baal opened a gateway and he and Lucifer managed to push Raphael through it. The Archangel was sent to the other side of the universe, leaving the evil pair to enter the chamber and bask in the brilliant golden light of the Power. What do you think happened next?"

Leo blinked, a bit thrown by Lucas' question. "I...I don't know."

Lucas grinned. "Oh, come on storyteller, you're good at this game. I heard you back in the restaurant. Entertain me."

He knew he should have asked how Lucas had been able to hear what was said in the noisy restaurant, especially when they had been so far apart, but as he was so enthralled in the tale, he just went with the flow. He considered the scenario for a moment, and then it became obvious.

"Baal had already agreed that Lucifer, being the Archangel, could claim the Power for himself, right?" Lucas nodded and smiled, so Leo continued. "But Baal, standing in the glory of the Power, became greedy. He wanted it for himself and challenged Lucifer for it."

"Bingo. Baal drew his blade and staked his claim. It's unclear how long they fought for, some say hours, but by the time Lucifer had bested Baal, the war was over. Michael and Gabriel returned to the chamber and, as you can imagine, were not best pleased to find Lucifer and Baal alone with the Power.

"An exhausted Lucifer was quickly defeated, and he and his fallen angels were brought before God to face His wrath. The Almighty banished each and every one of them to a new dimension called Hell."

Leo sparked up another cigarette before flinging one to Lucas. "The Power, what happened to it?" He was on the edge of his seat, his face a picture of scarcely contained wonder and excitement.

Lucas held the cigarette between his teeth and lit it. He took a long drag and exhaled a stream of white smoke. "The three remaining Archangels met the Divine, and it was decided the Power was too dangerous to remain in heaven; every angel knew of its existence, and it wasn't safe. Much discussion and heated debate took place between the Archangels about what should be done with it. Since it couldn't be bound back to its original source, the obvious choice was to give the Power to Michael, merge it with his own essence seeing as he was the strongest. Michael refused, claiming that any angel who tried to contain such a power would be corrupted.

"Raphael eventually came up with a viable solution that pleased them all: send it to Earth. So they did. A group of five were carefully chosen, and they were called the Elect. Divine powers were bestowed upon them, and they became masters in working with the elements and energy. They worked hard to create a vessel that could contain the Power on the earth's physical plane. With the vessel in place, they hid the Power deep underground and protected it with powerful spells and enchantments so that anybody who went looking for it would die before they ever reached it."

"Why do I have the feeling someone found it?" Leo asked, his stomach knotting.

"Baal." Lucas said, grimacing. "Baal had already fled and was in hiding. The fact he can open portals to anywhere made it impossible for Michael, Gabriel and Raphael to track him down. They knew he'd come here, to Earth, but he remained hidden for a thousand years. You see, when God banished Lucifer and his army of fallen angels, it wasn't forever. It was for—"

"A thousand years." Leo finished Lucas' sentence. Every time he'd picked up the Bible to read, he'd always felt there was something missing. Was Lucas' story the real deal? "Okay, I don't mean to be rude, your story is completely captivating, but what has this got to do with Daniel and myself?"

Lucas rolled his eyes while draining the contents of his glass for the second time. "Patience is a virtue, Leo. You gotta know the whole story. We're almost done, I promise."

"Sorry. Please, carry on."

"When the thousand years had passed, the fallen angels were permitted to venture back and forth between Earth and Hell. They'd come and carry out all sorts of evil deeds, and their behaviour earned them the title of 'demon'. Baal's reappearance came shortly after the demons returned, and he quickly began recruiting his old followers, determined to finish what he'd started. He'd have succeeded too if it wasn't for the Elect who had established themselves as a powerful force on Earth and had grown to vast numbers. The Elect used their magic and drove all the demons back to hell, apart from Baal. He was far more powerful than the Elect could handle. Nine Grandmasters have fallen at his hands."

Leo's eyes widened at this latest news. It was obvious to him that the Grandmaster was at the head of the Elect and therefore must be extremely powerful. It unnerved him to think that Baal had gone through nine of them.

"The last Grandmaster he killed," Lucas continued, "was the one to expose the location of the Power. She went up against Baal and was very nearly victorious. With his opponent wounded and powerless, Baal moved to the place where the Grandmaster's two children, a boy and a girl, were hiding. Pulling them roughly from their hiding place, he drew his blade and killed the boy instantly. He then placed his blade against the little girl's throat and gave the Grandmaster a choice: tell him where the Power was, or watch her daughter die.

"The very fact Baal gave the woman a choice showed just how desperate he was to find the Power. He's not one for giving choices.

"The woman obviously blurted out the location in order to save her daughter and, much to everyone's surprise, Baal kept his word. He tossed the girl to her mother and disappeared through a portal to the revealed location." Lucas sighed and shook his head. "The Grandmaster gave a false location; Baal's revenge was terrible. He hunted her down and brutally murdered her and her daughter, but not before the Grandmaster had carried out one last attempt to conceal the Power. Along with her daughter, the Grandmaster raced to the place where the Power was actually hidden and performed extraordinary magic. She changed the energy completely. She did something nobody had ever thought to do before. She gave it form, gave it life."

Leo gasped. "She made it human?"

"In a way, yes. She hid it in the soul of a newly conceived human so it would be born, live a natural human life, grow old and eventually die. When the human vessel dies, the Power finds another soul, conceived but not born, to bind itself to, and the process starts again. Reincarnation, I suppose. When you consider the number of women in the world who are pregnant at the same time, it was a very clever move on the Grandmaster's part. Baal only has a limited amount of time to search before the Power dies and is hidden for nine long months in the womb of an unsuspecting woman. Right now, even as we speak, his minions scour the earth looking for it."

"Why doesn't he search for it himself if he's so powerful?" Leo asked rather haughtily.

Lucas chuckled. "He can't. He's trapped in an enormous cavern underground. Centuries ago, the Elect managed to pull their magical strength together and bind him using a blood ritual. Basically, one of the members sacrificed themselves to imprison Baal. The ritual is linked to the bloodline of that particular member. As long as the bloodline exists, Baal will be stuck forever. Each day, he feeds on humans, and even other demons, to maintain his incredible strength."

"I have a question," Leo said, his brow furrowed as if he was trying to solve the world's hardest equation. "How did

Baal know the Power was on Earth? How did he know it had been turned human? I mean, if the Grandmaster's intention was to hide the Power, she wouldn't have told him it was human, right?"

For the first time since he'd arrived, Lucas looked uncomfortable. He shifted in his chair, reached over to the ashtray and put out his cigarette. "An angel told him, and that particular angel was a deluded fool who should have known better. But that's not important. What's important is that Baal knows what he's looking for and is extremely close to finding it, and when he does we're all fucked."

"Right, let's say I believe your story. What has this got to do with me and Daniel?"

"Think about it. You have magical abilities, and you are highly intuitive. Haven't you figured it out yet?" Lucas leant forward. "Not everybody has the gift of magic, Leo. That gift was bestowed on the ones God and the Archangels chose."

Leo was momentarily stunned as the truth dawned on him. "I'm...I'm part of the Elect." It wasn't a question. He just knew. "I'm one of them! And Daniel. He's one too! I knew it! I always felt that he was special, something unique. As a teacher you can't ever favour your students, but I always felt closer to him, like I wanted to—"

"Look after him?" Lucas interjected. "Protect him?"

"Exactly! You're one too, aren't you? That's why you've come. It all makes sense now." Leo's eyes twinkled with excitement as he stubbed out his own cigarette. He finally had the answer to why he'd never come across another person who could perform magic. The Elect were clearly a rare species. "Do you want another drink? I think I have wine in the fridge." He stood up and reached for the two empty glasses on the coffee table.

"Leo, you've got it wrong. Daniel isn't a member of the Elect." Lucas' voice was calm, controlled. "He's something much more than that."

Slowly, Leo turned around and faced the angelic looking man sitting on his couch. He knew what Lucas was going to say, but he was trying so hard to ignore his gut instinct. "What is he?" he asked breathlessly, his words coming out far too fast, his eyes searching Lucas' face for the answer he already knew.

"I think you've already worked it out," Lucas replied, standing up from the couch.

"I don't believe you," Leo whispered.

"You have this strong urge to protect him. Why? You don't know him any better than the other children in your class. Why him? I'll tell you why. You were built to protect him. Because of what he is. Daniel is the Power."

Lucas was standing right in front of him now, staring into his eyes. The two glasses slipped from Leo's hand and smashed into tiny pieces that scattered across the floor. "He can't be," Leo said, trembling. "This is crazy. You're crazy. None of this is true." He swallowed when Lucas cupped the side of his face.

"If you thought for a minute that it wasn't true, you'd have set me on fire and thrown me out already. The reason you haven't is because you know it, you feel it, and you believe it. You've always known deep down that you were meant for bigger things, and this is it. Daniel is the Power, or at least has the Power inside of him, and sooner or later, Baal will come for him. When that day comes, he'll need you."

"He's just a child."

It was insanity. Maybe he was going crazy after all. Here he was engaging with a complete stranger who'd broken into his house and told him that he, boring Leo Alexander, was a member of the Elect, a secret order handpicked by God to protect the Power that was in human form. Daniel form to be exact. It was madness.

Leo sat down again. He raised his hands to the sides of his head and rubbed his temples, willing his mind to process the vast amount of information he'd just received.

Eventually, he laid his shaky hands on his lap and cleared his throat. "Okay, so now what? What do you expect me to do?"

Lucas reached over and picked up his coat from the back of the couch. "That depends."

"On what?"

"On if you truly believe what I'm saying," Lucas replied, pulling on his coat. "If you believe, which I think you do, then you need to develop your magical potency as fast as possible. We need you at your most powerful for when Baal rears his ugly head." Lucas reached into the inside pocket of his coat, pulled out a little card, and handed it to him. "Father Cornelius O'Connor is the most powerful man in the Elect, aside from the Grandmaster, and will teach you everything you need to know," Lucas said as he walked towards the door. "You'll find him at the Cathedral. I suggest you seek his counsel first thing tomorrow. Thanks for the drink."

Leo was torn. The whole story was so unbelievable—fantastical even—and he wanted to believe that it was all a lie, and that this man, Lucas, was a complete and utter loony. Yet, the fact remained that Leo could perform magic and he'd never met a single person who could do the same. Lucas had provided a reason for this. There was also the fact that he felt undeniably protective over Daniel, and he cared more deeply than perhaps was professionally acceptable. It was true, he adored all of his students, but for some reason, he was inexplicably drawn to Daniel, and he could think of no reason why this was the case. Lucas had provided a reason "And what if I don't believe you?"

The question stopped Lucas, who was halfway out the door. He turned and looked solemnly at Leo. "First, your little boy Daniel will die, then everything you love in this world will be destroyed, and Hell itself will be unleashed. I may only be the messenger, but I know what's at stake. I wouldn't waste my time coming here if it wasn't crucial. Go and see Father O'Connor tomorrow morning. He'll be expecting you. I'll see myself out." Lucas turned and disappeared through the door.

Leo sat on the couch and stared at the spot where Lucas had been standing moments before. He heard the front door being unlocked and leapt off the couch. "Lucas, wait," he called as he ran into the empty hall. Seconds later, the front door swung open and piercing blue eyes gazed at him. "How close? How close is Baal to finding out who the Power is?"

"We don't know for sure, but we do know that he's never been closer. I'd give it a month at the most," Lucas replied.

Leo inhaled sharply. "About a month? Can't you be more specific?

Lucas stood for a moment, looking pensive. "When black wings flock around the holy place, that's when you'll know." And with that cryptic message, he closed the door and was gone.

After locking the door as quickly as possible, Leo walked back to the living room on shaky legs and flopped on the couch. He reached over for the vodka bottle, unscrewed the top, and took a large swig. After swallowing, a loud cawing sound made him leap off the couch.

He twisted his head towards the window and there, perching on the ledge and staring boldly in at him, was a large black crow. He put the vodka bottle down and proceeded to shoo the crow away by knocking aggressively against the window pane.

His eyes followed the crow as it flew off and battled against the wind and snow on its journey towards the Cathedral. When it reached the building, it circled the roof a few times before disappearing from view. A feeling of dread formed in the pit of his stomach until he remembered Lucas' warning had mentioned a flock of black wings, not a single pair.

Standing by the window, bathed in the soft silver light of the moon, he replayed the conversation with Lucas over and over in his head as bullets of icy sleet battered against his reflection in the window. He watched them slowly melt before they trickled down to form an icy pool on the window ledge where the crow had been standing moments before.

Chapter 3
Dreams of the Past

Leo drifted on a small wooden raft down a wide river that meandered before him, the banks on either side of it littered with an ancient civilisation. The houses he could see were made from some form of brick. Most of the buildings had one floor while a few had two or even three. Covering the doorways and windows of the houses looked to be a curtain made from dried out reeds. In front of and behind each house were little allotments full of black soil and sprouting greenery, evidence of growing vegetation. The people of this land were bustling around and carrying out their day to day activities under a cruel and punishing sun. Some worked the gardens, ploughing the rich, fertile soil; some worked down by the river, washing clothes and filling jars; others worked on little boats on the river, dragging nets through the water to collect fish.

The men and the young boys wore a white linen skirt that fastened with a belt, nothing more. Women and young girls wore plain, straight linen dresses with one or two shoulder straps. All of the very small children ran about naked, chasing each other in the relentless heat of the sunshine while their mothers scolded them if they got in the way of the hard work and toil.

Leo took in the sights as he floated serenely down the river, becoming very aware that he wasn't affected by the scorching sun. In fact, he was actually feeling comfortable and tranquil, wishing there was a cocktail in his hand. As he glided further and further down the river, the brightness of the blue sky began to dull. He tilted his head backwards and saw that the blue sky had been replaced by a canvas of dark grey. The women and men began shouting to their children before frantically packing away their farming tools, dragging their boats onto the banks and gathering up the washed clothes as day turned to night.

And then the heavens opened.

The rain came down in torrents as it grew darker still. The shouts from the locals who were running for shelter grew fainter and fainter until all he could hear was the rain lashing off the river. Like the sun, he was unaffected by the night time monsoon, and he remained bone dry.

After a few minutes of listening to the pounding rain, a flurry of movement to Leo's right caught his eye. He peered through the canvas of rain to see that a person was crouched at the river bank. It was a woman, and she was crouching before a small basket.

His raft came to a gradual halt, and the rain began to ease off. The moon came up giving him a clearer view of the woman. Her hair was black like the night sky, her eyes a deep brown with flecks of gold, and she was cradling a tiny bundle to her breast while weeping silently. After a few moments, she held the bundle away from her and gazed at it through watery eyes before kissing the top of it. He realised the bundle was a baby wrapped up in a blanket and watched as she placed him delicately into the small basket and set it off down the river.

The raft beneath his feet became mobile once more, and it followed the basket which was now drifting along the calm river. He looked back to the mother who never took her teary eyes off her baby until it veered around a corner and disappeared from sight.

He glided around the corner, and his jaw hit the floor when he was greeted with a spectacular structure that let him know exactly where his dreams had taken him. The pyramid standing before him was breath taking. He could appreciate the true beauty and enormity of the stone giant that towered above all else, understanding that there was divine architecture involved in its construction.

As the river swept him past the stone giant, the sun rose magnificently from behind the grand structure, illuminating it before rising further into the cloudless sky. The basket finally came to rest on a shallow part of the river which was overgrown with reeds. Leo's raft drew up alongside the baby. A piercing cry erupted from inside the basket and travelled through the air, forcing him to cover his ears. It didn't take long for the cries to attract attention. Soon, a trio of women came to investigate.

It was clear the women were local but even more obvious that they were wealthier than those women he'd seen working on the banks of the Nile. The linen dresses they wore were cleaner and crisper and looked far superior in quality than those of the working women. They were also decorated from head to toe with gold jewellery which gleamed and sparkled in the morning sunshine. One of the women, the one with the most gold on, ordered the other two to bring her the basket from the river which they did promptly. When the basket was brought to her, she picked up the baby and held it in her arms, soothing it with a gentle lullaby sang in a foreign language. The woman smiled down at the infant who was now silent and fast asleep in her arms. Still singing the haunting lullaby, the woman climbed up a nearby set of steps and was carefully followed by her two companions. Leo also followed.

Lying at the top of the steps was a massive square shaped courtyard which was being patrolled by six large men with swords. As he walked behind the women, the men ignored him. The courtyard was stunning in its simplicity; it had exactly four pomegranate trees in each corner, hanging baskets filled with beautiful jasmine, and a statue of the god Horus made entirely from gold. He gaped in wonder at the beauty offered by the courtyard, his eye drawn to the blazing statue that glittered in the sun. When he reached the statue, he stopped, marvelling at its astonishing craftsmanship. Each detail had been sculpted to perfection and was a truly wonderful sight to behold. Very tentatively, he reached out to Horus' face and pressed his hand against the warm gold. There was a sudden blinding light, and he was no longer in the courtyard.

He found himself in a glorious hall where the woman, the one who had carried the baby, was standing before a strapping man whose face was contorted into a deep scowl. The man sat upon a massive throne of gold, and Leo knew at once that this was Pharaoh.

"We can't take in every stray, Tuya! We already have a beautiful son of our own, we don't need another one!"

Leo watched in awe as the scene played out before him.

Tuya was too busy staring down at the baby boy in her arms to listen to her husband. She beamed when the baby took her finger and tried to shove it into his mouth. "Moses. We'll call him Moses," she announced to the Pharaoh. "Do you like that name, Seti?"

Seti let out an exasperated sigh. "Yes, it's nice, but we can't just take in an Israelite baby. What will the people say?"

Tuya snorted. "You are the Pharaoh! You can do whatever you want. Look at this baby. Look at him. Can't you see it?" she asked her husband, turning Moses around so Seti could get a better look.

"Don't be ridiculous, Tuya, of course I can see him. He's right in front of me!" Seti exclaimed.

Tuya laughed. "I know that, but can't you feel it? There is something special about this baby." Tuya moved closer to her husband and held out Moses, watching carefully as Seti took the infant and sat him on his lap. The Pharaoh's wife observed while moving to her own throne. She had to fight down the urge to giggle as Seti glared down at Moses as if he were an impossible problem that needed solved. It didn't take long until Moses won the Pharaoh over.

As Seti studied Moses, attempting to see whatever it was his wife could see, the little boy gazed back up at him with huge, brown innocent eyes. Moses let out a rasping laugh and then clapped his tiny little hands excitedly together. Seti couldn't supress the sudden wave of joy and love he felt for the baby and beamed down at him before turning to his wife. "He'll make a fine brother for our little Ramesses."

Leo watched as Seti and Tuya fawned over Moses until the flash of bright light returned and blinded him once again. When his sight returned moments later, he was in the same grand hall where everything was practically the same except for the couple who sat upon the thrones; a man, who was practically a younger version of Seti, and a beautiful dark haired woman were Egypt's new rulers. To the right of the woman was a young boy who was so strikingly like the Pharaoh that there was no doubt he was the ruler's son.

Before the three royals stood two men and a woman. One of the men carried a long wooden staff which Leo's eyes were inexplicably drawn to. The bottom of it touched the marble floor while the top of it stood at the same height as the man who carried it. Most of the staff looked to be formed by four slender pieces of gnarly wood that had been twisted together and then sanded down to an impossible smoothness. At the very top of the staff, the four pieces of wood split apart for a short distance, creating a small chamber before twisting together again. Fastened into the chamber was an amber crystal, encased by the split wood. Leo had the strangest feeling the man who carried the staff was a grown up version of—

"Moses, what brings you back here?" Pharaoh's voice boomed around the hall. "I didn't expect you to return after killing one of my father's citizens all those years ago."

64

The man with the staff stepped forward. "Ramesses, forgive me, but it was a necessity. Your father knew this. There are dark forces at work that you don't know about."

Ramesses let out a mirthless laugh as did his queen. "There is nothing that I, Pharaoh and ruler of Egypt, don't know about. It is my business to know everything."

The other man that was with Moses stepped forward. "Don't let your arrogance blind you, your majesty," he began. "We have come here to help you. Your kingdom is in grave danger."

Leo watched as the Pharaoh's hands tightened on the arms of his throne. "If you are referring to the armies of our enemies in the—"

"Don't be ridiculous!" the man interjected.

"How dare you interrupt the King of Egypt!" the Pharaoh roared, rising from his throne.

"Aaron, please be silent. Let your brother speak." The woman who stood with the two men spoke for the first time, her voice gentle and light. She caused a calmness to descend upon the group, and Pharaoh sat back down while Aaron allowed himself to be pulled back by the woman.

Moses turned and bowed his head in appreciation. "Thank you, Miriam." He smiled warmly at her before turning his attention back to Ramesses. "My brother, I beg you, please listen to me. Our father, the man who raised us, had a plan, and the time has come to fulfil it. The world is not as you know it. A darkness has fallen upon the world, and it has found its way to Egypt. My God has shown me."

"Your God does not exist, brother. Your monotheistic religion bores me," the Pharaoh said with a flippant wave of his hand. "But I am intrigued as to what you and my father were allegedly plotting."

"My God entrusted something to humanity a very long time ago," Moses said, his voice bordering on a whisper. "It's something powerful beyond anything the world has ever seen. The demons have crawled out of the darkness and are seeking it, Ramesses. If they get their wicked hands on it, the world will be pulled apart and everything will be destroyed. I am one of God's chosen, a guardian of the Power. God has bestowed…gifts to me."

The great Pharaoh wore an expression of pure boredom and exchanged a look with his wife. It was clear from their faces that they did not believe one word.

"And what proof do you have of this?" the Pharaoh inquired, penetrating Moses with a cold stare.

Moses stepped forward and placed his staff on the ground. Without warning, the staff turned into a gigantic serpent that reared itself up in front of the Pharaoh, its amber eyes glowing fiercely. The Pharaoh's wife and son gasped in surprise, but Ramesses merely raised an eyebrow.

"A nice trick, brother, but I have my own magicians. Raul! Tabith!" he bellowed.

Two men dressed in cloaks of black entered the hall from a doorway located to the left of the Pharaoh's throne. They walked with their hands held out before them, clasped together as if in prayer. Their hands were pale and thin, their fingers bony and long. "Your excellency?" the pair drawled, bowing their heads.

"Show how you can perform such magic tricks," the Pharaoh instructed. A grin appeared on Ramesses' face as the two magicians did just that with staffs they'd pulled from beneath their cloaks. Although Moses' serpent was much bigger, the Pharaoh had proved the magic could be replicated. The grin diminished, however, when Moses' serpent completely devoured the other two.

Moses reached down and picked up his serpent which transformed back into the wooden staff the moment his hand touched it. He drew himself up and set his eyes upon the two magicians. "Behold, Pharaoh Ramesses, the supreme power of the one true God," he thundered, keeping his gaze locked on to the two cloaked magicians. "You are done here, demons. Now, be gone before I show you the wrath of God Almighty!"

Leo was shocked when the two magicians suddenly sprouted huge black feathered wings. They reached above their heads and pulled large blades out of thin air. Each blade radiated an aura as black as their wings. Leo's vision blurred, and he soon felt like his spirit had left his body and was being pulled towards Moses. As he drew right up to Moses, he felt himself merge with the older man, two entities in one body, and was now seeing things from Moses' perspective. What he saw was two of the vilest looking creatures imaginable.

Chalk white faces, with black and crimson veins protruding from beneath the skin, snarled at him. The hideous snarling quickly turned into high pitched demonic shrieks that pierced his ears. Leo thought the demons' mouths of jagged and twisted teeth were truly terrifying until he noticed their eyes. The empty, black filled eyes were completely cold and devoid of any life and warmth, reminding him of a shark's. Then, like the world's most callous killer, the demons lunged straight at him. He felt the talon like hands grab him before he heard the unmistakable sound of steel scraping bone as they drove their blades through him repeatedly. Needle like teeth sank into his flesh and tore off big meaty chunks.

His eyes snapped open as his own screams of agony ripped him out of the dream world. He found himself thrashing about on the couch where he'd fallen asleep hours before, in the safety of his flat. After realising he was safe, he closed his eyes, sank back into the couch, and released a huge sigh while wiping the cool perspiration off his forehead. Once his heart rate had returned to normal, he dragged his legs off the couch and sat up. He yawned widely as he examined the living room. The vodka bottle sat precariously on the edge of the coffee table, the lid lying beside it. It was almost empty. Rubbing his eyes, he reached for it and drank what was left in one go. After thumping the bottle back down on the table, he swung his legs back onto the couch and tossed and turned restlessly for what seemed like an eternity before tiredness captured him and carried him off into a dreamless sleep.

Chapter 4
Truths

Leo was roused from his alcohol induced sleep by a dull ache in his head. Gradually, as he slipped back into consciousness, he felt its intensity increasing until it felt like someone was hammering away on his skull with an iron pole. He massaged his forehead with a gentle hand, groaning as he did so. The pain was still there five minutes later, so he gave up and opened his eyes for the first time. He instantly regretted it. A stream of golden sunlight scorched his eyeballs and made his head hurt even more. He squeezed his eyes tightly and put both hands over his face to block out the offending sunbeams while letting out a groan that was much louder and more aggressive. Sliding off the couch in a very ungraceful manner, he plonked himself onto the floor and dared to open his eyes again.

His line of vision was level with the coffee table, and an empty bottle of vodka stared at him, smugly reminding him that his current hangover was his own fault. If looks could kill, the bottle would have exploded. Once his eyes had adjusted to the daylight, he struggled to his feet, his balance a bit wobbly. The clock on the wall showed it was almost midday. He scooped up the empty bottle and then reached for the two glasses that lay beside it. His hand froze in mid-air.

"Two glasses?" he said to himself, temporarily mystified. The fog lifted like a veil, and the dreaded memory of Lucas and his dire warnings came flooding back to him along with a wave of fear.

"Leo...you've got it wrong... Daniel isn't a member of the Elect...You have this strong urge to protect him...you were built to protect him...Daniel is the Power."

Lucas' words echoed in his head and caused his heart to thump faster and harder. His throat became even drier, and his frozen hand had suddenly thawed.

"Stop it!" he told himself, clenching his quivering hand into a fist. "It was all a dream. Just a dream." He mentally willed his heart and hand to behave normally, repeating the mantra 'it was just a dream' over and over again until the logical part of his brain kicked in. It pointed out that if it had been a dream there would have only been one glass. There were two glasses; two glasses that were intact. He had a perfect memory of dropping those glasses and watching them smash against the floor. His heart palpitated again, and with a shaky hand, he grabbed the glasses with more vigour than necessary and stomped through to the kitchen where he deposited the bottle into the bin.

As he opened the dishwasher to put the glasses in, he gritted his teeth when he was faced with a pile of gleaming dishes that he'd yet to remove. He slammed it closed and placed the glasses on the worktop above. Reaching into the cupboard where he kept medical supplies, he popped three aspirins into his hand and swallowed them along with a glassful of water. His dehydrated body shook with relief. Placing the glass beside the tumblers, he eyed them uneasily before lumbering to the bathroom.

Leo spent a good five minutes brushing the vodka taste out of his mouth before rinsing with far too much mouthwash. He stripped off his work clothes from the day before, tossed them into the laundry basket, turned the shower on, and stepped under the powerful flow of hot water. The water ran down his toned body and began to wash away some of the self-inflicted hangover. His headache was already beginning to ease, and he was able to think more clearly about his meeting with Lucas. As he massaged shampoo into his hair, he began to analyse the facts.

Some random stranger breaks into his house and manages to convince him that one of his students, Daniel, is unknowingly housing the creative power of God in his body. A vicious demon named Baal, along with his army of demonic minions, is hunting for said power in order to destroy all of humanity. He, himself, is a protector of said power and has been gifted magical abilities in order to fight the demons who seek it. Baal, the vicious demon, is closing in on the identity of said power and is approximately a month away from finding out that Daniel is the one.

Having analysed the facts closely using his rational mind, he actually began to giggle as it registered with him just how absurd it all sounded. Lucas had been incredibly convincing, but after careful consideration, Leo was of the opinion that the guy was absolutely mental and had probably escaped from New Craigs, Inverness' home to the mentally ill.

'How did he know your name? How did he know Daniel? How did he get into your flat?'

His inner voice threw up some questions that he hadn't considered. He thought about them as he squeezed a blob of masculine smelling shower gel into the palm of his hand. It wasn't long until he'd figured it out.

'The guy is a psycho,' he told himself, 'This is what they do. They stalk someone for a long time before making their move. He could have easily been stalking you and listening in to your conversations in restaurants or clubs.'

That was it. If he was going to talk about any student to his friends when they were out socialising, he would talk about Daniel, and a psycho like Lucas would easily pick up on it by merely listening.

After washing the shower gel off, he closed his eyes and just stood under the jet of water, turning up the temperature until the water was almost too hot. And he just stood, letting the water blast onto him while he chanted a small incantation to release the tension from his body and mind. He focused on the sensation and the sound of the hot water pounding against his body, and he enjoyed the peace and tranquillity of the moment.

Five minutes later, he turned the water off and stepped out of the shower cubicle. The air in the bathroom was cold but not unbearable; it clung to his skin and rejuvenated him. He reached over and took the towel off the heated rail and wrapped it around his waist.

Exiting the bathroom, he felt a million times better with the crazy Lucas far from his mind. He grew more amused at his own stupidity for believing Lucas, and it definitely helped to lighten his mood. He hummed a tune while walking to the kitchen. The humming turned to whistling as he stepped onto the cold tiles of the kitchen floor and made his way to the fridge. He pulled out a tub of butter and a block of cheese before pushing the fridge door shut. The fridge door closed to reveal a familiar face grinning down at him. He jumped as if he'd just been electrocuted by a thousand volts. Following his frightful scream, the butter and cheese fell to the floor.

"What's for breakfast?" Lucas asked, amusement dancing all over his face.

Leo was far from enamoured. "Jesus Christ!" he raged. "What the fuck are you doing here?"

"Are you kidding me?" Lucas said, his expression one of mock hurt. "I had a great time last night. We saw each other at the restaurant, we had a drink together, and you spent some quality time with me. We both know that I am awesome. The least you could do is make me breakfast as a thank you for having the pleasure of my company."

"How the hell are you getting into my flat, you absolute psychopath?" Leo fumed, trying his hardest to melt Lucas with an acidic stare. "Did you get a key cut or something?"

Lucas appeared thoughtful. "Hmm, I never thought of getting a key cut. That would have been so much easier."

When he didn't elaborate, Leo opened his mouth to make a sarcastic comment but became distracted by twinkling blue eyes that had just scanned over his naked body.

Lucas seemed to notice he'd been caught stealing a glance and quickly changed the subject. "You haven't gone to visit Father O'Connor yet, and I wanted to know why."

Leo became very aware that he was naked except for the towel around his waist and instinctively placed one of his hands where the towel was tied together. He reached down and picked up the butter and cheese, placing them on the counter as he considered Lucas' question. "You want to know why I haven't visited Father O'Connor, fine. It's because—hey! Are you even listening to me?"

Lucas had just picked up the cheese and was studying the label intently. "Cheddar? Not my favourite, but it'll do."

"Oh, Jesus Christ!" Leo snapped.

"No, I'm Lucas, remember?" Lucas grinned, placing the cheese back onto the counter before crossing his arms. "I know Jesus," he said matter-of-factly. "Nice guy."

Leo had heard enough. "Ok! You are officially a *crazy person*! You don't just barge into a person's flat and invite yourself to breakfast! It's called *harassment*. Now, I'm going to get dressed, and I want you to *not* be here when I get back. Ok?"

Lucas unfolded his arms and clapped his hands together triumphantly. "Great! After you're dressed, we can go and speak with Father O'Connor."

Leo's growing irritation was beginning to make his head hurt again. "Hey! Nut-job! Read my lips. I. Am. Not. Going. Anywhere. With. You. Got it? Get out of here before I call the Police!"

Lucas sighed, and his shoulders sagged. He reached into his pocket and slapped a small piece of paper on the counter beside the butter and cheese. "My phone number. Use it when you've pulled your head out of your ass." The amusement that was on his face earlier was completely gone. "If I'd known that you were this stubborn and annoying, I'd have told Michael to go and shove this mission," he muttered. He walked past Leo and headed for the hallway. "Just go and see O'Connor. He'll have the proof you need."

"Who the fuck is Michael?" Leo demanded, but his question fell on deaf ears.

"Just go and see O'Connor," Lucas repeated as he left the kitchen and entered the hallway.

Leo followed him, walking briskly and continuing the argument. "Yes, that's exactly what I'll do. I'll go and see Father O'Connor right away and tell him that Lucas, the big crackpot, told me to come and visit him so we can discuss all of the crazy things that are in his head."

"Good, I'll let him know that you'll be at the Cathedral within the hour." Lucas was soon at the front door and unlocking it. "Don't keep him waiting. He's a very busy man," he said, stepping out onto the royal blue carpet of the hallway.

"I'm ever so glad that such a busy man could squeeze me into his busy schedule with such short notice so that we can talk about demons and the pending apocalypse." Leo's voice dripped with sarcasm, and as he went to close the door on Lucas' face, he stopped midway and opened it fully again to deliver a parting shot. "I'll be sure to tell him how entertaining you were and how I got to spend so much time in your awesome company."

Amusement returned to Lucas' face as he shrugged coyly. "You can tell him that if you really want to. It's entirely up to you. Personally, if I were you, I'd be more inclined to tell him that I'm having dreams about Moses."

Leo's jaw hit the floor, but he came to his senses quickly and did well to regain his composure. "Noted. I'll also tell him that you're a complete asshole. Have a nice day and don't come back." He slammed the door so hard that the walls around it came alive momentarily.

As he locked the door, he was sure he could hear Lucas laughing out in the hallway. Irritation flared up in him once more, and he pounded a fist against the door before storming down the hall and into his bedroom. He sat on the bed and massaged his temples to rid himself of the headache that had returned. He breathed deeply, trying his hardest to keep the rising hysteria at bay.

"Rationalise it, Leo," he told himself, placing his hands on his knees and drumming his fingertips against them. "Rationalise it," he repeated. But he had nothing. There may have been the slightest chance that Lucas had been an exceptionally good, albeit crazed, stalker who had picked up personal information about his life by secretly following him. He could then have used this information along with his exceptionally warped mind to weave a sinister and frightening story. Highly unlikely, but not altogether impossible. There was, however, no explanation for the fact that Lucas knew about the Moses dream. No explanation existed except for one: Lucas was telling the truth.

He stood up sharply from the bed and whipped off the towel from around his waist. He let it fall to the floor before marching to the wardrobe where he hauled out his clothes for the day: socks, underwear, a white tee, dark blue denim jeans and a tight fitting green hoodie. He threw on his clothes, his movements efficient and militant. Reaching under his bed, it took him a moment to locate a pair of tan boots. He pulled them on, laced them up, and was marching once more, bending to scoop the towel off the floor on his way out of the bedroom.

In the bathroom, he threw the towel into the laundry basket, half attempted to style his damp hair with an expensive hair gel, and then left the room as quickly as he'd entered.

He was on a mission as he strode into the living room to claim his duffle coat that was draped over the couch. As he pushed his arms into the sleeves, he stole a quick glance out of the window. The white rooftops of the churches and shops told him that it had snowed heavily during the night. Patting down his pockets revealed he had his wallet, cigarettes and phone.

Shortly after the regimented preparations to leave for the Cathedral, he was stood in the elevator. He was alone, and thoughts about Father Cornelius O'Connor were at the forefront of his mind. He had absolutely no idea what he was going to say to the man when he arrived at the Cathedral. That was, of course, if he even existed at all. He felt stupid, impulsive. It couldn't be real. None of it.

'Then why are you going to visit an old man at the Cathedral, you fool?'

Leo was usually very good at ignoring his inner voice when it was being sanctimonious, but in this instance, it had a valid point.

'You're going so that you can prove to yourself that Lucas is a raving lunatic who made the whole thing up. Then you'll be able to have a fabulous weekend. That's why you're going.'

It made him feel a lot better knowing he had a focus for visiting the Cathedral and that he was not going just because some nutcase told him to. The 'ping' of the elevator door pulled him out of his reverie of thoughts and stopped him scrutinising his own sanity for the time being. He stepped out into the main entrance vestibule of the building and was pleased to find it deserted. He didn't feel like making small talk with the neighbours. His sole mission was to prove that Lucas was insane.

The cold afternoon air gripped him tightly as he stepped out onto the street. The city was a hive of activity, considering it was early January. He figured most people would have been broke after the festive period, but he'd clearly underestimated the power of the January sales. The shoppers buzzed about, flying in and out of shops and clutching sacks of wonderful treasures. He tied the top button of his coat, tightened the scarf around his neck, and then took off towards the bridge that lay close by.

Stuffing his hands into his pockets, he trudged through the snow and ice, weaving in and out of the swarms of people who zipped past him and occasionally stung him on the elbow with their shopping bags. One shopper was so focused that she failed to see a dangerous patch of ice until her boots hit it. He could do nothing but watch as both of her feet slid from underneath her and left the ground altogether. He winced as she crashed to the floor, then immediately ran to help untangle the bags of shopping from her arms.

"Are you okay?" he asked while helping her to stand. He couldn't see her face as she was bent over slightly and dusting off the snow from her luxurious red coat.

"Oh my god! Yes, I'm perfectly fine thank you. Just hurt pride," the woman exclaimed with an embarrassed laugh. "You'd think I'd never seen a sale before. Wait until my husband and son hear about this, they'll be hooting for days!"

Leo laughed lightly. "Hey, it happens to the best of us. Anyway, the council should have had these pavements treated with grit. Easy to see they're trying to save money," he added, relishing the opportunity to take a swipe at his employers. The woman, having finished composing herself, looked up for the first time.

Leo's stomach somersaulted. "Mrs Macintosh!" he exclaimed, taking the woman by surprise. She was taller than him and had blonde wavy hair. Although he knew her to be almost double his age, a rigorous exercise regime, including various martial arts and tennis coaching, kept her in good shape. The only sign of aging was light wrinkling around her blue eyes and her forehead.

Mrs Macintosh looked at him properly and recognition set in. "Oh! It's you, Mr Alexander," she replied, her expression warming immediately. "Thank you for stopping to help me."

"If I'd known it was you, Mrs Macintosh, I'd have carried on walking," Leo joked, managing to step into his 'teacher' persona. There was a fine line between being friendly and being overfamiliar with the children's parents. He always remained professional while at the same time managing to inject his own sense of humour into such chance meetings. This particular meeting, with this particular parent, was not what he needed at the moment. He'd have to keep it short and sweet.

"Oh you are terrible!" she said with a hearty chuckle.

He couldn't help but notice her lavish jewellery as she reprieved him of the shopping bags. Her wedding ring, which he suspected was from Tiffany's, was a platinum band encrusted with sparkling diamonds. The bracelet of silver daisies dangling from her wrist had the elegant and unique stylings of Orcadian designer Judith Glue.

"Honestly, Mr Alexander, you're a gentleman. There are not many who would have stopped. Did you know that Daniel is always raving about you? Listen to what he said last weekend." Mrs Macintosh's eyes were twinkling as she recounted the story. "We were watching a Knight's Tale, and Daniel asked who I thought was a modern day knight. Naturally, I said it was his Dad and him. I asked him the same question and he said – Mr Alexander, because he cares for us, makes us feel safe, and protects us from the bullies. Now, isn't that high praise?"

Leo blushed. "Aw, what a sweet thing for him to say," he said, placing a hand lightly on her arm. "Well, if you're okay then I'll let you get on with your shopping. These sales won't last forever." He retracted his hand and placed it back in his pocket while taking a few steps in the direction of the Cathedral.

"No, they certainly won't. Thank you again, Mr Alexander. Wait until Dan hears about his Mum slipping on the ice in front of his teacher! And in such spectacular style too!"

"I won't tell if you don't," he said with a grin and put more distance between them. "Enjoy your weekend, and tell that boy of yours I owe him one. My desk has never looked tidier."

"You too. Don't worry, I'll tell him. Cheerio!" Mrs Macintosh called as she disappeared into the Judith Glue boutique.

'Of all the people to meet!' he thought as he reached the crossing just before the bridge. The traffic lights stopped the oncoming traffic and allowed him and some other pedestrians to cross. He was pleased for managing to act as normal as possible given the circumstances. If he hadn't acted normal, it would have confirmed to him that he was as bonkers as Lucas was. He amused himself as he crossed the bridge with thoughts of how it would have been if he'd told Mrs Macintosh where he was off to.

'Hello, Mrs Macintosh. How are you? Where am I going? Well, here's some school gate gossip for you and the other mums. Just heading to meet with Father O'Connor to discuss your son, Daniel. Did you know that very soon he will be hunted by demons because he is housing God's creative power which they want to use to unravel the whole of creation? Oh, and how's your husband?'

The grim thought entertained him as he stepped off the bridge and made a left which took him down the river side. His boots sank into the soft snow with a satisfying crunching sound as he walked.

He followed the river down towards the Cathedral and noted how high and fast it was with only about a metre of the riverbank showing above the racing water. His study of the river came to an abrupt end when he felt someone wrap an arm around his shoulders.

"I knew you'd see reason," Lucas said brightly as he walked in perfect sync with Leo.

Hearing Lucas' American accent in his ear annoyed him. "The only thing I can see is that you need psychological help," he snapped, shrugging the muscular arm from around his shoulders. "There is nothing reasonable about what I'm doing. It is the complete opposite of reasonable."

Lucas sighed. "The sooner you accept the truth, the faster we can put things in place to protect and hide Daniel."

Leo stopped walking and stared into Lucas' eyes. For what seemed like an eternity, he couldn't remember how to talk, or how to formulate a thought, or how to breathe. Those deep cerulean eyes held him captive, rendering him powerless. It was like the irises were alive, a constant ripple effect that repeated itself over and over. A car in the distance blared its horn, snapping him out of the hypnosis.

He remembered who he was again and managed to look pissed off. "The only thing I accept is that in order for you to leave me alone, I have to meet with some priest guy who'll tell me you're completely delusional." He turned on his heel and strode ahead.

"Whatever, Leo. I'm only trying to help you face facts. It'll be hard for you afterwards," Lucas said, easily catching up with him and falling back into step.

"Hard for me how?" Leo asked, his tone venomous.

"It'll be hard for you to listen to me say 'I told you so' after we're done speaking with Cornelius." Lucas let out a burst of laughter as Leo started to rant.

"I actually hate you. You are the most egotistical human being I've ever met! You really are an asshole." His hands swung wildly by his side. He worked extremely hard to ignore the butterflies in his stomach and the goose bumps on his neck that had appeared after hearing Lucas' angelic laugh.

"You may hate me now, dude, but that'll change. You'll grow to like me," Lucas said knowingly.

Leo snorted. "Oh really? So as well as being a psycho, you're also a psychic? I suggest you clean your crystal ball, Mystic Meg, and try again because unless you're getting a personality transplant in the very near future, my feelings towards you will not change." Lucas fell silent just as they turned the corner and the cathedral came into view.

The gothic building could be described in one word: stunning. He'd never really studied the architecture before, but it was hard to ignore, especially being this close to the stone giant. The main body of the Cathedral had been made from pink sandstone, and its entrance was flanked by two huge nave columns of granite. Flower beds and grassy areas surrounded the building like a moat. The grassy areas were home to various trees that should have stood tall and proud but were overshadowed by the grandeur of the towering Cathedral.

There wasn't anybody in the Cathedral grounds apart from a lonely man who looked to be very hard at work. He was throwing grit on the steps up to the entrance to combat the treacherous ice.

"Good afternoon," Lucas said cheerily, ascending the steps first.

The man carried on throwing grit, never lifting his head. "Is it? I wouldn't have noticed with all this snow," he grunted.

"Please ignore him, sir. He's an idiot," Leo said as he followed Lucas up to the double doors. He expected Lucas to hold the door for him, but he was mistaken. The heavy oak door swung back after Lucas had passed through and hit him on the shoulder. He rubbed his minor injury and watched as the door was pulled ajar slightly.

Lucas poked his head through the small opening, a look of concern etched on his face. "I'm sorry," he said, his look of concern switching to a wide grin. "It must be because I'm an idiot. Allow me to get the door."

It would have given Leo great pleasure to slap the grin off Lucas' smug face, however, he gritted his teeth and fake smiled while walking through the door which Lucas was now holding open. "Thank you," he muttered as he stepped through.

He had never once set foot in the Cathedral and was kicking himself that he hadn't taken the time to visit because the interior decoration was astounding. The first thing to catch his eye was an enormous bronze cross which was suspended from the roof directly opposite the doors he'd just walked through. He walked slowly up the aisle that had been created by the traditional wooden benches and admired the spectacular golden altar and a beautifully decorated reredos in front of him. The reredos depicted several biblical stories— the most prominent ones being of Moses and the exodus, Noah and the flood, and the Resurrection. In between every third row of benches stood stone pillars that were engraved with intricate religious symbols. The pillars reached up to merge with the ceiling which was remarkably plain in comparison to the rest of the interior. The east wall had three small stain glass windows, each one depicting one of the three higher archangels; Raphael was on the right hand window, Gabriel on the left, and Michael in the centre. The west wall had one large stain glass window showing Jesus ascending to heaven on a cloud while his disciples watched in amazement.

Lucas appeared at his side. "It's impressive, isn't it?"

"Yeah," Leo agreed, while marvelling at the magnificence of the Cathedral. He forgot for a moment that he hated the man. "It's beautiful."

"You should have seen it when it was first built."

"I can't imagine what it would have been like when it was brand new," Leo replied, glancing at the stone pulpit as he passed it. Then he remembered why he was even in the Cathedral and was suddenly all business like. "Right, lead the way to Father O'Connor," he said sharply. "Let's get this over with."

"Sure. This way," Lucas responded flatly and walked right up to the altar without another word.

He wasn't sure if he'd imagined it, but Leo sensed that Lucas had appeared a little dejected when he told him that he wanted to get it over with. It made him feel a little bit guilty.

'Oh for Christ's sake!' his inner voice boomed. *'Don't feel guilty about hurting the stalker's feelings! He broke into your flat twice and now has you visiting another potential fruitcake to prove that you haven't lost your marbles! Do not feel sorry for him!'*

He followed Lucas to the altar and was surprised to see a door on the west wall and another directly opposite. The door on the east wall had three thick wooden beams across it as well as a large metal bolt. There was also a keyhole underneath the round handle.

"Wow, security is tight for that room. What's in there?" When Lucas didn't answer, he turned around to discover that he was alone. He glanced back at the mysterious door, and his curiosity began to burn. Just as he considered peeking through the keyhole, Lucas reappeared.

"Hey, what's taking you so—oh, they're doing refurbishments in there. They've completely ripped out the entire floor and there's a ten metre drop to the basement. Anyone can come and visit the Cathedral at any time so we keep it locked. Can you imagine the grief this place would get if someone fell down there and hurt themselves? Compensation pay out would be massive."

Leo was half hoping there would be something a bit more exciting than simple refurbishment work, but he put his disappointment to one side and followed Lucas through the door and into a small square room.

The room was completely plain and quite derelict. There was nothing on the cream coloured walls apart from a painting of the crucifixion, and the only furniture in sight was a tiny desk and chair which was pushed into a corner. The chair was occupied by an elderly man dressed in plain black trousers and a marl grey knitted jumper. With the aid of a walking stick, the man stood upon seeing Leo, exposing how tall he really was.

"Welcome, Leo. I'm Father Cornelius O'Connor, but please, call me Cornelius. It's a pleasure to meet you at last."

The gentle Irish accent was pleasing to Leo's ears. Cornelius O'Connor was not at all what he'd been expecting.

He'd imagined a batty, shrivelled up mess of a human being who couldn't remember his own name. He couldn't have been more wrong. Cornelius, who appeared to be in his late seventies, had a youthful energy about him that was both strong and vibrant. He had a full head of hair which was completely grey and well kept. His eyes were a warm brown colour and sparkled with wisdom, while his smile was kind and genuine. If he'd met Cornelius on the street he'd have thought he was a sweet old man who would have made an awesome grandpa. As it was, he was here to prove that Lucas was a lunatic, and Cornelius' grandpa exterior would have to be brushed to one side.

"Hi, I'm sure it's nice to meet you too, Cornelius, but I'm afraid I can't stay and chit chat." Leo got straight to the point. "The thing is, Lucas here broke into my flat last night, and then again this morning. Not a pleasant experience, despite him being very easy on the eye." He caught sight of Lucas straightening up at this acknowledgement. "I'm really sorry to be taking up your time, seeing as you're so incredibly busy, but Lucas is convinced that I'm a member of some cult that's been handpicked by the Archangels to protect God's creative energy from a bunch of demons who want to use it to destroy mankind. I know, absolute craziness. If you could tell him that he is completely and utterly nuts, that'd be great. Then I can go home and get on with my life. Thank you so much."

Cornelius raised his eyebrows before turning his eyes to Lucas.

Lucas shrugged. "I told you."

The old man looked back to Leo. "Lucas speaks the truth. Is the fact that you have magical abilities not proof enough?"

"Listen, I had the exact same conversation with this wacko last night." Leo jerked his thumb in Lucas' direction. "I don't know why I can use magic. I just can. But what you're saying is absolute rubbish. I don't believe it, so could you please leave me alone to get on with my weekend?"

Cornelius bowed his head slightly. "As you wish, young man. Just pretend that Lucas never visited you and that you've never heard of the Power. To you, it doesn't exist."

Leo waited for Cornelius to say something more, and when it was apparent that the old man had finished, he nodded a few times. "Yeah, exactly. Thanks." He began backing out of the room while continuing to talk. "It was nice meeting you, Cornelius—not so much you, Lucas—but goodbye all the same. Don't take this the wrong way, but I hope I never see you again."

He was elated as he turned on his heel and took a step forward to leave the room. He was finally getting out of this madness, and the first thing he was going to do was call Wendy. No matter how sick she was, she *had* to hear about this drama.

He stepped back into the main body of the Cathedral and felt like a gigantic weight had been lifted off his shoulders. Just as he grasped his phone, the most horrific blood curdling scream filled the air. The sound paralysed him and rooted him to the spot. He'd heard a very similar sound once before, and his brain frantically tried to pinpoint when and where. The scream came again, and his hands shot up to cover his ears as he backed into the room where Lucas and Cornelius were. His eyes locked onto the bolted door where the screams were coming from. They weren't screams of help or screams of fear. They were screams of pure evil. His insides were frozen with fear; his whole body was shaking. In the small room, Lucas and Cornelius had moved into the centre of the room and were watching him intently with serious expressions.

"What's the matter, Leo?" Cornelius asked gently.

"That noise! What is it?" he demanded, his voice quivering.

Cornelius smiled sadly. "You already know."

Leo clutched his ears harder when another shriek erupted from behind the bolted door. "No, I don't! What is it? Make it stop!" he pleaded.

"You've had the dreams, you know what it is," Cornelius replied, stepping closer to him and resting a withered hand on his shoulder. "We didn't want to do this to you, but you've left us no choice."

Another scream. This time the scream was followed by a crashing sound. The locked door shook; something was battering it from the other side. He took a step back, his eyes wide. "Make it stop! You people are crazy! Stop doing this to me!"

"Lucas caught the demon last night and brought it back here," Cornelius explained. "He knew that in order to convince you of the truth, you would need real evidence. Well, here it is."

"There are no such things as demons! This isn't real," Leo whispered to himself, the screaming getting wilder and more regular. More crashing sounds came, and the door looked as if it was going to cave in at any moment. He felt a pair of strong hands on his shoulders, and the next thing he saw were *those* blue eyes. They were staring into his, penetrating his soul.

"Leo, I know this isn't easy for you, but you have to believe us. Everything I told you about Baal and the Power is true. I didn't want to frighten you, but I have to make you believe. You have to believe or we'll all die!" Lucas' voice was confident yet desperate. "Listen to me, Leo, focus on me. I want you to concentrate on your breathing. You need to calm down before we open that door."

Leo was slowly being pulled out of his terror by Lucas' calming voice until he heard the door was to be opened. "What!? Are you fucking crazy? You can't open that door!" he gasped, gripping tightly onto the man's strong forearms.

"And why not?" Lucas asked, still holding Leo's shoulders. "Why don't you want me to open the door?"

Leo was sure that in a matter of minutes, Lucas wouldn't need to open the door. "Because I believe you! I saw the demons in my dreams last night, and I believe you! They screamed just like that!" he confessed. "Please make it stop!"

Cornelius and Lucas exchanged a look. "Okay, but in order for it to stop, Lucas has to open the door and kill it," Cornelius explained.

Lucas put an arm around Leo's shoulders and squeezed gently. "It'll be okay. I can kill it easily. Just wait here with Cornelius." Lucas left the room and closed the door.

Suddenly, everything went deathly quiet. Leo could hear the pounding of his own heart. There was a loud clunking noise, and he knew that Lucas was taking away the wooden beams. The knot of fear in his stomach tightened. Two more beams hit the Cathedral floor with similar clunks. Silence. Then came the scraping of the metal bolt being pulled back. Silence. A key turning in an old rusty lock. Silence. A door handle being twisted. Silence. The creaking of a door being opened was followed by the sinister and demonic screaming which was louder than ever. Leo cowered behind Cornelius.

There was the unmistakable sound of scuffling followed by a barbaric war cry that drowned out the demon's shrieks. Next came several 'thudding' sounds like someone was bouncing a football. The silence that followed was deafening. Leo finally removed his hands from his ears and stood up straight. His eyes were locked on the door handle of the room that he and Cornelius were hiding in. The handle turned. He held his breath until the door swung open. Lucas filled the frame, looking mightily pleased with himself as he stepped through the threshold.

"See," he said with a shrug, "No big deal." He raised his arm to show Leo something that looked like a severed human head, except bigger. A substance, looking remarkably like blood, only it was inky black, dripped from where the neck used to be. "They aren't scary when they look like this." Lucas grinned smugly.

Leo couldn't take his eyes off the head that was being held up like a hunting trophy. Even in death, the demon's snarling expression was one of pure rage. The skin looked dry and papery, decorated with protruding black veins that lay frozen beneath. His hand shot to his mouth as a putrid aroma reached his nostrils causing him to gag.

"Fuck this!" he managed to say as he made a bid for the door. "Stay the fuck away from me!" he yelled, as he pushed past Lucas who had the decency to hold the demon's head away from him as he fled from the room. His gagging was not helped in the slightest by the sight of the beheaded demon corpse which lay face down in front of the altar like some freak offering to God. A pair of enormous black feathered wings sprouting from the demon's back were mangled and broken. The stench of rotting flesh and decay made his stomach lurch, and it wasn't long before he was tearing down the aisle.

He couldn't remember the journey from the Cathedral back to his flat. It was a blur. Despite the fact his legs had turned to jelly, he'd made it home. As he closed the front door behind him, he locked it and pulled the chain across before leaning his back against the wood. Standing with his eyes closed and his head resting against the door, he attempted to digest what he'd just witnessed. Within ten seconds of trying, he was sprinting through the hallway and into the bathroom where he fell to his knees in front of the toilet and vomited until there was nothing left in his stomach. Tears streamed down his cheeks as he continued to wretch, and with each heaving motion, he felt a stabbing pain in his side.

When his gag reflex eventually relented, he laid his head on the toilet seat, catching his breath and willing his heart rate back to normal. When he was sure his heart wouldn't burst through his chest, he hauled himself off the bathroom floor, turned on the cold tap, and splashed water over his face. He didn't realise he was still shaking until he reached for the small hand towel that hung on the rail next to the sink. After drying his face, he stared at himself in the mirror. It was clear he looked every bit as bad as he felt.

"What's happening?" he whispered to his reflection. "Am I going crazy?" His reflection offered no answer, so he returned the hand towel and walked wearily out of the bathroom.

After dragging himself into the living room, he walked over to the window and placed his head against the cold glass. His eyes were immediately drawn to the Cathedral where he watched a group of about ten crows flying erratically around the naves. The Cathedral still stood there, grand and magnificent, but it no longer held any kind of wonder or mystique for him. Instead, it was a reminder of the gruesome horror he'd witnessed.

The demon had shaken him to his very core. It proved that Lucas had been telling the truth about demons existing in the real world. This scared him to the point that he wanted to crawl into bed, curl up into a ball, and weep. If demons actually existed like Lucas said they did, it meant everything else that the demon killer had told him was true. While this terrible realisation sunk in, his vision became blurry, his stomach knotted for what seemed like the hundredth time since the previous night, and his heart grew heavy. Daniel. Beautiful, gentle, innocent Daniel. The boy whose whole world was probably going to be turned upside down, and he didn't even have a clue. He'd be plunged into a twisted game that he wouldn't be able to understand, let alone cope with. It was unjust and cruel; another Daniel had been thrown to the lions. Anger coursed through him at the unfairness of it all. How could a benevolent God have allowed this to happen?

"It's just sick," he muttered weakly to the empty room. Images of demons hunting Daniel flashed through his mind causing him to shake his head vigorously from side to side in an attempt to dispel them. He wanted nothing more than to protect Daniel, but he was beyond frightened. He remembered the way he'd reacted to the demon at the Cathedral. He'd fallen to pieces, and it was pathetic. What was he going to do against a demon?

'Light a fire and invite it to toast marshmallows,' he thought bitterly to himself.

He shut his eyes tightly and resigned himself to the fact that he was not going to be much help in protecting Daniel.

"…he cares for us, makes us feel safe and protects us…."

Out of the foreboding darkness, he heard Daniel's voice. The words that Daniel had spoken to his mother forced their way into his head and were ringing out loud and clear. His eyes opened and he wiped away the tears that lingered there. A new feeling of determination washed over him as he walked away from the window, striding with purpose towards the kitchen. If Daniel needed protection, he would not deny him it. Ever since he started practising magic, he was always wishing for something huge to happen in his life, some higher purpose. And now that it had arrived, was he going to suddenly start having panic attacks and wimping out?

"I don't fucking think so," he told himself as he walked into the kitchen.

He headed straight for the worktop where he'd placed the butter and cheese earlier. Next to them lay the small piece of paper that Lucas had left.

Lucas answered on the first ring. "Leo?" He sounded relieved and worried at the same time. "I'm sorry for what happened. It was too soon. I can't believe I thought it would be a good idea to spring a demon on you like that. It's just that we're running out of—"

"Lucas," he interrupted as he walked back through to the living room, "I'm fine. You were right to show me the demon. It made me realise that if demons were real, then you must be telling me the truth about Daniel."

"I am telling the truth. You've no idea how much I wish that it wasn't true, Leo, but it is. All of it. Baal is close."

Leo shuddered at the mention of Baal's name. "Yes, you said last night. At least we have a month to prepare." There was a sharp intake of breath followed by silence on the other end of the phone. He began pacing back and forth in front of the window. "Lucas? We have a month right?"

"It's happened." Lucas' tone had changed and had a sudden urgency to it.

Leo's mouth was dry, and he could barely speak. He felt like he was suffocating. While he waited for Lucas to tell him what had happened, he glanced momentarily out of the window as something big and black caught his eye in the direction of the Cathedral. It felt like someone had crushed his heart with ice cold hands when he realised what it was. He could feel bile rising at the back of his throat as his brain processed the horrific image of hundreds of crows swarming the Cathedral. Some sat on the rooftop, some flew in and out of the naves, and some dive bombed the pedestrians walking past. "Oh my god," he whispered. "Lucas, what is it?"

"Baal knows."

Leo gasped before the phone he'd been clutching slipped from his grasp and fell to the floor.

Chapter 5
Out of Time

"Baal knows."

The words rang loudly in his head, blocking everything else out. He didn't need to ask Lucas for any explanation; he understood. He felt it in his gut. Baal had identified his target.

"Leo? Are you still there? Leo? Hello?"

He could just make out Lucas' panicked words coming from somewhere on the floor. He reached down, picked up the phone, and held it to his ear. "I'm here," he said hoarsely. "Where are you?"

"Thank god!" Lucas said, sounding relieved. "Don't leave your apartment. I'm coming over."

"Okay," he replied, his voice betraying the fact that he was still in shock. "Door's open." He hung up and lingered by the window.

Suddenly, Lucas burst through the Cathedral doors and sprinted down the stone steps, his leather coat billowing behind him. He moved so quickly that the murder of crows swarming the building didn't have time to react to his presence. Leo was glad Lucas was rushing; the sooner he arrived, the sooner they could start to look for Daniel.

Finding Daniel would be a problem. Trying to get him away from his parents so they could hide him was an even bigger one. He had no idea how they were going to convince Mr and Mrs Macintosh to part with their son. Daniel's parents would think the whole story was insane and probably call the police, just like he had threatened to do to Lucas. No obvious solutions were jumping out at him, so he put the problem to the back of his mind for the time being. He had to get ready.

He moved away from the window and stepped out of the living room, pocketing his phone as he walked through the hallway and up to the front door. After unlocking it, he walked briskly to his bedroom, threw the wardrobe doors open, and dragged a large wooden chest out into the centre of the room. He knelt on the floor and opened the chest to reveal a variety of witchcraft books, an endless supply of candles, incense sticks, herbs, oils, ribbons, voodoo dolls, pentagrams, tarot cards and bags of mixed gemstones. He took the top book from the pile which was titled 'A Witch's Offensive' and stuffed it into a small black rucksack he'd retrieved from under his bed. He added in a few candles of different colours, three black linen bags full of gemstones, a handful of incense sticks, some ribbons, two voodoo dolls and two metal pentagrams. His hand found his favourite pack of tarot cards, and he lifted them out of the chest.

Leo remembered how he'd fallen in love with them the moment Ela, the owner of the New Age shop, showed them to him. The cards were beautifully decorated with the Archangels and were gold plated around the edges. He opened the box and slid a card out of the pack. Archangel Raphael stared up at him wearing a spectacular golden helmet that looked like it belonged on a Spartan warrior. The only other thing the angel was wearing was a white linen loincloth. His body had been illustrated to look magnificent with all the muscles accentuated in the right places by expert brushstrokes. He placed his index finger on the card and then ran it along the outline of Raphael's stunning golden wings. In his right hand, Raphael carried a huge blade that was glowing green like the aura around him.

"They don't really look like that."

Lucas' voice filled the room, making him jump.

"Actually, that's the closest depiction of Raphael I've seen," Lucas added, peering over Leo's shoulder at the card.

"He's beautiful," Leo stated, gazing into Raphael's sage green eyes. "He's always been my favourite."

"Really?" Lucas said somewhat huffily. "Well, I'm sorry to divert your attention from your favourite Archangel, but we have a crisis to deal with."

The bitterness in Lucas' voice drew Leo back into the room and away from Raphael's beauty. "Yes, I'm aware," he said coldly. He stuffed the card back into the packet and tossed them into the rucksack with the other magical items.

"Bag of tricks?" Lucas asked, his voice suddenly warmer.

Leo looked up from the rucksack that he'd just zipped shut. "Yeah, something like that." He looked up at the smiling Lucas, and his heart fluttered. "We have a problem," he continued as he stood up from the floor and hoisted the rucksack onto the bed. "We don't know where Daniel is."

Lucas looked dumbfounded. "How is that a problem?"

Leo put a hand on his hip. "If we can't find him, we can't protect him from the demons, can we?"

Lucas shook his head from side to side. "Wow, Cornelius is going to have a field day training you."

Leo was bewildered by the statement. "I'm sorry, I don't follow."

"Magic, Leo. You can use magic. Find him using magic for Christ's sake!" Lucas exclaimed.

"I…I don't know how to," Leo confessed, his cheeks flushing red. He fumbled with the zipper anxiously. Eventually, he unzipped the rucksack and began rummaging through his supplies. "Maybe there's a spell in the book I packed?"

"Holy Christ!" Lucas threw his hands up in the air and stomped over. "You don't need this!" he snapped, snatching the book out of Leo's hands. "And you certainly don't need any of this shit either," he continued, tipping out all of the rucksack's contents onto the bed.

Leo's temper flared up and began to override his embarrassment. "Hey! What did you do that for? Of course I need this stuff! That's why I packed it, crazy!" He snatched the book back and glared at Lucas.

"You don't need any of it. It's all an illusion."

Leo snorted derisively. "Don't be ridiculous. These tools give me the power I need to utilise the magic in the first place. I can't do it without them."

Lucas imitated Leo's snort. "Now who's being ridiculous?" he asked. "The power comes from within, nowhere else. All of this?" Lucas lifted a metallic pentagram and held it up. "It's an illusion. Have you ever thought about why the other people who shop at that New Age store can't do the things you can do despite having the same tools? They *can't* do those things because they aren't members of the Elect. This New Age gear is bullshit, and no matter how many candles or gemstones they have, they'll never be able to wield magic because they weren't born to. The reason you haven't really amounted to anything magically so far is because your mind is blocked. It remains suppressed by the belief that you require all of these tools to be able to work your mojo."

"And what would you know about it?" Leo asked venomously. "Oh, that's right, apparently you can do things that would put my pyrotechnics to shame."

"This isn't about me, it's about you," Lucas replied, his voice low.

"Just like I thought. All talk and no action."

"Last night, you didn't need any of this junk to use magic yet you almost cremated me. What does that tell you?"

"I don't know how I managed to do that. You had me backed into a corner, and I was scared. It just happened," Leo admitted, trying to avoid the fact that Lucas had a point. "I need to do a locator spell. Will you help me?"

Lucas didn't answer his question right away, and an intense silence descended on the room. Eventually, the American spoke. "I can help you, that book can't. It's like I said, the magic comes from within. You need to reach deep inside of you and feel it. I watched you from outside your classroom window after the children had gone. The cleansing energy you conjured was powerful stuff. I felt it from outside, and there were no tools, no gimmicks. Just you."

Leo shook his head and reached for a white candle. "We're wasting valuable time. I need to find Daniel before those monsters do. Get me some salt from the kitchen, please. I need to get the sacred space ready—"

He stopped talking abruptly when Lucas took his wrist and tugged his hand away from the candle. Before he could object, he was suddenly pulled against a solid muscular chest. His face flushed, his breath caught in his throat, and his entire body was suddenly wrapped up in a divine warmth that radiated from Lucas' body. A fiery passion stirred from deep within his solar plexus and spread through him like wildfire, scorching every fibre of his being.

"Listen to me," Lucas began, his silky smooth voice a soft whisper that Leo could feel brushing his cheek with every word. "You don't need anything to work the magic, except you. Get it, and get it fast. You have a powerful gift inside of you, and you need to learn how to use it or you'll be worse than useless against the demons."

"I don't know how to," Leo repeated, turning away from penetrating azure eyes, his mind clouded by the most intoxicating scent. He swallowed hard when Lucas' hand closed gently around his jaw and pulled his head slowly so their eyes met.

"Yes, you do, and I can help you. Do you trust me?"

Leo surrendered. "Yes."

"Close your eyes," Lucas said, his voice still soft.

As he shut his eyes, he became even more aware of the unnatural heat radiating from Lucas' body. He wanted to ask about it but knew this wasn't the time for questions, so he focused on the rise and fall of Lucas' chest against his own.

"Okay, go to the place you go just before you cast a spell," Lucas instructed. "Begin to feel the energies building up within and around you."

Energy work was incredibly easy for Leo. He had years of practise, and it was like child's play for him so it didn't take long to conjure up the required energy. It would have been even quicker if he didn't have the distraction of being pressed up against Lucas. He felt the familiar energetic charges ignite the air, crackling and fizzling noisily to let him know it was ready to be used.

"Okay, clear your head and picture Daniel as clearly as you can. Feel the desire to find him overwhelm and drown out all other feelings. Flood your whole mind, body and soul with the need to track him down and protect him. Feel the divine stirring in your soul. Embrace it. Succumb to its love and power."

Leo was lulled by Lucas' voice and found it easy to be guided by him. With every word that Lucas spoke, he felt his consciousness drifting off to another plane of existence.

"Seek him out, Leo. Release your mind. Believe that you can find him. Believe you and Daniel are connected and that you know where he is. You *do* know."

He could hear Lucas' voice perfectly yet couldn't feel his own body. It was like he wasn't even in it. He was suddenly aware that he couldn't smell Lucas' scent anymore or feel his warmth. It was just nothingness. He found himself enveloped in a blanket of complete darkness, and in this darkness lay an inner peace and calmness that he'd never experienced. He focused hard on channelling all of his thoughts and energy on locating Daniel, but after what felt like an eternity, he just seemed to wallow around in the nothingness he'd conjured.

He was about to give up when out of the darkness a familiar fragrance invaded his nostrils. He exhaled sharply in surprise.

"Where is he?" Lucas pressed. "Where are you?"

The unmistakable scent of grass continued to permeate his sense of smell, and Leo's heart fluttered with hope. "Grass. I can smell grass," he said in a monotone.

A whooshing sound filled his ears, and there was a roar that sounded like an army of ten thousand men. He tasted salt in the biting wind that was blowing around him and playing with his hair. His vision kicked in, and he was blinded by a sea of blue and red football shirts sitting in a large stadium. Beyond the stadium was a bridge looming in the background like a great metallic monster. He knew exactly where Daniel was. His eyes fluttered open as his consciousness returned to his body.

"He's at the football stadium," he announced before realising that he was still intimately close with Lucas. The warmth of Lucas' body, his musky masculine scent, and his hard muscular frame worked on Leo like an arousing cocktail of sexual desire.

A grin crept across Lucas' face. "I told you that you'd grow to like me, didn't I?"

"Whatever! You grabbed me unaware," Leo retorted, pushing himself off Lucas' chest and marching out of the bedroom. "We need to get to the stadium, and fast."

"You hate it when you're proved wrong, don't you?" Lucas said as he entered the living room, a slight swagger in his walk.

Leo shoved his arms into his duffle coat. "Of course I don't. It's the biggest thrill of my life being proved wrong."

"Why do your people always go to sarcasm first?" Lucas asked. His eyes lit up with mischief.

"My people? And what exactly do you mean by that?" Leo demanded. He twisted his scarf around his neck and yanked it a little too tightly.

"Gay people. I've met a few in my time, and you all

Use major sarcasm as a defence mechanism. It's…interesting."

Leo rolled his eyes. "I'm glad at least one person finds your observations interesting. Perhaps I'll suggest that the sarcasm of the gay population of Inverness be studied after I avert the fucking apocalypse. Can we go and get Daniel now? Or will we wait until Lucifer shows up and rips the kid's still beating heart from his chest?" He didn't wait for an answer and stormed out of the living room. He'd reached the front door when he heard Lucas call after him.

"It's Baal who wants to kill the kid, not Lucifer. Jeez, do you ever listen?"

Leo let out a few choice words in reply to Lucas' question, gripping the door handle tightly when he heard the American chuckling loudly.

The stadium itself was a ten minute drive to the outskirts of Inverness and lay at the edge of the Moray Firth, a triangular inlet of the North Sea. It was always freezing down by the stadium, even in the height of summer. Next to the stadium and crossing the Moray Firth, a massive bridge linked Inverness to the most northern parts of Scotland. The Kessock Bridge was notoriously busy with commuters but had been exceptionally busy recently due to important maintenance work. Leo was relieved it was the weekend as the traffic would be much quieter on the bridge.

He tried hard to concentrate on driving, but his mind was spinning wildly with what he'd just learned about himself. He apparently didn't need any of the so called tools of the trade when performing magic; it was already in him. 'I have enough bloody stuff to open up my own shop,' he thought to himself but only felt amusement, not anger. Perhaps the anger was surpassed by the sense of empowerment he was feeling as a result of being able to conjure up magic just by willing it.

He stole a glance at Lucas who was keeping himself content by looking out of the window and drumming his fingers against the dashboard.

"I know, I'm gorgeous."

Leo blushed. "Excuse me?"

"It's cool. Stronger people than you have fallen for this," he said, gesturing to his face with an open hand.

"It must be nice to have such a...healthy opinion of one's self," Leo replied. "I hate to tell you, but I was actually checking my mirrors." He knew the lie was completely transparent, but he didn't want to boost Lucas' already massive ego.

"Yeah, yeah. Whatever you say," Lucas chuckled, turning his head to look out of the window. "I don't blame you. Look at me, I'm magnificent."

"Oh my god! I've met some big headed people in my time, Lucas, but you are by far the worst. If you were chocolate you'd eat yourself," Leo said with no trace of humour in his voice.

Lucas laughed. "Really? Wow, that is high praise indeed, but I really don't think I'm more egotistical than Tyler."

"What the fuck? How do you know about Tyler? Have you been stalking me or something?"

Lucas laughed again. "I've been watching you for a while."

"For how long?" Leo was very unnerved by the thought that someone had been watching him go about his daily life while he'd remained completely unaware. It was true what they said—ignorance was definitely bliss.

"I actually started out watching Daniel. After we'd found out that he was the one we'd been looking for, we kept a very close eye on him. I've been watching him for almost a year now." Lucas stopped drumming on the dashboard and placed his hands onto his lap. "It wasn't until you took your class to Culloden Battlefield last September that I realised how strong the bond between you and him actually was."

"How could you have known? I treat every child in my class exactly the same," Leo said suspiciously, slowing down the car and eventually stopping at a red light.

"To the casual observer, yes, you do. But after a while, it was so obvious that you had a special bond with Daniel. At the battlefield, the two of you were inseparable. From the moment you stepped off the school bus until the moment you were back on it, he was by your side. Both of you are unaware of it because it's all happening subconsciously. I knew then that there was something about you, but I couldn't put my finger on it. I began watching your every move, tried to suss you out. And then I saw you performing magic for the first time, and I knew exactly what you were. It explained the closeness of you and the boy."

The traffic light went green, and Leo set off again. "Ok, can you stop talking now? I'm a little freaked out that you were watching me and I didn't have a clue. It's…creepy." Leo squirmed in his seat.

"Not as creepy as watching you throw yourself at that Tyler guy," Lucas said. "You could do so much better than him."

Lucas' words made him squirm even more. "I don't throw myself at anybody," he protested somewhat lamely. "And for the record, he's into me too. It's just…Tyler is finding his sexuality difficult to get to grips with."

"He has no problem getting to grips with yours. Interesting."

"Okay, whoa! First of all, that is none of your business, and secondly, this conversation is over." He crunched the gears on the approach to a roundabout and cursed.

"Would you like me to drive?" Lucas asked politely. "I see you're having trouble with the gears."

"No, I would not like you to drive!" Leo snapped. "Anyway, we're here.

Lucas sat upright and began looking around in all directions. "The traffic isn't as bad as I thought it would be," he said, suddenly all business like.

Leo looked at the clock which lay just below the speedometer. "The game started half an hour ago so

101

everybody will be in already. Football fans are never late for the kick off. We just need to find a place to park."

"Look, car park for the home fans," Lucas said, pointing to a large white sign with black writing on it.

"Nice one." Leo sped up and drove past the front of the stadium where the entrance to the club shop and VIP area was. The car park for home supporters lay just beyond the entrance, and he wasted no time in reaching it. He pulled into the enormous car park and began driving down the side of the stadium. Every so often, bits of gravel would clink against the side of the car. Signs indicated that they were currently driving along Row A. Dozens of stewards wearing bright yellow jackets darted around like cockroaches, directing late comers.

"I can't see a space," Leo whispered, as if the stewards were going to hear him.

"Stop the car," Lucas said and unclipped his seat belt.

Leo complied immediately. "What is it?" he asked, his whole body tense.

"I'll get out here and start looking for Daniel while you park the car. I'll call you in ten minutes."

Before he could respond, Lucas opened the door and practically flew out of the car. Once the door was closed, Leo drove off quickly and sent pieces of gravel everywhere. He couldn't see any spaces at all and was beginning to get irritated by the distance he was having to travel away from the stadium. Upon seeing that he was now in Row M, he followed the exit sign and was soon motoring along the main road again. He turned back into the car park and restarted the search for an empty space in Row A once more. A young female steward stepped out from between two parked cars and began signalling at him to drive towards her.

"Please be a space! Please be a space!" he prayed aloud. As he drew nearer to the steward, he saw that she was indeed pointing to an empty space. "Hallelujah!" After praising the Lord, he swung his car into the space, quickly shut off the engine, and leapt out. The car made a beeping sound and the lights flashed momentarily when he pushed the button on his key to lock the doors.

"Sir! Excuse me, sir! That'll be five pounds parking fee!" a shrill female voice shrieked after him as he took off towards the stadium at high speed.

He turned his head to look back at her. She was carrying a ticket machine and had begun jogging after him.

"I'm only going in for five minutes!" he shouted back before going into a sprint. After a couple of minutes in sprint mode, he dared to look back to see if the steward was chasing after him. She wasn't.

Upon reaching the stadium, there was a set of turnstile gates that one had to walk through in order to access the football pitch and the stands. He chose gate number five and pushed forcefully against the cold metal. The gate didn't budge.

"Oi! Watch my turnstile," a voice croaked from the small booth at the side of the gate. "You gotta pay to get in ya know!"

Leo was suddenly struck by the overwhelming desire to tell the elderly man that he'd never, and would never, pay the extortionate prices to watch twenty two overgrown boys do a variety of "skills" that they were grossly overpaid to do including; kicking a football around a field, occasionally rolling around on the grass clutching at their legs, pushing and shoving each other at any given opportunity, and using atrocious language while in full view of impressionable young children. He resisted the urge to voice his opinion and instead dug his hand into his pocket to retrieve his wallet.

"How much for one half?" he asked the man.

"Twenty quid," the old man replied, giving him a hard stare.

"Twenty quid! For one half of a football match? Are you serious?"

"Deadly," came the tender's reply. "Everyone comes to watch the *whole* game, not just one half. Never heard the like in all my life, and I've been doing this gate for twenty five years!"

Leo opened his wallet and pulled out a ten pound note. He thrust it onto the small wooden counter of the booth. "More fool you for sticking it out so long. There's a tenner," he said and attempted to walk through the turnstile. Once again, the turnstile didn't budge. "Oh, come on! I'm only going in for five minutes! Please let me through," he pleaded with the tender.

The elderly man's expression remained the same. "Twenty quid," he repeated and continued to look at Leo as if he were something unpleasant.

If it wasn't an emergency, he would never have handed over another tenner. The tender gave him a triumphant look as another tenner went onto the counter. A clicking sound came from the turnstile, and Leo pushed his way through without thanking the old man.

When he emerged from the turnstile area, he was greeted with a sea of football fans not unlike his earlier vision. They were in a stand directly opposite him and were all transfixed on the enormous green football pitch that was currently home to two football teams. The players were getting stuck in and testing each other to the limit. Both sets of fans had been whipped up into a frenzy and were singing songs with very explicit lyrics. The teacher in him wondered if any of these grown up buffoons had considered that there were children present.

An arctic blast of wind whipped up the ends of his scarf and tugged at his jacket as he hurried along the front of the northern stand. He scanned the crowds of football fans who were all either cheering, singing, swearing, clapping, or stamping their feet loudly. He stopped dead at every set of steps which were roughly thirty metres apart from each other, his eyes scanning the spectator seats all the way to the back. The sting of disappointment hit him every time he saw a young boy around eleven years old with black hair; they'd turn around and it was never Daniel. He thought

104

about shouting Daniel's name but knew his voice would be lost amongst the wind and the racket from the army of supporters who had now gone into a Mexican wave.

By the time he'd covered the entire northern stand, he was beginning to lose hope. There were just far too many people, and it was like looking for a needle in a haystack. He ran a hand through his hair and looked towards the other three stands. His heart grew heavy when he saw they were even bigger than the one he'd just searched. He couldn't see any empty seats either.

'Think, Leo!' he told himself while tapping his forehead in the hope that it might knock the answers into his head. At that moment, his phone vibrated against his hip.

"Lucas?" he shouted into the phone.

"Yeah...me...I haven't found...yet."

He could barely make Lucas' words out. "I haven't found him either. Where are you?"

"I'm...east stand...this place...crawling...demo... Where are—"

The rest of Lucas' words were swallowed up by an almighty roar from the home fans. The stadium went berserk.

"In between the north and east stands!" Leo bellowed. The fans quietened down to their loud state, and he could hear Lucas more clearly.

"Stay wh... you are...I'm close..." Lucas hung up.

Leo had picked up enough of what Lucas had said so returned his phone to his pocket and decided to wait where he was. Just then, a young male steward came striding towards him in an orange fluorescent jacket. He looked in his early twenties at the very most but had the confidence of somebody double his age.

"Sir, you can't stand here. Please return to your seat," the steward said in his best authoritative voice and placed his hand on Leo's shoulder.

"Hey, hey! Could we have a little more decorum, please?" Leo said, jerking his shoulder away from the steward's touch. "I'll just be here until my friend joins me. He's literally on his way," he explained to the steward who had now pulled out a radio from his pocket.

"Ground unit to control. Can I get police back up at the north to east junction? I have a gentleman refusing to move."

Leo's mouth fell open. "Are you for real?"

"Roger that. Back up dispatched," the radio buzzed loudly before the smug steward returned it back to his pocket.

"Was that really necessary?" Leo demanded, glancing around and looking for any signs of Daniel or Lucas.

"I'm just doing my job sir," the steward replied with an arrogant shrug. "Just doing my job."

"Fine. Look, I'm sorry. You can call off the police. I'll move, okay?"

The steward raised an eyebrow before narrowing his eyes. "You're really going to move?" he asked, not bothering to hide his suspicion.

"My friend is almost here, and we were just leaving anyway," Leo said. "See!" He pointed to Lucas who was running towards them. The steward retrieved his radio once more.

"Ground unit to control. Police back up not required anymore, gentleman cooperating."

Leo couldn't help but roll his eyes. "You really love your job, don't you?"

The steward grinned. "Yeah, how can you tell?"

He was about to respond with something extremely cutting when the stadium's tannoy system crackled into life.

"Call out for Daniel Macintosh. That's a call out for Daniel Macintosh. Please report to north turnstile, gate five."

A hand touched Leo's shoulder for the second time. "Look, asshole! I already told you that I was about to move." He spun around to find a bemused Lucas in front of him. "Oh, it's you. Sorry, I thought it was—"

"Never mind that," Lucas interrupted. "We need to get to Daniel."

"Yeah, I heard the announcement," Leo said. "That was genius. I never thought about putting a call out for him."

Lucas looked troubled. "That wasn't me."

The colour drained from Leo's face as the realisation set in. "Shit! Move!" he yelled and shoved past Lucas. His legs had never worked so hard in their life as he bolted back along the north stand. Lucas caught up easily.

"Where is gate five?" he asked.

"All the way to the end of the stand and turn right," Leo panted, trying to ignore the fire that had ignited in his lungs. "It's the gate I just came through."

Lucas became lightning and streaked to the end of the stand.

Despite the intense pain rising from his lungs and making its way into his chest, Leo kept thundering on, his gasping reminding him that he should probably give up smoking. Everything was a blur as he sprinted towards the north turnstiles and gate five. He was almost at the end of the stand with about a hundred metres to go when something blue and red came jumping out of the stand and right into his path. He had no idea how he managed it, but he somehow contorted his whole body while side stepping to almost avoid running into the blue and red object. His right leg clipped it, and he flew into the air and landed on the ground. There was an audible thud before he came skidding to a halt.

His left hip took the brunt of the fall, and he could tell his hands and knees were skinned because they were burning badly. His knees also felt wet which was a sure indicator that they were bleeding. He hauled himself up from the ground and dusted himself off. Some of the fans who had witnessed his spectacular fall were applauding and had burst into a chorus of, "He fell over! He fell over!" Crimson faced, he held out his skinned hands and gave a little bow to entertain the crowd despite the agonising pain. They whooped and cheered. He straightened up again while rubbing his hands together to get rid of the tiny stones that had embedded themselves into his skin.

"Mr Alexander?"

Leo stopped when he heard the familiar young voice calling out his name. He would recognise the sound anywhere, but he didn't dare believe that it was Daniel. Slowly, he turned around to locate the owner of the voice.

And there he stood, at five foot three, managing to look both pleased and concerned at the same time. He wore the blue and red football top that belonged to the home team over a black skin tight under armour that all the kids seemed to wear. Black hair protruded from beneath a blue woolly hat and flopped down to sit above youthful and vibrant blue eyes. His skin was unblemished and had a beautiful olive complexion.

"Are you alright? I'm so sorry," Daniel said, moving towards him.

When Daniel was in reach, Leo pulled him into a smothering bear hug and squeezed him tightly for a moment. Relief flooded his body, and all of the pain was forgotten. He released the boy but held him at arm's length.

"It's okay, Daniel. It was my fault. I wasn't watching where I was going," he said and placed a hand on the boy's shoulder. "Don't worry, I'll be fine."

Daniel smiled. "What are you even doing here? You hate football," he pointed out, a puzzled expression appearing on his face.

Leo laughed. "I do hate it. I'm actually here looking for somebody," he explained, rubbing his hip tentatively as the pain returned. It felt like it was bleeding too.

"There's just been a call out for Daniel Macintosh. I'm just going to check it out, see if it's me."

"It is you," Leo lied. "I put the call out."

"Why?"

"It's nothing to worry about. Your Mum had a little fall in town this morning outside my flat on black ice, and she had to go to hospital to get checked over. I said I'd come and get you."

The boy raised an eyebrow. "Why didn't my dad come for me?"

"He's in meetings all day, and his phone is off." Leo hadn't realised he was such a good liar. "They'll keep trying to contact him, but for now, I've to take you to the hospital." He could almost see the wheels in Daniel's head turning as he processed this information. He inwardly sighed with relief when the boy shrugged.

"Okay. Cool. Do we have to go now?"

Leo nodded. "Yeah. Who are you here with?"

"Joe, Alfie and Will. I'll just go and tell them I have to go."

After he'd told his friends he was leaving, Daniel walked beside him quite happily, keeping one eye on where he was going and the other on the game. Leo was trying hard not to celebrate finding Daniel alive and well just yet and focused solely on making his way to the east turnstile. His brain was already working out where they were going to exit the stadium in relation to the car.

"One of my friends is with me. I'll just call him and tell him to meet us outside," he told the boy who was more interested in the football than anything else. Seeing Daniel so fixated on the football brought a smile to his face. He dialled Lucas' number but the call rang out and went to voice mail, so he hung up and redialled. Leo's smile disappeared when the call rang out and went to voice mail again. The feeling of dread churned around in his stomach as he dialled the number for a third time. This time, the phone was answered. Before he could speak, the home team scored another goal, and the crowd went ballistic, including Daniel who began jumping up and down and punching the air as he walked.

"Hello, Lucas?" he called into the phone, placing a finger in his other ear to try and drown out the savage noises that the football fans were making. As the crowd died down again, the sounds of metal scraping metal filled his ear, steadily becoming louder and more regular. "Lucas! Are you there?" He felt a tugging on his sleeve.

"Mr Alexander, we're almost at the gate," Daniel announced.

He looked down at Daniel, trying to keep the terrified expression off his face. "Excellent. I'm just trying to call my friend now," he said, his voice sounding a tad hysterical. It must have been noticeable because Daniel was now staring up at him with a bewildered look on his little face. "It just keeps going to voice mail," Leo explained, forcing his voice to sound more natural as he hung up and redialled once again. He held the phone back to his ear just in time to hear an all too familiar screaming that snuffed out every bit of warmth in him. It made the blood in his veins run cold.

Overcome with terror that something gruesome might be happening to Lucas, his voice was explosive as he screamed down the phone at exactly the same time the home team scored a third goal. "Lucas! Answer me!" His cry of terror was lost in the roar of the home fans, however, Daniel was close enough to have heard it and was staring open mouthed at him.

"Mr Alexander?" he said meekly.

Leo clutched the phone to his ear and turned to Daniel. He was about to reassure him that everything was okay when he heard Lucas' voice from the other end of the phone.

"Leo!" Lucas called. He sounded breathless, like he was in pain.

"Lucas! What's happened? Are you alright?"

"I'm fine. Have you got Daniel?"

"Yes, he's with me now. We're heading to the car," he replied, reaching over and squeezing Daniel's shoulder and giving him what he hoped was a reassuring smile.

"Good. I'll meet you at the—oh fuck."

The line went dead. Leo's insides turned to stone.

He reached over to Daniel and pulled him close. "Daniel, there's no time to explain what's going on right now, but I will once we're out of here. I need you to stay close to me, okay?" Daniel nodded but looked positively bamboozled by his teacher's bizarre behaviour. "Good boy."

When they reached the turnoff that would lead them to the exit, a distant figure, one that was dressed in black leathers and a metallic black biker's helmet, caught Leo's eye. The muscular curves and feline stance clearly indicated a female. He stopped dead as she lifted her slender hands to her head and removed her helmet. A curtain of jet black hair fell across her shoulders and snaked itself down to the base of her back. An invisible frost made its way from her cold grey eyes and constricted his insides in an unyielding grip. The only thing warm about this woman was her thin ruby red lips.

Even as the frost crept up Leo's spine, he stared back into those lifeless eyes for what seemed like an eternity. In that moment, he felt something he'd never felt before: hatred. It coursed through him, all directed towards this woman who he'd only just laid eyes on. He'd no idea how, but he knew she was his nemesis. She was his enemy, and he knew she felt it too. A cruel and calculating smile split her porcelain face but failed to reach her eyes, eyes that were now focused on Daniel. The smile disappeared in an instant, and her expression became predatory. It was precisely then that a familiar orange jacket popped up behind the woman in black and diverted her attention momentarily.

With the snotty steward distracting the sinister woman, Leo grabbed Daniel's hand and hauled him towards the exit. While he ran, he was aware of something vibrating in his hand and realised it was his phone. He answered it without looking at the display.

"Lucas?"

"Yeah, it's me. You need to get Daniel out of this stadium right now!"

"I'm working on it," Leo wheezed.

"Get a move on! Things just got a whole lot worse."

"Are you crazy? How can things possibly get worse?"

There was a short silence before Lucas answered. "Because the Templars are here."

Chapter 6
The Templars Cometh

Leo ushered Daniel through the turnstile as fast as humanly possible, waiting impatiently for the boy to reach the other side. As soon as Daniel reached the other side, Leo burst through the turnstile to join him, his head spinning back and forth as he tried to get his bearings. "This way, quickly!" he urged, and broke into a run. He kept his arm locked tightly around Daniel's shoulders as they ran, doing his best to guide him away from the stadium while trying to ignore his injuries.

"I can run faster without your arm around me," Daniel said, shrugging off Leo's arm but still staying close to him. "What's going on? Who's the scary looking witch lady?"

"Just keep running," Leo said, wheezing with every step. "We have to keep going!"

"Tell me," Daniel insisted.

"I'll tell you once we get you somewhere safe. Don't stop running until we get to the car."

Leo wasn't surprised to feel his heart hammering against his chest once more. His heart had probably done more work in the last twenty four hours than it had done in the last ten years. He felt a heart attack was imminent.

'Then you wouldn't have to worry about demons and Templars!'

There were times when Leo's inner voice made him laugh and times when it drove him crazy. Today, it was driving him crazy.

"Almost there," he announced, although he wasn't sure if the running commentary was for Daniel's benefit or his own. When they finally reached the car, Leo unlocked the doors. "Quickly, get in and get your seatbelt on," he instructed, glancing back at the stadium and checking for any signs of Lucas. Nothing. He clambered into the driver's seat, clicked his seatbelt into place, and switched the engine on before throwing the gearstick into reverse.

He shot out of the parking space and sped down the gravel track of the car park, dropping his speed before swinging out onto the main road. He slammed the accelerator to the floor, and the car lurched forward while his eyes alternated between the rear view mirror and the road ahead; both were clear.

As he approached the turn off to the away supporters' car park, his eyes dropped to the speedometer for a split second before returning to the rear view mirror again.

"Look out!" Daniel screamed.

Leo looked ahead to see a red motorbike zipping out in front of him. He yanked the steering wheel to the right and veered onto the other side of the road. "Bloody hell!" he yelled, steadying the vehicle and returning to the correct lane. He glanced at Daniel to see him peering into the wing mirror.

"That's her!" the boy cried.

"Who?"

"Scary looking witch lady."

"Are you sure?"

"Yeah, I can tell by the hair. She really shouldn't be riding without a helmet."

Leo looked in his mirror to see that the rider had a mane of black hair. It flapped wildly in the wind as she gave chase.

"Oh bugger!"

"Daniel! Mind your language," Leo scolded. "What is it?"

"She's got friends," Daniel replied anxiously.

Leo checked his mirrors once more to see that six black motorbikes had joined the woman. The riders were dressed head to toe in black except for the visors of their helmets which were emblazoned with a white rectangle. In the centre of the rectangle was a thick red cross.

"Oh bugger!"

"Mr Alexander! Mind your langua—"

The roaring of engines drowned out the rest of the boy's words as the woman caught up and glided smoothly alongside Leo's window. A flash of silver caught his eye, and he turned his gaze to see a razor sharp double sided axe in her left hand. The blades gleamed as she drew it back across her chest and swung it violently.

Glass rained down on him as he jerked his head to the side. The axe grazed his scalp, and he felt a trickle of warm blood running down his face. There was no glass in the window to block the woman's next attack, and he was getting the distinct feeling that she was a pro with this particular weapon. He knew the next strike would hit its target, so he did the first thing that came into his head: swerve. His plan worked. The woman had to return her axe wielding hand to the handle of her bike and steer away from danger. She shot him a spiteful look before speeding off and manoeuvring herself in front of the car.

"They're trying to box us in!" Daniel squeaked. "And they all have weapons."

Leo's eyes swept across all mirrors and quickly assessed the situation. There were two bikers to his left, two to the right and two taking up the rear.

"Hold on, I'm going to—" he started to say but was cut off when his back windscreen and two back passenger windows were shattered by a range of medieval weaponry. "That's my car, you bastards!" In his blind fury, he jerked the steering wheel left and felt a grim satisfaction when he heard a clunking sound followed by the scraping of metal.

"Nice one, Mr A! Two down," Daniel commented helpfully.

"And repeat," Leo said through gritted teeth and jerked the wheel right. There was no clunk this time, but his action made the other two veer so much that they swayed too close to the pavement. Before they could react, their front tyres struck the high concrete kerb, and they sailed over their handlebars.

"Four down, two to go. Ouch!" Daniel said. "That looked sore."

"Good!" Leo said harshly. "Now, for my next trick. Brace yourself!" He stomped on the brake pedal, and two motorbikes slammed into the back of his car. The impact of the collision travelled through his entire body.

"Six down," Daniel said in a quieter voice.

"Yeah, but there's still her," Leo replied, his eyes staring straight ahead at the female biker who had initiated the chase.

She had stopped about a hundred metres ahead and was facing them, her face expressionless as she revved the bike's engine several times.

"What's she doing?" Daniel whispered.

Leo swallowed. "I think she wants to play." He revved his own engine. "Hold on."

Two sets of tyres screeched against the tarmac and sent smoke billowing into the air. Leo's heart was a jackhammer in his ribcage as his speed increased and the gap between them closed. With seconds to spare before the collision, he watched in disbelief as the woman jumped up onto her seat and turned the bike sharply to the left before propelling herself into the air. She landed on the bonnet with the poise and elegance of an Olympic gymnast, and then leapt out of sight. The roof at Daniel's head creaked, and Leo's eyes widened.

"Get your head down, now!" he yelled at Daniel.

Daniel's window exploded as the axe head crashed through it. The boy screamed in surprise and covered his head as shards of glass showered him. A hand grabbed a fistful of his football shirt and tried to haul him through the open window. Leo swung a fist and pounded on the muscly arm of the woman but to no avail. Every time he swung, the car swerved dangerously to the opposite side of the road, and he had to use both hands to prevent them crashing. The only thing saving Daniel from being pulled out through the window was his seatbelt.

"Help me!" Daniel shouted while trying his best to detach the hand that was pulling at him.

Leo could see the boy's small fists were doing nothing to deter the woman who was becoming more aggressive each time she hauled at him.

"Daniel, bite the bitch!"

An audible shriek filled the air as Daniel sank his gleaming white teeth into the woman's hand which was withdrawn from the car with surprising speed.

"Take your belt off, get onto the floor, and stay low," Leo ordered. Daniel complied immediately just as the axe appeared in a smooth flowing arc before Leo's eyes. The windshield shattered completely and ice cold winds tore at his face as he was sprayed with glass for the second time. "Fuck this shit!" he shouted and performed another emergency stop.

As expected, the female attacker flew off the roof, slammed onto the hard tarmac surface, and tumbled for a couple of metres. After the sixth tumble, she rolled to her feet with astonishing grace and fluidity, axe still grasped firmly in her hand.

"You've got to be kidding me," Leo muttered to himself while noting how exceptionally tall she was. He estimated her to be well over six foot.

The woman wasted no time in continuing her assault and marched forward in the direction of the heavily damaged car, her piercing stare freezing him in place. When she had significantly closed the gap between herself and the car, she elegantly drew the axe behind her head and thrust it forward with terrible ferocity. He could only watch as it flew with deadly accuracy towards him.

And then everything around him seemed to happen in slow motion; the wind that gently caressed his hair and stroked his face, the graceful spinning of the axe, the whirring sound it made as it soared towards him, and even his own heartbeat seemed to be happening at a snail's pace. He felt complete and utter terror as the axe drew closer and it had nothing to do with his own imminent death.

In the seconds he had left, he turned to look at Daniel who was cowering on the floor of the car with his arms wrapped protectively over his head. Who would protect the boy from these lunatics when he was gone? With that horrific thought in mind, he lifted his head and gazed back to the oncoming axe which glinted with every turn as it reflected the light of the sun.

A flash of movement to the left of the car caught Leo's eye, and suddenly, a black leather coat blocked his view of the airborne axe. His perception of time returned to normal, and he realised the coat cladded figure was Lucas.

His eyes were unblinking as he watched Lucas snatch the axe out of the air and hurl it back at the woman. She twisted her body in an attempt to dodge it, but she was too slow. She spun through the air and hit the ground hard with the axe embedded in her shoulder. This time, she didn't get up.

Lucas appeared at Leo's window and placed a hand on his shoulder. "God, Leo! Look at you, you're shaking. Are you okay?" he asked, a look of deep concern on his face.

Leo could only nod.

"You're bleeding too."

Leo felt Lucas' hand on his head. "I'm fine, it's just a scratch," he said, moving away.

"And the boy?"

"I'm here," Daniel piped up from the floor, giving Lucas a little wave.

Lucas peered down at Daniel and grinned. "Ah, there you are. Do you see all the fuss you've caused, little man?"

Daniel shrugged. "It was Mr Alexander's driving that caused the fuss."

"I can see why you're Mr Alexander's favourite," Lucas chuckled.

Leo was about to respond but noticed a large amount of blood on the white t-shirt beneath Lucas' leather coat. There were two colours of blood: red and black. He reached over and pulled the coat open a little more. "You're hurt."

"I'm fine, just a scratch," Lucas replied, echoing Leo's words back to him and pulling away. He looked over at the woman who was now beginning to stir. "I think it's time to go. Quick, little man, into the back."

After Daniel had scrambled into the back and Lucas had taken up the front seat, Leo put the car in gear but kept it stationary, his glacial stare fixed on the woman who had just attacked them. She was trying to get to her feet.

"Leo, what are waiting for?" Lucas asked. "This chick is dangerous. We need to leave."

"Mr A, come on, let's go," Daniel said.

Leo cleared his throat, his eyes still locked on the woman who was now on her feet. "Daniel, shut your eyes, and don't open them until I tell you."

"But Mr—"

"Daniel, close them now." He looked into the rear view mirror to see Daniel shutting his eyes tightly and then covering them with his hands.

"Leo, you need to get us out of here," Lucas urged.

"We're going," he told Lucas, slamming the accelerator to the floor and making the tyres screech noisily.

The woman turned around to see the vehicle charging at her like a metal rhinoceros. She made a move to jump clear, but the car was too fast. She went up into the air momentarily and then came crashing down onto the bonnet before rolling off and bouncing along the ground.

From his mirrors, Leo could see her writhing on the ground and allowed a small smile to form on his lips. After basking in his small victory, he turned his attention back to the road and concentrated on putting as much distance as possible between them and the stadium.

"She'll be back," Lucas said grimly as he sank back into the chair in his usual casual manner. "We need to get back to the Cathedral so I can check in with Cornelius."

"Okay, two questions, if I may?" Leo started. "Who—"

"Can I open my eyes now?" Daniel interrupted.

"Yes," he told Daniel before returning to quiz Lucas. "Who ordered the hell's angels back there, and who in God's name is the axe loving psycho bitch?"

"They're the Templars," Lucas said simply. "They're protectors of the Church and Warriors of the Light."

Leo snorted. "Warriors of the Light? Really? And do Warriors of the Light usually go around trying to kill innocent children?"

"Look, if you're going to go all sarcastic Suzy on me, forget it. You can find out who they are by yourself," Lucas retorted and folded his arms across his chest.

"No! No way are you pulling this shit on me after that, so start talking," Leo demanded, giving Lucas a sideways glare.

Lucas let out a burst of angelic laughter and turned to face Daniel. "Is he always this intense and uptight?"

Daniel ignored Lucas' question and spoke to Leo instead. "Mr Alexander, I want to go to the hospital to see my mum."

"I know you do, but your mum isn't there. I had to lie a little bit to get you out of the stadium and away from those men," Leo replied, keeping his voice as gentle and kind as he could.

"You said those men were trying to kill me. Why?" Daniel asked, sounding as if he was going to cry.

"I don't know," Leo lied, feeling the threat of tears himself. Beside him, Lucas sat up.

"You have to tell him, Leo. He has a right to know."

Leo felt the first pangs of anger rising within, but he remained calm. "We'll contact his parents first, meet up with them, and tell them everything. They can decide whether or not to tell him."

"This boy has the power of—"

"No!" Leo exploded, causing the other two to jump in their seats. He took a deep breath, fighting hard to control the rage. "Not yet, Lucas. This isn't our decision to make. We tell his parents, and then it's up to them."

Lucas slouched back into his seat. "Okay. We'll do it your way. But sooner or later, he has to know."

"Know what? What do I have to know?"

Leo turned his gaze to see Daniel's head poking between the two front seats and looking expectantly up at him. "Do you see what you've done now?" he huffed at Lucas before softening his expression and speaking to Daniel. "Dan, sit back and put your seatbelt on. I might have to drive faster if She-Ra and her bikers appear again."

"But what do they want?"

"Listen, little man, do what Leo said and put your seatbelt back on, then I'll tell you what you need to know," Lucas said, causing the boy to sit back and buckle up in seconds.

"I've got my seatbelt on," Daniel announced.

Leo opened his mouth to protest but felt Lucas' hand on his arm. He took his eyes off the road briefly and faced the handsome man.

"Trust me."

The sincerity in the azure eyes won Leo over, and he found himself nodding. "Okay," he said, reluctantly returning his eyes to the road. Lucas squeezed his arm gently.

"Okay, little man, listen up. I'm only gonna tell you this once. No interruptions, okay?"

"Okay."

"Good. So, those people back there are bad news. They think I have something that belongs to them, and they want to destroy it. I'm protecting it, and Leo is helping me."

"What is it? What do they want to destroy?"

"You. They think you are somebody with a lot of power."

"But I'm not," Daniel stated simply.

"Yeah, we know that, but those crazy bikers don't. They're hunting the wrong person," Lucas explained patiently.

"Why can't we just tell them that they've made a mistake? Or call the Police?" Daniel asked.

Lucas laughed lightly. "They're dangerous men, Daniel. Look at the lengths they've just gone to with smashing up Leo's car. This is not something the Police can deal with. We have to play this very carefully. Once we know exactly who the Templars are supposed to be looking for, we can sort it out. Until then, you and your parents have to go into hiding for a little while."

"For how long?"

"I don't know, little man. A couple of weeks, maybe a month. But don't worry, your parents will be with you."

If Leo didn't know any better, he'd have believed every single word that came out of Lucas' mouth. It was like the man had a golden tongue when it came to weaving lies. What was it he'd said before?

The best lies are the ones in which there are some truths...'

Leo found Lucas' ability to create such effective lies a bit unsettling, but the important thing was that Daniel seemed to buy it for now. From the mirror, he could see that the boy was sitting back and staring out of the window with his brow furrowed. Every so often, the breeze coming in from the smashed out windows ruffled the black hair poking out from underneath his blue hat. Leo tore his gaze away from Daniel and felt the sting of tears.

"Are you okay?" Lucas asked, placing his hand on Leo's thigh.

"Yeah, I am," Leo replied, brushing Lucas' hand away.

"Okay, no worries. By the way, good thigh muscle."

Leo blushed furiously and quickly changed the subject. "Do you have a plan?"

Lucas pulled a phone from his pocket and handed it to Daniel. "Call your parents. Tell them to come to the Cathedral as soon as they can."

Daniel took the phone and began swiping and prodding the screen.

"We'll head to the Cathedral and speak with Cornelius," Lucas said. "He'll advise us from there."

Before Leo could answer, Daniel started speaking.

"Dad, it's me. Listen, something's happened. No, no. I'm okay. I need you and Mum to meet me at Inverness Cathedral…"

Leo didn't bother to listen any further. He knew that the Macintoshes would come running if they thought their only son was in trouble. As he drove deeper into the city, he let his mind analyse everything that had happened in the last twenty four hours. Between Lucas' breaking and entering, to the crazy axe woman and her bikers, it had been eventful to say the least. He couldn't help but wonder what the next twenty four hours would bring, and it did not fill him with joy. The meeting with Daniel's parents wouldn't be pleasant at all. He was not looking forward to explaining the details of who Daniel was.

'How do you break that kind of news?' he thought to himself.

His inner voice was unusually quiet, no sarcastic answers or remarks. An image of the raven haired woman appeared in his mind, and a blanket of cold fear enveloped him. Who was she? And why had Leo felt like there was history there? He'd never hated anybody that he'd met before, let alone a complete stranger. He was desperate to find out all the answers, but as long as Daniel was near, he'd have to wait. He didn't want to scare the boy even more.

"Okay, Dad. See you soon. Love you."

Daniel's voice pulled Leo from his analysis of the day's events.

"Dad said he'll be there in just over an hour. He's going to pick up Mum on the way."

Nobody said anything.

'Great,' Leo thought bitterly to himself, 'another two lives will be ruined today.'

And with that discomforting thought, he guided his smashed up car through the busy Saturday streets of Inverness.

Chapter 7
Warming Up

Like the master of all thieves, the night was beginning to creep up from behind the horizon in preparation to steal the daylight. Streetlights glowed softly as they warmed themselves up, ready to fend off the invading darkness when it finally reached them. The sun had begun a hasty retreat westwards, rolling across the sky and away from the gathering snow clouds that seemed to be working with the approaching darkness to impose winter's cruel regime. It was impossible for Leo not to feel the onslaught of winter as the bitter wind rushed through the glassless windows and attacked them unmercifully.

"It's so cold," Daniel whimpered.

"Wrap this around you, little man." Lucas took off his leather coat and tossed it into the back.

"Wow, your jacket is like a radiator."

Leo glanced in the mirror and saw Daniel pulling the coat around himself, tucking in all the edges so no heat could escape.

"Thanks, Lucas."

"You're welcome, dude."

Although Leo had the heating on full power, the cold air continuously blew in from the broken windows. By the time they reached the Cathedral, he was absolutely frozen despite wearing his thick duffle coat and scarf. To add to his misery, the pain in his hip was getting worse with each passing minute.

He drove into the Cathedral car park just as the first snowflakes of the evening began to fall. Soon, the three of them were climbing the steep stone steps up to the Cathedral's entrance. "Are you not cold?" he asked the t-shirt clad Lucas as they climbed.

Lucas shrugged. "I don't really feel the cold."

"Lucas, it's the middle of winter, and it's snowing. How can you not feel the cold?"

"I just don't. Here, feel."

Leo stopped walking when Lucas placed two toasty hands gently on his face.

"See, I'm always warm." The American's cerulean eyes sparkled.

From the moment he was touched, Leo felt a warm sensation spread across his whole face. It journeyed to his neck and chest before manoeuvring its way around the rest of his body. "That's…impossible," he stammered. Red hot desire ignited inside him, and his mind flashed back to the last time he'd gotten this close to Lucas.

"What can I say? I'm hot stuff," Lucas said with an impish grin.

Leo pulled away from Lucas' touch, dashed ahead of the inexplicably hot man, and caught up to Daniel who had just reached the Cathedral door. Just as the boy's hand reached the heavy oak, the door swung open to reveal Cornelius, his wrinkled face awash with relief.

"Leo! Lucas! Thank heavens you're alright," the old man exclaimed. "And you must be Daniel. Quickly, come in before you catch your death," he fussed, stepping to the side and ushering the three of them inside.

"Lesser demons and a few demons at the stadium," Lucas reported immediately. "And…the Templars are here."

"I know, I can feel their presence," Cornelius said, pushing the doors closed and securing them with a metal bolt. "They know."

"How could they know?" Lucas asked, his voice irate. "There is absolutely no way they could have known unless…" His face darkened. "We've been betrayed."

"Impossible. I trust all of mine implicitly." Cornelius said the words, but it was clear by his expression that he was plagued with doubt. "Follow me."

Lucas didn't move. "*She* was with them."

Lucas' words stopped Cornelius dead. He stared into Lucas' eyes for what seemed like an eternity. "We'll talk about her later. We must move quickly."

Leo took up the rear of the group as they walked into the draughty main hall where the temperature wasn't much warmer than outside. The howling wind pushed itself into the vast room through any openings it could find. Massive fabrics that were decorated with religious symbols hung down in various places and moved silently when the draughts reached them.

Cornelius walked smartly down the aisle towards the pulpit, his walking stick rhythmically clicking off the stone floor. Leo was anxious as the old man led them to the east door at the back of the hall beside the altar. The recent memory of seeing his first demon played in his mind making him want to flee the building, however, he'd promised himself he was going to protect Daniel no matter what.

Swallowing his fear, he kept a hand on Daniel's shoulder as they passed through and entered a long narrow corridor that contained seven other doors. He glanced back at the east door and immediately wished he hadn't. The once handsome door was damaged beyond repair with scratches and claw marks. They were embedded deeply into the wood and ran up the entire height of the door. Large splintered areas showed where the demon had been trying to smash its way out.

'And how the hell are you going to win against one demon, let alone hundreds, maybe thousands?'

His inner voice had reawakened. It always asked the tough questions, the ones that required an answer, even if the answer wasn't the one he wanted to hear.

'Magic, perhaps? Maybe take a crash course in burning demons alive. That should do it. Boil their blood.'

He winced at the memory of the demon's blood and how bad it had smelt. It had been vile: a thick, black, vulgar and putrid substance that was no doubt a result of the evilness that lay within. Shuddering at the thought, he concentrated on following Cornelius and Daniel down the corridor, ignoring the fact Lucas had hung back to walk with him.

As they walked further down the corridor, Leo counted six doors, each marked with a golden number. One, three and five marked the doors on the left while two, four and six lay to the right. Ahead of them was a numberless door.

"These are the Cathedral dormitories, the door in front of us leads to my chambers, the lounge area, the dining hall, the kitchens, and the courtyard," Cornelius explained, striding through the corridor. "Only dormitories one and two are occupied. The others are vacant and will be where you'll stay for the night. I'll have Mrs Ellen prepare the rooms after dinner."

"Mrs Ellen?" Leo enquired.

"Mrs Ellen is the housekeeper and the cook," Cornelius replied.

Leo sniggered unpleasantly. "I'm glad to see the Church still have enough money during the recession to employ servants. Although I suppose the maid is better paid than me and gets free accommodation. How very…Christian."

The clicking of the walking stick stopped abruptly. Cornelius spun around and faced Leo who had no option but to stop.

The old man's usually warm and kind face was now hard and stony, the sparkle in his eyes dead and gone. "Contrary to common belief, the Church does not have the vast wealth it once had, nor does it have to employ servants," he said sharply. "Believe it or not, Mr Alexander, there are souls in the world who still adhere to and uphold the traditional values of the Christian faith and who, quite frankly, set an example to the rest of us in this wicked, lost and sinful world."

"I'm sorry, I didn't mean to—" Leo began.

"And yet, you did," Cornelius interrupted abrasively. "You, like so many others, seem to think you have a perfectly clear understanding of how the Church community works, delighting yourselves in picking fault and besmirching our reputation. It would surprise you, I'm sure, to know that Mrs Ellen chooses to serve in this Cathedral because she has devoted herself to our Lord. Mrs Ellen also chooses to wander the streets of Inverness in the freezing cold of winter to collect homeless people and bring them back to the Cathedral. She gives them food and warmth because she believes they are God's children who deserve to be shown compassion and kindness. She also visits sick children and their families every Saturday in the hospital and brings them faith, hope and love. She has also singlehandedly raised over two hundred thousand pounds by organising bake sales, jumble sales, and other community events that have fostered love, kindness and overwhelming generosity. The funds raised went to children's hospitals, cancer charities, and other projects that work hard to provide for those in need. Mrs Ellen has never taken a single penny in the forty years of her life in which she has dedicated herself to our Lord and to helping the less fortunate.

"I, myself, have risked the safety of Mrs Ellen and the others who reside within these walls by taking you and this boy into their home. The Templars and demons would launch a devastating attack on this building and burn it to the ground to get to this child, yet Mrs Ellen and the others, who you see fit to mock, would rather die in the flames than allow any harm to come to this boy and yourself. Please, if

129

you don't think that is Christian behaviour then could you so kindly explain to me what you think Christian behaviour is?"

Leo had the decency to look very ashamed of himself. "Cornelius, I...I don't know what to say except I'm sorry. I clearly don't know what I'm talking about. I'll keep my mouth shut in the future." He didn't know if it was his genuine apology or the fact that Cornelius was a genuinely decent man, but whatever the reason, the sparkle flickered once more in the old man's eyes.

"And I'm sorry too," Cornelius said before letting out a long sigh. "I understand only too well the Church has a lot to answer for in terms of its many past indiscretions. But I do get defensive when decent, honest, and hardworking people like Mrs Ellen are tarnished with the same brush as those who defile the Church. You must trust there are still Christian people who are just that—Christian. Now, shall we continue?"

Without another word, Cornelius turned on his heel and the walking stick clicked off the floor once more.

Leo's eyes met with Daniel's, and he had to supress a laugh when the boy exhaled loudly, pointed in the direction of Cornelius, and mouthed the word 'crazy' before scampering off after the old man.

"The kid is very funny."

Leo was not expecting to hear Lucas' voice so close to his ear, and it caused him to jump.

"Am I standing too close?" Lucas asked, his ocean blue eyes sparkling with mischief.

"Just a little," Leo snapped, shaking his head before continuing on without another word.

"You boys will be pleased to know that Mrs Ellen has a fire on, and I'm sure she'll be more than happy to fix you a hot drink," Cornelius said, leading them through the remaining length of corridor and into a dimly lit room.

The stone walls of the room were bare except for the one which housed the fireplace. Two red armchairs, a red couch and a coffee table sat in front of a glorious burning fire that roared merrily in the hearth. The fire was the main source of light in the windowless room alongside some candles that lay on the coffee table. There was another entrance into the lounge which was directly opposite the door they'd just walked through.

"We will converse in here," Cornelius announced, patting the armchair that was closest to the fire. "Daniel, perhaps you'd like to warm up."

"Thank you," Daniel replied politely, walking over to the chair and plonking himself down.

Cornelius smiled and placed a hand lightly on the boy's head. "Am I right in thinking a hot chocolate might help in warming you up?"

Daniel's eyes lit up. "Can I have marshmallows?"

"Daniel!" Leo said reproachfully.

"Oh, sorry. Can I have some marshmallows, please?"

Cornelius and Lucas both laughed warmly. At that precise moment, a woman entered the room through the other door. She held a dish towel in her hand and walked to Cornelius' side. She was about Leo's height, he reckoned, and she was a very plump woman with a rosy, well rounded face. Her clothes were very plain: a simple black dress, a white apron fastened at the waist, black tights and black plimsoll shoes. Her greying red hair was fastened into a tight, well sculpted bun.

"Ah, Mrs Ellen," Cornelius said brightly before making introductions. "These are our guests for the evening. This young man is Daniel, and that's Leo."

"Oh, what a delight Father," Mrs Ellen said in a broad Irish accent. "I'm Mrs Ellen, pleased to meet you both, so I am. Goodness gracious, you've been in the wars, Leo," she said, her eyes roaming up the side of his face and up to his head. "I'm sure Lucas will show you where to get cleaned up. Will you be having your tea with us tonight?"

"Yes, they will, Mrs Ellen," Cornelius answered, taking her flabby hand in his and smiling adoringly down at her. "What will you be serving, my dear lady?"

"Chilli sausages with mash and roasted vegetables. It's one of Lucas' favourites, so it is," she said, beaming over at Lucas with enchanting sage green eyes.

Leo watched as Lucas gave Mrs Ellen one heart stopping smile. His full pouting lips were pulled back to display dazzling white teeth, and the light from the candles radiated off his tanned face, outlining the perfection of his chiselled features. He'd always thought Lucas was incredibly good looking. Ever since he'd set eyes on him at the restaurant, he'd most definitely put him at the top end of the handsome scale. He wasn't entirely sure if it was the candle light or the tight, blood stained t-shirt, but as he watched Lucas standing there, he realised he'd never seen anything more beautiful. An unfamiliar feeling awoke from deep within him and made his stomach knot. Whatever the feeling was, he couldn't identify it because he'd never felt anything like it in his life. The only thing he could compare it to was when he'd been pressed up against Lucas back at his flat, but even then, that feeling had been more primal. The carnal feeling was still there, certainly, but it had been joined by something else—something deeper.

"It certainly is, Mrs E," Lucas said enthusiastically while looking over at Daniel and Leo. "You two are gonna love it."

Leo dropped his eyes to the floor when Lucas looked over at him. He silently cursed himself because the action was too obvious. "I'm sure we will," he replied with a smile in Mrs Ellen's direction. The old woman looked genuinely delighted.

"Right, young man, I think we have some hot chocolate and marshmallows in the kitchen. I'll need help to make it," she said to Daniel.

Daniel promptly hopped up from the comfy armchair he was sitting in, pulled off Lucas' coat, and handed it back. "Thanks for letting me use your coat. Do you take marshmallows in your hot chocolate?"

"You're welcome, little man," Lucas responded, ruffling Daniel's hair. He made a fist and held it out. Daniel also made a fist and bumped it against Lucas'. "As for the hot chocolate, I'll take as many marshmallows as you can fit in the mug."

"There'll be none of that now. You don't want to be setting a bad example to the young lad," Mrs Ellen interjected, giving Lucas a stern look.

"Sorry, Mrs E," Lucas said with his head bowed down like a child who had been reprimanded by a parent. "I promise I won't do it again."

Daniel giggled when Mrs Ellen broke into a grin and swung the dish towel in Lucas' direction, hitting him on the back of the head.

"Hey! Assault!" Lucas cried and hid behind Cornelius who was looking on with feigned dismay.

"Daniel, let's get out of here before that badly behaved American teaches you any more bad manners," Mrs Ellen said, placing her arm in a motherly fashion around Daniel and leading him into what Leo assumed to be the kitchen.

He waited until Daniel and Mrs Ellen had disappeared out of the room before breaking his silence. "Not that I don't appreciate the break from all the doom and gloom, but I really think we should be devising a plan rather than fooling around and making hot chocolate."

"Oh, come on Leo, lighten up," Lucas said as he threw himself down onto the couch and sprawled out in front of the fire.

"I would love to lighten up, Lucas, but unfortunately there are demons and mad Templar bikers trying to kill us."

Lucas sighed, swung his legs off the couch, and straightened up. "Okay, so what plan did you have in mind?"

"I don't know," Leo snapped. "How about one that keeps Daniel and myself alive?" He was going to continue ranting but was silenced when he felt a hand on his shoulder.

"Be at peace, child," Cornelius said softly. "We know the danger is great, but you are safe as long as you reside in this Cathedral. I have secured the entire building with enchantments."

Leo raised an eyebrow. "Enchantments?"

"Did Lucas not tell you? I'm also a member of the Elect and have been my whole life. Trust me, no demon or Templar will get near this building without me knowing about it. You have much to learn about your abilities, and I look forward to watching you develop them. From what Lucas tells me, you've already tapped into them."

Leo merely shrugged. "I thought I was quite good actually, but Lucas told me my powers were nothing but pyrotechnics."

Cornelius fixed his gaze on Lucas. "Did he really? Well, between you and me, Lucas lets his mouth and ego run away with him."

"Yeah, I can't argue there," Leo agreed with a smug smile, looking pointedly in Lucas' direction.

"Uh, hello? I'm still in the room!" Lucas said sulkily.

"Yes, I can see that," Cornelius retorted while turning his back on Lucas and walking towards the door that Mrs Ellen and Daniel had gone through moments earlier. "I will return to my chambers for now. I must contact the Grandmaster and fill her in on the afternoon's events. She may well want to meet with us all in person to discuss possible strategies. By the time I'm done, I'm sure Daniel's parents will have arrived, but should they get here before I'm finished with the Grandmaster, bring them to this room and wait for my return. Do not start without me. I fear they may not react in the way we would like them to. Make yourself comfortable, Leo. Something tells me it's going to be a very long night."

And with those words, Cornelius was gone, and Leo was left alone with Lucas. He stood awkwardly, arms still folded. Lucas was watching him intently.

"You're allowed to sit down," Lucas said at last, swinging his legs back onto the couch and returning to the sprawled out position he'd adopted earlier.

Leo walked slowly over to the chair furthest away from Lucas and attempted to sit down. As he bent down, a burning pain erupted from his hip and both his knees. He inhaled sharply and clutched his side, holding it until he was sat in the chair.

"Are you okay?" Lucas asked, lifting his head up from the couch.

"I'm fine. I tripped over Daniel at the stadium and landed on my hip," Leo said while unbuttoning his duffle coat. He sat forward and tried to pull his coat off when the burning pain in his hip fired up again. Gritting his teeth, he sank back down into the soft armchair.

"Let me take a look at it," Lucas said, once again swinging his legs off the couch.

"It's fine. It's just a little graze, nothing more."

Lucas' eyes narrowed. "If it's just a little graze, how come you can't take off your coat without looking like you're in agonising pain?"

"It's not agonising."

"If it isn't agonising, take off your coat."

"Fine!" Leo huffed, realising that Lucas was not going to give up. "I'll take the damn thing off." He pulled the coat open and sat forward again. Several attempts later, he admitted defeat and had to stand up to get it off without it hurting his hip. Once he'd removed his coat, he tossed it over the back off the armchair along with his scarf, and turned to gloat at Lucas. "See, it's nothing."

"Leo, look."

"What?" Leo followed Lucas' gaze to his hip where a large patch of blood had marked his hoodie. "It's not as bad as it looks, don't worry," he said, sitting back down.

Lucas stood up. "It's seeped all the way through two layers. I'm taking a look at it, it might need stitches."

Resigned to the fact that Lucas wasn't going to let this go, he got to his feet with a lot of mumbling and moaning. "It's just a cut, Lucas. I won't die." He tugged the bottom of his hoodie and t-shirt, and yelped.

Lucas was on his knees in a flash. "Your t-shirt is stuck to the cut. Hang on."

Leo gritted his teeth as the material was carefully peeled away from the wound.

"It's bleeding again," Lucas piped up from the floor. "But you're right. You're not going to die," he confirmed.

"Told you," Leo said, his eyes rolling.

"It is quite deep though. You'll need to have it cleaned. Come, I have a first aid box." Lucas jumped to his feet and headed through to the dormitories.

Still holding his hoodie and t-shirt away from the bleeding wound, Leo followed. When he entered the long corridor, Lucas was nowhere in sight.

"Number one!"

Leo scanned the doors down the right hand side as Lucas' voice echoed around the corridor, and he saw that the very last door was ajar and had a golden shiny number one on it. He dragged himself to the door, knocking lightly when he reached it.

"Come in," Lucas called from the other side.

Slowly, he pushed the door open. The first thing he noticed once he'd stepped into the room was Lucas' scent. It was everywhere. The room, although very spacious, had very little furnishings. There was a double bed, plain black curtains draping down in front of a small window, a wooden chair, a single desk, a chest of drawers, and a flat screen TV hanging on the wall. Lucas was half under the bed, rummaging around.

"Cool room," Leo said.

"I love it. I have everything I need in here," Lucas replied, his voice muffled.

"You *need* a TV?"

Lucas laughed his beautiful laugh. "Of course I need it. If I miss the soccer, I become unbearable," he chuckled, emerging from beneath the bed with a small green box in his hands. "Got it."

Leo sat on the bed and watched Lucas as he tipped the contents onto the duvet and tossed the box onto the floor. "How come you're making a fuss of my wound when you have one of your own?" he asked, pointing to Lucas' chest.

"Because it wasn't my blood," replied Lucas. In one swift motion, he pulled his blood stained t-shirt over his head and threw it beside the first aid box. "See. Woundless. Now, let me fix you up."

There was nothing Leo could do to stop himself gawking at the incredible set of abs and broad muscular chest that was on display. When Lucas walked, his muscles rippled underneath his skin like a well-oiled machine. It was only when the topless man knelt down and tore open an antiseptic wipe that Leo was able to take his eyes off the toned torso. He held his breath and gritted his teeth as the wipe drew closer to his hip.

"This will sting a bit," Lucas said softly before gently cleaning the wound.

Leo briefly observed the wound being cleaned before another part of Lucas' anatomy caught his attention: his arms. The man had amazingly huge arms. With every wiping motion, the bulging biceps became more appealing, and he knew that if he focused any more on the flexing god, his growing arousal would become extremely obvious. He felt a mixture of relief and disappointment when the wound was finally cleaned.

"All finished," Lucas announced cheerily. "I'll just put a dressing on it."

"Whatever you think," Leo replied, clearing his throat and trying to sound as normal as possible even though he was almost hyperventilating. When Lucas turned around to get some dressing pads and tape from the bed, Leo decided to check him out from behind. When his eyes fell upon

Lucas' naked back, he had to stifle a gasp. "Lucas! What happened to your back?"

It was clear Lucas hadn't intended for him to see the markings on his back because he immediately froze when Leo had asked the question. Two almost identical white scars, about half a metre long, ran vertically from each shoulder blade and stood out against the tanned flawless skin that covered the rest of his back.

"My father," Lucas said eventually, swiping the packet of dressing pads and tape off the bed. He turned back around to face Leo and closed the gap between them. "I did something terrible when I was young, so he punished me for it."

"Punished you? How?" Leo couldn't mask his horror.

"It doesn't really matter. The point is, I deserved it." Lucas placed a large pad over the wound with one hand while using the other one, along with his teeth, to rip off strips of tape and secure the dressing.

"Jesus, Lucas! That's terrible. What did your mother say?"

"My mother died when I was a baby. I never knew her." Lucas bent his head and kept his eyes firmly locked on the dressing. "I deserved it."

Leo shook his head vigorously, anger stirring within him. "I don't believe it. What could you have possibly done to deserve being mutilated as a form of punishment?"

Lucas looked up at him from his position on the floor, and his eyes were glistening. There was no sign of an ego, and all of the American swagger was gone. Lucas, for the very first time since Leo had met him, looked vulnerable and terrified.

"Lucas, what did you do?" he asked, not entirely sure he wanted to know the answer. He continued to hold Lucas' gaze for what seemed like a lifetime but no explanation came.

Lucas forced a smile onto his face, laughed lightly, and jumped to his feet. "There, all done," he said, turning his back on Leo and returning to the bed. "How are your knees?" he asked, while packing up the first aid box.

"They're fine," Leo responded immediately, unable to stop staring at the scars on Lucas' back. "Tell me, what did you do?"

"I told you, it doesn't matter," Lucas said, his tone flippant and blasé.

"I know, but I'm curious now. Tell me."

"I don't want to tell you," Lucas fired back, throwing things into the box with increasing aggression.

"Why not? We all make mistakes and do stupid things when we're young. Tell me."

"Drop it, okay."

"Fine, but give me one good reason why you won't tell me."

Leo jumped as the first aid box sailed across the room. It crashed into the wall with such speed and power it split in half, spilling all of the medical supplies across the floor.

"Because you'll fucking hate me even more if I tell you!" Lucas exploded, his thunderous voice echoing around the room. He was clenching and unclenching his fists repeatedly, and his entire body was shaking.

Leo was stunned into silence. When it was obvious that Lucas had no intention of moving or talking, he walked tentatively over to the first aid box and knelt down on skinned knees. He ignored the pain and started picking up the contents of the box, piling them into one of the halves. As he was joining the two halves back together, Lucas finally spoke.

"I despise them," he said, his voice shaky and hoarse. "They're ugly and repulsive...like the person I am."

"You're not ugly and—"

"You know nothing, Leo. I can't tell you what I did, ever. Just know it was something unspeakably wicked and something I'm deeply ashamed about." Lucas turned around and faced Leo, his eyes still glistening with unshed tears.

139

"Okay," Leo agreed, picking up the box and getting to his feet. "It's none of my business, and I won't ask you again." He walked over to Lucas with the box clasped in his hands. "But can I say one thing?"

"What?"

"I don't hate you—hey! Don't look at me like that, I really don't!" Leo said, irritated by the doubtful expression on Lucas' face. "Okay, I admit I wasn't crazy about you when you broke into my flat and gave me the worst possible news ever, but can you really blame me for that?"

The mood lightened, and the flicker of a smile flashed across Lucas' lips. "I guess not."

"And you have gone out of your way to irritate me and make me squirm ever since we met."

"I have not!" Lucas protested, sounding more like himself.

"You cut off a demon's head and held it in my face."

"I only did that so you'd believe my story," Lucas said, rolling his eyes. "And I apologised for it."

"You nearly gave me a heart attack in my kitchen this morning when you broke into my home for the second time."

"I thought you'd overslept for your appointment with Father O'Connor."

"You let the Cathedral door slam into me on purpose."

"You called me an idiot to a complete stranger."

Leo was growing hot and flustered the longer the conversation went on. "Oh my god, you never take any responsibility, and you are so immature! Hey, you might be right after all! I do hate you!"

Lucas smirked at him. "You don't have a sense of humour, and you're uptight."

"I am not uptight!" Leo was so wound up that his words came out in a hysterical squeak. He cleared his throat and adopted a more relaxed posture. "I am not uptight," he repeated coolly.

Lucas laughed so much that he doubled over, clutching his stomach. "Okay, maybe I was wrong. Maybe you do have a sense of humour!" he hooted.

Leo tried his best not to join in, but it was impossible to resist Lucas' infectious laughter. It wasn't long until tears were streaming down his face. After the day he'd had, this was a welcomed release of all the tension and fear he'd been feeling.

"Listen, I have to thank you for everything you did for Daniel and me," he said after they had both calmed down.

"No, you don't. I didn't do much," Lucas said modestly.

"You helped me find Daniel at the stadium, you killed demons that would have ripped me and Daniel to shreds, you saved me from an axe that would have decapitated me, and you kept Daniel warm by giving him your coat." He looked up at Lucas who appeared pensive.

"Now that you mention it, yeah, I did do all that. I guess that makes me kinda awesome," he said with a massive grin.

Leo found himself grinning back. "Yeah, as much as it pains me to admit, I guess you are a little bit. I'm glad you're here to help us."

"Careful, sounds like you're complimenting me," Lucas said, raising his eyebrows.

"Don't push it," Leo laughed, shoving Lucas playfully before turning serious. "But seriously, I owe you." He smiled and held out the box. It was then he noticed that Lucas' whole demeanour had changed from playful and mischievous to one that he couldn't quite fathom. His heart skipped a beat when Lucas stepped forward and eradicated the space between them.

"A compliment and a debt owed. I guess it's my lucky day," Lucas murmured.

Leo stopped breathing when Lucas reached out, placed his hands on top of his, and pushed the box gently down so their chests were practically touching. "I," he started to say but found that he didn't have any words. Lucas' heavenly scent overwhelmed his senses. Inexplicably warm hands travelled up his arms and began caressing his neck. The first aid box hit the floor as his own hands found their way onto Lucas' firm hips.

He swallowed hard as the angelic face inched closer to his, the bluest of blue eyes bewitching him. His heart was pounding, his mouth was dry, and his stomach was twisting in a million different ways. Once again, that indescribable feeling returned to his solar plexus, bringing a lust infused carnal desire with it. His eyes closed of their own accord, and his mouth waited in eager anticipation for Lucas' approaching lips.

"Lucas." Cornelius' voice invaded the room and shattered the moment.

Leo instantly pulled away. "Thanks for fixing up that wound on my hip. Feels better already," he babbled before pretending to notice Cornelius. "Oh, Father O'Connor. I didn't see you there."

"Evidently," Cornelius replied, his tone and expression unreadable.

"I'll…um…head to the lounge now," Leo said and walked hastily to the door in which Cornelius stood.

"Daniel's parents have just entered the car park. I shall meet them and escort them to the lounge," Cornelius said, stepping to the side to allow Leo passage into the corridor. "Grab a chair and get comfortable."

Leo almost collapsed with relief when he stepped out into the cold corridor. He had only taken a few steps away from the room when he heard Cornelius' voice.

"Whatever game you're playing, Lucas, it ends now. He is off limits to you," the old man said calmly although there was no mistaking the hostility in his voice. "This is a house of the Lord, and as long as you are living under this roof, you will treat it as such. Do you understand?"

Whatever Lucas' response was, Leo didn't hear it as the door to the room was slammed shut. He couldn't help but linger and try to eavesdrop, but the thick stone walls and heavy oak door prevented him from hearing anything.

With his heart still hammering in his chest, the result of yet another close encounter with Lucas, he made his way to the lounge where he had the unpleasant task of telling a father and a mother that their only son was now the target of evil demons and crazy Templars.

Sometimes, life could be a real bitch.

Chapter 8
Answers

As Leo predicted, Daniel's parents were not thrilled. After making the necessary introductions and explaining that Daniel was safely having dinner in the kitchen, Cornelius spent thirty five minutes telling them the entire story. Initially, Mark and Ruth Macintosh thought the whole thing was a joke for a comedy television show. It was only when they realised the three men in the room were deadly serious that they stopped laughing.

"Are you kidding? Mr Alexander, come on, the joke is over," Ruth said, the humour on her face being slowly replaced with doubt.

The Macintoshes sat together on the large couch while Cornelius sat in the chair closest to them. Lucas was perched on the arm of the second chair, and Leo was standing, arms crossed, by the fireplace directly opposite Mark and Ruth. He could feel the gentle warmth from the dying fire on the back of his calves, and it would have been quite relaxing if he wasn't in this horrendous situation.

Leo let out a long sigh. "Mrs Macintosh—"

"Call me Ruth."

"Ruth, I know how insane this all sounds, believe me, I know. I felt exactly the same when Lucas told me last night. I didn't believe any of it either."

"And now you do?" Mark interrupted.

Apart from thinning hair and a pair of designer glasses, Daniel was most definitely a mini version of his father. He gazed across the room with the same eyes as his son, searching Leo's demeanour for any sign that this was all a huge wind-up.

Leo nodded his head sadly, wishing he could tell the Macintoshes what they wanted to hear, what *he* wanted to hear. But he just couldn't. There was too much at stake. "Yes, I believe it," he replied. "I didn't want to, but I've seen things that I can't even begin to explain. Last night, I was feeling exactly the same as you are now: Daniel doesn't have the creative power of God within him, demons don't exist, there is no such thing as the Elect, and Baal and Lucifer are figments of this lunatic's imagination," he said, pointing at Lucas.

"What made you change your mind? Have you joined the lunatic's asylum as well?" Ruth asked, fixing her fiery gaze upon Leo.

Leo sighed again, took a step forward, and unfolded his arms. "First of all, I want you to think about the implications of my actions this afternoon. I abducted your son. If you wanted to, you could kill my career with a phone call, but I don't care about that. What I do care about is what will happen if those demons and Templars find Daniel."

Mark laughed coldly. "Will you listen to yourself? You're absolutely raving mad! Demons? Templars? Give me a break! I don't know what the hell is going on with you three, but I want my son back now so we can get out of here." Mark stood up on the last word and stepped towards Leo. "Where is he?"

"Will you please listen?" Leo pleaded.

Ruth stood up and joined her husband. "No, we've heard enough of this nonsense. Give us Daniel back, and we might allow you to keep your job." Ruth's eyes were steely, a sure sign that her protective mother instinct had kicked in, and she was prepared to do anything to protect her young.

Lucas stood up and walked to Leo's side. "You should listen to him. He cares deeply about Daniel and would do anything to protect him. He's an Elect."

"Oh yes, an Elect. A protector of the Power, right? And I suppose you can do magic too? Go on then, pull a rabbit out of a hat," Mark scoffed.

"Sneer all you want, but this man would die to protect your son!" Lucas yelled. "In fact, if it wasn't for him, the Templars would have killed Daniel already."

"What a load of shit!" Mark snapped.

"I'm calling the police," Ruth announced, pulling a phone out of her pocket.

The tension in the cosy room was palpable, the silence toxic. Both Macintoshes looked ready to erupt while Leo stood silent, struggling to come up with anything that could help the situation. He glanced at Lucas to see him glaring back at the Macintoshes. A tapping noise broke the silence and caused all four in the stand-off to turn their heads.

Cornelius was tapping his stick against the stone floor and staring absentmindedly into the hearth where the last embers of the fire had just died out. "Leo?" he said.

"Yeah?"

Cornelius shuffled forward in his seat. "Would you be so kind and light us another fire, please? Lucas, would you put the logs on while Leo gets ready."

"Cornelius, I don't think I can—" Leo started to say but was silenced when Lucas placed a firm hand on his shoulder.

"You know how to summon fire," Lucas told him, "so do it."

Leo knew it was the only way to get the Macintoshes to start believing. He gave Lucas a small nod before closing his eyes and trying his best to concentrate on the element of fire.

He was very surprised when he felt the fire energy begin to stir instantly.

"Hello? Yes, hello! Police please. Don't touch me! Let go!"

"Get your hands off my wife!"

"Lucas, stop at once!"

Leo managed to focus despite the sudden commotion in the room. He could feel the heat of the element within him, and he was confident he could manifest it in the physical plane.

"Hello, Police?" Ruth said. "Yes! I'm at the—oh my god."

The air around Leo ignited with orange and red sparks that crackled and popped noisily as they spiralled down to the palm of his right hand.

"No fucking way," Mark gasped.

Leo knew Daniel's parents were now witnessing his magic, so he opened his eyes to reveal two blazing emerald orbs. "Do you believe now?" he asked, his voice sounding otherworldly.

Without waiting for a reply, he spun around and unleashed a ball of fire from his hand, watching as it exploded into the hearth. The logs burst into flames and emitted a pleasant heat, and Leo knew his task was done. He dispelled the mystical energies before allowing his eyes to revert to their normal state. When he set his eyes back on Mark and Ruth, his heart sank because he saw the terrible realisation hit them: the truth.

"I'm sorry, there's no emergency. I don't need the police. My mistake."

Ruth hung up the phone and sat down on the couch where she was joined by her husband. Mark took his wife's hand and clasped it in his. They both looked at each other before fixing their gaze upon Leo.

Leo's eyes were drawn to Ruth's neck where a solid crucifix hung on a chain; both were expensive gold. She was rubbing the crucifix between her thumb and index finger while staring at him. There was something in her expression, like she had just figured something out, like suddenly everything made sense. He was about to call her up on it but her husband started talking.

"What are you?" Mark's voice was a mixture of awe and fear.

"He's an Elect, Guardian of the Power. This man is your son's protector," Lucas said sharply, "so you better listen to what he has to say."

"Lucas, that's enough," Leo said sternly. He walked over to the couch and knelt before the Macintoshes, having nothing but empathy for the couple.

Their whole world had just been turned upside down, and they were going to have to spend the rest of their lives living in fear of what might happen to their only son who they loved more than life itself. It was cruel.

Cornelius rose to his feet with the help of his walking stick. "Lucas, let us see if young Daniel has finished eating his dinner. Like myself, I'm quite sure he'd relish some of Mrs Ellen's apple crumble."

And with that, Cornelius led a very reluctant looking Lucas out of the lounge giving Leo a chance to speak with the Macintoshes alone.

Still kneeling on skinned knees, Leo saw the disbelief, shock and fear written on their faces. He rested his hand on top of their joined ones and felt the glittering diamond ring that decorated Ruth's wedding finger beneath his palm. He looked up at them with warm and sympathetic eyes.

"You've had some very shocking news. I can't even begin to imagine how you must be feeling, being his parents and all, but you have got to accept that this is happening."

Ruth stared back at him with questioning eyes. "Was it something we did?" she asked. "Did we do something wrong? Are we being punished?"

Mark shook his head vigorously from side to side. "No. We are good parents," he said, reassuring his wife. "We go to Church, and we work hard. We do the best we can for Daniel."

"He's right," Leo agreed. "You have done nothing wrong."

There was a small silence before Mark spoke. "Why Daniel?"

"I don't know much more than you do at the moment," Leo replied, standing up and moving to sit in the armchair that Cornelius had just vacated. "I only got told last night, and believe me, you are coping a lot better with it than I did. Apparently, nobody knows why the Power selects who it does. It just does."

"What happens now?" Mark asked. "I mean, if you say this demon, this Baal, is after our son, why isn't he here? What's he waiting for?"

"Lucas explained to me that Baal is trapped underground somewhere, imprisoned by the magic of the Elect. He can't get out yet, but he has demons everywhere. That's it. That's all I know."

"And the Templars? I thought they were protectors of the Holy Grail," Mark said.

Leo bit his lip as he tried to organise his thoughts. "I did too, but I guess we're wrong," he replied with a shrug. "Cornelius hasn't filled me in on them yet. I suppose we should ask him when he comes back."

A door opened, and Daniel's voice echoed around the room. "Mum! Dad!" He came rushing into the room and threw himself at his parents who hugged him tightly.

Leo couldn't help but smile. It was a scene to warm the iciest of hearts. He thought the love between a parent and their child was one of the most beautiful things to behold. As he watched, the smile began to slowly disappear, and an expression of deep longing replaced it. The sadness came out of nowhere, blacker than the shadows and twice as looming. He felt it hug him like it was his parent, a parent who had reared him to accept the fact that he would never have one of his own. He didn't like the idea of meeting the man of his dreams, buying a house, getting married and then paying a surrogate to carry their baby. In a perfect world, his baby would have his genes and also his husband's genes, but nature didn't allow it. Society had finally allowed same sex couples to have children, but Leo had vowed years ago that he'd never adopt a child for fear they'd grow up to be taunted and teased for having two fathers. It would break his heart to see his kid tortured and made fun of because of his selfish desire to have a family. He knew that lots of gay couples were raising children and were perfectly happy. But he couldn't do it. He'd find it unbearable if he was the cause of his kid's misery.

"Leo."

Cornelius' voice pulled him out of his reverie of dark and bitter thoughts. He turned to see Cornelius and Lucas standing by the door.

"Daniel didn't want dessert, he just wanted to see his parents. Poor lad has had a bit of a fright. I think it would be best if you went with Lucas to the dining room. You and I need to have a long chat about the power you possess, but you'll be no use to me with an empty stomach. I will look after the Macintoshes for the time being while you eat. Mrs Ellen has plated you up a wonderful dinner."

Although he longed to stay close to Daniel, he knew that it was important for them to have time alone as a family. Mark and Ruth had a lot that they needed to think about and prepare for. From now on, they were going to have a new and uncertain life, and he figured that it was best to leave Cornelius to deal with explaining the finer details of what that new life would entail.

Leo got to his feet. "I'll catch you guys later," he said to the Macintoshes, before walking towards the kitchen. He stopped when he reached Cornelius. "Don't let them tell Daniel anything about what he is. He's too young to know."

Cornelius smiled warmly and placed a hand on Leo's cheek. "Trust me, child, I've broken this news once before. I know exactly what to say," the old man said.

While Cornelius walked towards the Macintoshes, Leo followed Lucas out of the lounge.

The dining room was large, its walls decorated lavishly with hanging tapestries depicting more Biblical stories. A huge marble dining table, twelve feet in length, sat in the centre of the room upon a stone tiled floor. It was a grand room, and everything in it looked expensive. Golden candlesticks littered the table, and Leo could see that one place had been set with cutlery and napkins. Lucas skipped past him to the table place and pulled out the black chair from beneath.

"Table for Sir," he said, gesturing with an open hand to the set place.

Leo's attention was grabbed momentarily by the candlelight reflecting in mischievous azure eyes. "Thanks," he said while taking the chair offered to him.

"Can I do anything for Sir?"

"Yeah, you can stop calling me Sir," Leo said with more tetchiness than he'd intended. Lucas' face fell, and Leo felt a pang of guilt. "Sorry, I'm just tired and hungry."

Lucas perked right up. "I'll go and get your plate. Do you want a drink?"

"Yes, please. Can I have a bottle of vodka and a straw," Leo said flatly, causing a burst of musical laughter from Lucas.

"No vodka I'm afraid. We have wine though."

"Perfect."

"Great. Be right back."

Minutes later, Lucas reappeared with a hefty plate of food and a substantially large glass of red wine which he placed down in front of Leo.

"Thanks," Leo said as he took the glass of wine and gulped it down in one go. He placed the glass back on the table. "I feel much better. May I have another one, please?" he asked while wiping his mouth with the back of his hand.

Lucas raised his eyebrows to the ceiling. "Sure you can, but not until you eat. You haven't eaten anything all day, and it's almost eight o'clock. Cornelius will not be impressed if you get hammered."

Leo wanted to argue, but Lucas was right. There was no point in getting drunk and hoping that everything would go away. He did that last night, and it had done him no favours. He picked up the knife and fork and attacked the sausage. After cutting off a big bit of the meat, he popped it into his mouth and chewed slowly. The hot chilli flavour of the sausage filled his mouth, but it was bearable. After a few more mouthfuls of delicious chilli sausage, he realised that Lucas was looking at him, or rather, looking at his hands.

"What?" he asked through a mouthful of mashed potato.

Lucas shrugged. "I just noticed you hold your knife and fork the wrong way around."

"And I've noticed that I'm eating, and my wine glass is still empty," Leo retorted.

"Wow. You're a barracuda, aren't you?" Lucas said. "Remember when you were being the nice Leo, about an hour ago in my bedroom? Remember when you were being all concerned about my scars and wounds? Can't you be that Leo?"

Leo shrugged. "I could be. But since you told me you did something really evil and deserve to have those scars, I'm thinking you don't deserve my kindness."

"I'll get the wine," Lucas said coldly, getting up from the table. "Don't be surprised if I poison it first," he added as he stropped off to the kitchen.

Leo was still tucking into the sausage and mash when Lucas returned. Regardless of the fact that he'd been less than pleasant, the man was still kind enough to fill up his glass with more wine.

"Thank you," he said, picking up the glass and raising it. This time, he only took a few sips before setting it back down.

Lucas was silent while Leo consumed every bit of the incredible meal. When he was finished, he set his cutlery down onto the empty plate and pushed it away before taking a large gulp of wine. "What's the deal with demons then?" he began, his fingers running up and down the stem of the wine glass.

"What do you want to know?" Lucas asked, looking on eagerly as if he couldn't wait to answer Leo's questions.

"How do you kill them?"

Lucas' eyes hardened. "I find decapitation the best method, but fire will get the job done."

Leo considered this information for a moment. "That sounds easy enough. I can do fire."

"You'd be dead before you could conjure one spark," Lucas said matter-of-factly.

"Did you not see me lighting the fire back there?"

Lucas waved a hand dismissively. "Oh yeah, that was pretty and everything, but you had time to prepare. You're not as strong as you think you are. You've got to let the divine in, feel it in your heart and soul; if you succumb to the supreme divinity, the magic happens itself. Do you think the demons will spare you a minute so you can summon fire?" he questioned. "I don't think so. Demons are fast, deadly fast. They may not have any magical abilities like the Elect, but what they lack in hocus pocus, they more than make up for in strength, speed and combat. I've seen a group of five demons obliterate over twenty Templars in less than two minutes."

"You're exaggerating," Leo said before draining his glass and setting it down on the table. "But I get it, demons are dangerous."

"This is no time to be flippant, Leo. Cornelius wanted me to give you more details, so could you shut up and listen?" There was no trace of humour in Lucas' voice, no mischievous glint in his eye. "One demon is extremely dangerous. More than one, and you, right now, are pretty much dead. The demon you saw yesterday was in his true form. The black veins, the black eyes, the wings and the pointed teeth are all part of the package."

"True form?"

"Yeah, true form. Demons can alter their appearance to fit in with humans. They don't like doing it, but they can't risk exposing themselves to the human world. Also, it's the easiest way for them to get what they want."

As intrigued as he was, Leo was a little bit frightened talking about demons, but he knew he had to get over his fear. He had a feeling that demons would be featuring heavily in his life in the very near future, so now was the time to get informed.

"What do demons want exactly? Besides killing and maiming innocent humans."

"Not all demons are like that," Lucas snapped.

Leo snorted. "Really? Do you know any friendly demons?"

"As a matter of fact, yes, I do," Lucas replied tartly while refilling Leo's glass. "But that's not important just now. Have you heard of Succubi and Incubi?"

Leo nodded.

"And what do you know about them?"

"According to demonology," Leo recited, "a succubus was a demon who took on the female form of a woman and had intercourse with a man. Incubus was the opposite, a male demon that seduced women."

Lucas looked impressed. "You really do know your stuff."

Leo picked up his glass of wine. "I've always been into demonology, mythology and anything to do with the supernatural."

"Of course, all you Elect are. Part of your programming," Lucas said with a smile. "Anyway, you're spot on about them. That's exactly what they do, and it's how they reproduce. They breed half demon and half human offspring. We call them lesser demons. We reckon that one in a thousand of the world's population are lesser demons."

Red wine sprayed from Leo's mouth. "Are you fucking kidding me? That's like seven million!"

Lucas nodded grimly. "Yeah, at least. They don't inherit much from their demon parent though. Most get blessed with advanced strength, agility, speed, and healing. They're mortal and will age as a normal human does. On their own, they don't pose any real threat. But in packs, they can be dangerous."

Leo wiped his mouth with a napkin as he considered what Lucas was saying. "When you say lesser demons are mortal, does that mean proper demons are immortal?"

"In a way, yes."

"What happened to the demon you killed this afternoon? If he's immortal, how come I saw his very dead body?" Leo's head was beginning to spin. He had no idea if it was because of the information Lucas was giving him, or the wine.

"When Lucifer and his angels were first cast down into the abyss and banished for a thousand years, Lucifer spent the entire time planning how he could rain down vengeance on humanity," Lucas explained. "When the thousand years were up, he used his incredible angelic power to tear holes in the dimensional fabric between his world and yours. His demons journeyed through them and unleashed many evils upon the earth. When the demons were first vanquished by the Elect, their bodies were destroyed, but their spirits survived. The spirits travelled through the veils that Lucifer had created and back home to the abyss."

"And they can never walk on the earth again, right?" Leo said, sounding hopeful.

"I'm afraid they can. When a demon loses their body in this world, it's lost forever along with a great deal of their power. The spirit, like I said, returns to the abyss but can return to the earth by possessing a human. The body you saw today used to be human. When the demon takes full possession, it can use its demonic energy to return to its original form. Although a lot of their power has gone, they are still extremely powerful and dangerous. There is some good news you'll be glad to know."

"Thank god. For a minute there I was beginning to get worried," Leo said drily.

Lucas grinned. "The demons who have never been killed on earth rarely venture here."

"And this is a good thing because…"

"Because those pure demons still have their original strength and power. Those Templars chasing us today? One pure demon would rip every single one of them to bits in less than ten seconds."

Leo had the decency to look scared by this news. "Okay, that really is a good thing," he agreed, straightening up in his chair and attempting to process all of this new information. "Let's see if I've understood you so far. Lesser demons are demon offspring with advanced strength, speed, agility, and healing. A demon who comes to earth and is killed loses its physical body and some of the original power it had. Its spirit travels back through the abyss and lingers there until it decides if it wants to possess a human which it usually does. Pure demons are bad news. Run when I see one."

"Correct," Lucas confirmed.

Leo pulled his lips together and puffed out his cheeks before exhaling noisily. "Right, next question. How does a demon possess a human?"

"There are two ways. The first one is the hardest for a demon. When a human is asleep, their spirit wanders the astral planes and leaves their body an empty shell. The demon can force its way in and take control. The human's spirit is then forced to walk the astral planes forever."

Leo looked horrified. "That doesn't sound hard for the demon at all."

Lucas leaned back in his chair so that it balanced on the back legs. "Believe me, it is. Most humans don't travel too far from their bodies, and the closer the spirit is to the body, the harder it is for the demon to break through. The demon also has to break through the eight foot energy field that every human has."

Leo nodded to show he was following. "Okay. What's the second way?"

"After a human dies or is on the brink of death, a demon can possess the body easily. There is little strength to break in a dying human's energy barrier and none at all after they've died. When—"

"Wait a minute," Leo interrupted. "If the body is dead, then surely there will be a post-mortem and then a funeral. People would notice if there was no corpse at a funeral."

"Nobody can play dead like a demon," Lucas explained. "All they have to do is wait until the night before the funeral, break out of the coffin, fill it with something heavy, and nail it shut again. The family don't have a clue." Lucas leant forward and placed the two front legs onto the stone floor with a resounding thud.

"Man, that's sick!" Leo exclaimed, grimacing at the thought of those families burying a coffin full of stones and mourning as they lowered it into the ground. "I think I've heard enough about demons. I'll figure the rest out as we go along."

Lucas chuckled as he stood up and began tidying up Leo's dinner plate. "There's not much more to be honest. I think we covered it all. The main thing is, if you come across a lesser demon, or a demon who has possessed a body, then burn it or cut its head off. If it's a pure demon, run like hell."

"How will I know the difference?" Leo asked.

Lucas' answer was simple. "You'll *feel* the difference."

With all the dirty dishes in his hands, Lucas didn't say another word and walked out of the dining room, leaving Leo alone with his head buzzing.

'Three kinds of demon,' his inner voice piped up in amusement. *'Scary lesser demons, terrifying possession demons and run like fuck and don't look back pure demons.'*

He closed his eyes tightly for a few seconds. It was a lot to take in, but he did feel better about having more information.

The door to the lounge opened, and he turned to see Cornelius standing in the threshold. The old man closed the door and walked towards the table, his walking stick clacking off the stone tiles.

"How did you enjoy Mrs Ellen's famous chilli sausages?" he asked, his face aglow with its usual warmth.

Leo patted his stomach. "They might have been the best sausages I've ever eaten," he replied.

"Glad to hear it, my boy. Now, what has Lucas told you so far?"

"I know way more than I ever wanted to know about demons. Honestly, I'm not loving them."

Cornelius smiled sadly. "I know the feeling," he said, the sadness reaching his eyes.

In that moment, Leo couldn't feel or see the youthful and vibrant energy that had been there when he'd first met Cornelius. There was only exhaustion and weariness. "Cornelius, are you okay?" he asked.

"I'm just tired, Leo. It's been an eventful day, and those enchantments I placed around the Cathedral have worn me out. I'll be as fit as a fiddle after a good night's sleep."

"I know how you feel, I could sleep for a week. How are Daniel's parents?"

"They're both in a deep state of shock as one would expect. I feel for them," Cornelius said, sighing deeply. "It's never easy delivering that kind of news, but that's what I signed up for. They're in room number five. Mrs Ellen is just fetching freshly laundered bed linen and towels for them. She'll make sure they're well looked after."

"I don't doubt it. What happens now?"

"We get a goodnight's sleep in preparation for the meeting with the Grandmaster. She'll be here first thing tomorrow morning. Lucas will watch over the Cathedral while we rest," Cornelius explained, just as Lucas reappeared from the kitchen with a tray of drinks consisting of a glass of water, a glass of red wine, and a cup of tea.

While Cornelius continued talking, Lucas handed the glass of water to Leo and placed the cup of tea in front of Cornelius. He sat down on a seat next to the old man before picking up the glass of red and taking a long drink.

"We might be safe from demonic attacks while we remain in the Cathedral, but the Templars are a different story, especially when they have Morgana leading them."

Leo was in mid-sip when Cornelius mentioned Morgana. Very slowly, he lowered the glass. "Morgana, as in the bitch who tried to lodge an axe in my head?" He remembered those cold, grey eyes and the long raven hair. Both Lucas and Cornelius nodded. "Who the hell is she?"

"She's the leader of the Templars," Cornelius said.

"I don't mean to be rude, but I kinda gathered that," Leo replied. "Why did she try to kill Daniel? I thought the Templars were protectors of the Holy Grail?"

Cornelius shook his head despondently and sighed. "Ah yes, this is where it gets truly complicated. The Templars think they're doing God's work and unfortunately, that's what makes them so dangerous. They were first set up to protect the Power in medieval times. History is laced with stories of their secrecy and deception. As I'm sure Lucas has already told you, the best lies are those woven with elements of truth.

"Today, there are many theories regarding the Templars and what their role in history has been. The truth is they were protectors of the Power and worked with the Elect for centuries to keep it secret and safe. However, one particular Templar had very different ideas from those of the Elect. René Bordeaux convinced the Templar High Council that the only way to ensure the Power remained hidden and out of Baal's hands was to kill the human who contained it."

Leo gasped. "Oh my god! Why?"

"Did Lucas tell you what happens to the Power once the human who is carrying it dies?" asked Cornelius.

"Yeah, he did. Doesn't it find a newly conceived soul to attach itself to?"

"Yes. You see, the Templars believe the Power is best hidden when it's in the womb, and they are, in a way, correct. If you consider the sheer amount of women who are pregnant in the world, you can be certain that the demons will never be able to find the Power. Thus, the Templars find the Power and kill it no matter if it's a man, woman, teenager, child or baby."

"And they believe that's what God would want?" Leo asked in disbelief.

"I'm afraid so," Cornelius replied.

Leo shook his head from side to side in disgust. "They're no better than demons!" he spat. "In fact, they're worse!"

"Agreed," Lucas said.

Leo couldn't believe that anybody would deliberately hunt down and kill another human being, let alone a tiny, helpless baby. "How many of them are there?" he asked. The look exchanged between Lucas and Cornelius didn't fill him with joy. Neither did Cornelius' answer.

"We can't be certain, but somewhere in the region of nine hundred thousand, maybe more. They're like roaches. You kill one and three more pop up."

Leo opened his mouth a few times as if he was going to say something, but he didn't have any words. Then he had a thought. "But wait a minute, they're only human, right? They're not as scary as pure demons, even lesser demons. Yeah, there might be a million of them, but that's not so bad if they don't have any special powers."

Lucas and Cornelius shared another look as both of their faces darkened.

Leo decided that he'd had enough bad news for one evening. "I don't even want to know what that look was about. Don't tell me anymore!" he said dramatically and stood up, pushing the chair back with his legs.

"All of them are experts in medieval weaponry and hand to hand combat—" Lucas began before being cut off.

"Didn't I just say I didn't want to hear anymore?" Leo said, holding his hand up in protest. It did little to stop Lucas from continuing.

"Back when Bordeaux convinced the High Council to slaughter the person whose soul harboured the Power, the majority of the Elect were outraged, and the two allies became warring factions. Unfortunately, some of the Elect agreed with Bordeaux and joined the Templars."

Leo placed his hands on the dining table and hung his head in defeat. "Lucas, are you telling me that some of these Templars can use magic?"

"That's exactly what I'm saying."

"If this wasn't so fucked up, it would be funny," Leo stated, lifting his head and alternating his gaze between Lucas and Cornelius. "She's one of them, isn't she? Morgana. She's an Elect."

Lucas looked down at the floor for a brief moment before turning his beautiful cerulean eyes on Cornelius. "Yes, she is. But she's also something more."

Leo rolled his eyes. "Of course she is!" he exclaimed. "So, what is she? An indestructible hybrid of Templar, Elect and bad ass demon?" The sarcasm dripped of his tongue, but Cornelius and Lucas didn't react to it. They were too busy looking incredibly awkward. "Well, go on then, tell me. What is she?"

Cornelius cleared his throat and uttered three words that caused Leo's jaw to hit the floor.

"She's my daughter."

Chapter 9
Warnings

"I can't take any more of this tonight! I need to sit in a dark room, alone," Leo yelled, storming to the lounge door and yanking it open. A chair behind him scraped against the stone floor. "No, Lucas! Don't follow me. I need to be alone to get this fucked up shit sorted out in my head. I'll see you in the morning."

"Mrs Ellen prepared room three for you," Cornelius said softly.

"Thank you. Goodnight," Leo responded sharply.

Without another word, he left the dining room and walked through the lounge, quickly moving through it and emerging into the corridor where the bedrooms were. He stopped outside door number five and, as discreetly as he could, pressed his ear against the wooden door. The density of the wood prevented any sound being heard. He wanted to check in with them, make sure they were okay. He also didn't want to trouble the family anymore so he moved on to door number three.

Room three was almost identical to Lucas' apart from there was no TV fixed to the wall. As he stepped into the room, his eyes were drawn to a small pile of white towels lying on the bed. He walked over and sat down next to them, noticing a small note was sitting on top of the fluffy pile.

Here are your towels, Leo. Freshly laundered today, so they were! The shower is easy to use and self-explanatory. I've left new shower items such as toothbrush, shampoo and shower gel in the bathroom, so please help yourself. Scrambled eggs on toast for breakfast. Sleep well. Mrs Ellen. X

Leo managed a small smile after reading the note and placed it on the bedside table. He lay back and sprawled across the bed, shutting his eyes and placing his hands on his forehead. He couldn't stop thinking about the dramatic new additions to the story and how they only complicated matters even further. The more the story unravelled, the more it twisted erratically like a massive ball of knotted wool. Any more shocking news from Cornelius and he feared the old man would send him over the edge.

With a great big sigh, he lifted himself off the bed and undressed down to his underwear before taking a small towel from the pile and walking barefooted to the bathroom.

The bathroom was very small and housed only the bare essentials: a toilet, a sink, and a shower cubicle with a curtain. Next to the sink was a full length mirror which also happened to be opposite the shower cubicle. It was obvious from the plasterboard walls that the ensuite had been an added feature. Above the sink was a small wooden shelf that had been drilled into the plasterboard. Like Mrs Ellen's note indicated, there was a new toothbrush, toothpaste, and a variety of shampoos and shower gels.

He smiled to himself as he thought about Mrs Ellen. She was a complete stranger to him yet so transparent that he felt like he'd known her his whole life. 'I bet she makes a mean scrambled egg,' he thought to himself as he began tearing open the packaging from the new toothbrush.

After brushing his teeth and using the toilet, he peered into the mirror and inspected his war wounds. A good chunk of his hair was stuck to the cut on his scalp. Running a finger around the dressing on his hip, the images of Lucas' scars flashed in his mind's eye.

He felt revulsion and disgust towards the so-called father who had inflicted the horrific injuries upon his own son. Lucas said he deserved them, but Leo didn't believe it for one minute. There was something about the man he couldn't quite figure out, however, he instinctively felt that Lucas wasn't capable of a crime meriting such a punishment. It would have been a lie to say he wasn't curious about the scars, but now wasn't the time to ponder. With one last look at his bumps and bruises, he switched off the bathroom light and returned to the bedroom.

Before climbing into bed, he walked to the small window and reached for the curtains. He paused for a moment, staring into the darkness and wondering what lay beyond. Although he'd walked past the Cathedral many times, he'd never been into the building before. The light from the bedroom illuminated a few feet out into the night but not enough to let him get his bearings.

It was snowing heavily now, and he could see the snowflakes relentlessly streaking through the air like white bullets. He could hear the wailing wind piercing the silence of the night, angrily hammering against the window and making it rattle. He shivered and drew the curtains.

Despite the room having old stone walls, it was pleasantly warm. He would usually have considered the reasons as to why this was, but as tiredness gripped him in an unyielding hold, he was merely grateful for the soothing heat. Without another thought, he slipped beneath the thick duvet, rested his head on the impossibly soft pillow, and closed his eyes. Within minutes, his chest was rising rhythmically as tiredness consumed him, pulling him effortlessly into the world of sleep.

*   *   *

He found himself on a hilltop, looking down on what looked to be a small country village populated with men, women and children. The people were dressed in clothes made from various materials that ranged from linen and wool to animal skins and silk. They bustled around and conversed with each other, but there was no sound to be heard. Leo strained his ears, but it was in vain. It was like somebody had pressed 'mute' on the remote control.

While walking between the small mud-brick houses that had been built closely together, he observed the local villagers. They were extremely excited. There was a definite buzz in the air, and something had them riled. Small children darted into their houses and emerged moments later with their parents in tow, bounding up and down like puppies on their first walk while heading deeper into the village.

Leo followed the crowd right through the village and into a forest. The forest floor had tree roots pushing up from beneath the soil making it uneven and treacherous to walk upon. It did little to impede the villagers' progress as they walked briskly onwards, getting deeper and deeper into the thickening foliage of the forest. Eventually, the dense greenery opened out into a clearing where the villagers were congregating.

He made his way carefully through the gathering crowd, his curiosity driving him forward. The crowd's excitement appeared to have rubbed off on him, and his own desire to find out what was going on was peaking. As he emerged from the throng, he stopped dead in his tracks when he finally saw what had been causing the fuss.

A small group of people, who Leo recognised to be a family, were working tirelessly on the biggest wooden structure he'd ever seen. Even though he was impressed by their skilled labour, the villagers were ridiculing them mercilessly. The family, seemingly undeterred by the taunts and jeers, continued to work while the crowd grew and filled the entrance to the clearing. A number of them dispersed themselves along the forest line while others climbed the trees to get a better view.

After careful scrutiny of the structure, Leo decided it was some kind of containment unit as it had a large entrance way with a long wooden walkway leading up to it and no windows at all. His eyes looked beyond the unit, and he marvelled at the stunning scenery that lay there. It was a mass of green and stony grey with the surrounding areas coming together in a collage of mountain, hill and flat grassy land.

He'd gazed up to the sky at one point and saw the sun moving swiftly across it, a lot faster than normal. The moon came up shortly afterwards and moved at the same speed as the sun while the stars sparkled and glittered in the darkness. Somebody had pressed the 'fast-forward' button on his dream. He stood some distance away from the unit and continued to watch the man and his family work at super speed. After several repetitions of the sun and moon chasing each other playfully across the sky, time reverted back to normal, and the man and his family stood before the completed structure. The sun took centre stage in the cloudless sky and shone brightly down on everything it could reach.

Leo felt the heat caress his face as he walked around to the other side of the completed structure and studied it further. He realised he'd been right about it being a containment unit as this side was identical to the other.

It was then he noticed the man and his wife standing at the foot of the walkway holding hands, their sons and their wives beside them. It should have been a moment of pure pride and satisfaction on what was a gloriously sunny day, but the men looked anxious, the women scared. At first he thought the family were staring at him, but he quickly realised they were staring past him. When he turned to see what they were looking at, clarity descended.

Two of every type of animal he could ever imagine were either marching across the land, slithering over the earth or flying through the air towards him. Some he recognised, some he didn't. He turned, wide eyed, to look at the older man who was now staring directly at him.

"Noah?" Leo said, but no sound came out of his mouth.

The man smiled and nodded.

When the animals reached the Ark, the family stepped aside to let them walk, gallop, slither or crawl up the walkway. It seemed like hours had passed when the last of the animals disappeared into the great depths of the Ark. The family followed them inside except for Noah who started towards Leo with the aid of a long walking stick.

When the man got closer, Leo instantly recognised the walking stick he carried, its amber stone glinting in the sunlight. Noah extended his hand, and Leo clasped it firmly, gasping when his vision blurred momentarily. When it returned to normal, he saw that he was back where he'd started with the forest and crowds behind him and the mountains and hills facing him. About four hundred metres away, the villagers continued their ridiculing from the forest and the trees. He dropped Noah's hand and looked up at the man to see that his lips were moving.

"I'm sorry, I can't hear you," Leo said with an apologetic smile.

"How about now?" Noah asked.

After the initial shock of suddenly hearing again, Leo cocked his head and took in Noah's appearance. He was a very tall and broad man with greying hair and a long greying beard. He was strong and muscular, despite his age, and his skin was sun kissed, attributes that were probably from the amount of time and effort he'd spent out in the blistering sun working to complete the Ark.

"Yes, I can hear you now," Leo replied, relieved that he could hear his own voice again. "You're Noah, aren't you?"

Noah nodded and smiled. "I've been waiting for you, Leo Alexander. Although, I'm not the only one who has been waiting. Someone has been waiting even longer, but that's none of my business. I'm supposed to tell you something, something secret."

Leo immediately wanted to be elsewhere. So far, everything that Lucas and Cornelius had told him had been emphatically bad. The dream with Moses had started out nice enough, but then the demons had shown up and ruined it. Even in the dream world, he wasn't safe from the dread that began to slowly asphyxiate him. "I know I'm going to regret this," he moaned, "but what is it you have to tell me?"

The smile on Noah's face faded away to sadness. "The demons are coming for him, Leo."

The moment the words were out of Noah's mouth, the sunlight faded, and a sudden gust of cold wind slapped Leo's cheeks. "I know that," he said flatly. "Lucas and I will protect him."

"And you will fail to protect it in its current guise. He will foresee it."

Leo threw his arms up into the air. "Oh *He* will, will *He*? Well, if *He's* going to see it then what is the bloody point in this whole charade? Why doesn't *He* just stop all this?"

"He can't stop what he did not create, Leo. His gift is his curse."

The amber stone in Noah's staff began to glow, and large drops of rain fell from the darkening sky, drumming on the dry hard soil and bouncing off the Ark. A clap of thunder sounded in the distance, and the villagers looked up nervously to the sky.

"We don't have much time. I shall tell you what you need to know. You'll be deceived by an agent of the Beast. When the Power takes on its next guise, it will be its last."

The words 'next' and 'guise' did not sit well with Leo, and their meaning prevented his brain from processing the word 'Beast'. "Wait, are you telling me that Daniel will die?" he exclaimed as the rain ran down his face.

Noah merely nodded before continuing. "When you find the Power in its final disguise, you must get ready for battle. The final battle is coming, and the forces of hell are preparing their final onslaught. They are desperate now, they sense time is running out. The pure demons will walk the earth once more, corrupting mankind and reigning their evil down on the good and righteous. You must stop them."

"How? How can I possibly stop them?" Leo asked hopelessly. A second clap of thunder boomed above their heads, and the rain fell even heavier.

"Yours is the gift to change, Leo. That is the first thing you must understand. Secondly, the Power has a great ally which will come to its aid when it needs it most. We, the Elect of my time, created this ally, but it requires a firm hand to control. It remains buried deep underground beneath a liquid mass."

"Who is this ally?"

"You'll know when you see it," Noah replied. "You'll feel it."

Leo did not feel reassured by the man's words and pushed his saturated hair out of his eyes. Before he could ask another question, screams of terror filled his ears, and he glanced over his shoulder to see the villagers scrambling away from the forest line and stampeding towards the Ark. He caught sight of various movements at the top of the trees and saw the villagers who had chosen to sit up in the branches suddenly disappear. Panicked, he turned to Noah.

"Noah?" Leo blinked; Noah was gone.

He looked again at the charging villagers, his eyes drawn to those at the forest line who were being hauled back into the trees by an invisible force. Another clap of thunder filled the air as demons exploded out of the forest and gave chase to the humans. He could only gasp when several villagers disappeared, screaming and terrified, under monstrous black wings.

His eyes fell back on the Ark where he saw Noah's sons pulling the walkway inside. Once it was in, the sons followed, and an enormous wooden door was pulled across the entrance as a deafening fourth clap of thunder shook the air.

Leo took off in the direction of the Ark feeling like his legs were made from lead as he tried to run away from the stampede that was quickly gaining on him. From the top of the Ark, there was a flash of amber light, and he looked up to see Noah standing on the roof, staff in hand.

"Help me!" he screamed at the biblical man, knowing that it would be impossible for Noah to hear him above the thunder, the rain and the screaming villagers who were being massacred by the demons.

'I am helping you.'

Noah's mouth didn't move yet Leo heard his voice.

'Before we part, I have one final piece of information for you. You must find Eden's Gift. It is your weapon to wield and will bestow great power on you.'

The effort he was putting into running wasn't worth the tiny distance he was covering, so he stopped and rooted himself to the spot.

"What's Eden's Gift?" he bellowed.

'It's a gift, from Eden,' Noah's voice echoed in his head.

Never before had Leo wanted to tell somebody to fuck off more than he did now. He was tired of all the cryptic messages.

The villagers were roughly a hundred feet away from him. He could see the demons clearly now. Despite them being hideously ugly and horrific, there was something majestic and beautiful about their black feathered wings. Noah's voice boomed in Leo's head.

'Genesis 6:7 - And the LORD said, I will destroy man whom I have created from the face of the earth; both man, and beast, and the creeping thing, and the fowls of the air; for I am sorry that I have made them.'

The crucial part of the story came to the forefront of his mind: the flood. He watched helplessly as Noah flung his head backwards and thrust the staff high up into the air. A dazzling beam of white light shot out from the amber stone and straight up into the sky, lighting everything up so gloriously that Leo thought heaven itself was going to fall upon the earth. After a minute, the white beam was sucked back into the stone, and Noah vanished.

'It is done.'

As well as the voice in his head, Leo was conscious of the ear-splitting screams coming from the villagers who were either being slaughtered by the demons or running past him to pound their fists against gopher wood. He watched one desperate man make it to the roof of the Ark only to be carried off by a winged demon who ripped him apart in the air.

Blood splattered across Leo's forehead just as a sinister humming noise began to drown out the sounds of the massacre. The humming had started off softly, reverberating through the air gently. It quickly and gradually grew louder until it became a constant roar that made the ground tremble.

He watched in complete reverence as an ocean of water fell from the heavens and came crashing down on the Ark, sweeping away any villager and demon in its way. He stood rooted to the spot as the water formed a wall and came racing towards him. With his eyes shut tightly, he opened his mouth to scream, but the sound was lost in the roaring depths of the tidal wave as it ripped through him and pulled him off his feet.

When he opened his eyes again, he was in crystal clear water that was oddly serene given the fact it'd been so turbulent seconds before. He allowed himself to float leisurely, occasionally waving his arms and kicking his legs. Above him, he could see the enormous Ark moving away from him at great speed. He stared lazily at it and watched until it was out of sight.

It was peaceful in this place, and he preferred it here. He closed his eyes and was just about to savour the moment when he suddenly felt a presence that struck fear into every fibre of his being. He wasn't alone in the water. Even though his eyes were shut, he knew there was something in front of him—something huge and dangerous. It was

171

something so frightening that he didn't want to open his eyes, but he was too curious for his own good.

It was worse than he'd imagined. Huge red gleaming eyes set in an olive coloured serpentine head stared greedily at him. The creature opened its jaws to reveal four foot long razor sharp teeth. After a short time, it closed its jaws before pulling its lips back in a psychotic and terrifying grin. It had a body shaped like a plesiosaur, but instead of flippers, it had short stubby legs with wicked looking talons on the end of its feet.

Leo tried to scream, but no sound came out. The last thing he saw was the creature's powerful jaws opening wide, and then everything went black.

Chapter 10
The Grandmaster

Snowflakes floated serenely through the dark sky and landed gently upon the pristine blanket of snow that covered the Cathedral grounds. Inverness was dormant. It was late enough that the Saturday night revellers were tucked up in bed in an alcohol induced coma, but early enough that the church goers hadn't risen for their hymns and morning prayers. A cold breeze ruffled the bare branches of the trees before coming spiralling down to tug at Leo's clothing.

He leaned against the stone wall situated in the small alcove of the main door, wrapped up in his coat and scarf, and wearing yesterday's clothes. Bringing his second cigarette of the morning up to his lips, he stared across the river at his flat which lay in complete darkness. It was alone and abandoned, just like Daniel; the boy who had been thrown to the lions by a God who supposedly loved him. Daniel was truly alone. Nobody could ever explain to him how it felt to carry such a power because anybody who'd ever experienced it was dead.

The anger bubbled and made his face grow hot despite the black and bitter morning. He'd never felt a fury like it before, and it boiled his blood. It was molten lava; it needed a vent. He feared if he didn't let it out soon, he was going to erupt like Vesuvius.

While he'd gone through the torturous process of cleaning his half healed wounds in the shower earlier this morning, his mind processed the endless information it had received over the last thirty hours or so. He deduced that two people were solely responsible for the whole fiasco.

The primary culprit was, of course, God Almighty. As far as Leo was concerned, if He'd preordained everything like the Bible claimed He did, then He already knew this would happen yet hadn't acted upon it. It was infuriating to think that a benevolent deity could stand by and allow this curse to befall innocent children.

Then there was culprit number two: The Grandmaster who had cast the spell in the first place. What had she been thinking? Did she even think about the ramifications her magic would have? Did she actually stop to think about the danger she was putting innocent people in?

'She was being hunted by a sadistic pure demon who had already killed her son in front of her eyes, and then threatened her daughter. Cut the girl some slack!'

He exhaled a large stream of smoke from his nostrils before dropping the cigarette end to the ground and crushing it into the snow. His inner voice did have a point, but he chose to ignore it. At the present time, it felt good to blame somebody.

The early morning breeze managed to get beneath his scarf, chilling his neck. Against his flushed skin, it was most welcome as it caressed and soothed. He loosened his scarf to get the full benefit before delving into his pocket to retrieve another cigarette.

"Three cigarettes and it's not even seven yet. Tut, tut, Mr Alexander." Lucas appeared at the Cathedral door and slipped into the alcove beside him. He wore his leather coat, dark blue denim jeans and brown boots.

After lighting his cigarette, Leo reopened the packet and held it out to Lucas. "If I give you one, will it shut you up?" he asked drily.

Lucas grinned. "It will."

Leo cupped a hand around his lighter and flicked it to ignite the flame. After several attempts, it was clear the lighter was broken. The irises in his eyes sparkled momentarily as he raised his index finger to the cigarette that Lucas had placed between his shining white teeth. A tiny red spark burst from his finger followed by a little flame.

"Clever boy," Lucas praised. "The more you use the magic, the stronger you'll become no matter how little it is."

"I'm trying to get used to conjuring without my magical supplies. I think I might like this way of casting. It's less hassle," Leo said with a wry smile.

"The light you carry inside of you is powerful and will chase the demons back into the darkness. Believe it." Lucas paused to exhale the smoke, murmuring as he did so. "Nothing like a cigarette to start the day. Did you sleep well?"

"No."

"How come?"

"I just didn't," Leo replied. He was thoroughly enjoying the cigarette despite the gritty feeling at the back of his throat.

"The dreams are quite intense, but you'll get used to them."

Lucas' words made him cough and splutter. "How do you do that?" he demanded after regaining his composure. He took a few deep breaths before inhaling a fresh lungful of smoke.

Lucas shrugged. "I've been around the Elect for a long time. A lot of the members who go on to become the most powerful have always had the dreams. I'm told they're extremely vivid. A long time ago, a Grandmaster said the dreams were messages from the Divine."

Leo considered this for a moment. "That's the second dream I've had, and I don't want anymore," he said emphatically.

"What was it this time? Cain and Abel? Adam and Eve? The parting of the Red Sea?" Lucas' eyes burned with curiosity.

"None of the above," Leo answered. "I'll give you a clue - huge wooden boat, older man with a stunning wife and handsome sons, two of every animal, and an ocean of rain."

Lucas finished his cigarette and flicked it on the ground. "No way!" he chuckled. "Noah? I've never heard of anyone getting him before. Was he rocking the bearded look?"

"Yeah, he was actually," Leo said. "It was more of a nightmare than a dream though.

"How come?"

"Noah told me the Power has one more human guise. I don't believe him because that would mean Daniel will have to die, and that's not going to happen." Leo said the words with so much conviction even he believed them. He would die first before he'd let anyone harm a hair on Daniel's head.

"Did he say anything else?"

As Leo concentrated on recalling the dream, his brow furrowed, and he bit his bottom lip. "He said a few things but nothing enlightening."

"Tell me anyway, I'm interested."

"He said the demons would come after me and Daniel which we know already. There was something about being deceived by an agent of the beast, but I wasn't really paying much attention because I was still reeling from what he said about Daniel."

Lucas raised his eyebrows. "Really? Did he say who the beast was?"

"Funnily enough, no he didn't," Leo answered, dropping his cigarette and standing on it. "The divine apparently thinks it's much more fun for me to guess who the little Judas might be."

Lucas frowned. "We'll have to keep our eyes and ears open. What else?"

"Something about pure demons walking the earth again, which filled me with glee, and the Power having an ally buried deep underground. Then a group of demons ripped a bunch of villagers to shreds. Oh, and something about Eden." He closed his eyes and tried to pluck the name from his memory.

"Eden's Gift?" Lucas suggested.

Leo opened his eyes. "Yes! That's it. Noah said it was a weapon. Have you heard of it? Do you know what it is?"

Lucas nodded. "And I believe you've already seen it."

"I have?"

"Yup. Noah might have used it in your dream last night, but you'd have definitely seen it in your dream about Moses."

Leo mulled both dreams over in his head, but there was nothing jumping out at him. "Moses and Noah didn't use any weapons in my dreams. No swords or blades of any kind. They both used magic, so I'm guessing they were both Elect."

"They were Grandmasters," Lucas explained. "Both of them are among the most powerful men that have ever walked this earth."

"Yeah, I got that impression. Moses turned his staff into a snake and—" Suddenly, Leo was back in both dreams simultaneously. Moses transforming the staff into the snake, Noah holding the same staff to the sky to open the heavens. Eden's Gift became as clear as day. "The staff!" he exclaimed, grabbing Lucas' arm. "It's the staff!"

Lucas smiled and nodded. "Bingo. Eden's Gift is exactly what its name suggests, a gift from Eden."

Leo rolled his eyes. "That's what Noah said."

Lucas chuckled. "When Adam and Eve were banished from the Garden of Eden, Adam snapped a small branch off a very special tree and took it with him. He shaped it into the staff you saw and used it as a walking stick. Guess which tree."

"The tree of the knowledge of good and evil?" At that moment, Leo's knees began to shake, and his teeth started to chatter. The winter morning had finally cooled his rage.

"Correct, but before I tell you anymore, let's get inside," Lucas said, rubbing the side of Leo's arm. "You're freezing."

Once back in the soothing warmth of the Cathedral, he followed Lucas half way up an aisle and watched him squeeze his muscular frame into one of the pews.

"As I was saying, Adam kept the walking stick with him until he died. It was passed down to his son Cain, however, Adam never told Cain exactly what it was. Cain carried the family heirloom until he died, and it was passed onto his son who did the same. Eventually, it came to a man called Methuselah.

"Methuselah was a very intuitive member of the Elect, and from the moment he touched the staff, he knew it contained divine power. As well as the staff, Methuselah's father, Enoch, passed down an amber crystal. Enoch was gifted the crystal by the angel Uriel who had imbued it with angelic power. Combining the gemstone with the staff, Methuselah created an extraordinary weapon of light to use against the demons. Very few humans that have lived can harness its power."

"Were they Grandmasters?" Leo asked.

"Yes. It's a heavenly weapon, so technically angels are the only other entities who can use it. Unfortunately, that means demons can too," Lucas added grimly.

Leo rubbed his hands together and blew into them. "Where is it now?"

Lucas' face fell. "Noah didn't tell you?"

"What do you think?" Leo sighed and slumped back into the seat. "Messages from the divine? Yeah, right! Why does it always have to be cryptic bullshit? Can't they just tell it like it is?"

178

"Eden's Gift hasn't been seen for millennia," Lucas continued. "The last person known to have it was Moses. If everything written about Eden's Gift is true, then it has phenomenal power. If you got your hands on it you'd be virtually unstoppable."

Leo snorted rudely. "Thanks for the vote of confidence, but what the hell am I going to do with the staff?"

"What couldn't you do? Leo, you don't have a clue about the power you have within you. I can't wait until the Grandmaster starts training you because then you might actually start believing in yourself."

"I guess we'll just have to wait and see I suppose," Leo replied, his face flushing.

Lucas got to his feet. "The Grandmaster will be here in an hour. I think Mrs Ellen is doing scrambled eggs on toast, and you don't want to miss that."

"No, I really don't," Leo said sincerely while Lucas squeezed past him and stepped into the aisle.

"If you remember anything else useful about the dream, let me know. I'm just gonna check in with Cornelius, see what he wants me to do. I'll catch you later."

He remained seated as Lucas started walking towards the dormitories. Suddenly, a picture flashed in his mind. His body trembled, and it had nothing to do with the cold.

"Lucas!"

Lucas stopped and turned around. "Yeah?"

"At the end of my dream, I was underneath the water. Everything was beautiful and peaceful. Then out of nowhere, I suddenly got these bad vibes, and every part of my body felt this presence behind me. I turned around and this enormous monster was there." Leo did not like the look of alarm on Lucas' usually cheerful demeanour.

"What did it look like?" Lucas asked, his jaw tightening.

"It was gigantic, and it had scarlet eyes and olive skin. It had a serpent-like head on the end of a long neck and the body of a plesiosaur. Kinda like Nessie."

"Did it have wings? Was it a snake? Did it communicate with you?" Lucas fired off his questions in rapid succession while striding back to the pew.

Leo slid over to allow Lucas to sit. "Um, I'm not sure if it had wings—"

"You need to get sure! This is important, tell me exactly what you saw."

"Lucas, you're scaring me."

On the back of the pews there was a small wooden shelf for bibles and hymn books to sit on. Lucas snatched up the closest hymn book and opened it. From the left pocket of his coat, he pulled out a pen and sketched erratically on the blank inside cover. Leo could do nothing but wait.

"Is this what you saw?" Lucas finally asked, holding out the book.

Leo's instincts told him that he didn't even need to look at the drawing; he knew it would be identical to the one from his dream. He grasped the hymn book with a quivering hand, not looking at the sketched image straight away.

"Come on, Leo. This is critical!"

"Why?"

"Just look at the fucking picture!" Lucas snapped.

Leo complied and let his eyes fall ever so slowly onto the paper. There, in blue ink, was the exact same beast from his nightmare; the feet, the neck, the teeth, the eyes and the head were all perfect replicas. The only difference from the dream version was a giant pair of wings. The rest of the sketch was identical to the beast he'd seen.

"Well?" Lucas urged.

Leo closed the hymn book and placed it back on the tiny shelf. After taking a deep breath, he looked at Lucas who was quivering in anticipation.

"Yes, down to every single feature apart from the wings. I can't be sure about them. I never saw any."

"Did it communicate with you?"

"No, it just floated in front me for a while and sort of grinned manically. Then it opened its jaws and went for me."

Lucas nodded curtly and stood up. "Promise me that you won't mention this to anybody for the time being."

"Why?" Leo felt the familiar sensation of his heart and stomach sinking at the prospect of yet more devastating and potentially terrifying news.

"Can't you just do what I ask, for once?" Lucas asked, sounding exasperated.

Leo folded his arms in defiance. "How about you give me one good reason why you want me to keep it to myself, and then I'll consider."

"Because if this means what I think it means then everything has changed. I can't explain it right now, walls have ears. Please, promise me."

Leo gave into the bewitching blue eyes. "Fine, I promise. But the next time we're alone, you better tell me what it's all about," he answered with a pout.

Lucas smiled. "You're really cute when you're pissed off," he said before turning serious again. "I'll explain everything to you after I speak with the Grandmaster. Don't even tell Cornelius."

He was a little thrown at Lucas' use of the word 'cute' to describe him, but he didn't react outwardly to it and simply nodded. "Got it. Mum's the word."

"Thanks. Now, go and eat breakfast. I have some calls to make. I'll come and get you when the Grandmaster arrives."

Before Leo could answer, Lucas strode towards the main door with his phone clutched to his ear before disappearing through it and leaving him alone with his thoughts about the beast. He sat for a moment and stared at the altar, silently praying that the beast didn't physically exist in the real world.

Just like you wished that demons didn't exist? Good luck with that.'

Ignoring his snide inner voice, he picked himself up off the pew and made a quick visit to his dormitory. He cast off his coat and scarf, noting the dried up blood on his favourite green hoodie. Just like last night, he stopped outside room number five and pressed his ear against the door. He couldn't hear a single sound and assumed they were still asleep, so he went searching for breakfast.

He found Mrs Ellen in the dining room where she was busy bustling about with plates, cutlery and serviettes while humming to herself. When she saw she had a guest, she offered a pair of bright eyes and a warm welcoming smile.

"Top of the morning to you, Leo. How are you feeling today? Now, you'll be having scrambled eggs on toast for breakfast. White or brown bread for you?"

Her lilting Irish accent filled the room with such a genuine and homely warmth that he forgot he was in the back rooms of the Inverness Cathedral. Her energy transformed the grand and exquisite ambiance of the dining room into a more quaint and cosy one, much like that of a small cottage. She pulled out a chair as he approached and ushered him into it.

"Good morning, Mrs Ellen," he said, sitting in the chair and returning her smile. "Thank you. Scrambled eggs on toast sounds great. White bread, please."

"Excellent!" Mrs Ellen beamed, placing a chubby hand on his shoulder. "What would you like to drink? I have tea, coffee, orange juice or water, and I think there's lemonade left over from last week's Sunday school."

"I'll have an orange juice, please. Is there anything I can do to help in the kitchen?"

Mrs Ellen squeezed his shoulder gently. "Oh for heaven's sake, no! You'll sit there and eat your breakfast, so you will, and you won't lift a finger." For a moment, the old woman sounded as if she was offended by his offer to help but was back to being bright and bubbly seconds later. "Now, do you want tomato sauce with your eggs?"

"Can you eat scrambled eggs without it?" he joked, laughing when Mrs Ellen swatted him gently on the back with her tea towel.

"Oh, you're terrible, so you are! I'll just get your orange juice and then get going with breakfast."

She vacated the dining room briefly and returned with a large glass of orange juice and a plate containing six pieces of buttered toast. "There you are son. That'll keep you going until I get the eggs ready, so it will. Enjoy!"

"Thank you, Mrs Ellen," Leo said before she disappeared back into the kitchen.

He picked up a slice and tore a piece off. The bread tasted like it was homemade, and he considered that it might be the best bread he'd ever tasted in his life. It reminded him of the bread his mother used to make and was the only memory that hadn't faded over time.

Every morning his father would come into his room, wake him up and carry him through to the kitchen where his mother would be fussing over a delicious breakfast involving freshly baked bread. Everyday up until he was five years old, the same routine was played out. The painful memories of his parents made his vision blur and caused a hard lump to form at the back of his throat. They always caught him unaware, but he was skilled at quickly burying them deep in the back of his mind where they'd stay until they tried to claw their way back out again.

Leo had eaten his third slice of toast when the dining room doors opened, and the familiar sound of Cornelius' walking stick clacked off the stone floor. He was about to greet the old man when a woman that he recognised only too well entered the room and caused him much surprise.

"Ela!" he exclaimed, standing up at once. "What are you doing here?" He rushed over and hugged her.

"The same reason you are," Ela replied, smiling radiantly and returning his hug. She was a tall and slender woman in her fifties with blonde curly hair that was greying slightly.

Although she carried the same air of wisdom as Cornelius, Ela's energy was far more celestial.

Leo was puzzled by her response. "You're here to protect Daniel?"

"I am indeed, my darling," she said, taking his hands. The sleeves of her long flowing white top tickled his wrists, and her lavish bangles jingled and jangled pleasantly. "Come, sit for a moment."

He allowed Ela to direct him back to his seat, marvelling at the way her skirt trailed across the ground, the beautiful turquoise colour shimmering as she floated across the room. She took the seat directly next to him while Cornelius chose to sit opposite her, his face expressionless and his eyes fixed firmly on the table.

"Are you an Elect too?" Leo asked, taking a large bite of toast.

Ela smiled warmly. "Yes, I am."

"Why didn't you tell me? I'm never out of your shop."

"Would you have believed me?" she countered, gazing at him softly. Her eyes were an unusual yet stunning shade of light blue.

"No, probably not," he replied, stuffing the rest of the toast into his mouth.

"Exactly. It wasn't my place to tell you, and it wasn't Lucas' either, although I understand why he did it."

"If Lucas hadn't told me, I wouldn't have a clue about anything that's going on." He picked up his glass of orange juice and gulped it down.

Ela nodded. "True, but the Elect must find their own way to the path. You were almost there, but Lucas did what he thought was best."

"Yeah, he did. Do you know when the Grandmaster is going to get here?"

Ela looked amused. "Leo, my dear, I'm the Grandmaster."

Orange juice came spraying out of his mouth like a hose. Luckily, he was quick enough to turn his head so that it only sprayed the floor.

"Are you serious?"

"Of course. I came to this city almost twelve years ago to watch over Daniel and his family. He was only two months old when I opened my shop."

"How did you know the Power was bound to him?"

"The same way you found out about Eden's Gift, dreams and visions. They're not for the—"

The door to the kitchen swung open, and Mrs Ellen came into the room with a silver tray containing a small plate of toast, a small jug of milk, a bowl of sugar, a teapot, two cups and two spoons.

"Good morning, Father. Good morning, Lady Ela," she said charmingly, placing the tray in front of Ela. "Here's your breakfast."

"You are too kind, Mrs Ellen. And please, it's just Ela. I've never been one for titles," Ela said with a smile, picking up the teacups. After she'd poured hot tea into both, she passed one over to Cornelius. "There you are, Father O'Connor."

Cornelius took the cup without thanking her.

"The eggs are almost ready, so I'll go and get our other guests," Mrs Ellen announced.

After Mrs Ellen had left the room, Leo sat patiently while Ela added four heaped teaspoons of sugar and a tiny drop of milk into her tea. The spoon clinked pleasantly against the china cup as she stirred.

"The dreams and visions are not for the faint hearted, but they're vitally important to us. They always point us in the right direction." Ela paused and took several sips from her cup. "One particular vision taught me that every human vessel of the Power was born with a mark."

"What kind of mark?"

"Daniel's mark is on his lower back at the base of his spine. It's purple in colour and is the symbols for alpha and omega. I've seen pictures from other vessels, and at first glance one would think it's merely a birthmark, but to someone who knows, the symbols are unmistakable. You, along with Cornelius and I, are the only ones who know about this mark." She took another sip from her tea, the expression on her face indicating her pleasure at the taste.

Leo's brow creased as he speculated on the meaning of the alpha and omega symbols. He was up on most things biblical, but the significance of the symbols alluded him.

"Why alpha and omega?"

Ela held the cup at her mouth and cast a glance in Cornelius' direction.

"Revelations 1:8 – 'I am the Alpha and the Omega,' says the Lord God," the old man said, his tone far from warm. "The alpha and the omega symbols are Greek in origin. They mean the first and the last and refer to the eternality of the one true God. A very fitting symbol for the vessel of His power."

Ela placed her teacup on the table. "Very fitting," she said curtly before changing the subject. "Lucas said you had a dream."

Leo's gaze wavered between the Grandmaster and Cornelius. "Yeah, that's right," he replied and gave a detailed account of the dream, staying true to his word and omitting the part about the sea monster.

"Fascinating," Cornelius commented, his voice slightly warmer. "It would appear the divine is pointing you towards Eden's Gift."

"Lucas and I think the same. Ela?" Leo looked over expectantly at his friend, the Grandmaster posing as a magic shop owner.

"I concur," she said. "I believe the divine is working very hard to bring you to Eden's—"

"If that's the divine's will, then so be it," Cornelius interrupted, standing up and taking a step back from the table. "It's imperative that you find that staff, Leo. You must begin the search as soon as possible."

"But we have no idea where it is," Leo pointed out. "Noah didn't show me a map or anything."

"Maybe he will in the next dream," Ela said with a grin.

"I don't want any more dreams, so he'll have to send me a text," Leo said drily.

Ela chuckled.

"Seriously, they're far too intense for me," he complained. "Do they ever stop?"

"I'm afraid not, but they get less intense with each one. You'll soon learn to immerse yourself in them and really understand what God is trying to tell you."

Leo sighed. "Why does He need to communicate this way? If He's that powerful, why can't He just appear before me and actually tell me Himself? It would save a lot of hassle."

Once again, Ela chuckled. "Believe me, He could easily do that, but humans weren't built to witness the enormity and complexity of what God is. Not on this plane of existence anyway. Think of a computer's hard drive. What happens when it is given too much data and information to process?"

Cornelius snorted rudely and banged his walking stick against the stone floor. "Are you really comparing our Lord and Creator to the cheap world of technology?"

The warm and homely atmosphere that Mrs Ellen had created in the dining room perished as an ice age formed between Ela and Cornelius. There was a painfully long silence as the pair tried to freeze each other with ice cold stares, entirely forgetting that Leo was even there. His skilled powers of intuition kicked in, and he could feel a deep loathing between the two that could only come from a long and bitter history. It shouldn't have intrigued him, but it did.

"We live in the twenty first century, Cornelius, and it's about time you realised it instead of desperately clinging to the old ways," Ela replied, her voice rich with underlying menace.

"If it wasn't for the old ways and our Lord, you'd still be a lady of the night. You should be gracious and grateful to the old ways instead of belittling and mocking them!" Cornelius' face was puce.

"I'll always be eternally grateful to the old ways and the part they played in my redemption, but times have changed, and so have I. The old ways will never die as long as the Elect continue to use their gifts for the purposes intended."

"Oh yes," Cornelius sneered, "I forgot you'd managed to convince the High Council that you'd changed. A leopard never changes its spots, Ela, and neither does a common whore."

Leo was stunned. He looked over at Ela who was still seated, her eyes locked on Cornelius, her hands clasped firmly together. Her face was impassive, but her hands were trembling as she barely contained her fury.

"For somebody who preaches forgiveness," she said calmly, "you should try and practise it. They made me Grandmaster, Cornelius, it's time to get over it."

Cornelius battered the end of his walking stick against the stone floor. "I will never forgive the High Council for choosing a common whore over a servant of the Lord! You bewitched them! All of them! You sold yourself on the street for money and cavorted with the incubi. You're unworthy of the title Grandmaster!"

Ela's hands shook more violently with every word Cornelius said. "I was young and foolish back then. People change, and you should know that better than anybody."

Cornelius's face went from puce to white as he gritted his teeth. "I had no control over Morgana's actions. She made her own choices, and she chose to turn her back on the Elect. It was grossly unfair that I was punished for her choices by being denied Grandmaster in favour of a common whore!"

"Perhaps if you'd been a better father, she wouldn't have strayed to the Templars," Ela pointed out.

Without warning, Cornelius launched a big blue ball of energy with ferocious swiftness. Ela raised her hand, and the energy collided with her palm. The blue orb shattered and sprayed tiny shards of ice over the table.

"Hey, hey! Whoa!" Leo exclaimed, standing up from the table. "Can we all just calm down please?" He took a couple of steps back when Ela got to her feet.

"You forget who I am, Cornelius," she said. "I'm your Grandmaster whether you like it or not."

"You're not my—"

"I'm not finished talking yet!" Ela roared, incandescent with rage.

The room darkened and a clap of thunder boomed as Cornelius was thrown against the stone wall, held in place by an invisible force. A vicious howling wind swept around the Grandmaster causing her long flowing clothes to billow about her.

"Take this as your warning, Cornelius O'Connor; do not push me. If you ever try to use magic against me again, it will be the last time. Do you understand?"

Leo was pressed up against the door that led to the lounge and was willing Cornelius to back down. He could feel the might of Ela's magic, its purity and power raged through the room, and knew Cornelius didn't stand a chance. Relief flushed through him when the old man finally nodded his head, and Ela's magic ceased instantly.

After adjusting her clothes and hair, the Grandmaster returned to her seat. "Now," she said, completely at ease again, "where were we?"

Cornelius cleared his throat. "Eden's Gift," he said, shuffling back to his seat and acting as if nothing had happened. "We need to determine its location."

"Okay," Leo said while moving towards the table, "I don't know what the hell just happened, but if it's going to happen again then I'd be grateful if you could let me know beforehand so I can leave the room. I don't need any more drama—"

The lounge door burst open, and a frantic Mrs Ellen came charging in.

"Father! Father!" she wheezed. "Come quick, it's the Macintoshes!"

Leo's stomach somersaulted. "What about them?"

The old woman turned her panicked gaze onto him. "They're gone!"

Chapter 11
Lambs to the Slaughter

Leo flew from the main Cathedral doors like he'd been fired from a gun. He was a blur of green and dark blue as he rocketed down the treacherous icy steps leading to the car park. As he barrelled through the snow towards his car, he clicked the button on the keys to unlock the doors. He reached out and grasped the handle of the driver's door.

"Leo! What's wrong?"

From out of nowhere, Lucas was at his side looking every bit as alarmed and anxious as Leo was feeling. "The Macintoshes didn't stay here last night! You were supposed to make sure they didn't leave their room, and now they're probably all dead!" he yelled.

"I stood guard outside their door all night, and nobody left that room. I would have known about it," Lucas said calmly.

"They're not here! Daniel is not here!"

"There is no way they could have sneaked past me. It would have been impossible unless they can walk through walls or…" Lucas' face fell. "They never stayed here last night. They must have done a runner after Mrs Ellen had sorted them out with their bed linen and stuff."

The situation was far worse than Leo had imagined. He yanked the car door open, but Lucas pushed it closed, leaving his hand pressed firmly against the ice cold metal.

"Where are you going?"

"I'm going shopping! Where the fuck do you think I'm going?" Leo fumed, the sarcasm pouring out of his mouth like acid. "I'm going to drive to Daniel's house and hopefully find him there in one piece. Get out of my way."

"How do you know they'll be there?"

"I don't, it's a guess! But I have to try, so move your fucking hand!" Leo tried his best to pull the door open, but Lucas' hand remained welded to it.

"We don't have any time to waste on guesswork. We need to be absolutely sure." With his free hand, Lucas retrieved his phone from his coat pocket and began swiping at the screen before holding the handset to his ear.

"Hello, Mr Macintosh?" Lucas said, disguising his American drawl behind a convincing Glaswegian accent. "Yes, hello. This is Detective Simmons returning the call you made to the police station. It's regarding the allegations you've made against Mr Leo Alexander."

At first, Leo was mystified as to how Lucas had gotten Mr Macintosh's number, but the memory of Daniel using the phone yesterday came back to him. He was impressed but didn't let it show.

"Yes, I understand that you came into the station and gave a statement, but the officer who took the statement made a few errors," Lucas went on. "My sincerest apologies for that. I'll need you to come back to the station so we can take another statement." A brief pause from Lucas. "I understand that you don't want to leave your family alone given what must have been a terrible situation yesterday." Another pause. "Would it be helpful if we came to you? It would be no trouble at all, Mr Macintosh. And could you please confirm the address?" Lucas paused for the final time and looked expectantly at Leo. "Fourteen Manse Road?"

Leo nodded.

"Great, we'll be with you in half an hour. See you soon." Lucas hung up.

"That was risky. How did you know he called the police?" Leo asked.

A wry smile played at the corners of Lucas' perfectly shaped mouth. "I didn't. It was a guess. I had to try," he said with a wink.

"I thought we didn't have time for guesswork?"

"It paid off, didn't it? And besides, Daniel is safe for the moment." Lucas pointed out. "Are you driving or—" Lucas stopped talking abruptly and slumped against Leo, pinning him to the car.

"Lucas!" Leo gasped, as the man fell to his knees and sank into the snow covered ground. His stomach twisted when he saw the small throwing axe lodged between Lucas' shoulder blades.

"Get inside!" Lucas hissed through gritted teeth, using Leo and the car to drag himself to his feet.

"I'm not leaving you!" Leo said firmly, allowing Lucas to lean on him.

"You'd be wise to listen to him, Leo Alexander."

Leo had never heard such a heartless voice in all his life. Despite only hearing it for the first time, he knew exactly who it belonged to. When he looked up, Cornelius' daughter stood twenty feet in front of him.

The winter breeze tugged at her long raven hair, making it flap gently behind her. She stood and tossed a throwing axe up and down in her hand while a small army of leather clad men, who were armed with swords, spears and axes, stood behind her. Leo quickly counted twenty.

"Where's the boy?" she demanded.

"He's not here," Leo replied coolly. "And even if he was, you wouldn't be getting him."

A hollow chuckle, devoid of any happiness, sounded from her blood red lips. "I always get what I want, little boy."

"It'll be over my dead body."

"That can be arranged," Morgana said with a ravenous look in her steely grey eyes.

With cat like reflexes, she hurled the throwing axe towards him. He watched it become a heat seeking missile, hurtling through the air and honing in on its target. Without thinking, he lifted his hand and summoned a powerful energy barrier that rippled when the axe bounced off it. For a few seconds, the barrier rippled like a heat wave on a scorching summer's day before becoming invisible. Although he'd shocked himself by conjuring the shield to his defence, he tried his best to look like he'd meant it.

"I see," Morgana began. "If you wanted to play with magic, all you had to do was say."

She whipped her hands forward, and two balls of fire rocketed towards him. They found their mark and exploded against his barrier. Although they didn't get past it, he felt an agonising burning pain deep in his solar plexus that made him want to scream.

Morgana grinned. "Hurts, doesn't it?" she sneered, firing off another fireball.

Leo staggered back after the third fireball collided with his line of defence. The same intense burning pain hit him in the exact same spot, and he bit his bottom lip to keep from screaming.

Morgana stalked forward, her tight leather outfit creaking with every step. "Your barrier is pathetic as are you, little boy," she taunted, unleashing two more fireballs.

When the fireballs crashed into his barrier, it sizzled into the ether, and he let out the scream of agony he'd been containing. While clutching his stomach with one hand and holding Lucas up with the other, he leant against the car to stop himself from toppling over.

"They warned me you had power, little boy," Morgana said, her tongue trailing across her top lip. "You do have power, that can't be denied, but it's a shame nobody has taught you how to use it. Such a waste. And to think, the Seers told me you'd be my equal." She tilted her head, studying him like he was an insect that she was considering squashing. She quickly lost interest. "I'm bored. Kill them both," she said, waving a hand flippantly in the air. One Templar obediently stepped forward and drew back his spear.

Still leaning against the car and trying to recover, there was nothing Leo could do to protect himself. He was still suffering from the internal fire that was raging on in his solar plexus while beside him, Lucas was trying to grasp the handle of the axe that was in his back. When he looked into those ocean blue eyes, he expected them to reflect the same thoughts and emotions he was experiencing, but he was mistaken; Lucas' eyes were full of defiance, courage, determination and hope. Fear was absent. And then he heard the whisper.

"Get down...now!"

Leo was shoved forcefully to the ground and several angry shouts filled the air. He sat up just in time to see the spear wielding Templar fall backwards and land with a muffled thump in a thick cushion of snow. Blood oozed from the dead Templar's forehead where an axe, the one that had previously been stuck between Lucas' shoulder blades, was now embedded into his brain. Leo scrambled to his feet when Lucas stepped towards Morgana.

"Stay back," Lucas ordered. "Get in the car."

Leo stopped in his tracks. He didn't argue and slowly backed off towards the car, his eyes drawn to Lucas' back. Through holes in the clothing made by the axe, he was astonished to see there was nothing but perfectly tanned skin; there wasn't even a blemish where the axe had been. He didn't get the chance to think any more on this strange anomaly because Morgana had begun striding towards Lucas. She stopped at the body of the murdered Templar and smiled coldly

"Are you sure you want to do this?" Lucas asked her, his tone condescending.

Morgana let out another hollow chuckle. "Oh, I'm very sure."

Lucas held out his hands and shrugged, putting vast quantities of arrogance into the action. "Okay, but it'll be your funeral. Are we gonna do it the old fashioned way?"

Morgana's eyes were steely. "Fine with me. Weapon?"

"Sword, of course."

"Of course," Morgana repeated with a curt nod of her head. "Thomas! Give this imbecile your sword."

Thomas, a burly man who hid his identity behind a biker's helmet, promptly complied and marched over to Lucas. If he was afraid of Lucas, it didn't show.

Some of the Templars moved forward.

"Stay where you are," Morgana barked. The men halted immediately. "Take this," she commanded, callously kicking the corpse lying at her feet. "Take it back to the temple. It's of no use to me. Now, leave us!"

Leo had just clambered into the driver's seat when the Templars picked up their dead comrade and carried him away from the Cathedral. He turned the keys in the ignition, and the engine spluttered to life. The lack of windshield allowed him to hear the words exchanged between Lucas and Morgana, even above the purring of the engine.

Lucas swiped the sword expertly through the air a couple of times. "And what will your weapon of choice be, ma'am?"

Morgana reached behind her back and drew out two more throwing axes, twirling them in perfect circles as easily as if she were twirling spinning batons.

"You can still back out of this you know," Lucas said, speaking as if he was talking a friend out of doing a dare. "There's no shame in yielding to someone like me."

"You obviously have no idea who I am if you think I will yield to your kind," Morgana retorted, closing the gap between them with a few confident strides.

Leo watched as the two enemies circled each other. Morgana was the first to strike. She swung both axes at

Lucas who parried them away with visible ease. Lucas followed the parry with a swing of his own, and his sword clanged against Morgana's axes, the impact causing her arms to shudder.

"Come on, Morgana, make your death worthwhile," Lucas said snidely. "Give me everything you have."

Infuriated, Morgana began swiping the axes through the air with fast and furious precision. Lucas moved incredibly fast and parried the tirade of attacks, but Morgana showed no signs of tiring. In a move that took Lucas by surprise, she changed strategy and sent one of her weapons through the air. His reactions were too slow, and the axe collided into the hilt of his sword and knocked it out of his hand. Morgana took full advantage of the situation, and Lucas barely had a chance to recover as her relentless onslaught continued.

Leo watched anxiously as Morgana drove the disarmed Lucas back towards the car. They were almost battling on top of the bonnet when the tide of the fight changed drastically.

Morgana misjudged one of her ferocious swings and found Lucas' hand wrapped around her wrist. She tried to break free from his iron grip, but the panic in her eyes suggested that he was far stronger than she'd been expecting. Lucas stared at her icily before viciously twisting her wrist. Leo's blood ran cold when he heard the sound of snapping bone followed by Morgana's agonising scream.

"It seems you've been outfought," Lucas said without a trace of humour. A darkness spread over his angelic face as he pulled her close to him and set his hands upon her head—one grasping firmly under her chin, the other positioned at the side of her forehead. "Without your magic, you're nothing. Your time on this plane ends here."

Shivering in the driver's seat, Leo turned away and closed his eyes. As much as he hated this woman, he didn't want to watch Lucas snapping her neck.

"Lucas! Stop!"

Leo opened his eyes and poked his head out of the gap where the windshield once was to locate the source of the thunderous voice. Cornelius stood at the top of the Cathedral steps, leaning on his walking stick and looking shell shocked. Ela was there too, arms folded and staring at the scene before her with an unreadable expression.

"Let her go, Lucas," Cornelius commanded.

Lucas looked up at the old man as if he was crazy. "Let her go?" he shouted, his voice betraying his disbelief. "Cornelius, she's the enemy!"

"I don't care. I've given you an order! Obey it."

"Listen to yourself! This bitch would kill every single one of us without remorse!"

While listening to the two men arguing, a flicker of movement caught Leo's attention, and he looked on in horror as he saw Morgana grabbing Lucas' crotch. A blinding flash of electric blue light filled the air causing him to shield his eyes. When he dared to look again, he saw Lucas writhing on the ground at Morgana's feet, clutching his manhood. Leo threw the car door open and swung his legs out.

'Do not get out of the car. She'll kill you.'

Ela's voice rang inside his head. He never suspected telepathy was possible, yet he could hear the Grandmaster loud and clear. He wanted to ignore her and go to Lucas. The feelings bubbling up within him were surprising and intense; they threatened to override his rational mind. Against all of his instincts, he exchanged a look with Ela from the confines of his car and nodded.

"Cornelius, thank you so much for distracting this poor creature," Morgana said, looking down at Lucas in disgust. "However, he is a worthy opponent. That shock should have knocked him out for a week, so credit where credit is due." She gave Cornelius an ugly grin as she knelt down and placed a porcelain hand on Lucas' forehead. "Perhaps another blast should do it?"

"Morgana, please! I beg you. Stop this madness at once," Cornelius pleaded.

"Madness?" The grin dropped from her face as she stood up. "You call doing the Lord's work madness?"

"If killing an innocent child is what you call the Lord's work, then yes, its madness." Ela spoke for the first time, and she was met with a look that could melt iron.

"And your opinion matters because…"

"Because I am the Grandmaster of the Elect," Ela said softly.

Morgana's eyes widened before a wickedly sinister smile spread across her features. She held her hands up to the sky. "Well Hallelujah, praise the Lord!" she crowed, bringing her hands back down to her hips and bowing her head. "We meet at last. I'm Morgana, pleased to meet you, Grandmaster. I'll be killing you in the very near future."

Ela's expression conveyed how unimpressed she was. Still, she appeared calm while looking down on Morgana with nothing but pity. "I know exactly who you are, Morgana, but I'm afraid I won't be dying just yet."

"You don't sound so sure," Morgana said as she moved to the bottom of the stone steps. When Ela didn't reply, she continued talking and climbed the first step. "I've waited a long time to meet you, Grandmaster. It's said you're the most powerful woman in the world."

"Morgana, stop this at once!" Cornelius shouted.

Morgana whipped her hand through the air, and Cornelius fell to the floor, clutching his face. "Shut up, you old fool!" she hissed, never breaking her ascension. "The girls are talking." She turned her attention back to Ela. "As I was saying, it's said you're the most powerful woman in the world."

Ela considered this. "Whoever said such a thing would probably be correct."

"They've never met me," Morgana fired back.

'Leo, get Lucas into the car, and get moving. You must find Daniel.'

The sudden sound of Ela's voice in his head gave Leo a jolt. He didn't need telling twice and burst out of the car. He sprinted through the snow towards Lucas who was now on all fours and trying to get to his feet.

"Lucas, come on," he said urgently, wrapping his arm around Lucas' middle. "We have to find Daniel. After three, try to stand up – one, two, three."

"Fucking Elect magic," Lucas cursed as he stood on shaky legs. "Always hurts us like hell!"

Leo gently patted Lucas on the back while guiding him to the car and helping him in. "You still sound like yourself, so we can rule out brain damage."

"I hope Ela kills the bitch," Lucas said as he clicked his seatbelt in place. He pulled out a packet of cigarettes and held one out. "You want one?"

"In a minute," Leo replied while glancing quickly up at the Cathedral to see Morgana was almost at the top of the steps.

'Go!'

He thrust the gear stick into reverse and slammed his foot on the accelerator. The four wheels screamed noisily and spun on the snow, desperately trying to grip the concrete underneath. Eventually, the tyres burrowed through, and the car shot backwards. He wrestled with the steering wheel and managed to whirl around in a perfect one hundred and eighty degrees to face the car park exit. He couldn't resist looking over at Lucas while he shunted the car into first gear.

"That's what I'm talking about!" Lucas chuckled while applauding ecstatically. "Let's get outta here."

Leo grinned as they barrelled forwards and onto the main road. "Did you see what happened to Ela?" he asked as the adrenaline wore off.

"I didn't, but she'll be fine. She's a tough lady and more than a match for Morgana," Lucas answered while holding a cigarette between his teeth and lighting it.

He didn't detect any doubt in Lucas' voice but still feared the worst. Morgana was ruthless, but she was also clever and resourceful which made her even more deadly. Adding to his anxiety was the pressing matter of the runaway Macintoshes. The Templars didn't have a clue where Daniel was, but the same couldn't be said for the demons.

"Can I have one of those please?"

"Sure." Lucas handed over the cigarette he'd been smoking and lit himself a new one.

"Thanks." Leo took a massive drag and exhaled loudly, giving a little moan of pleasure as the nicotine did its job.

"Is it just me, or are the main roads actually clear?" Lucas wondered aloud.

Leo hadn't noticed the state of the roads until Lucas had mentioned it. Sure enough, when he looked out of the non-windshield, the roads were practically black. "Maybe the Highland Council are organised this winter," he replied with a shrug. "Makes a change. Works for me though. Means we can get to Daniel's house quicker."

"That's the spirit. Stay positive."

Leo couldn't help but laugh. "Stay positive? I've only been up for an hour, and we've had three major dramas already! I'm a ball of positivity."

"Wow, only three? What were they?"

"Finding out the Macintoshes were gone, Morgana and the Templars showing up, and…" The third one evaded his memory. "There was definitely a third, I'm sure of it. Oh! Ela and Cornelius had a huge spat in the dining room this morning."

Lucas didn't appear surprised. "Yeah, those two hate each other. Well, to be fair to Ela, she doesn't hate him, but Cornelius despises her."

"It's to do with the whole Grandmaster thing, right?"

"Yup. Cornelius can't stand the fact she got Grandmaster over him. He hasn't forgiven the High Council for choosing her either despite her past…transgressions. Her colourful past doesn't matter anyway, she'd still have got it. The woman has the strongest connection to the divine I've seen in millennia. She's probably wiping the floor with Morgana as we speak. As for Daniel, we'll get to him before anything happens. Trust me."

"I hope you're right," Leo said grimly, falling deeply into a sea of negative and frightening thoughts. Somewhere in his mind, there was something bothering him about Lucas' use of the word millennia, but it wasn't the time to ponder; they had a child to find.

*　　　　　　　*　　　　　　　*

After twenty five minutes of driving in silence, Leo pulled up to Manse Road. It was one of the more affluent streets in the area where everyone had their own uniquely designed house. From the shape and colour of the front doors, right down to the cars that sat upon the large black islands of tarmac that made up the driveways, the residents of Manse Road did their upmost best to ensure that nothing was the same as the neighbours, heaven forbid

"We're here," he told Lucas as he killed the engine.

Lucas sat up and peered out of the window. "That's number four. I thought it was number fourteen?"

"It is, but I don't want Mark and Ruth to see us coming until the last second," Leo said while unclipping his seatbelt. "How are you feeling now? Are you going to be able to hold back Mark until I grab Daniel?"

"Don't ask stupid questions," Lucas replied arrogantly as he exited the car.

"Jeez, sorry for asking, asshole," Leo muttered under his breath while opening the door and stepping out.

"Did you say something?"

"Christ!" Leo yelped when hearing Lucas' voice in his ear. "Stop doing that! You're gonna give me a heart attack."

Lucas smirked. "I'm sorry, it's the unfortunate side effect of being an asshole."

Leo slammed the car door closed. "You *are* an asshole!"

Lucas adopted a serious expression and brought his index finger to his lips. "Sssshhhh!" he stage whispered before adding, "We don't want them to know we're coming."

Leo shot him a dirty look. "This is not a big joke," he growled, pointing to the house they'd stopped at. "There is a little boy in that house who could be murdered by vicious demons any second because of something he has no control over. Stop fooling around!"

"Daniel doesn't live at that house, he lives at that one," Lucas pointed out, gesturing to the next property.

"Oh, fuck off!" Leo fumed, stomping off and ignoring the American's chuckling. When he reached number fourteen, he stopped and placed his hands on the red gate. Beside him, Lucas began sniffing noisily. "In the nicest way possible, what the hell are you doing?" he asked, his face completely bemused.

"Shit!" Lucas muttered as he grabbed Leo's wrist and yanked it off the gate. He inspected it carefully in the light of the streetlamp that towered above them.

"Hey!" Leo exclaimed when Lucas licked his hand. "That's gross!"

"Look," Lucas instructed, turning Leo's wrist to display his palm.

Leo's eyes bulged when he saw that his hand was bright red. "What the fuck is that?"

"Lamb's blood. It's on the gate," Lucas said, pushing Leo out of the way and lifting his leg. The sound of crunching wood echoed through the deserted street when Lucas kicked the blood covered gate off its hinges.

"What does lamb's blood mean?" Leo's voice shook as Lucas pulled him up the concrete path towards the front door. His heart pumped adrenaline infused blood through his body.

"It means the demons have beaten us here."

Upon hearing those words, Leo broke free from Lucas' grip and overtook him. He was soon at the red door of number fourteen and tugging at the golden handle. It was locked.

"Daniel!" he screamed, ramming the door again and again with his shoulder.

"Leo, there's blood on the door."

He felt Lucas' hands trying to pull him out of the way, but his fear for Daniel had taken over, and he shrugged them off. "I don't fucking care!" He let out a howl of fury and unleashed a powerful blast of energy from his hands. The door exploded into splinters that crunched under his feet when he charged over the top of them like a rampaging bull.

"Leo, be careful!" Lucas yelled after him.

He struggled to breathe as he stormed through the long hallway of the Macintosh house. The blood was everywhere. It was matted into the carpet, splattered up the walls and dripping from the ceiling.

"Daniel!" he continued to shout as he burst into the living room, the stench of death overpowering him the moment he entered. The violent and horrifying scene that lay before his eyes silenced his screams.

Mark Macintosh was sat in an armchair with a bottle of whiskey and an empty tumbler at his feet. Surrounding the bottle and tumbler was a deep crimson pool that was soaking into the fluffy cream carpet. The pool was being topped up by little red droplets that were falling from the bottom of Mark's pyjama trousers which were saturated in his own blood.

Leo gagged when he saw Mark's torso. The skin of his whole upper body had been flayed and ripped apart like curtains to expose his entire insides. The bones of a smashed up rib cage remained and protruded at awkward angles, protecting nothing but fresh air. All of his internal organs had been removed and were nowhere to be seen.

And then there was his face. The demons hadn't touched it, but it was the most shocking thing of all. Mark's face was frozen forever, pulled into an expression of pure pain and unadulterated terror from having his insides ripped out of his body while still alive.

Lucas entered the room just as Leo tore his eyes away from Mark's corpse and covered his mouth with his hand. Lucas rubbed his back while he gagged.

"Keep it together, dude, we still have to find Daniel," Lucas reminded him. "I'll check the rest of this floor. You wait in the hall."

Leo allowed himself to be directed out into the hall and away from the horrors of the living room. He leant against the banister and breathed deeply while Lucas disappeared into another room. While he did his best to regain control of his emotions, his mind fixated on the fact he was stuck in the goriest, most ruthless nightmare imaginable, and that it was real; this brutal reality that he couldn't escape by waking up was all real. As he stared into nothingness, he wondered what would have happened if he hadn't gone to the Cathedral yesterday. Would this hell have found him? He waited for a reply from his inner voice: nothing. Perhaps it was feeling exactly the same as he was: numb. He'd felt lots of emotions in his life, but this was painfully new to him. Numbness was infiltrating every part of his existence.

"Nobody here."

Lucas was back, gazing into Leo's soul with azure eyes. A strong hand cupped the side of his face, and he closed his eyes, the warm touch giving him much needed comfort.

"Are you okay?" Lucas asked, rolling his eyes immediately afterwards. "Sorry, that was a stupid fucking question. Of course you're not okay. Listen, stay here. I'll look upstairs. You've seen enough."

"No," he croaked, shaking his head vigorously. "I need to do this. Daniel is my responsibility."

He could tell Lucas didn't think it was a good idea, but his mind was made up. Just as he placed his foot on the first step, he heard a muffled cough coming from upstairs. "Did you hear that?"

Lucas nodded.

Leo took the steps two at a time, not bothering to avoid the blood covered walls and banisters. Four doors waited for him when he reached the top; three to the right and one to the left. The solitary door was partially closed while the other three were wide open, revealing the bedrooms lying beyond. He moved slowly to the door on the left. Lucas walked closely beside him, coiled and ready for action.

As he drew nearer to the half open door, he could see there was someone lying on the white duvet covered bed with their hand hanging off the side, almost touching the floor. The delicateness of the hand indicated it was a woman, and there was a white imprint on the left finger where a large diamond wedding ring used to be.

"It's Ruth," he said to Lucas and pushed the door so it was fully open.

Ruth Macintosh had met a similar fate as her husband. She lay with her head at the foot of the marital bed, barely recognisable as the beautiful and stunning woman she had been. As far as he could tell, Ruth's organs were all intact; the once white coloured blouse she was wearing hadn't been tampered with. Her face, however, was an entirely different story. Her eyes had been plucked out of her skull, and all that remained were the optic nerves which hung limply out of the sockets. Her entire bottom jaw had been completely ripped off and unceremoniously dumped on the floor leaving her tongue to loll about in the huge gaping hole that was her mouth. Whoever had carried out the gruesome act had angled her head so she was looking at the door. The inhumanness of it disturbed Leo greatly, but he now knew what he was up against.

"Bastards," Lucas cursed from the threshold of the bedroom door. He took off down the corridor and across the landing to investigate the other rooms.

On the edge of the bed, underneath Ruth's head, was a cream coloured blanket. Leo carefully pulled it out from beneath her and unfolded it. "I'm sorry," he whispered, touching her hand. She was still warm. He realised the cough he'd heard from downstairs had been her dying breath. With that painful thought, he cast the blanket over her. He stepped back and wrapped his arms around his body in order to protect himself from the horrors of the Macintosh house, but it was useless. A floorboard creaking behind him made him turn. It was Lucas. "Any sign of him?"

"Nothing," Lucas replied.

"I guess that means they've got him."

"It doesn't mean anything. He could have gotten away."

"Gotten away?" Leo repeated angrily. "Look at this place! It took those savages less than twenty five minutes to do this. An eleven year old boy wouldn't stand a chance against those monsters. Get a grip, Lucas!"

"Get a grip? You're seriously telling me to get a grip? Jesus Christ, Leo!" Lucas yelled. "Haven't you got any hope? Can't you hope that maybe, just maybe, Mark and Ruth were able to get Daniel out of the house before the demons attacked?"

"Look at this fucking place!" Leo exclaimed. "My guess is they lasted ten seconds each, tops, and then those animals carried Daniel away. And to answer your question, no, I don't have any hope left in me anymore. It's dead, Lucas. Gone!" He folded his arms around himself once again, embracing the numbness and hopelessness.

"If he was dead, you'd feel it," Lucas said, his voice softer. "Do you feel that he's dead?"

Leo sighed and rubbed his quivering hands across his face before placing them on his hips. "I don't feel anything, Lucas. I'm numb. I can't feel anything because if I do then it means that this is all real, and he's dead and it's all my fault." Out of nowhere, the emotions punched through the wall of numbness, and his entire body heaved with great big sobs. The next thing he knew, Lucas was pulling him into a tight hug.

"It'll be okay. Everything will be okay."

"How can it be? The demons have Daniel. They'll take him to Baal, and the world will be ripped apart," Leo wailed, holding onto Lucas with every ounce of strength he had.

He didn't know how long Lucas held him or how long he'd cried for, but he was grateful for the support and comfort. After a while, he lifted his head off the muscular chest and pulled away. "What do we do now?" he asked, wiping his face. "When will we know that Baal has the Power?"

Lucas gave a light shrug. "No idea. We should head back to the Cathedral and speak to Ela. She'll have prepared for this scenario."

Leo nodded. He was on auto-pilot and could feel the numbness taking hold of his soul once more. It was preferable to grief. Lucas walked out of the bedroom and into the hall. Leo followed. A massive black cloud hung over his head, and a crushing weight pushed down on his chest as he stepped into the hallway. As he dragged his feet along the carpet, the unmistakable sound of someone coughing cut through the darkness, the despair and the defeat that had enveloped him. Lucas was already halfway down the stairs but had stopped dead.

"Did you hear—" Lucas didn't get a chance to finish his question.

"Daniel?" Leo bellowed. He stood like a statue, not daring to breathe. After what seemed like an age of silence, he heard Daniel's muffled voice.

"Mr Alexander?"

"Yes! It's me! Where are you?"

"I'm up here!"

Daniel's voice was distant, but Leo could hear every word. A shuffling sound came from overhead, and he gazed up at the ceiling. It was then he saw the faintest outline of a hatch door. There were a few scraping noises followed by a single click before the hatch door opened to reveal a black depthless hole. Leo held his breath until a familiar face appeared at the hatch.

"Oh my god, Daniel!" he exclaimed, fresh tears spilling down his cheeks. "Don't worry. You're safe. We need to get you down."

"Mr Alexander, I heard screaming. Are my parents okay?"

The question brought him back to earth with an almighty thump. He wanted to tell the boy the truth, but the words were stuck in his throat. How could he tell this child that his parents had been brutally murdered by demons? How could he tell this child that he was an orphan?

"Mr Alexander?" Daniel repeated, panic rising in his voice.

"Hey, little man," Lucas said, appearing at Leo's side. "I need you to come down first, and then we need to leave here as fast as we can in case those bad guys come back. You got a ladder up there?"

There was a loud clattering noise, and moments later a ladder was lowered from the hatch. Lucas caught it and held it firmly while the boy climbed down.

Leo lifted him off the ladder as soon as he was in reach and pulled him into a tight bear hug. He was grateful when Lucas walked over to the master bedroom and closed the door.

"Why did you close that door?" Daniel asked. "Are my parents in there?" He wriggled down from Leo and moved towards his parent's bedroom.

Lucas stood firm. "You can't go in there, buddy."

"I want to see my mum and dad!" Daniel yelled, his eyes glistening with tears.

Leo cleared his throat. "Daniel, you can't. They're..." The boy stared at him, his bottom lip quivering. There was no power on earth that could make him utter the words, but he knew Daniel was a smart kid and had already figured it out. He was selfishly glad to be spared the burden of telling the eleven year old boy the worst news of his life.

"No," Daniel whispered with a violent shake of his head. "You're lying!" he shouted. "They're not dead!"

Lucas stepped forward and placed a comforting hand on Daniel's shoulder. "I'm sorry, Daniel. Your parents are gone."

When Daniel sank to his knees and cried a river of tears for the mother and father he would never see again, Leo knelt on the floor and held him tightly. With every strangled sob of grief that escaped Daniel's mouth, another piece of Leo's heart and soul shattered, and he didn't think he had the strength to be Elected, to be one of God's chosen. Just as he was about to slip into a state of complete catatonia, he felt a hand on the back of his neck and glanced up to see Lucas gazing down at him. The bright blue eyes seemed duller somehow, more indigo than cerulean, but the message they conveyed was clear: that he was strong enough to protect this child.

And although the strength was borrowed, in that moment, it was enough.

Chapter 12
A Gathering Most Evil

The crow swooped expertly down the spiral stone stairwell at great speed, its wings never touching the slime covered walls on either side. It finally reached the bottom and swept through the small alcove and into the vast cavern where its master was waiting expectantly. Below the soaring bird, two demons and five lesser demons made the perilous journey across the ivory bridge which rocked dangerously from side to side as they drew nearer to the lonely grey rock. The crow flew past the demonic group and began its descent towards Baal who sat on his throne of death with an outstretched arm. It executed its landing perfectly, opening its sharp talons and closing them with precision around white leathery skin.

Baal extended a bony finger and stroked the breast of his faithful pet. After a few moments of petting, he lifted the crow up to his ear and closed his eyes. The crow's coal coloured beak snapped open and shut as it divulged all it had learned since their last meeting. When it was done, Baal opened his soulless eyes and smiled unpleasantly. "This news pleases me, my clever little friend," he whispered, resuming the stroking of his spy's breast. "Ah, and look, we have guests. Your reward will have to wait."

Both Baal and the crow turned their black eyes to the small party, the last of which had just stepped off the bridge, and observed them as they formed a line in front the throne. All of them dropped to one knee and bowed their heads, awaiting to be addressed by the pure demon who looked quite entertained at the display. "Such a…humble and honourable way to address power," he said softly, lifting his arm and kissing the bird on its feathered head. "Tell me, Izeel, why do they come back to me childless? Hmm. Do you think their excuses for their failure will appease me, my faithful companion?"

The crow, sensing its master's rising fury, hopped onto the arm of the throne and began preening itself.

"Natalya, speak," Baal snarled.

The group consisted of two demons: a large, bald headed male and a shapely, red headed female. Natalya rose from the ground clutching a small brown leather bag and moved to stand directly in front of Baal. The body she'd possessed had belonged to Dee, a woman in her twenties with an obsession for the Ouija board. Dee also had a cocaine addiction. Playing around with the Ouija board while under the influence of powerful drugs made possessing the healthy, strong and youthful body a walk in the park for a demon as powerful as Natalya.

"Master, we carried out your orders and attacked the home of the family believed to be concealing the Power." Her voice was husky, alluring and seductive all at once.

There was practically no fear from Natalya, not like the lesser demons who quivered where they knelt, but she wasn't a fool. Baal was unpredictable, cruel and evil to the core. Nobody was indispensable to him, and she knew it. Her saving grace was the fact she'd enjoyed many sexual exploits with Baal, performing acts that would make the Devil himself blush. It didn't mean she was safe from his wrath, but it was something she could use to her advantage.

S.R. FRASER

"And?" Baal asked, his hands gripping the arm rests of his throne so tightly that the bones creaked under the pressure.

Natalya tossed the little brown bag at Baal's feet. "The Power is down two protectors thanks to myself and Motaris."

At the mention of his name, the male demon stood up and sauntered over to Natalya, his brawny six foot plus frame towering over the petite red head. Motaris had acquired his body from thirty nine year old Brian, a loving husband to Martha and a doting dad to three strapping boys and three beautiful girls. Conveniently for Motaris, Brian was diagnosed with a rare form of lung cancer and was given four months to live. Motaris had been drawn to Brian for a long time. He'd tried many times to possess the human while he slept next to his delectable wife who he'd lusted after, but the human had a strong energy field that he couldn't penetrate. Luckily for him, the doctors got it wrong and Brian passed away two months after diagnosis. Motaris relished the possession and his greatly anticipated return to the earthly realm. He, like his demonic father, had a thirst for cruelty and pain. A week after getting used to his new human body, he reappeared at Brian's family home where he slaughtered all of his children, making a hysterical Martha watch as he did so. And then, after all his waiting, he defiled the woman in the bed she'd once shared with her dutiful and devoted husband.

"Motaris, you come back empty handed. I'm disappointed."

"You've always been disappointed in me, Father," Motaris said petulantly.

Baal moved swiftly and soon had his hand wrapped around his son's throat. The red flecks in the centre of his black eyeballs pulsated. "Then don't give me reason to be disappointed, you pathetic excuse for a demon!" he roared, digging his talon like nails into his son's neck until blood began to flow.

213

Motaris' expression remained sullen as he held up a small silk pouch. "For you, Father."

Baal's eyes softened. As he released his grip on his son's throat, his mask of rage was replaced with a smile that didn't belong on his evil face. "A present? For me?" He took the small pouch into his hands and clutched it to his chest like it was the most precious thing he'd ever seen. "My youngest son, bringing me presents!" he exclaimed, the happiness in his voice sounding alien. "What a lucky father I am. You must forgive me, my son. You could never disappoint me."

Motaris rolled his eyes. "I regularly disappoint you, just like all your sons and daughters. Although, there is one son whose disappointment we could never match."

The memory of his favourite son's betrayal clouded his face, and he cast a lengthy glance at the white feathered wings that decorated his throne.

"Motaris!" Natalya scolded. "Why did you have to bring that up? You know it upsets your father."

"It's quite alright, Natalya. Motaris only speaks the truth. No one could deceive me like he did. Even after seven hundred and five years, the disappointment and hurt is still raw."

Motaris huffed, folding his arms before launching into a rant. "That backstabbing bastard wouldn't know family loyalty if it came up and slapped him across his disgustingly handsome face. How many of us have lost our pure demon bodies by his hand?"

Natalya snarled. "Too many!"

Baal wandered slowly back to his throne, scooping up the brown bag that Natalya had thrown at his feet earlier. Cradling both bag and pouch, he climbed the three steps and took a seat, settling himself down comfortably while placing his gifts on his knees. "The Deceiver will be held accountable for his treachery, make no mistake about that. Each of my children, the ones he has wronged, will have the opportunity to take vengeance upon his pure demonic form in any way they see fit, as will you, Natalya."

"A most considerate and pleasing offer, master. I shall look forward to having my day with that disloyal worm," Natalya replied, bowing her head.

"And of course, the Deceiver's death will be at the hand of my youngest, Motaris. That's my will."

Motaris swelled with pride. He strode over to his father and dropped to one knee. "Father, your will is overgenerous but well placed. Nobody will take greater pleasure in killing the Deceiver than I! After all the hurt and pain he's caused you, I will make him suffer." Motaris lightly took his father's wrist and pushed the sleeve of the black robe that hung there, revealing a muscular forearm with protruding crimson veins. He planted a firm kiss on the back of his father's hand then gently turned it around and kissed the palm.

"And it will give me great pleasure to watch you, my son. Now, where were we," he pondered, casting his eyes over the five lesser demons who hadn't moved from their kneeling position. The corners of his hacked lips curved upwards as he watched the small group tremble. Beads of sweat trickled down the sides of the teenager's face until they reached her chin where they fell off and splashed into the dried dusty soil.

"What were your orders, lesser demons?" Baal's tone was venomous.

None of the five dared to speak or lift their heads. They knelt in silence, their bodies shaking violently.

"We are very quiet tonight, aren't we? No volunteers? Very well," Baal said regretfully, placing the bag and pouch next to Izeel. "Watch over our gifts, Izeel. This won't take long."

The crow stopped preening itself when it heard its name and fluttered onto the brown bag, cawing excitedly when the master rose from his throne.

With strength and speed that defied his great age, Baal whipped his hand through the air and conjured a scarlet whip of demonic energy which, in the blink of an eye, became coiled around the teenager's neck. He hissed with laughter when he hauled her forwards and she landed heavily at his feet; he shivered with pleasure when he commanded the whip to tighten and she gasped for air.

"Sssshh, everything's okay," Baal lulled. "Asphyxiation is supposed to cause fear and suffering, your reaction is perfectly natural. Let me help you up."

Standing at her full height, she barely reached his chest. He held her in an awkward hug and sniffed the sweetness of her blood that was seeping out from beneath the whip. It was virgin's blood, and it made him want to feed on her there and then, but he fought the urge. She was weeping silently, the tears running down her face and dripping off her chin.

"What's your name, my dear child?"

The girl's words failed to reach her supple lips.

Baal shook his head and cupped the girl's face, much like a parent would do to console their upset child. "My darling!" he chuckled heartily. "Here I am asking questions that you can't answer because of all the asphyxiation going on. Forgive me!" Taking his time and being as gentle as he could, he removed the offending whip from his victim's neck before speaking to her in soothing tones. "There, that's better. Now, tell me, what's your name?"

"Sarah." Her voice was small and weak.

"Sarah. What a beautiful name. And how old are you, Sarah?" Baal asked, still sounding like a concerned father.

Sarah took a deep breath. "Fourteen, Sir."

Baal turned to Natalya and Motaris who were loving every minute of this performance. He mouthed the word 'fourteen' with an expression of mock surprise before returning his attentions back to Sarah. "Fourteen year old Sarah, can you please explain to me why five lesser demons couldn't manage to retrieve a small and unprotected human boy?"

"The boy wasn't there," Sarah answered quickly. "It was just his parents. We searched everywhere, Sir. No room was left unturned." She lowered her head to avoid eye contact with the monster interrogating her.

"You searched...everywhere?" Baal repeated, the parental tone vanishing and being replaced with one much more suited to his darkening visage. "That's very strange, Sarah, because Izeel tells me that the Power was escorted out of the house, the exact same house that you seemingly left no room unturned during your search, I hasten to add, by none other than the Deceiver and one of his Elect fools who now have him under their protection."

Sarah blurted out the first thing that came into her head. "Motaris and Natalya couldn't find them either! We assumed that if they couldn't sense the boy's presence, then he wasn't there."

Baal gave her a look of pity while running a skeletal finger down her cheek. "We must never assume anything, nor should we deflect blame onto others, my lovely sweet Sarah. Who was given the job of killing the boy's parents so that they wouldn't impede the capture of the Power, and did they succeed in doing so?"

"Motaris and Natalya," Sarah whispered, defeated. "And yes, they succeeded."

"And who had the simple task of finding the weak, pathetic and defenceless human child and bringing him back to me?"

"Myself and four others."

"Yourself and four others," Baal repeated coldly. "So, what I'm hearing, Sarah, is that the parents were dealt with accordingly by Motaris and Natalya which would mean they did as they were commanded yet you, accompanied by four others, failed. Oh dear, Sarah." He moved his face slowly towards hers until he could feel her warm breath on his lips. "Was I not clear on what the punishment would be if you were to return here without the boy?" he asked, his tone beyond perishing.

Sarah's tears fell faster as Baal snaked his hand around her neck and clamped the other on top of her head, entwining his fingers tightly through her thick auburn hair. She realised there was nothing she could say, but it didn't stop her from begging. "Master, please! We searched—"

A horrendous ripping and crunching sound echoed around the vast chamber, followed by the dull thud of Sarah's body crumpling to the floor and Izeel's rapturous squawks. When she hit the ground, a small cloud of dust rose into the air and formed a veil around her and Baal momentarily.

"Fix your eyes upon me!" Baal roared, holding his hand skyward.

The remaining four lesser demons obeyed immediately. When the dust settled, four pairs of eyes witnessed a most disturbing scene. Baal stood before them holding Sarah's head which still had her entire spine attached to it. The pure demon shivered as the euphoria of his terrible act reached orgasmic heights. He dropped the head and watched it bounce down the steps and roll off the platform's edge where it was swallowed by the monstrous black hole. The spinal cord rattled off the stone ledge, sounding like out of tune chime bars, before it was pulled into the darkness and out of sight.

"Each and every one of you failed me, and as you can see, I do not tolerate failure. You bring shame on the demon who spawned you! But I will not end your wretched existence," Baal announced, watching the relief sweep across the four faces. "Motaris and Natalya will." A fresh ripple of pleasure ran through him when he felt their terror. "After all, demons need to eat too." He snickered and returned to sit upon the bones of his Elect victims.

Izeel flew onto his shoulder while he lifted the bag and pouch off the floor. He opened the large brown one first, rummaging about for a moment before stopping to look at the group who still knelt before him. "I'm not as unmerciful as some might think. I'm giving you a sporting chance. You have two minutes to see how far you can run. If you're quick, you might just make it to the top of the steps that lead into the church." Baal continued rummaging about in the brown bag as the lesser demons scrambled to their feet.

"Look, Izeel! Organs! We have liver, kidneys, lungs and…" Baal pulled out a dripping heart from the bag and ran his forked, charcoal coloured tongue across it. After lapping up all the blood on the outside, he wrapped his mouth around one of the arteries and used it like a straw until he'd drank every last bit of the thick red liquid. "My favourite—so very sweet," he murmured before ripping into the heart with his sharp and crooked teeth. He tore off a large chunk and swallowed without chewing. "I think there might be something in here for you, Izeel," he crooned and tossed the black pouch onto the floor. It landed beside Sarah's headless corpse which was still pumping blood onto the ground from the gaping hole where her head used to be.

Izeel dove down on top of the pouch and began pecking furiously at the drawstring. Within seconds, the bird had removed the drawstring and had emptied the contents onto the floor. Two eyeballs with blue irises squelched out of the pouch and rolled in circles before coming to rest against each other. Opening its beak, the crow picked up one of the eyeballs and tossed it down to the back of its throat where it then slipped down its gullet.

Baal cast the bag to the side and stood up when he'd finished eating the heart. He fixed his eyes on Motaris and Natalya. "Izeel tells me a woman visited Cornelius O' Connor in the early hours of this morning. Hair full of curls, an unusual shade of pale blue eyes. Izeel isn't good with human ages, but he thinks this woman was of a certain age…*her* age. Unfortunately, they spoke in the confines of his chambers with the windows closed and the curtains drawn."

"You don't suppose?" Motaris gasped. "Why would she come here? She'd be a fool to show her face at this stage in the game."

"If it is her, we must strike now."

"Then Natalya and I will go after her!" Motaris declared with a deafening clap of his hands. He began jumping up and down on the spot.

"Yes, you will," Baal agreed.

"I don't want to rain on your parade, master, but are your sources accurate?" Natalya asked. "This woman could be anybody. What if we're mistaken?"

"A minor detail," Baal answered with a flippant wave of his hand. "At worst, you'll have rid the world of one of those Elect fools or a useless human. But if it is her…"

Natalya wasn't convinced. "I don't mean to be pessimistic, master, but do we want to risk going up against the Deceiver and whatever Elect army is residing at the Cathedral only to find out it isn't her? We need to be sure."

"The Deceiver and the Elect are nothing, Natalya! They'll fall at our hands," Motaris scoffed, still bobbing up and down.

"He is not nothing! He took our purity away from us!" Natalya snapped, clenching her hands into fists. "Do you not remember how long we had to linger in the abyss before we were able to possess these bodies?"

Motaris' jumping on the spot came to a sudden halt. Her words, as deflating and unwelcome as they were, happened to be true. "I remember," he said quietly.

"Like I said, Motaris, I would happily go with you to kill this woman, but we need to be absolutely sure." Natalya placed a hand on his shoulder and squeezed lightly when he stroked her face.

"Look at you!" Baal sneered. "Look at how *human* you've become. Too long you have spent in the company of humans and lesser demons. It's made you weak! You've forgotten who and what you are. You are demons! I'm convinced this woman is the one. You will go to her, rip her insides out and feast on her blood like the demons you are. I'm not prepared to wait for another forty years until she dies of old age."

The finality in Baal's tone left no room for Natalya to question. "As you wish, master," she reluctantly agreed.

"It is my wish, my dear. You must trust me. It's her. I can feel it. Her resurgence into the human world means the Elect are in dire need of direct leadership. The Templars have launched their latest assault and Morgana O' Connor is leading the charge. The tensions between the Grandmaster and Cornelius are delicious. Nothing causes discord like jealousy, and where there is discord, there is weakness. My time is coming! I'll walk the earth once more and eradicate the race of man from this god forsaken world. And when I have the Power in my grasp, heaven and hell will have no choice but to bow to me!"

Natalya gazed lustfully upon Baal, all prior reluctance gone, and applauded his monologue. "Master, your words make me feel so…" Her hands travelled up and down her body, sliding beneath the garments concealing her nakedness.

"Sinful." Baal finished her sentence and brought his blood covered hand to her mouth. "Can I trust that you two will take care of this?"

Natalya lapped up the blood like she was a kitten drinking milk from a bowl, and nodded enthusiastically.

"Consider it done, father," Motaris said.

Baal whipped his hand away from Natalya and turned to the bridge. The lesser demons had crossed it and were now disappearing through the entrance way and into the alcove that lay beyond. "Perhaps they might just make it to the Church," he commented. His snake like tongue swiped the blood from his chin as he turned to Motaris and Natalya. "I think they've had enough of a head start. Remember, save the heads. I want their covens to know what happens when they fail me. Go!"

On his command, Motaris and Natalya sprouted enormous black wings and took off, the force of their flapping feathers sending torrents of dust spiralling through the air. In no time at all, they were both zipping into the alcove like streamlined killing machines with their wings folded perfectly to enable them access to the stone stairwell. So skilled were they in flight that neither of them so much as grazed a shoulder on the walls.

Moments later, Baal heard the first screams. "It's true what they say, my most faithful," he said to his pet who'd just finished ingesting the second eyeball. "There's no better taste in this world than the blood of a virgin. Bon appetite."

And then, in the darkness of his chamber, Baal and Izeel began feasting on the remains of fourteen year old Sarah.

Chapter 13
Two Faces

The return journey to the Cathedral had been a deathly silent one. Having bundled a grief-stricken boy into the car along with a suitcase of his belongings, Lucas took to the wheel while Leo sat in the backseat next to Daniel. For the whole time they travelled, Daniel held Leo's hand but never made any attempt at talking, instead fixing his anguished eyes firmly out of the window. Every so often, Leo would feel his hand being squeezed so would turn eagerly to the youngster expecting communication of some sort. It wasn't long until he realised that the boy was making sure someone was close by, someone that he trusted and knew cared for him.

'What a poor consolation prize for the boy: Leo Alexander.'

The return of his inner voice didn't fill him with joy, especially when it was right. He could never be what Daniel needed him to be. He wasn't equipped to be a parent. He was efficient in the classroom and managed extraordinarily well considering he'd never had much experience in dealing with youngsters but children behaved differently in school. They conformed, or the majority of them did at least, and there were rules for everybody to abide by. As far as he knew, there wasn't a parent manual for dummies. *'Perhaps it* will be enough to simply be his friend,' he thought as he copied Daniel and stared out of the window.

While ignoring the scenery, he struggled to process what had transpired in the last two days, his mind only just coping with the information overload. It'd been an emotional rollercoaster to say the least, and he suspected things weren't going to get any easier. As he lay his head against the soft head rest, a beam of sunlight burst through the window and dazzled him.

He shifted his head and peered up at the sky. Apart from a few wisps of white cloud, the sky was completely blue. It was the first time the sun had shone in weeks due to winter's blizzards holding court over the festive season. He couldn't help feel that this beautiful day was wholly out of place. How could Daniel enjoy such a stunning day? The sunlight reflected against the fields of snow causing them to sparkle magnificently, and the gentle heat of the sun, caressing the faces of those it reached, felt welcomed after the recent arctic conditions.

He tore his eyes away from the white diamond encrusted blankets and decided that God couldn't possibly foresee the future. If He could, then surely He wouldn't have allowed for all these terrible things to happen: the death of Daniel's parents, his own parents' death, Lucas' abusive and violent father, and on a grander scale; the Twin Towers, two World Wars, and the never ending conflict in the Middle East where atrocities were regularly carried out in His name.

A stabbing pain shot across his forehead warning him that it was not the time to dissect his whole belief system and analyse the flaws and foundations of modern religion. Right at that moment, an entourage of three police cars and two ambulances sped past in the opposite direction. Their sirens squealed noisily as they flew past, kicking up the stray black slush that the snow ploughs hadn't managed to fully push into the side of the road. He felt Daniel's hand squeezing his own again, this time the pressure was intense. The boy knew exactly where the emergency services were off to. Leo felt a pair of eyes on him, and he looked up to see Lucas peering at him from the rear view mirror.

Their eyes met, and Leo conveyed his gratitude for how strong Lucas had been at the Macintosh house. It was Lucas who'd held it together while he tried desperately not to fall apart. It was Lucas who'd helped Daniel pack a suitcase of clean clothes and a few other belongings, including a picture frame of Daniel and his parents at Disneyland Florida. It was also Lucas who'd called the police.

Fortunately, the Elect had infiltrated the police a long time ago, and it was Detective Carlos Rodriguez who took the call. Rodriguez had been a member of the Elect since he'd been old enough to speak. His grandfather, Carlos Senior, had been Grandmaster before Ela St Clair succeeded him. He'd been fiery, passionate, a force to be reckoned with until old age caught up with him. Predicting the crisis which was now upon them, he sent his grandson to the United Kingdom to work with the next Grandmaster. Carlos' position in the police force aided the Elect greatly in such troubled times. He assured Lucas that everything at the Macintosh house would be taken care of. Lucas trusted Carlos, and that was good enough for Leo. A full blown murder investigation was a problem he didn't need right now, especially with a heart broken child to console.

The silent journey finally came to an end, and Daniel exited the car without a single word and began climbing the stone steps up to the Cathedral. Leo felt it was only minutes ago that he'd watched Morgana climb up them. As expected, Cornelius was there to meet them at the front door.

"Daniel! Thank heavens you're alright, my child," he fussed, placing a hand on the boy's shoulder. The old man looked relieved to see Lucas and Leo too. He peered beyond them. "Mark and Ruth?"

Leo shook his head from side to side, words escaping him. He was glad that Cornelius read the signals and changed the subject.

"The Grandmaster bested Morgana and is recovering in one of the dormitories. Morgana has retreated for now. I'll share more details after you've had time to rest."

Leo only slightly relaxed when the large Cathedral doors closed behind them and Cornelius, while saying a prayer, fortified the building with an enormous energy barrier. He and Daniel gawped as a sphere of white light formed in Cornelius' hand and expanded rapidly, passing through the giant stone walls of the Cathedral and encasing the entirety of the gothic structure. Daniel quickly lost interest in Cornelius' display of power and returned to looking mournful while dragging himself through the main hall towards the dormitories where Lucas had gone.

Leo, however, couldn't take his eyes off the white barrier and moved to the window to get a better view. It shimmered in the morning sunlight and then faded away. Even though it was invisible, he could feel it was still there due to a constant vibration and buzzing that it seemed to emit.

"That's quite a barrier," he commented.

A crooked smile formed on Cornelius' face. "Thank you. I've been doing this for a long time now, and I'm not too bad at it." The old man winked. "If anybody walks through that barrier, Templar or demon, I'll know instantly."

A significant amount of people, Leo noted, were walking in the vicinity of the Cathedral, but not one of them showed any signs that they'd seen the barrier. "Why can't they see it?" he asked.

Cornelius smiled softly. "I would like to say it's because they aren't Elected and that only those who are chosen can see such things. The truth is…" his words tailed away as a deep sadness washed over him. "They don't see because they don't *want* to see. Every human has the capacity to see God's gifts, but they choose to live their lives completely wrapped up in themselves, selfishly wondering what can be done to further enrich their own existence.

"These people run around with the best of everything. They have I-Pads, I-Phones, brand new cars, houses and swimming pools, and they still aren't happy. Not even close. Parents worship their children, second only to themselves of course, and inflict upon society selfish little creatures who are incapable of compassion and decency towards other human beings, existing only to take what they can to satisfy their own needs. Parents behave in this way because they see their child as a 'mini-me' and believe it's their right to have the best.

"The majority of humans are smothered by the belief that their lives, and indeed the lives of their spouses and offspring, are somehow worth much more than the lives of others. They're completely and utterly devoted to themselves and only themselves." Cornelius let out a long sigh, and it sounded like he'd regretted sharing his thoughts.

"I'm so sorry you think like that," Leo replied, his face expressing disappointment.

"Am I wrong?"

Leo shrugged. "I don't think all people are like that. Sure, you do get a lot of parents who turn their children into spoilt little monsters by giving them everything they want, but even then, they do it out of love, don't they?"

"Are you saying that love is materialistic?"

"Not at all. I'm saying that some parents love their children so much that they can't help pandering to them and giving them everything they want to make them happy. Wanting your children to be happy isn't a bad thing. They want them to be happy because they love them so much."

"Such an unhealthy expression of love, don't you think? The man who gets everything handed to him without earning it can never truly appreciate anything, Leo. But the man who goes out and earns things for himself appreciates and takes great care of what he has. It depresses me to say it, but the world has fallen into a new dark age. To be selfless simply doesn't exist anymore. Everyone thinks they're entitled. I always thought greed was the worst of the seven deadly sins."

Leo smiled. "I see your point, but I don't think the world is as bad as you think. And that's why we, the people who know what's important in life, should lead by example by being kind, selfless and compassionate."

"Wise words for someone so young," Cornelius praised. "And even after everything that you've experienced in the past few days, you remain optimistic and positive. You must hold onto these kinds of thoughts, Leo, for they fight off the darkness. You have a bright light within you, and it's powerful and strong."

Leo shrugged off the compliment and changed the subject. "I agree with you, greed is the worst. That's why I opted for lust."

Cornelius chuckled. "As amusing as that was, I'll pretend I didn't hear it, young man, especially on the Sabbath. Shall we see how young Daniel is doing?"

Leo allowed the old man to wrap an arm around his shoulders and guide him through the hall towards the dormitories.

"I didn't mean to sound so negative," Cornelius said as they walked. "I'm aware there are many beautiful and worthwhile things in life that outweigh the bad ones I just mentioned. I'm not cynical enough to believe everybody is like that. I've just reached the age where there is nothing quite like a good moan. Of course there are wonderful things like love, laughter, friendship, being of sound mind and health to name a few…"

Leo let the old man chatter on as they entered the dormitory hallway and smiled when the list of life's beautiful and worthwhile things grew and grew, giving the impression that Cornelius wasn't cynical after all. Lucas came through the lounge door as they were approaching it, putting an end to Cornelius' extensive list. He was alone.

"Where's Daniel?" Leo asked immediately.

Lucas held up his hands. "It's okay, he's with Mrs Ellen in the kitchen. He asked if he could help out. We put his suitcase in your room. I offered him a room to himself, but he wanted to be with you. He feels safer."

"His trust in you bodes well for us," Cornelius said. "We don't have to worry about him running away. I think the best thing is to let him help Mrs Ellen in the kitchen, keep him as busy as possible. She'll talk him through his feelings, let him begin the grieving process. Mrs Ellen knows a few things about grief.

"In the meantime, I suggest you take some time to regroup. Recent events will begin to take their toll on you if you don't look after yourself, and things are only going to get tougher. Why don't you go and lie down? Perhaps some meditation? The Grandmaster has suggested we meet at three o'clock to devise a plan of action. The next few days are going to be crucial, and you need to be fit and ready."

Leo exhaled. "I don't think I could meditate for a second with all this buzzing about in my head, and there's no way I could relax right now...but it won't kill me to try," he added after a stern stare from Cornelius. "Seeing as Daniel is here in the Cathedral, the safest place for him to be right now, I'm going to run home and grab a few things." He gestured towards the sleeve of his green hoodie which was covered in lamb's blood. "I'll also need to grab toiletries. No offense, but I like having my own."

"None taken. Lucas, you'll accompany him."

"Um, I don't need Lucas to come with me. It's literally right across the road."

"You're now a deadly enemy of the demon world, Leo, not to mention the Templars. It's not safe," Cornelius explained.

"Thanks for your concern, but I really don't need Lucas to come with me. I'm just going across the road to pick up a few things. I'll be less than fifteen minutes."

"Suit yourself," Cornelius said tartly. "If something happens to you, on your own head be it." He made his way to the lounge door and stopped just as he reached it. "Oh yes, there is just one other thing. The Grandmaster has summoned every member of the Elect to the Cathedral for an emergency meeting tomorrow night. Some may start arriving first thing in the morning so expect to see some unfamiliar faces wandering the corridors. If anyone should need me, I'll be in my chambers."

"You're not going alone," Lucas said the second Cornelius was out of earshot.

Leo rolled his eyes. "Don't start."

"No, don't *you* start," Lucas fired back. "Have you forgotten what they did to Mark and Ruth?"

"Lucas, it's only across the road. A demon isn't going to attack me in a public place."

"And what about the Templars?"

"Cornelius said they've retreated. I'll be fine."

Lucas narrowed his eyes. "Yesterday, you were freaking out when I showed you a dead demon's head, and now you aren't remotely bothered by the thought that several live ones could show up in your apartment?"

"I guess the thought of demons doesn't frighten me anymore," Leo replied with a half-hearted shrug.

"They should frighten you," Lucas said, pointing his finger. "You'd last five seconds against a lesser demon never mind a pure demon. I'm coming with you whether you like it or not."

"No, you're not. I'd feel better if you were here keeping an eye on Daniel."

"You just told Cornelius that Daniel couldn't be any safer in the Cathedral. You're not going alone, end of story. I'm coming."

"Why do you want to come so badly?" Leo snapped.

"Because I couldn't live with myself if anything bad happened to you!"

Leo was more than a little surprised by Lucas' admission. He cleared his throat and tried to speak but discovered he didn't really know what to say. Eventually, he tried to make light of it. "To be honest, I thought you'd be grateful for the peace and quiet you'd get if I wasn't around." He gave a little laugh. "But seriously, don't feel you have to look after me because Ela and Cornelius tell you to. I'm fine to go to my flat by myself."

"Fine!" Lucas yelled, making Leo jump. "Go yourself! Get killed! But don't expect me to take care of the boy when the demons have used your blood and guts as wallpaper!" Without another word, Lucas stormed into his room and slammed the door shut.

Feeling completely bamboozled by Lucas' outburst, Leo fetched his scarf and coat from his own room. The cogs in his head turned manically as he tried to figure out Lucas' motives. He stopped by the bed where his garments lay, delving into recent memories of the interactions he'd had with Lucas since first meeting him.

The first was yesterday morning when he'd just gotten out of the shower. He was certain Lucas' eyes lingered over his naked torso, but he'd chosen to ignore it. Why? Secondly, when he'd been packing up what he thought were the tools and catalysts of his magic, Lucas had been there to help him tap into the gift he didn't know he had within. Lucas was adamant that he didn't need any tools. Lucas had taken him by the wrist and pulled him against his body so their chests had touched, the synchronicity of their breathing had been unmistakable. He'd chosen to ignore it. Why? Later when Cornelius had berated him for his less than fair comments about the Church, he'd turned around and Lucas was there, practically resting against him. Lucas himself had made a joke about it. Ignored once more. And then during the first aid session in Lucas' room, Lucas confessed he'd done something terrible, something so bad that his father deemed it acceptable punishment to mutilate and scar his own son. He wouldn't tell Leo what he'd done because he was convinced Leo would hate him even more than Lucas thought he already did. Leo didn't ask himself, or Lucas for that matter, why it should matter if Leo hated him or not.

Finally, Lucas had attempted to kiss him. Or had he? Leo knew he had a penchant for romantic fantasy and always got way ahead of himself which was why he hadn't given the moment a second thought until now. They hadn't actually kissed because they'd been interrupted by Cornelius. He closed his eyes and reconstructed the scene in his head.

He was holding the first aid box he'd just finished packing after Lucas had smashed it into the wall. He was now agreeing with Lucas that he was awesome for all he'd done to help that day. Lucas was stepping forward, his hands pushing the first aid box down. He was feeling Lucas' hands running up his back and coming to rest on his neck; he could feel their warmth. Lucas' eyes, holding him in place, were coming closer and closer. Lucas. Lucas. Lucas. It was always Lucas doing the instigating. Now Lucas was furious with him for wanting to go to his flat alone in case something happened to him. His eyes fluttered open. Was Lucas trying to tell him something?

'Oh for fuck sake! Give the idiot a medal! I place the sole blame onto you for this ridiculous self-esteem issue.'

He bit his bottom lip. Was his inner voice right? Had Lucas been sending out signals? The chiselled, drop dead gorgeous, divinely handsome Lucas? He shook his head vigorously. There was absolutely no way that Lucas was giving him the come on. Even Cornelius had asked Lucas what game he was playing. Lucas was just like Tyler. It was all a big game to them. As sad a fact as it was, he knew that people like Lucas wouldn't look twice at people like him. Lucas was A-List material while he was D-List at best.

'Yeah, D-List as in the dunce list! Get a fucking grip. He cares about you, moron!'

He let this sink in for a moment. A small butterfly fluttered in his belly. "Stop!" he told himself while placing both hands firmly on his stomach, determined not to let the fantasy corrupt his judgement. He didn't like Lucas; Lucas didn't like him. End of story.

As he pulled his coat on, he saw Daniel's suitcase at the foot of the bed. The reality of the youngster's situation came skipping up to him and slapped him across the face, pushing all thoughts of Lucas out of his mind and forcing him to consider Daniel's total isolation from the world. Until this morning, the boy had two loving parents. He wondered what their last moments as a family had been like. Why had Mark and Ruth left the Cathedral last night, their only place of sanctuary and protection? They'd believed; he'd seen it in their faces after he'd conjured the fire. Was it the shock of it all? What had been their intentions? It was clear they'd phoned the police and made allegations against him, but then what were they expecting to happen? How did they know to hide Daniel? Did they see the demons coming? Had Mark, having saw them coming up the front path, gotten the intuitive feelings they were coming to carry out something terrible? Did he know that he and his wife were going to suffer excruciating deaths?

Leo shuddered at the thought while wrapping himself up in his scarf. He exited the room without another thought about Lucas or the Macintoshes' untimely demise. There would be time later to put an end to the speculation surrounding the latter and hear it from Daniel first hand. He believed it was important for the boy to talk about what happened so he could attempt to deal with it, accept it, and move on as best as he could.

Leo scanned the environment carefully for enemies as he walked along the riverside, cigarette in hand. It wasn't until he'd stepped beyond the protective stone walls of the Cathedral and through Cornelius's invisible enchantment that he realised Lucas was right: he needed protection. Looking at the human faces he passed, an alarming fact, one he'd never given any thought to amidst the chaos of the past two days, was brought to his attention by his inner voice.

'Anyone of them could be a demon. Anyone of them could have an evil, twisted and terrifying demon lingering just beneath the surface of their skin. You'd never know until it was too late.'

"Shit," he muttered to himself while quickening his pace and bustling across the road towards the bridge. Beneath his coat and scarf he began to feel hot and sweaty despite the fact the sun had taken early leave. The bright blueness of the sky had been smothered with black clouds. While scurrying over the bridge and weaving in and out of pedestrians, he focused solely on reaching his flat in one piece and tried not to let his paranoia take over. He was already more than halfway to his flat, so it would be stupid to turn back now. He had to stop his eyes from erratically darting from one person to the next as it was earning him funny looks from passers-by. It was only when he pulled the door open to the empty lobby and reception area of his flat that he began to settle.

"Leo!"

His head spun wildly around to locate the voice. Tina, the receptionist, smiled at him from behind her desk. She was younger than him and had blonde hair, blue eyes, and a slim figure, attributes that would get her far in the game of life. Tina openly admitted she'd no real aspirations and was quite happy doing the job she was doing. It paid the bills and fed her partying habit. She was a regular on the Inverness clubbing scene which was where he'd met her.

"Jesus, Tina! You almost gave me a heart attack," he gasped, wiping away the sweat from his forehead with the back of his hand.

Tina giggled. "I didn't see you leave this morning, Mr. Is this you just getting in from a night of partying?" Tina's sparkly, mascara bordered eyes lit up as she eagerly awaited his gossip from the night before.

He imagined her reaction if he'd launched into the events that had befallen him since Friday night. If he wasn't so paranoid about being savagely murdered by demons and Templars, he'd have found the thought very amusing. He could easily have pawned her off with a lie and said he'd stayed at Wendy's, but as it was, he couldn't resist the excitement that lay in her eyes at the prospect she was about to get some juicy gossip.

"And what a party it was," he said with a wink.

Tina was elated. "Who was the lucky man?" she asked, settling down into her black leather chair and resting her elbows on the shiny marble desk.

He brought his finger to his nose and tapped it three times. "That, my darling, is for me to know and hopefully for nobody else to ever find out." He was at the elevator now and had pressed the button.

"Oh, you're so bad!" she giggled. "I didn't get out myself—was on the early shift this morning."

The elevator pinged behind him, signalling its arrival. "Count yourself lucky you don't have the hangover or the deep hollow void where your self-esteem, pride and dignity used to be," he joked, stepping backwards into the lift.

"I'd rather suffer from those knowing I had a fabulous night! See you later," she called just as the elevator doors closed.

Everything from the humming noise of the elevator to the sound of the button being pressed all seemed louder than usual which was perhaps caused by the fear, paranoia and adrenaline gushing around his body and heightening his senses. The doors opened with the usual 'ping' and within a minute of leaving the elevator, he was in his flat and locking the door with both key and chain.

He slumped breathlessly against the door with his head leaning back against the cool wood. It wasn't the only thing that was cold. The entire flat was an ice box. He'd only been gone a day yet the place felt like it hadn't been lived in for months. Pushing himself off the door, he made his way down the small hallway and into his bedroom while removing his coat and scarf. He tossed them onto the bed along with his blood stained hoodie and then himself, moaning in pleasure as he sank into the softness of the duvet and mattress. Just as he was really relishing the comfort of his own bed, there was a knock at the front door.

He bolted upright, his eyes staring through the open door of his bedroom. He pulled himself off the luxurious bed and took a few tentative steps into the hall, pausing for a moment and listening. The only sound he could hear was his heart beating against his chest. Maybe he was hearing things. The knock sounded again, firmer this time, and he found himself turning out the pockets of his coat until he located his phone. He walked slowly back into the hall and found Lucas' number on his call log. He held his thumb over the dial option as he stalked towards the door.

"Leo, I know you're in there. The receptionist told me. Open up. It's Tyler."

He breathed a huge sigh of relief and opened the door to reveal Tyler standing there, hands on his hips and grinning.

"Hey man, what happened to you?" He cast his warm brown eyes over the blood stains on Leo's top.

"This? It's just paint. I was helping Wendy to decorate…her living room." He was never good at lying. "I just got home."

"Can I come in?" Tyler asked, running a hand through his dark brown hair, his eyes sparkling with mischievous intent. "It's been awhile since we…played."

Standing in the threshold of the door, Leo had never been more tempted, and he didn't know if it was entirely down to the six foot, athletically built handsome man standing in front of him, or if it was the desperate need to reclaim the feeling of normality after such a crazy two days. He really liked Tyler, and despite what Wendy thought of him, no other man had ever shown him any interest. So Tyler wasn't committing just yet, but they were both young. Wasn't it natural to experiment and have fun?

He was about to say yes when Daniel's face popped into his head, plaguing him with guilt. "I'm sorry Ty, but I can't today. I have somewhere I need to be, and I have to take a shower. Maybe some other time?" Even as he was saying it, he knew there'd never be another time. He doubted he'd ever see Tyler again.

"Aw come on, Leo. I missed you last night in the club, looked everywhere for you too." Tyler stepped forward and closed the gap between them. "Can't you be a little late?"

Leo swallowed when he felt a hand on his neck and another on his hip. His eyes betrayed him by closing as he gave into Tyler's touch. "No, I can't be late. And I..." He was quickly losing his train of thought when Tyler's lips found his neck. "I have to shower, I don't have time." His protests came out in croaky whispers that were hardly convincing. He knew Tyler could sense that he was close to submitting.

"How about I join you in the shower?" Tyler whispered, his tongue traveling up Leo's neck. "That way, everybody wins."

Tyler's persistence, along with his expertise in seduction, had broken through his defences the way they'd done so many times in the past. He was a goner. He cleared his throat and was just about to invite Tyler to come inside when a hostile American voice came from inside his flat.

"Hey, asshole. I believe he said no."

Leo turned his head to see a bemused Lucas standing by the kitchen door.

"Ah, I get it," Tyler said as he released Leo and took a step back. He folded his arms and smirked unpleasantly.

"It's not what it looks like," Leo said, mirroring Tyler's stance.

"Really? It looks like you've got yourself a brand new play mate. Did you meet this loser last night?"

"He's not a loser," Leo said sharply. "And we met on Friday, but it's not like that. We're just...friends."

"You expect me to believe that bullshit?"

"Believe what you want. What does it matter? You said we were just having fun, remember?"

"Yeah, you're right," Tyler said, nodding in agreement, "we were just having fun. But just so you know, I was having much more fun with two hot chicks I scored with last week, but they had to leave town on business this weekend."

Leo felt like he'd been punched in the stomach.

"You're a lousy fuck, but you're better than my right hand," Tyler sneered. "I'll see you around." He gave Leo a light slap on the face before turning abruptly on his heel.

A flurry of footsteps erupted behind Leo. He immediately turned around to see a feral and furious Lucas baring his teeth and flying towards him.

"Lucas, no!" Leo yelled as the American barrelled past him, knocking him to the floor.

Before Tyler could react, Lucas had wrapped a hand around his throat, lifted him clean off the ground like he weighed nothing, and slammed him against the white walls of the lobby, leaving a deep indent in the plasterboard.

By the time Leo had picked himself up from the floor, Tyler's face was cherry red, and the vein in his forehead was throbbing as he desperately tried to prise Lucas' hand away from his throat. "Lucas! Stop!" he yelled. "Let him go! Lucas, he's not worth it!" He had both hands clamped to Lucas' arm and was using all of his strength to loosen the death grip, but his attempts were futile. The beautiful blue eyes had misted over with rage. It was only when Tyler's face began to turn purple that Leo began to truly panic. "Lucas! Stop!"

When Lucas ignored him for the third time, Leo moved his hands from Lucas' arm to his chest, and a sound, not unlike a firework exploding, tore through the air. Lucas went flying backwards in a shower of white sparks while Tyler crashed to the ground and began sucking in as much oxygen as his shallow breaths would allow. Lucas landed on all fours in the doorway of Leo's flat.

"Jesus, Lucas!" he exclaimed, taking a step towards him. "What the fuck? You could have killed him!" No response. He was about to chastise him again but was interrupted by a burst of movement behind him.

Tyler, who had begun to revert back to his normal colour, had scrambled to his feet and was staggering to the elevator. He pounded the 'call lift' button as soon he reached it. "You fucking psychos!" he spluttered. "Stay away from me!" He flung himself into the elevator, and the sound of him furiously punching the buttons to get the elevator doors closed soon followed. Seconds later, the doors drew together and he was gone.

Relieved that Tyler would live to see another day, Leo turned his attention back to the fallen Lucas who was still on his hands and knees with his head lowered. "I'm so sorry, I didn't mean to hurt you," he said softly, walking to Lucas and kneeling beside him. "I thought you were going to kill him. Are you okay?" He placed a comforting hand on Lucas' back.

Lucas emitted a low growl and recoiled from his touch. "Get away from me!"

"Please don't be like that, Lucas. I'm really sorry," Leo said, reaching out and touching him again. Lucas lifted his head and snarled ferociously, his feral face completely unrecognisable.

Gone were the ocean blue eyes; they'd been replaced by empty soulless lumps of coal with a single red fleck in the centre. Gone was the smooth, sun kissed skin, replaced by a white crumpled leathery sheet that was heavily decorated with blood red veins. Instead of the angelic, divinely sculpted visage that Leo knew, Lucas had transformed into a terrifying and monstrous demon.

While staring into the callous eyes of the thing he feared above all else, Leo let out a blood curdling scream.

Chapter 14
Lucas' Secret

Leo didn't scream for long and came to his senses surprisingly quickly. He spun his body away from the demon with the intention of sprinting to the fire exit. He'd barely taken a step when he felt two muscled arms around his waist. His vision blurred as he was hauled backwards into the flat at frightening speed. The front door was closed with a thunderous slam, but it was the following silence which was truly deafening.

He fixed his eyes firmly on his bedroom door at the end of the hallway and forced himself to concentrate on breathing. His heart battered around in his chest, and he wondered how many more shocks it would take for it to stop beating altogether. Realising he was completely powerless, he let his body go limp and prayed that Lucas would be merciful. Lucas was a demon. Were demons capable of bestowing mercy?

'It's just Lucas. He won't hurt you.' His inner voice was doing its best to calm him down even if it didn't believe what it was saying.

For a while, the only sound in the hallway was Leo's heavy and erratic breathing. His breaths came out in long drawn-out rushes and sounded as though he was on the brink of a panic attack.

"I'm not going to hurt you."

'Told you!'

Leo's body tensed when Lucas spoke. He still found the voice to be spine tingling but in a completely different way. It sounded cold, reptilian even. He thought that if snakes could talk they'd probably sound similar to Lucas' demonic tones.

"I'm not going to hurt you," Lucas repeated. "But if you start screaming or try to use magic, you will leave me no choice, and I'll have to silence you. Understand?"

Leo nodded.

"Good boy. I'm going to let you go in a second. Before I do, I need you to listen very carefully, okay?"

He nodded again, noting that Lucas' voice was thawing. The more he spoke, the less he sounded like a frosty viper.

"I know this is a huge shock to you, but you've nothing to fear from me. Yes, I'm a demon, but I'm not going to hurt you, I swear it. If I let you go, do you promise not to scream the place down like a big drama queen?"

Despite the fact he was still terrified, Leo couldn't stop himself from rolling his eyes. He nodded for the third time and stayed rooted to the spot while he was slowly released. After being freed, he remained standing with his back pressed against Lucas' hard body and psyched himself up. Eventually, he turned around, and much to his surprise, he was looking up at sparkling azure eyes. It wasn't a demon; it was Lucas.

Placing his hands on Lucas' face, he studied every inch of it and found there were no traces of demon, only deep shame and self-loathing. It caused his heart to ache so much he thought it might break. It was all there in Lucas' eyes. Suddenly, Leo felt his own shame. How could he have been so selfish that he didn't see what was so obvious now? Lucas' pain. Lucas' sadness. Lucas' burden.

He removed his hands from Lucas' face and took a step back, already doubting that Lucas had turned into a demon. It was hard to believe when he looked so stunningly angelic. Leo was seriously considering the possibility that he'd either been hallucinating or that he'd gone mad, and given the catalogue of recent events, the latter was highly probable. But he knew better. It had happened. Lucas was a demon, but did he want what the others wanted? His eyes searched Lucas' face once more, silently asking the question that burned inside of him.

"If I wanted it, he'd be dead already," Lucas said. "Besides, if I was a threat, do you really think Ela and Cornelius would let me near him? Or you?"

Leo digested this for a moment, and then shook his head. "No, they wouldn't. Do they know you're a demon?"

"Of course. I told them the minute I met them. They wouldn't have trusted me if I hadn't been honest from the beginning. With their vast knowledge on demonology, it wouldn't have taken them long to figure it out."

"Why didn't you tell me?"

"I was scared," Lucas replied instantly.

"Of what?"

"Of your reaction," Lucas confessed, turning his head away and taking an interest in a picture of Monet's water lilies hanging on the wall.

"What makes you think I would have reacted badly?"

Lucas, still gazing at the artwork, scoffed. "Are you kidding, Leo? I've lost count of how many times you've condemned demons. You hate them. Remember yesterday when you saw your first demon? You were a quivering mess, and that was only hearing its screams. You weren't ready to know…and I wasn't ready to tell you."

"Why do it now?"

"You think I wanted to?" Lucas said, turning his head sharply towards Leo. "I never meant to frighten you. It was the last thing I wanted to do. I just got mad at the way that asshole spoke to you and flipped out, and then you zapped me with your magic."

"So, you're like the Hulk," Leo said.

"Huh?"

"You know, when you get angry you turn into a monst— I mean a demon." Leo corrected himself quickly and gave Lucas an apologetic look.

Lucas laughed. "Don't worry about it. I am a fucking monster. And no, it doesn't work like that. I can shift into my demon form at will. Anger has nothing to do with it."

"You did change deliberately then," Leo stated, accusation creeping into his voice.

"No!" Lucas shook his head vigorously. "It was your Elect magic that caused me to change. You see, the Elect can force a demon to reveal its demonic nature using magic. When you zapped me, your divine energy reacted with mine, and it brought my demon form out. I had no control over it. It's just what happens."

"Did it hurt?" Leo asked sheepishly.

"A little, but the pain didn't last long. I suspect that's because you haven't reached your full potential yet. You're just getting started, so I'm counting myself lucky that you're not at maximum strength. I'd still be on my back if you were."

Ignoring yet another one of Lucas' appraisals of his apparent power, a new thought entered his head which intrigued him. "Morgana," he said.

"What about her?"

"She used magic against you earlier today, remember? She electrocuted your...balls," Leo pointed out, flushing slightly. "It's Elect magic, right? Why didn't you turn then?"

Musical laughter filled the hallway where they stood. "Yeah, she did get me in the balls, and it fucking hurt like hell!" Lucas winced as if the mere memory caused him great pain. "She can use Elect magic, but it's tainted. She takes it to a very dark place where it loses its divinity. Your magic remains pure because you're pure."

"None of us are pure, Lucas."

"Maybe not, but your intentions are pure and have always been for the greater good," Lucas explained. "The gift inside of you can differentiate between the likes of you and the likes of Morgana."

"But what makes us different? If I have to kill a demon, lesser demon or even a human with my magic, what makes my killing different to hers? Murder is murder, right?"

Lucas maintained intense eye contact. "She relishes it. Every time she takes a life she's filled with endless joy and pleasure. You will kill out of necessity, because it's the only way to protect this world. We're at war, and killing is inevitable, but that doesn't mean it has to be enjoyed. I've killed more times than I care to admit. I've killed for both sides of this war, but I've never gained enjoyment out of a single one. Do you think you'll take enjoyment out of ending a life?"

Leo's answer was instantaneous. "Yes."

"Lies," Lucas shot back.

"The demons who made Daniel an orphan. I'll take great delight in ending their miserable existence."

"You say that now, but I wonder if you'll say that when the time comes."

Leo looked doubtful but didn't say anything further on the matter. "What happened to you anyway? How come you're helping the Elect? I thought all demons were out to get the Power. If you're not after the Power, then what do you want?"

"That's a lot of questions," Lucas said with a laugh before turning serious. "Look, I want to protect this world. I want to protect all of humanity, not that every human deserves it, but I want to save them all nonetheless."

"You're a demon, you're supposed to hate humanity."

"Believe it or not, I actually *like* humans."

Leo snorted. "Yeah right, *I* barely like humans! Why would you like them?"

Lucas shrugged. "They're human."

"Really?" Leo cast a serious look of doubt towards Lucas.

"Yes, really," Lucas said with a roll of his eyes. He looked down at his watch. "I'll tell you everything you want to know later, but right now, we should be getting back to the Cathedral. Cornelius will be wondering what's happened to us."

Leo's brain kicked into overdrive at the mention of the priest. "Oh shit! Daniel!"

"Daniel will be just fine," Lucas said, taking a step forward. "I'm more worried about you. You've had a lifetime's supply of shocks and surprises in the last two days, and I think it'd be best if you rest properly and cleared your head."

"Yeah, I suppose you're right. I was going to shower here, but I'll do it at the Cathedral. Give me a minute until I pack a bag."

"No worries, I'll wait in the living room."

Lucas disappeared, leaving Leo alone with his thoughts. He couldn't quite believe he'd missed all the signs that Lucas was a demon. Perhaps he was more self-obsessed than he realised.

'No shit, Sherlock.'

Ignoring his inner voice, he walked into his room and started chucking various clothes into a holdall. Deodorant, shampoo, a toothbrush, a tube of toothpaste, hair gel, moisturiser, and a phone charger followed. As he zipped the packed holdall closed, his mind started bombarding him with a new set of thoughts.

How had he missed something so huge? Lucas was a demon. It was as if his brain had to keep repeating the statement over and over until he got the message. While he threw his scarf and coat on top of the sealed holdall, he replayed the past two days in his mind's eye at super speed. With the benefit of hindsight, he could see all the clues staring him in the face.

Lucas had killed a demon all by himself. He'd appeared in the nick of time when Morgana had launched her axe and snatched it out of the air. There was also the fact there'd been no wound on Lucas' back where the axe had embedded itself between his shoulder blades. It was so obvious now.

"Wow. If I'd known that you were this stubborn and annoying I'd have told Michael to go and shove this mission."

Lucas' words from the previous day echoed loudly in his head. It made complete sense. Archangel Michael. On the night when Lucas had broken into his flat and told him the entire backstory regarding the Power, he remembered how Lucas had radiated powerful emotions, particularly when he'd been talking about the angels. There'd been definite melancholy and feelings of loss, regret and sorrow. They had come pouring out of him. Had Lucas been there at the Fall of Lucifer? Was he that old? Had he been an angel of God or born a demon? Was he carrying out a mission given to him by the Archangel Michael? The questions bounced around in his head, and curiosity burned through him as he grabbed the holdall and left the bedroom.

When he entered the living room, Lucas was slouched back on the couch with his feet on top of the coffee table, reminding Leo of their first meeting. Lucas greeted him with a grin that stretched from ear to ear.

"And what's amusing you?" Leo demanded. It seemed that Lucas' revelation of being a demon had not altered his sense of humour.

"Nothing," Lucas replied, removing the grin. His twinkling eyes, however, deceived him.

Leo dropped the holdall at his feet along with his coat and scarf. He folded his arms and glared. "Okay, out with it. I've just learned that you're a demon on top of everything else that's happened in the last two days. I could do with a laugh."

"Well," Lucas began while leaning forward and resting his elbows on his knees, "look how far you've come in two days."

246

"I don't follow."

"If I had changed into a demon in front of the Leo I met on Friday night, he would have dropped dead. I sensed your fear when Cornelius and I were trying to convince you that demons were real. It was pure, unadulterated. But look at you now. You're cool, calm and collected. Maybe you're getting more resilient?"

Leo shook his head and unfolded his arms. "I'll always fear demons. I watched the Exorcist as a child and was traumatised when the girl became possessed. The whole demon thing has always terrified me."

Lucas peered up at him with thoughtful eyes. "Have you ever gotten to the root of the fear? Maybe if you understand what it is about demons that scare you so much, then you could learn to control it."

"I understand my fear perfectly. Demons frighten me because they're evil. They speak evil, they practise evil, and they embody evil. End of story."

Lucas straightened up. "Not all of us are like that."

"What are you? The demon who cares?" Leo replied sharply. The tension in the room took a sudden spike. "Demons are evil."

Lucas winced but tried to cover it up by sinking back into the couch and adopting his usual arrogant posture. "That's funny," he said without a trace of humour. "Up until about ten minutes ago, you didn't think I was evil, did you? In fact, before you discovered that I was a demon, you were getting hard anytime I came near you."

Leo's jaw hit the floor.

"Admit it. You want me," Lucas continued. "You have done from the second you met me, and even though you know what I am, you still want me."

"Maybe I did, so what? And you're wrong. Everything's changed now, and whatever I felt has gone."

A carnal hunger flashed across Lucas' face, and he raised both eyebrows to the sky. "Is that so?"

"Ye…yes," Leo stammered. "I'm sorry, but it's gone. You're a demon."

"Don't kid yourself," Lucas said seductively. "You want me now more than ever. I'm the forbidden fruit."

"You keep telling yourself that. Whatever floats your boat. I'm leaving." Leo said, turning away.

In the blink of an eye, Lucas was behind him, wrapping his huge arms around his chest. He let out a short gasp when he felt the demon press himself up against his back.

"Such a shame you don't feel anything for me anymore," Lucas purred.

When hot breath caressed his ear, Leo started to tremble. A heat from deep within his solar plexus ignited and spread like wildfire to every inch of his body when Lucas' strong hands moved from his chest to his abdomen where they stroked and teased.

"Lucas, stop," he protested weakly.

"Make me," Lucas replied, his voice low and gravelly. "I'm just an evil demon, right? And those feelings you had for me are gone, right?"

Leo was about to answer, but his breath caught in his throat when Lucas' hands slid under his t-shirt and touched bare skin. He gasped and felt himself leaning into the demon. He'd lost control of his body and was powerless to stop Lucas from pulling the garment over his head.

"Do you want me to stop?" Lucas asked as he discarded the t-shirt. It fluttered through the air and landed without a sound on the laminate floor.

It took a few moments for Lucas' question to filter through to him as he was lost in the pleasure of having lips brushing against his neck. His eyes closed of their own accord and heightened his other senses. His ears took in the low alluring sound of Lucas' voice as well as the erratic beating of his own heart. His nose faced an onslaught of Lucas' divine musky scent and whatever pheromones the demon was emitting. Both spiralled through the air and gathered like a lustful cloud around his head, bewitching him. The areas of skin where Lucas had stroked were aching and burning with the longing to be touched over and over again. His tongue wanted to taste Lucas so badly that he bit down on it to kill its shameless desire.

Leo felt Lucas' lips working their way down his naked back, and he shuddered with pleasure. "Lucas!" he gasped when the demon's hands slipped beneath the waistband of his jeans. Lucas retracted his hands, and Leo felt himself being spun around.

"Tell me to stop," Lucas growled. "Look at me and tell me you want me to stop."

Being spun around so forcefully brought Leo back down from the high. His eyes flew open, and he had to tilt his head back slightly so he could gaze into Lucas' eyes. They were still magnificently blue, and they smouldered, as did the expression on Lucas' face. He tore his gaze away from those burning blue eyes and looked at the floor.

Lucas had been right; he'd wanted him from the second he saw him, and nothing had changed. All of the options he had available swirled around in his head, and he cursed the indecision that was currently plaguing him. There was sudden movement, and he altered his gaze to see Lucas bending down and picking up the t-shirt, dejection written on every inch of his divine face.

"Don't stop."

Lucas, from his kneeling position, suddenly turned his head up and met his eye. "What did you say?"

"Don't stop," Leo repeated in a stronger voice. He maintained eye contact with Lucas as the demon returned to full height and peered down at him.

"Are you sure?"

"I'm sure. Don't stop."

Leo had stopped shaking. He had a determined look in his eye, and he could feel Lucas scanning his demeanour, looking for signs that he might not be utterly resolved in his decision. It was then that he realised it was Lucas who was unsure and stalling.

"I don't want you to do something you're not sure about," Lucas said. "I'll understand if you don't—"

Lust overwhelmed Leo. He grabbed the demon by the neck and silenced him with a deep passionate kiss. He'd no idea where his confidence and strength had come from, but suddenly, he was in control and wanted nothing more than to feel Lucas' lips on his. His insides became a blazing inferno as he was thrust onto another plane of existence.

He wasn't prepared for the rush of heavenly pleasure that surged through him, but he embraced it. The kiss became heated very quickly, and soon his hands were exploring every inch of Lucas they could reach. Lucas' hands travelled down his back all the way to the base of his spine where they disappeared under the waistband of his jeans and underwear. A violent tremor of ecstasy powered through his body, and his knees trembled and threatened to buckle. To stop himself from getting carried away too quickly, he distracted himself by bringing his mouth to Lucas' neck, and then sank his teeth repeatedly, in a playful fashion, into the demon's tanned skin. Lucas inhaled sharply.

With his teeth happily engaged, Leo's hands found their way to the buttons on Lucas' shirt and discovered they were snap buttons. He yanked hard and exposed a smooth, rock hard chest and stomach. His hands roamed over the defined muscles that had been hidden beneath the black material while his mouth journeyed back to the demon's lips. Burning desire coursed through his veins like molten lava, driving his actions and consuming every part of his brain so that nothing else mattered except this moment. He'd truly lost all sense of reality.

And then everything changed.

A more aggressive growl coming from Lucas punched through the red haze and brought Leo closer to the real world. But it was a sizzling sound coupled with the smell of burning flesh that really snapped him back from heaven. He pulled away from the kiss and opened his eyes to see black and emotionless eyeballs set in a porcelain mask—a mask painted with red spindly veins—looking back at him. Before he could open his mouth to scream, his eyes were drawn to the hissing smoke rising from underneath his hands which had come to rest on Lucas' broad chest. He pulled them away and winced as he looked at the red scorch marks they'd left behind.

"What's wrong?" Lucas asked, his ink black eyes blinking in confusion.

"You're all...veiny and stuff."

Lucas looked down at his papery white hands. "Fuck!" He covered his face with his hands and turned his back. "Don't look at me!"

He stood watching while Lucas wrestled with his demons. He wanted to help, but it was apparent his divine energy was somewhat of a hindrance, so he busied himself by putting his t-shirt back on.

A minute later, Lucas turned around revealing his human guise. "Sorry about that, I didn't know that was going to happen." Lucas stepped towards him, his face alight with lustful intent.

"I'm sorry," Leo said immediately, his eyes drifting across Lucas' chest where the handprint wounds glared angrily up at him. They looked as if they'd been put there with a branding iron, and he couldn't help but grimace at the sight of them. "I can't...I mean...I don't think it's a good idea."

The words stopped the demon in his tracks, and a cloud of rejection descended upon him. Lucas cleared his throat and avoided eye contact. "I understand," he said, buttoning up his shirt while walking towards the door. "I'm a fucking monster. Why would you want to?"

"Lucas, it's not that—"

"You don't need to explain. I'll wait for you outside." As Lucas crossed the room, he bent down and scooped up the holdall lying at Leo's feet.

Leo grabbed the holdall as it was lifted into the air and tugged at it to stop Lucas from running off. "Can you just stop and listen to me for a second?" he pleaded, inwardly sighing with relief when Lucas stopped. Although the demon still avoided eye contact, Leo was glad they were still in the same room. "I don't think it's a good idea because my divine energy obviously hurts you," he explained.

"It doesn't hurt at all," Lucas grumbled.

Irritation flitted across Leo's face, but he was determined to avoid another argument. "Look at your chest. I've literally branded you with my bare hands! That must have hurt."

"I never even noticed."

"Bullshit! I could feel the heat, and you can still smell burnt flesh in here. It must have hurt."

Lucas finally turned his head and looked at him, giving a half-hearted shrug when their eyes met. "It stings a bit now, but when we were kissing before, I didn't feel a thing."

"Lucas, come on."

"I'm serious! I didn't feel your hands burning my chest. The only thing I felt was…" Lucas hesitated, and his eyes shifted from side to side.

"What? What did you feel?"

"Nothing. It doesn't matter. I can't tell you."

"Oh for Christ's sake, of course it bloody matters! Just tell me! What did you feel?"

"I can't tell you," Lucas repeated, his low and gravelly tone indicating his agitation had reached dangerous levels.

"Just fucking tell me!"

"I can't fucking tell you!"

The volume of the roaring didn't frighten Leo, but when Lucas' angelic face morphed into its demon counterpart before his very eyes, he staggered backwards, tripped over the coffee table, and landed in a seating position in the softness of his black leather couch. The fear in his eyes must have triggered something in Lucas because immediately his expression softened, and he became breathtakingly beautiful again.

The agonising regret and remorse that cloaked Lucas' face shattered Leo's heart, and his terror dissolved immediately. "I'm sorry, Lucas. It's my fault. I need to learn not to push things." To his dismay, this added to Lucas' anguish, and the demon threw his hands on his head and pulled at his hair. Over the past two days, Leo had known the happy Lucas, the mischievous Lucas, the scary Lucas, and the angry Lucas.

"Stop apologising like *you're* the monster! *I'm* the monster! *I'm* the one who should be apologising for being an ugly creature from hell," Lucas cried before falling silent.

As the words poured out of his mouth, Leo was now getting to know the raw and emotional Lucas. It was clear that Lucas was the type of being who never allowed his emotions to take over no matter how strong they were. Judging by the look on the demon's face, it was clear his emotional outburst had even taken him by surprise. Leo stayed quiet to allow Lucas to compose himself. He watched as the demon closed his glistening eyes and took deep breaths, his diaphragm swelling grandly underneath his ribcage, his shoulders rising and falling. A shroud of calmness seemed to envelope Lucas, and his eyes eventually fluttered open, still shining with unshed tears and conveying a depthless sadness.

"Leo," he began in a steadier voice, moving to sit on the couch next to him. "I didn't feel any burning pain on my chest when you touched me, I promise. I was feeling something else, but I can't tell you what it was."

"Why not?"

"I can't tell you because I don't know. I've never felt anything like it before, so I've nothing to compare it to. All I can tell you is, it's the best feeling I've ever felt in my entire existence, and that's coming from somebody who used to be an angel."

"You were an angel?"

"Yeah, until I joined my father and fought on Lucifer's side during the war in heaven."

"Okay, now I'm really confused! I thought your father was *thee* Father, as in God."

"Angels can have offspring if they want to, just the same way demons can. I won't go into the details though," Lucas said with a small smile.

"We can get to those details later. Tell me, who's your father? And please don't say Lucifer," Leo said jokingly. He let out a hearty chuckle at his own outrageousness.

Lucas' smile disappeared. "Not quite. Lucifer is my Grandfather," he announced, causing Leo's mouth to fall open. Lucas took a deep breath and exhaled slowly before he uttered his next sentence. "My father is Baal."

A monastic silence exploded in the living room and consumed everything in its wake. A dumbfounded Leo sat forward, clasped his hands together, and digested Lucas' latest offering. His gaze never left Lucas who was biting his lower lip and shuffling his feet. There were a few times when Leo opened his mouth to speak, but words and their meanings eluded him, and he couldn't find any that came close to expressing how he felt.

An uncomfortable amount of time passed, and he could do nothing but stare at Lucas, trying his best to process the entire saga of the Power while taking this new information into account. A part of him wanted to combust, to explode with fury and let loose a rage fuelled tirade of Elect magic just to vent his frustrations.

Do it! chimed his inner voice. *Blow it all to hell!*

Without warning, Leo started to convulse, and uncontrollable howls of laughter came hurtling out of his mouth. When he saw Lucas glaring over, he tried to supress the laughing but found the harder he tried to contain it, the more uncontrollable and louder it became. It wasn't until he was blinded by tears, doubled over on the couch and pounding his fist into the cushions, that he heard Lucas' melodic laugh joining in with his own.

"Fucking hell!" Leo wheezed, clutching at his stomach, "you couldn't make this shit up!"

'That's it, laugh it up real good!' his inner voice said with that annoying way of always sounding superior. *'At least you're not crying about it.'*

Through the hysteria, he knew his inner voice was once again right. If he didn't laugh about it now, he would have crawled into bed, assumed the foetal position, cried a sea of tears, and ultimately given up. So he had to laugh.

Eventually, he repressed the hysteria and stifled the laughter. When he straightened up, he gave Lucas an apologetic look. "I'm sorry. I don't know where that came from. It's not even funny," he said, wiping away the last of his tears.

Lucas smiled. "It wasn't the reaction I was expecting," he admitted, "but I'll take it."

"Man, you must have one hell of a story to tell."

Lucas did his usual shrug. "I'll tell it to you sometime, but to be honest, you had it pretty much nailed back in the restaurant when you and your friend were playing your little game."

It took a second for Leo to understand what Lucas was talking about, but when it clicked, he grinned. "I actually had a feeling you could hear me at one point, but I told myself it wasn't possible."

"An accountant? You really thought I looked like an accountant?" Lucas screwed up his face in mock disgust while standing up and reaching for the holdall. He took the coat and scarf that lay on top and tossed them to Leo before stepping into the centre of the room.

"No, I was just messing about with that one," Leo grinned, getting to his feet and wrapping himself up in his coat and scarf.

"I'm way too cute to be an accountant," Lucas said, the American charm and swagger back in place.

"If you say so," Leo replied. "After dinner, I want to hear your story from the very beginning."

Lucas looked uncomfortable at the idea. "You sure you want to? I mean, I don't want you to end up hating me."

Leo placed a hand on his shoulder. "You just told me that you're the son of the psycho demon who is trying to cause an apocalypse by killing a child who I love dearly, and that you're the grandson of Satan. I haven't bailed yet. What does that tell you?"

"That you're a terrible judge of character?"

"Uh, if memory serves, didn't I say in the restaurant that you were a fallen angel?"

Lucas nodded.

"Exactly! My judgements are spot on. Anyway, let's get back. I want to check on Daniel," Leo said, heading towards the door. When he got to the threshold, he turned back to face Lucas who was still standing in the middle of the room.

"Just wait until Wendy finds out how accurate I was. She'll love it," he said and spun on his heel before stepping into the hallway.

In the living room, unseen and unheard by Leo, Lucas shook his head lightly. "Accurate alright, kiddo. Right down to the stories they're gonna write about us." And with that, the demon gave a massive sigh and began the arctic journey back to the Cathedral.

Chapter 15
I'm Ready

On arriving back at the Cathedral, Leo had immediately checked in with Mrs Ellen who had been cooking up a storm in the kitchen. Her report indicated that Daniel was barely okay; she'd tried to talk to him but had gotten nothing. Deciding it was best to leave him be, she'd distracted him by putting him to good use in the kitchen. Leo knew there was a chance that Daniel would never fully recover from the grisly events of his parents' death, but the boy was showing remarkable courage and strength despite the circumstances.

'He's bottling it,' his inner voice warned.

It was probably true, but until Daniel opened up, there was nothing anybody could do except be there for him.

"I have to cater for the Elect members who have started arriving, so I do! Sixty of them already," Mrs Ellen had proclaimed the moment she'd finished her whispered report on the boy. "But with the help of young Daniel, it'll be an easy task, so it will." She smiled in her usual warm manner before thrusting a whisk into a metal pale which sat in the deepest sink Leo had ever seen.

The kitchen itself was exactly what Leo would have imagined Mrs Ellen's kitchen to look like. It was an expansive rectangular room with a mid-tone oak flooring.

Natural light invaded the room from one gigantic window and emphasised the gorgeous golden honey shades of the floor. The window, which was directly opposite the only door to the kitchen, was situated above the sink. Lying to the right of the sink was an enormous black Aga cooker, which had four deep ovens and two huge hotplates, and two worktops cluttered with various appliances and utensils. On the wall adjacent to the kitchen door and the window were three cream coloured dressers containing expensive looking china. Plates, teapots, saucers, cups and jugs sat grandly upon the shelves and gleamed brightly for any potential admirers. A large kitchen island which was surrounded by four wooden stools sat proudly in the middle of the room. From the chopping boards and knives lying on its surface, it was clear that this was where Mrs Ellen did most of her food preparation.

After speaking with Mrs Ellen, Leo found Daniel in a small partitioned area of the kitchen which lay to the far right of the door and beyond the island. The partitioned walls stood about five foot tall and created a rectangular shaped work space which housed a massive fridge freezer and two large metal machines that he didn't recognise.

One of the contraptions had a tall cylinder shaped base that supported a large silver sphere. On first glance, the machine looked like a giant metal lollipop except it had a black rubber lid on the top and a big rectangular door on the side. A lever was situated directly above the door and looked as if it was used to open and close it. He suspected the machine was loaded through the top and emptied via the little door.

The other machine was almost as tall but looked like a silver box standing on four legs. Like its neighbour, this one had an opening on the top for loading and one on the side for emptying. Instead of a door and lever mechanism for unloading the machine, there was a narrow metal chute that led down to a large plastic barrel.

"Hey, Dan."

Daniel, who was sitting on a plastic bucket and peeling a potato, peered up through his long dark fringe. "Hey, Mr A," he replied, offering the tiniest of smiles, his bloodshot eyes lacking their usual sparkle.

"Need a hand?"

The boy nodded in the direction of the floor where seven large baskets of peeled potatoes sat. "It's cool. I've only three tatties left."

"My god!" Leo exclaimed, gawping at the baskets. "There must be hundreds of potatoes there! Did you peel all of those by yourself?"

Daniel pulled his tiny smile into a very sincere and solemn expression. "I did."

"Of course he peeled them all by himself, so he did," Mrs Ellen called over from the sink. She smiled across at Daniel from her pale of water which she was currently adding some golden flour to.

Leo laughed. "I'm sure he did."

"The tattie peeler might have helped me a bit," Daniel confessed, patting the lollipop shaped machine, "but it broke, so I had to do this bucket by hand. Mrs E says she'll have it fixed by next week."

"You've done a great job, my boy," Mrs Ellen praised while whisking the flour and water together with the vigour of a woman half her age. Through her frenzied whisking, she continued to talk without difficulty. "It's a batter mix for the fish tomorrow," she explained to Leo who was looking curiously over at the pale and its contents. After a few more vigorous whisks, she stopped to scoop in more flour and was rapidly whisking for her life once again while still managing to give instructions.

"Daniel, your next job is to put the peeled tatties into the chipper. It'll cut the tatties into chips and spit them out into the barrel. You turn it on and load it in exactly the same way as you did the peeling machine. Once you do the last basket, there's a hose in between the machines for filling the barrel with water. Maybe Leo can help you to lift the baskets?"

"Of course I can," Leo said while walking over to Daniel who'd just thrown the last peeled potato into a basket. "Go on then, Dan, fire her up."

Daniel got to his feet and pressed a green button that was on the wall behind the chipper. It sprung to life and started to emit a slashing sound. Daniel had to stand on his tiptoes to reach the lid on the machine. When he pulled it off he became a curious little puppy and jumped up repeatedly to catch a glimpse of what was inside. Leo felt himself grinning as he watched the inquisitive youngster.

"Woah! Dan, get down," he exclaimed, his teacher instincts suddenly kicking in when Daniel mounted the machine and peered into its whirring depths.

"But I wanna see what it's like inside," Daniel pouted as he climbed back down.

"Fine," Leo sighed as he walked across to the kitchen island and picked up one of the wooden stools. He carried it back to the machine and placed it against the side. "Here, climb up, but don't fall in." Contentment and happiness washed over him when the boy's face lit up. He watched in amusement as Daniel scrambled up the stool and examined the belly of the machine.

"Coooool!" Daniel's eyes were like dinner plates.

"Can I see?" Leo asked, poking his own head into the machine after Daniel had moved out of the way. Peering inside, he saw that the potatoes slid down a metal chute towards five menacing blades that sliced back and forth noisily and turned them into chips. "We better be careful if we don't want to lose a hand," he said grimly.

Daniel, unperturbed by the danger, hopped down to the ground and grabbed a handful of the newly peeled potatoes before clambering back up onto the stool. "Watch this," he said excitedly and fed the potatoes to the hungry machine. The blades devoured them in seconds before spitting them out onto an external chute that led them down to the barrel. "Ha ha! That was immense," Daniel exclaimed before scampering down off the chair to fetch more potatoes.

"Wait a minute," Leo said. "I think you're supposed to tip the whole basket in."

Daniel's eyes widened. "The whole basket?"

"Yup, the whole basket," Leo repeated, grabbing the nearest one. "Okay, put your left hand on the handle like this, and then hold your right one under the basket like this," he instructed. Daniel followed the instructions perfectly, and soon the pair of them were holding the basket above the circular opening of the machine.

"After three," Daniel commanded. "One, two, three!"

On three, they angled the basket so all of the potatoes tumbled down the chute and into the direct path of the five blades. There was the most satisfying slicing sound as the knives slashed through potato flesh with ease. Daniel was off the stool in a flash and went to stand by the barrel as the chipped potatoes slid down the chute and thudded into the barrel.

"And that's how chips are made," Leo stated in his teacher voice.

"I didn't even know they had machines that did this," Daniel smiled.

"Come to think of it, neither did I," Leo confessed, placing the empty basket onto the floor and picking up one of the full ones. "Do you want to do this one?"

"No thanks, I'll just watch from here. I love the way the machine spits the chips out."

When they had chipped all the potatoes, Daniel retrieved the hose and held it over the barrel while Leo turned the tap on. He turned both the tap and chipping machine off once the barrel was filled with freezing cold water.

"That's a job well done, so it is," Mrs Ellen said as she appeared in the partitioned room with her pale of batter mix. She carried it to the fridge and placed it on the bottom shelf before closing the door firmly behind her. "Right, that's all the preparations for tomorrow's lunch done. Hmm, battered fish and chips. There's nothing like it! I hope you boys like fish and chips," she said with a bright smile, her eyes crinkling at the sides.

"I actually don't eat fish. In fact, I don't eat anything that comes out of the sea, so I guess it'll be just chips for me," Leo chuckled. He placed a hand on Daniel's shoulder. "What about you, Dan? Are you a fan of fish?"

Daniel turned his head up, and his black floppy fringe swept across his eyes. "I love fish, I take after Da—"

The boy's whole body went rigid, and his usually olive skin turned frightfully pale; it was like he'd suddenly developed rigor mortis. Then the trembling started—a small shudder at first that quickly developed into uncontrollable shaking followed by huge gut wrenching sobs. He brought his small hands up to his face and covered his anguish.

Leo was over in a split second, wrapping his arms around the boy and holding him tightly against his chest. Words eluded him. He was clueless. What words did one use to comfort an eleven year old who'd just lost his parents in a brutal blood bath? He knew exactly what had triggered Daniel's reaction, and a glance over at Mrs Ellen let him know that she understood as well. Having lost himself in the mundane of the normal world, Daniel's excitement at working the machine had caused him to forget. Reality's merciless punch had hit the boy hard and had brought the realisation that his parents would never get to taste fish again. They were gone from this world forever. Leo closed his eyes and fought his own desire to lose it while Daniel continued to sob into his chest. Eventually, the muffled sobs stopped.

"I'll take him to lie down," Leo told Mrs Ellen. "Thanks for looking after him while I was gone."

"It was my pleasure," Mrs Ellen replied. She turned to Daniel who had now stepped away from Leo's hug. "I'll bring you something to eat in a couple of hours. You go and lie down, and get some rest." She reached over and stroked the top of his head. "Off you go."

"Thank you, Mrs Ellen," Leo said. He hardly knew this woman but already loved her like a grandmother. Placing a comforting arm around Daniel's shoulders, he guided the boy out of the kitchen and back to the dormitories.

When they arrived at his room, he led Daniel in and closed the sturdy wooden door behind him. He took a deep breath as the boy trudged to the bed and sat down on it.

"Are you okay?" Leo asked. He immediately regretted it. "Wow! That was a stupid question. Of course you're not okay. I'm sorry." He bit his bottom lip anxiously and silently prayed that he would be able to support and comfort this devastated child.

"It's okay, Mr Alexander," Daniel said, staring at the floor.

"Please, call me Leo. We're way past student and teacher boundaries now," Leo said softly.

"Leo." Daniel tried out the name before looking up and giving Leo a small teary eyed smile. "Sounds funny." He brought his arm up and wiped his eyes and nose with his sleeve. "I didn't want to leave here last night. It was Mum and Dad. They said—"

When Daniel began to open up, Leo was taken aback, but he didn't show it. He remained silent and joined him on the bed when his little voice cracked. After crossing his legs and resting his hands on his knees, he gave Daniel a nod of encouragement. "Only tell me if you want to. You don't have to do this now." Deep down, he selfishly wanted Daniel to spill the entire story so he could find out just how much his parents had told him.

"I have to do it now," Daniel said urgently, as if he might change his mind at any moment. "I need to tell someone what happened."

"Okay, take your time. If it gets too much for you, stop." He squeezed the boy's shoulder lightly.

"When Mrs Ellen showed us to our room," Daniel began after taking a deep breath, "I went straight to the bathroom. Mum and Dad tried to talk quietly so I wouldn't hear them, but the walls are really thin, and I heard every word. Dad called you all a bunch of crazy freaks, especially you, and that he wanted nothing to do with any of it. He said Cornelius' story about the Power was lies. Mum thought it might be better if we stayed here where it was safer, but Dad didn't agree. He kept saying we couldn't trust anybody, and that we should go to the police. Eventually, Mum agreed.

"When I came back from the bathroom, Mrs Ellen was there with bed sheets and clean towels. After she left, we snuck out and drove to the police station where Mum and Dad talked to some officers. They wrote everything down and told Dad they'd be sending somebody out to speak to you, Lucas, and Cornelius about my abduction. Mum and Dad signed some papers, and then we went home.

"When we got back to the house, Dad sent me to bed straight away. I did as I was told, but I kept my bedroom door open and lay right beside it so I could listen in. I knew they'd want to talk about what had happened, and I wanted to know more. They said some stuff about you."

Leo raised his eyebrows. "Really? What did they say?"

"They thought you might be a demon because you summoned fire." Curiosity burned brightly in Daniel's eyes. "Are you a demon?"

"No."

"Oh."

Leo couldn't mistake the disappointment in the boy's tone. "But I can summon fire." He smiled as Daniel's eyes lit up the way they always did when something excited him.

"Can you do it now?" he asked eagerly.

"I could, but the truth is I'm not very good at using magic," Leo admitted. "I might end up setting us both on fire, and that wouldn't be good, would it?"

Daniel smiled and shook his head. "No, I guess not."

"What else did they say about me?"

"That was pretty much it. They talked about demons and Templars and something to do with a group of people called the Elect. I must have fallen asleep because I remember

264

waking up and being in my bed, not on the floor. I could
hear Dad downstairs. I knew it was him because I could
hear the whisky bottle clinking. I guessed Mum had come
upstairs and checked to see if I was asleep on her way to
bed. She must have picked me up and tucked me in. I
looked at the clock on my bedside table. It wasn't even six
yet, so I decided to go back to sleep. And that's when I
heard the voices."

Leo lifted his hands from his knees and uncrossed his
legs, placing them firmly on the floor as he folded his arms
tightly across his chest.

"My bedroom window is at the front of our house, and it
looks out onto the street. That's where I thought the voices
were coming from, so I got out of bed, and I peeked out of
the curtains. I saw a group of eight including the dead lamb.
They were using the lamb's blood to paint our gate. I knew
they were demons straight away."

"How?" Leo asked, the word barely making it out of his
mouth.

"One of the men and one of the women had these huge
wings. They were like an angel's wings, only black."

"What did you do once you saw them?"

"I got Mum. She came back to my room, and we looked
out of the window. I could tell she was terrified. She
grabbed my hand, and we ran downstairs to the living room
where Dad was. He'd just gotten off the phone to the police
when we told him the demons were outside. He went over
to the window and peeked from behind the curtain just like I
had done. Everyone says we're very alike." An unbelievable
sadness coated Daniel's words. "He was very calm, but I
could tell he was scared too. I'd never seen my parents
scared before. Parents aren't supposed to get frightened.
It's always bad news when the adults are scared, isn't it?

"And then Dad came rushing over to me. He fell to his
knees and grabbed me by the shoulders. *'Daniel,'* he said,
*'Listen very carefully to me. I need you to be brave. There are some
really bad people out there, and they can never find you. If you do as I*

say, everything will be okay. You have to hide up in the loft. Whatever happens, you stay there until one of us comes to get you.'

"I didn't want to. I wanted him to hold me and tell me I was safe. I was so scared—" His voice broke, and he let out a strangled sob.

"Oh, Daniel," Leo comforted, reaching out and rubbing his back.

"Dad wouldn't let me stay with them. I told him to phone the police again, but he said they wouldn't be able to help in time." The words came pouring out in a rush of chokes and sobs as the floodgates opened. Tears spilled from Daniel's eyes as he clasped his hands together. "He and Mum held me tight, and I knew it was the last time I'd get to hug them. I just knew. They told me they loved me over and over again and that I was to come and find you if anything bad happened to them.

"Then Mum took me upstairs and helped me into the loft. She told me I had to be quiet and stay there until you came for me. She was so sure you'd come. Before she closed the hatch, she took off her necklace and gave it to me." Daniel put his hand into his pocket and pulled out a golden chain with a solid gold cross on it.

"It's beautiful," Leo said, running a finger along the cross. The design was simple but elegant. Some of Daniel's tears landed on it and rolled onto Leo's finger.

"I took the cross, and I looked down at her. She didn't look scared anymore even though she was crying. She was smiling at me like she always did, although this time it felt different. She put her hands on my face, and she said, *'I knew you were something special from the day you were born.'* Then she put her hand on my heart and said, *'No matter what happens to me, I will always be in here. I love you forever, my beautiful boy.'* And then she was gone.

"I locked the hatch, found the furthest away corner I could, and sat there. I sat waited in the darkness." Daniel's hand closed around his mother's cross. "I heard her screaming. She screamed for ages, and I wanted to go to her, I really did, but she made me promise. I should have gone to her! I should have saved her! But I didn't, and I'm a coward! I sat in the loft covering my ears like a coward."

There was nothing Leo could do to stop his own tear ducts from opening when Daniel buried his head into his chest and unabashedly bawled his eyes out. He'd wanted to stay strong for the boy, strong enough to not shed any tears, but it wasn't to be. To appease his failings, all he could do was hold the grieving boy as long as he needed to be held. While Daniel wept uncontrollably, Leo became absorbed in thoughts of injustice, and he suddenly felt his aching heart turn to stone. His inner voice sprang to life, vicious and accusatory.

How could an almighty being get it so wrong? Look at this boy's pain! God isn't the all-powerful entity that everybody makes out! Fuck Him! Fuck Him all the way to hell!'

Leo didn't know how long Daniel had cried for, but eventually his tears ran out. He waited for a short time, formulating exactly what he wanted to say in his head before he said it to the boy. When he felt it was the right time, he gently released Daniel from the hug, placed a hand under his chin, and titled his head.

"I need you to listen to me, Daniel Macintosh," he began, peering into red and puffy eyes. "What happened to your parents was so bad that I don't have any words to describe it, but I do know three things, all equally important. Number one: your parents loved you more than life itself. Two: none of this is *your* fault, and I don't want to ever hear you say it is or I'll put you in detention for a year, got it?"

The tiniest of smiles and a nod.

"Excellent. The third thing I know is that you, Daniel Macintosh, are one of the strongest, bravest and most courageous young men I've ever met. You managed to stay quietly hidden from a pack of bloodthirsty demons while they did all those horrible things to your mum. Do you have any idea how many grown men would have been screaming hysterically? You stayed strong, Daniel. You listened to your parents, and they would be so proud of you. I'm proud of you."

Daniel's bottom lip quivered, and he pulled his watery gaze away.

"Hey, look at me," Leo said softly. "You should be proud of yourself." He took his hand away from Daniel's chin and dropped it to the boy's shoulder.

"But I hid. I did nothing."

"You did exactly what you were meant to do. Your parents knew what would have happened if those demons had found you, so they had to pretend you weren't there. I bet you anything they died telling those demons that you weren't in the house. Think about it. If the three of you had tried to run, the demons would have easily caught you." Leo squeezed Daniel's shoulder.

"But they're gone now, and I'll never see them again."

"I know, Dan, I know," Leo said, pulling Daniel into another hug while he fought back his own emotions.

"It hurts, Leo. I can't stand it. It hurts so much," Daniel said through heart wrenching sobs.

Leo, blinded by his own tears, held the boy. He'd lost his own parents when he was only five years old, and it was a struggle to remember anything in great detail from that time. He couldn't tell anybody what the funeral was like or what he did on the day he found out they'd died. But he'd never forgotten the pain of losing them.

"Will it ever stop hurting?" Daniel asked after he'd controlled his sobbing.

Leo took a deep breath and wiped his eyes. "It gets easier, over time. You're always going to miss them, Daniel, and you'll probably have the pain of losing them in your heart for the rest of your life. Time is a great healer, and you'll find that the pain you feel now will fade until there's nothing left except a dull ache."

"Do you promise?" he sniffed.

Leo nodded. "I promise."

Another sniffle. "Leo?"

"Yeah?"

"Will the demons come back?"

Leo stiffened. "Yes, but they won't get near you because Lucas and I will always be standing in the way." He felt Daniel hug him tighter.

He could tell the youngster was engaging in the torturous process of making sense of the hostile and cruel new world he was now facing. A world where he was being hunted by demons and Templars who, in Leo's opinion, weren't all that different from each other. These thoughts fuelled the angry fire that had been burning inside him since his early morning cigarettes, and that anger was directed towards the Grandmaster, who had altered the Power in the first place, and God.

'There's enough anger in here to go around.'

It was so much easier to get his thoughts in order and to take action when he and his inner voice were on the same page. After witnessing the extent of Daniel's heartbreak and suffering, everything had become crystal clear.

Daniel stirred and removed his arms from around Leo's middle. "I'm tired."

"I'm not surprised. You've been through a lot," Leo replied, rising to his feet and walking over to the light switch. "You can sleep here. I'll come back and check on you in a bit," he said while dimming the lights.

"Where are you going?" Daniel asked, a fearful expression flashing across his face, "Don't leave me!"

"It's okay," Leo said gently. "I'm just going to have a talk with Ela, Cornelius and Lucas. We need to decide what we're going to do next."

Daniel glanced anxiously towards the door. "I don't want to be alone."

"Then I won't leave you," Leo said as he walked back to the bed and sat down. "Kick off your shoes, and get under the covers."

Daniel did as he was told.

"You comfy?"

The boy nodded.

"Good. Close your eyes, and try to rest. You'll feel better after a good night's sleep."

"It's like five thirty," Daniel pointed out, rubbing his tired eyes. "I'll only need a nap. I'll be awake for dinner."

Leo grinned. "If you say so." For a long time, the only thing he could hear was the sound of Daniel's breathing. Just when he thought the boy was sound asleep, his little voice whispered the question Leo had been dreading.

"Leo, why do the demons and Templars want me?"

The answer didn't come right away, but when it did, Leo knew it was the right one for the time being. "You have something they desperately want."

"What?"

"I don't know for definite, but when I do, I'll tell you. Okay?"

"Okay."

"Now, sleep. You can barely keep your eyes open." And Leo wasn't exaggerating. He watched Daniel fight a losing battle. The boy kept trying to force his eyelids open, but the onslaught of sleep was relentless, and it was overpowering him.

"Leo?" Daniel murmured sleepily.

"I thought you were wanting to nap."

"I do, I just wanted to say thank you."

"What for?"

"For protecting me," Daniel whispered, before sleep carried him off to the dream world.

On hearing those words, a strong determination penetrated the hopelessness Leo had felt since the night Lucas had inflicted this terrible duty upon him. He reached over and delicately caressed the side of Daniel's face. "You're welcome," he whispered, leaning over and kissing the boy on the forehead.

He stayed for another ten minutes to make sure Daniel was sound asleep. When he was sure the boy wouldn't waken, he got up from the bed, tiptoed to the door, and left the room.

Once the door was closed behind him, he paused, placing a hand on the solid wood. His love for Daniel, if it was at all possible, had just grown deeper. The tragedy that had befallen the youngster did have one silver lining: it made Leo finally understand and accept his purpose.

Without further hesitation, he whipped his hand away from the door and marched down the dormitory corridor. He swept through the lounge and dining room before stopping opposite the kitchen where he could hear Mrs Ellen humming to herself. He glanced right to see a narrow stairwell spiralling up to another level of the Cathedral.

He strode towards it and took the steps two at a time, ascending into a gloomy darkness that was only broken by a single window half way up. When he reached the top, he was faced with an ancient wooden door that hadn't been closed properly.

Without pausing, he took in the appearance of the obstacle. A rusty iron plaque had been nailed into the wood about a third of the way down, and someone had engraved the name 'Cornelius O'Connor' expertly into it. He raised both hands and pressed them firmly against the wood. It was cold, soft and rotten. With one great big push, he flung the door open and stepped into the room.

Cornelius, Ela and Lucas all turned to gawp at him from a table littered with mountains of documents.

Lucas stood up from his chair. "Leo? Is everything alright?"

"I'm ready," Leo stated.

"Ready for what?" the demon asked.

Leo's burning eyes moved from Cornelius to Ela before settling back on Lucas. "I'm ready to be Elected."

Chapter 16
The Road to War

Snowflakes drifted lazily through the evening air and into the Cathedral courtyard. The golf ball sized flakes landed silently on the previous fall of snow which had become hardened by the plummeting temperatures of late January. It hadn't snowed for almost a month yet the city of Inverness lay smothered beneath a frozen white quilt. The day after Leo's epiphany, a freezing fog and an unrelenting frost had forced itself upon the city and prevented the snow from thawing. He'd never experienced coldness like it, and every time he had to venture outside, he'd breathe in the sharp winter air only to feel its icy hand travel into his lungs where it would constrict without mercy. It wasn't a pleasant feeling.

But today had seen a breakthrough in the arctic siege. He was glad to see the fog lift and feel the temperature rise at last. Although he was fed up with the snow, the reprieve it offered from the severe sub-zero conditions was most welcome, especially now seeing as he was standing in the Cathedral courtyard wearing only a thin black pullover and a pair of denims.

The courtyard had become his training ground where he'd transformed his magical powers beyond recognition.

Ela and Cornelius, despite their fraught relationship, had worked tirelessly together to come up with a gruelling programme for him in order to strengthen and hone his abilities. The Grandmaster and the priest had succeeded.

Before his training, he'd been under the delusion that he was proficient in the use of magic; he could summon the elements, he was a natural. When he saw the older Elect members in action, he realised just how insignificant and pathetic his magic was in comparison and had thrown himself into the training. It had been exhausting. It had been painful. It had been one of the toughest, most intense experiences he'd gone through in his life, but he regretted none of it.

By the end of the first week, he was threatening to quit. He'd been burnt by fire and ice, blown about and suffocated by ferocious winds, battered and beaten by chunks of earth, and almost drowned by water. Everything his mentors threw at him in the first week hurt like hell. In the beginning, the only line of defence he had at his disposal was his energy shield. He'd discovered he could conjure this when Morgana had attacked him in the Cathedral car park. At the time, his shield had blocked each and every one of her fireballs. During his initial training, however, each time he'd tried to conjure one to defend himself against Ela and Cornelius' magical onslaughts, he found the shield was worse than useless. The magical attacks would simply pass through the energy barrier and smash into his body. He'd sworn an impressive number of times during his initial training, much to Cornelius' dismay.

When the first week ended, it became apparent to Leo that his attitude and motivation were critically low. His own tiredness and the freezing weather had played a big part in making him miserable, and being constantly afraid of losing Daniel to the demons had also contributed to his wallowing misery.

Then there was Lucas. Ever since Leo had found out what he was, Lucas had kept his distance, and his behaviour towards him had been as cold as the January frost. He noticed the day after he'd found out Lucas' true identity that the demon only spoke to him when he really had to and refused to make eye contact. To make matters worse, it was only him that was getting the cold shoulder. Whenever Lucas was with Daniel, he'd be laughing, joking, fist bumping, and clowning around like he'd normally do. The minute he noticed that Leo was there, the icy demeanour would reappear, and he'd mumble something and take off.

As well as being extremely hurtful, Leo found it most confusing. He felt he'd been more than accepting of Lucas' lineage, and despite his own personal fear of anything remotely demonic, he'd kissed Lucas *after* finding out he was a demon. There'd never been any opportunity to discuss the issue with Lucas because they were never alone together. Lucas only ever appeared when there were other people present, usually Cornelius, Ela, Mrs Ellen and Daniel, all of whom he'd interact with in his usual cheeky manner.

During the first week of training while walking through the lounge, Leo had come across Lucas and a young woman chatting animatedly by the fire. He recognised immediately that the woman was Elect. She'd sat in the armchair nearest the fireplace while Lucas had sat on the armrest. He only saw the back of the girl's head and was treated to a thick mane of straight, shimmering blonde hair. Her frame from behind looked petite, and he imagined her to be absolutely stunning, especially if she'd managed to catch Lucas' eye. Lucas appeared enthralled in whatever she was saying, but when he saw Leo enter the room, he tore his eyes away from the beauty's face and gave him a cold smirk. Leo had felt jealousy plunge her cruel dagger into his heart and hadn't realised just how much Lucas had gotten under his skin until that moment. The training session that followed had been the worst one ever.

Another problem for Leo was that with the increasing number of Elect members arriving at the Cathedral, it was impossible to get any privacy or peace and quiet. There were exactly one thousand, three hundred and ninety four members of the Elect, including himself, and most of them had arrived. It was a mystery to him how they all managed to fit in the Cathedral. Yes, the gothic building was impressive in size, but he was sure it wasn't big enough to house almost one and a half thousand people. With all the new faces, it was complete pandemonium on a daily basis, and it was driving him insane. The only positive of the invasion was the Elect members had brought their children with them which meant Daniel had company.

When the children of the Elect had arrived, Leo was optimistic in thinking they might make him feel better, but he was sadly mistaken. The children, lovely as they were, only made him realise how much he missed school, and thinking of school made him think of Wendy, who he'd been fiercely instructed not to contact under any circumstances. It had been heart breaking for Leo to comply with this instruction, but he knew it was important for Wendy's protection. As far as everyone was concerned, the less she knew, the safer she was. Leo had agreed to break all contact with her on the condition that a strong member of the Elect worked in secret to protect her at all times.

The last time he'd communicated with Wendy was the night he'd marched up to Cornelius' chambers and declared he was ready to be trained. It had been a simple text, nothing too dramatic or out of the blue. It stated he'd caught a virus, he'd be off work until he recovered, and she wasn't to worry. For the rest of week one, she'd bombarded him with phone calls, text messages and voice mails, each one growing more irate and concerned about the fact she hadn't heard from him. Wendy's wedding was coming up, and he knew she'd be dying to include him in all the details. It killed him to think how hurt she would be, and it made him feel like shit.

There was no escape from the busy Cathedral either as a carefully orchestrated plan had been put into action which prevented him from going anywhere other than the courtyard. As far as the demons and Templars knew, Daniel had gone on the run with Leo and Lucas. It was Ela who had masterminded the entire deception, and it had worked perfectly. Two groups of Elect members, each one consisting of two adults and one child, had snuck out of the Cathedral in the early hours of the morning. They'd taken off in separate cars and were currently leading their enemies on a wild goose chase across the globe and as far away from Daniel as possible. Regular contact with the two groups had been maintained through Cornelius, and after weeks of being on the run, one group was reported to be in Paris with the hounds of hell snapping at their heels, while the other had made it to Sweden with a mob of leather clad Templars hot on their tail. Although Leo was beyond relieved to learn their enemies had fallen for their trick, he knew deep down it was only a matter of time before the plan was foiled, and they'd be back. The thought was unsettling, and he found he was never completely relaxed.

Going into week two, he'd reflected on all of these aspects and realised they were impacting greatly on his magical growth and development, particularly the Lucas issue, so he took action and spoke to the one person who everybody seemed to go to in times of desperation: Mrs Ellen.

"First thing you need to do is focus on getting a good night's sleep, so you do. You're absolutely no use to anybody if you're tired. How on earth do you expect to get better with magic if you're walking about like a zombie? Honestly, I've never seen anybody looking so tired in all my days," she'd lectured, skilfully ladling hot soup into a bowl while giving him a stern look.

"Secondly, you'll want to clear that head of yours. So many thoughts! I can practically hear them all the way over here, so I can. Meditation will sort that. A quiet place is all you need. When young Daniel is helping me with the tea, you get yourself into your room, and shut your mind off to everything. Them walls will block out a herd of thundering elephants, so they will, so no excuses. You won't hear a thing. When you start to feel His presence, you'll know what to do. Here you are," she'd said, placing the bowl of soup in front of him.

"And lastly, don't you be taking any notice of Lucas now, you hear? That one is a very mixed up little soul, so he is, and he has lots of issues to work through, so don't be taking it personally. He likes you, so he does, I can tell. Just give it time."

He hadn't been sure how to react to Mrs Ellen's advice regarding Lucas. Did she mean 'like' as in *'like'* or was she merely referring to friendship? Whatever she meant, he didn't question it and pondered over her guidance carefully while enjoying the homemade soup. When he'd gone to bed that night, he felt a million times better and had slept soundly.

The next day's training went far better than he could have imagined. He deflected most of Cornelius' attacks, and even Ela had to up her game in order to land any blows. His mentors had been elated at the sudden turnaround and questioned him on the reason for his remarkable improvement. He'd kept quiet about the whole thing, not uttering to anybody that Mrs Ellen had been the catalyst. He'd followed her advice religiously and really looked after himself by making sure he ate properly, got enough sleep, and meditated to keep his thoughts in order. He also started working on trying to feel indifferent towards Lucas by constantly telling himself that he was nothing more than an ugly evil demon. He might have been lying to himself but the feelings of hurt, anger, and frustration became less intense as the days went past.

By the time his third week of training had come to an end, his conjuring and elemental control rivalled that of Cornelius. He could create blazing infernos out of nothing and twist them into all sorts of shapes, his favourite being a flaming unicorn. He could also summon howling winds, raging storms, and lightning bolts. No trial was too much, and no tribulation was too challenging; he excelled in them all. Although his ability to wield magic had surpassed all of his expectations, and indeed the expectations of Ela and Cornelius, he was told he had one more trial to pass, and this final one would be the toughest.

"It's one thing to practise using magic in a non-threatening environment where you have time to prepare, but it's a whole different ball game when faced with an enemy who is unpredictable and deadly," Cornelius had told him on the morning of the trial. "Be in the courtyard for ten tonight. Don't be late."

Leo had assumed the final trial would involve a duel against Ela and Cornelius, both of them bringing every ounce of magical power they possessed to the table. Despite his extraordinary transformation, he wasn't expecting to win a battle against two of the most powerful members of the Elect, but he was determined to give it his best shot. Even if he could take out Cornelius, that would be a great achievement in itself.

And so, in the numbing coldness of late winter, after a full month of rigorous and brutal training, Leo did as he'd been instructed and was waiting in the frozen courtyard, staring dreamily at the falling swarm of snowflakes as they fell past him. He'd been waiting for the two elders for twenty minutes and was beginning to think he'd been given the wrong time.

While he waited, he took in the scenic sights of the courtyard that he'd spent most of the past month in. He'd never truly appreciated its beauty before. The courtyard was exquisite, its simplicity reminding him of the one he'd seen in his dream about Moses. It was a perfect square, its area approximately one hundred and sixty square metres. A grand marble fountain with a square base stood in the centre depicting the virgin cradling her infant while the archangel Michael watched unseen from behind. The angel's wings, even in sculpture, were glorious. He realised that whoever had carved the statue must have witnessed the divine beings themselves because the wings were almost identical to the demon ones he'd seen, and as Lucas had told him, demons were technically angels. At each corner of the courtyard was an apple tree, pruned to perfection and ready to provide a fruitful supply of apples in the summer. Two large boulders with snow covered tops flanked each bare tree. From his observation, he could see that the eight rocks were identical in shape and size.

The main body of the Cathedral lay directly in front of him. To his left and right were two smaller buildings that he hadn't been in before, and he had no idea what lay within. According to Daniel, the building behind him was where the members of the Elect were crammed into. It was significantly larger than the two side buildings but nowhere near the size of the Cathedral. He couldn't see how over a thousand people could possibly fit into it.

After admiring his surroundings, he checked his watch to see it was almost ten thirty. He took a step towards the main building when a sudden movement to his left caused his eyes to dart back and forth across the gloomy courtyard. There was nothing there. He wondered if it was one of the gigantic flakes catching the corner of his eye but quickly realised that they were beginning to ease off and had shrunk considerably in size.

An unexpected rush of wind brushed the back of his neck, and in a split second, he was alert and focused. He used the slippery snow beneath his feet to turn one hundred and eighty degrees with the intention of startling his enemy. When he spun around, there was nobody there to startle. He was convinced he'd felt somebody blowing on the back of his neck, but after a couple of deep calming breaths, he told himself he'd imagined it. That all changed when the same thing happened a second and third time.

Trying to refrain from visualising a terrifying demon about to gut him, he cleared his throat. "I know you're there," he called out, his voice as cool as the winter air. Silence. He took another step forward. His eyes roamed the courtyard, but they found nothing. He went to take yet another step when a deep voice rang through the darkness, causing him to freeze.

"It's pretty obvious that you're not alone."

He recognised the voice instantly. "Lucas?"

A light thudding noise came from behind him, and he turned to see Lucas crouching in the snow several metres away, his cerulean eyes studying him intently. He wore black jeans, nothing more. He stood up to his full height, his muscles rippling beneath his skin, his eyes never leaving Leo's. The demon blocked the entrance way to the Cathedral, and Leo wondered if it was deliberate.

For a long time, they just stood and stared at each other. The snow had come to a complete stop, revealing a night sky speckled with glittering stars that twinkled and shone across the galaxy. The moon threw her silver light down, illuminating the courtyard like floodlights at a major sporting event.

"Where's Ela and Cornelius?" Leo asked, unable to tear his eyes away from Lucas' torso which was currently bathed in splendorous beams of moonlight. The effect was mesmerising, hypnotic.

"Were you expecting them?"

"Yeah."

"Why?"

"For the final trial. It was supposed to start thirty minutes ago."

Lucas grinned. It didn't reach his eyes. "It did, and you're failing."

Leo narrowed his eyes. "Failing? Don't be ridiculous. They aren't even here yet."

"The trial started thirty minutes ago. I've been watching you this whole time."

"Really? And would you mind telling me how I'm supposed to participate in a trial when I don't have a clue what the trial is?" Leo asked, folding his arms and glaring.

"It's easy. All you have to do is go into the Cathedral and find Daniel."

"What's the catch?"

Lucas chuckled coldly but didn't answer.

"Okay then," Leo said uncertainly. He lifted his foot to take a step forward when Lucas unexpectedly reached above his head with his left hand and snatched the air. His heart skipped a beat, and his stomach twisted into a tight knot as he stared down at the magnificent sword that Lucas held.

'Cornelius and Ela done good, kiddo. What better way to assess your magical capabilities than against a real life scary mother fucking demon?' his inner voice chirped in his head. Leo had to agree, it was the perfect test, and Lucas was playing the role of evil demon flawlessly.

The long samurai style blade, which was almost as tall as Lucas, was blue in colour and looked like it had been polished everyday of its existence for hours at a time. Moonlight bounced off every part of it, highlighting its perfection majestically and illuminating the diamonds that were encrusted into the platinum hilt.

Lucas swung the blade three times with such stunning elegance and ease that it was almost like the sword was a part of him. "Forged in heaven itself," Lucas said, placing the end of the sword into the ground and trailing it gently through the snow. "This sword has ended the lives of many demons, angels...and humans." He lifted the blade and rested it on his shoulder while staring at the thin trench he'd made in the snow. Flames, bright blue and half a metre tall, sprouted from the trench and licked the cold night air.

"I thought you said angels and demons couldn't be killed," Leo said, marvelling at the way the fire burned brightly in the demon's eyes and intensified their blueness even more.

"I didn't say they couldn't be killed. I just never told you how to do it," Lucas answered softly. He continued to gaze dreamily into the flames as if they were the most important thing in the world. "Any blade that was forged in heaven or hell can do it. Put it through any demon's heart and that demon will cease to exist."

"That sounds simple enough." Leo couldn't help his arrogance. It often reared its ugly head when he felt intimidated. He'd always put it down to the fact his star sign was the proud lion. He carefully watched as Lucas lifted his head and set his blazing blue eyes upon him.

"You underestimate my kind." Lucas' tone was threatening. He turned his attention back to the flames which had risen to the same height as his waist, and were continuing to rise.

"I'm stronger now," Leo said sharply. "I think I could hold my own against a demon."

Lucas bared his teeth in what could have been a grin. It was as hostile as the bitter winter that had embraced the city. "After watching you train over the last four weeks, I'd agree. I reckon you'd crush lesser demons without a problem, and you'd certainly be able to 'hold your own' with a demon, but…"

"But what?"

"But how would you fair against a pure demon?"

"A pure demon?" Leo repeated, squinting to see Lucas through the inferno which had grown to chest height. The heat radiating off the small bonfire reached him, stroking his face and bringing relief from the icy coldness of the courtyard.

"That's right," the demon chuckled, his jaw now concealed by a flickering curtain of blue fire. "A pure demon, like any other demonic entity, can be destroyed forever if their hearts are pierced with a heavenly forged blade—"

"Like any other demonic entity?" Leo interrupted. "Sounds to me like pure demons aren't so special if they can be killed like any other demon. Just saying."

The grin vanished from Lucas' face instantly. "Okay, let's see what you make of your first pure demon."

"How stupid do you think I am? Ela and Cornelius wouldn't allow a pure demon anywhere near this cathedral, even if it was for training purposes."

"You're right, they wouldn't let just *any* pure demon into the Cathedral," Lucas replied, his mouth twisting into a chilling sneer. The flames leapt up to cover his face and completely hid him from view. "But they would let *me*."

The meaning of Lucas' words hit him like a double decker bus. In the blink of an eye, he was coiled and ready to spring. The mystical energy residing within him rushed through his body in seconds, firing him up.

The blue fire was sucked back into the ground, and the demon was no longer there. A rush of air hit the back of Leo's neck, and he whirled around to find Lucas standing right in front of him. Lucas' fist slammed into his chest and launched him backwards with incredible velocity. When he landed, he continued to skid along the ground until he came to a stop under one of the apple trees, and for the first time this winter, he appreciated the depth of the snow. While lying on the ground, he tried to overcome the agony in his chest by breathing through the pain but was quickly interrupted by Lucas, who towered over him with his sword raised above his head.

"I thought you would have lasted longer against a not so special pure demon. Just saying," Lucas mocked before driving his blade downwards.

As the blade fell, Leo thrust his hand forward and summoned an energy shield. The blade ricocheted off the mystical barrier, crackling noisily and sending showers of blue energy everywhere. He quickly launched a fireball that exploded against Lucas' bare chest and blasted him off his feet. With Lucas temporarily incapacitated, Leo scrambled up the side of the apple tree while keeping his eyes locked firmly on his enemy.

By the time he'd gotten to his feet, the demon was up and charging towards him, closing the gap at frightening speed while dragging his heavenly blade in the snow behind him and leaving a trail of blue fire. In his panic, Leo stepped to the side and almost fell over one of the large snow covered boulders. Suddenly, a voice bubbled up from the deep recesses of his mind.

"Become one with the world; it's God's gift to us. Nature is our weapon."

Reaching out with his magic, he allowed it to consume the rock like Ela had taught him. It was his to command. The boulder flew from the ground and became a grey missile that streaked through the air with incredible swiftness. The mass of grey struck Lucas on the head with a sickening crack, knocking him clean off his feet and sending him spiralling into the air above the fountain. A second cracking sound resounded through the courtyard as Lucas' skull cracked off the corner of the marble base when he landed. The demon rolled onto his stomach and became still.

"Oh fuck!" Leo's hand shot up to his mouth in horror. "Fuck, fuck, fuck! Lucas! Are you—oh thank god!"

Lucas was stirring.

"I'm so sorry, Lucas, I panicked!" He was by Lucas' side in seconds. "Are you alright?" he asked, placing his hand on the demon's back.

There was a flash of movement, and Lucas' hand, which was now pale and lined with crimson veins, was wrapped around his throat and lifting him off the ground.

"If you think a rock is enough to stop a pure demon then you need a serious fucking reality check," Lucas growled.

"Lu…cas!" Leo croaked, clawing at the demon's hand.

Apart from pulsating flecks of red, the onyx eyes were dead and empty. It was one of Leo's greatest fears—the thought of nothing after death—and that is exactly what he was reminded of when he looked into the demon's eyes. He kicked out and tried to scream for help but couldn't make a sound.

Lucas cocked his head to the side and narrowed his eyes. "You still think you can handle yourself against my kind?" he snarled. "This is what you're up against, Leo. This is what you have to face. Look at you! You're a pathetic quivering mess! Even after all your training; the blood, sweat and tears, you still let your ridiculous fears rule you."

Leo's lungs burned as he tried in vain to free himself. His insides turned to ice when Lucas drew him closer and their noses touched.

"You're on the road to war, and you're nowhere near ready to walk it."

When the demon forced him to look into those lifeless orbs, he stilled as their emptiness consumed him. While staring down into the hollow abyss, a calmness crept over him, and suddenly his fear began to retreat, his eyes closing as he succumbed to the tranquillity.

The light you carry inside of you…its powerful Leo, and it will chase the demons back into the darkness where they came from.

How ironic, he thought, that it should be Lucas' words that he heard right now. In his moment of clarity, he understood what Lucas had been trying to tell him from the day they had met. He had no reason to fear the demons; they should be fearful of him. He was divine, or at least the magic inside of him was, and it was now he realised that he was going to pass this trial.

"You're weak!" Lucas hissed, "I might as well go and hand Daniel over to Baal now and get it over with!" With those words, he tossed Leo across the courtyard.

Leo kept his eyes closed and braced himself for the impact. His ribs slammed into something solid, and there was a loud cracking noise before he slumped to the ground. The pain was excruciating, but he refused to scream.

In his mind's eye, he visualised himself enshrined in a white light speckled with gold. He heard Lucas' feet crunching into the snow and knew the demon was heading for the Cathedral. As he lay there, he felt the divine power knitting the cracks in his ribs back together. Under the flesh, his muscles repaired themselves and became strong again while the pain of Lucas' attack ebbed away to nothing.

'What if Lucas was the enemy?' his inner voice chided. *'What if he was Baal and he'd just kicked your ass and was now going to rip Daniel into tiny little pieces? What would you do right now, in this scenario?'*

Leo knelt down and pushed his hands deep into the snow until they touched the earth underneath. His dazzling eyes shot open as he used his mystical power to pull himself gracefully to his feet. By his command, a massive wall of rock pushed itself up from the ground and blocked the entrance way to the Cathedral. Lucas stopped, turned around, and flashed a toothy grin.

"You'll have to kill me first," Leo said, his voice carrying power and strength.

Still in his demon form, Lucas pointed the tip of his blade at Leo. "That can be arranged," he said, running his forked tongue along his bottom lip.

"I don't want to embarrass you by kicking your ass all over this courtyard, Lucas, but if that's what I have to do to pass this trial, then so be it."

Lucas laughed loudly, its musical sound only slightly audible through the demonic gruffness. "I knew you'd fight back eventually. Cornelius was adamant you'd crack under the pressure, but I told him he was wrong. Ela was confident you'd best me in the end...I guess I'll have to prove her wrong too."

Leo prepared to defend himself as Lucas turned and ran full speed at the mound of rock, sprinted half way up it and used his powerful legs to push himself off. The demon twisted in mid-air and flew towards him like a demonic torpedo. Leo calmly dropped to the floor, and the torpedo flew harmlessly by.

"You missed," Leo said. He stood up slowly and gazed over at Lucas who was clinging to one of the smaller buildings.

"Did I?"

An icy blast of wind hit Leo's back, causing him to shiver. Snaking his arm behind his back to investigate, he swept his hand over exposed skin and drew it forward to inspect. No blood.

"It would appear you did," Leo replied, looking back up at his opponent.

Lucas snorted. "If I wanted to, I could have sliced you into little Leo pieces."

"I dare you to try."

"This is a trial. I'm not trying to kill you. If I was you'd be dead alre—"

Leo didn't give Lucas the chance to finish his sentence and threw two fireballs at him. They exploded on either side of the demon who gave a yelp of surprise and lost his balance. Lucas manipulated his fall beautifully and somersaulted to land delicately on the balls of his feet, looking very smug until the falling debris from the fireball blasts came tumbling down on top of him. Leo, not caring that Lucas was buried under a ton of bricks, took the opportunity to sprint towards the blocked Cathedral door.

As he ran, he willed the offending rock to disappear, and it was sucked back down into the earth until it was gone. The grass and soil where the rock had punched its way through looked undisturbed, and Leo was fairly impressed with his own work.

When his hands touched the Cathedral's heavy door, he felt relief; he was going to make it. Grabbing the metal handle, he pulled it down and yanked the door towards himself, but it didn't budge.

Push it!' his inner voice screamed.

Leo threw his shoulder against the wood, and when the door remained intact, his heart and determination sank. He leant his forehead on the doorframe and let his shoulders sag.

"Oh dear, did someone lock the door?"

Leo regained his composure before turning to face Lucas. "I don't suppose you have a key?"

"As a matter of fact," Lucas said, putting a hand in his pocket and pulling out a large silver key, "I do, but I'm afraid

if you want it, you're going to have to come and get it."
With an impish grin, he returned the key to his pocket.

Leo grinned back. "Or, we could try this," he said, thrusting his hands in Lucas' direction, knowing that nothing was going to happen.

Seeing Lucas' demonic features display puzzlement and confusion made the demon's face appear less scary; Leo found it almost cute. He did not, however, surrender to his amusement and focused on what he was trying to accomplish. He could sense his magic enchanting the two boulders that lay beyond Lucas. They shook slightly as his will gently shrouded them, consuming them in a quilt of divinity. Lucas hadn't noticed yet; he was too busy looking entertained by Leo's seemingly failed magical attack.

"Uh oh," Lucas said unpleasantly. "The homo's lost his mojo."

"Really? You're going to go there?" Leo asked, giving the demon his sincerest look of pity while lowering his hands.

"I like rhyming," Lucas shrugged before slicing the air with his sword. "My blade is hungry, and it looks like your batteries are dead. If this was real, you'd be demon food."

"I wouldn't if I were you," Leo warned as the demon stepped forward.

Lucas stopped. "The door is locked, I have the key, and you're burnt out. I think I've won," he said pompously.

"God, arrogant much?" Leo retorted. "Let me tell you one thing that you don't know about humans, my dear Lucas."

"And what would that be?"

Leo's irises ignited. "We're a lot smarter than demons."

The two boulders he'd enchanted were ripped from the ground and magically propelled through the air. One flew straight at Lucas while the other went right above the demon's head and towards Leo. As expected, Lucas sensed the danger and spun around, swinging his greedy blade at the boulder coming directly at him and slicing it in half as easy as if it'd been a watermelon. The two halves landed at the demon's feet and spun wildly on the snow like two giant spinning tops.

With Lucas momentarily distracted, the other boulder had gathered up an astonishing speed and was hurtling towards Leo like a mini comet. At the very last minute, he stepped casually to the side, and the rock pummelled into the door, decimating it entirely. With the door no longer a problem, he fumbled through the dust and wreckage and stumbled into the gloominess of the Cathedral.

"You almost made it," Lucas whispered in his ear.

Without thinking, Leo flung out an elbow and the sound of crunching bone filled the corridor.

"Motherfucker! My nose!" Lucas howled, his hands covering his face.

Leo quickly placed his hands onto the demon's bare chest. Seconds later, the aroma of charred flesh came alive in his nostrils as the papery skin sizzled. Lucas screamed, and his blade fell to the ground with a clatter. Just as Leo reached out to grasp the platinum hilt, he felt a powerful hand grab him by the scruff of his neck. The stone wall shook as he was slammed against it.

"Still think you're smarter than me?" an enraged Lucas hissed.

Leo felt the cold metal blade slide beneath his chin and come to rest under his throat. He stared death in the face, and it was staring back at him through furious black eyes.

"Trial's over!" the demon growled, a manic glint giving some life to his dead eyes. "You lose."

Wide eyed with terror, Leo let out a tiny gasp as Lucas swiped the blade across his throat.

Chapter 17
I've Been Waiting Forever

After Lucas had drawn the blade across his throat, Leo prepared himself for a world of pain and panic, but he needn't have bothered. He realised in the anti-climax of the moment that he was unharmed.

Lucas was grinning. "I'm impressed. You almost had me."

"Fuck you!" Leo fumed.

"Aw, come on," Lucas protested. "You know I was just acting. There's no need to be a sore loser. No human has ever bested me."

"That's good to know," Leo said sarcastically. "But if you're just acting, why is this blade still at my throat?"

"Because I know you secretly like it when my weapon presses against you," Lucas replied with a low chuckle.

"You really are an arrogant bastard, aren't you?"

The demon smiled and closed his eyes, leaving the question unanswered. The dark crimson veins that marred his face gradually disappeared, and the papery white skin became more supple and tanned. Once his entire face had reverted to its normal beautiful self, Lucas opened his eyes. Leo couldn't help thinking the change in the demon's eyes made the transformations all the more shocking. One minute they were chillingly black; the next they were radiant and alive, glittering like the stars in the cosmos.

"Don't I get a prize seeing as I won the game?" Lucas asked, his eyes smouldering. "A kiss, maybe?"

Leo swallowed. "We can't."

"Why?" Lucas demanded, bringing his blade down to Leo's chest and slowly beginning to saw through the fabric of his pullover.

"You know why," Leo said, his face flushing when Lucas' lips touched his ear.

"No, I don't," the demon whispered seductively. "Give me one good reason?"

With Lucas' lips brushing against his earlobe, Leo found it hard to concentrate. "It burns, remember? Then you turn into a demon. It doesn't work." Cold air blew against his naked chest as Lucas' blade finally cut through his pullover. His heart skipped a beat when Lucas' lustful gaze fell upon his naked torso.

"It won't happen this time," the demon said, his voice thick with desire.

Leo jumped a little when Lucas' blade fizzled into the ether. "How won't it?"

"You have total control over your power now," Lucas explained, inching closer. "It won't be the same, I promise."

Leo's eyes closed of their own accord when Lucas kissed him, and he inhaled the demon's mind blowing scent, allowing it to cloud his senses and bewitch his mind. Just as he was starting to get into the kiss, Lucas pulled back.

"See, no demon face," he said. "No burning, no pain."

"I…I don't understand," Leo stammered, still dizzy from the kiss.

"Four weeks ago, you had no control over your gift," Lucas explained. "Whenever we were close, you were attacking me without meaning to."

"How is that even possible? How can I have attacked you without meaning to?"

"Subconsciously, Leo. The magic inside of you is very powerful, and when we kissed in your apartment last month, it sensed my demonic nature and acted in self-defence because you weren't in full control. But now that you've mastered your gift and surrendered to it fully, we won't have that problem, and we can…you know." Lucas wriggled his eyebrows mischievously.

Leo's mind processed what he'd just heard, and it all made perfect sense. But something completely unrelated was creeping into his mind, and it had nothing to do with the relationship between divine and demonic energies. Why had Lucas ignored him for a month? Why had he been so cold? Why had he flaunted the blonde haired girl in front of him? Why was the arrogant bastard now wriggling his eyebrows like everything was fine after avoiding him for so long? A month's worth of anger and frustration sprung up from his solar plexus and into his chest where it writhed around like a ferocious beast.

"You're a fucking asshole!" Leo snapped, shoving Lucas away. "Stay away from me!" He pushed past the startled demon and stormed down the corridor towards the dining room and kitchen, his arms swinging wildly with every stride. It didn't take long for Lucas to catch up, and when he did, Leo saw him reach out a hand. "Don't touch me!"

"Jesus Christ! What's all the drama for?" Lucas asked, perplexed. He sounded tetchy but still rushed ahead and held open the dining room door.

Leo marched through the door without thanking the demon and stomped his way through the dark room. He ignored Lucas' pleas until they were in the dormitory corridor. Lucas rushed past him and stood in front of the bedroom door leaving him no choice but to engage.

"I'm not moving until you tell me what your problem is," Lucas said quietly, his arms stretched out over the doorframe.

"Are you seriously asking me what my problem is? I thought it was pretty obvious, you moron!"

"I'm not skilled in the art of mind reading, you big drama queen! So instead of behaving like a hormonal school girl, just fucking tell me!" Lucas shouted.

"Keep your voice down! Daniel is asleep!" Leo hissed, his eyes flashing with anger.

Lucas took a deep breath. "He won't hear a thing through the door, it's solid," he said, lowering his voice. "Let's go to my room and discuss this like adults."

"There is nothing to discuss."

"Okay then. I guess we're camping out here tonight."

"Fine!"

"After you."

By the time Leo got into Lucas' bedroom, he was bristling. He stood in the centre of the room, his body tense, and his arms folded rigidly against his chest. While Lucas closed the bedroom door, his eyes pierced the demon's back.

"Right, I can see that you're a little upset," Lucas said quietly. He shut the door and turned the key in the lock before facing Leo.

"A little upset? I'm fucking furious, and I can't believe you don't know why!"

"Is it because I was talking to that girl?" Lucas asked, a smile playing at the corner of his mouth.

"Don't you dare laugh at me," Leo warned. "Of course it isn't because of some cheap blonde floozy!"

"Look me in the eye and tell me I'm wrong."

Leo hesitated. He was a terrible liar and always had been. "It isn't because of her," he lied, his eyes dropping to the floor for a split second.

"Look me in the eye," Lucas repeated with a grin.

Leo scoffed. "What are you, the Body Language Expert? Okay, so that's maybe a little bit of why I'm upset," he admitted grudgingly.

"I thought you said you were furious," Lucas pointed out.

"Oh, forget it!" Leo fumed, storming towards the door and reaching for the handle. He pulled it only to find it was locked. As his hand grasped the key, Lucas was wrapping his arm around his shoulders.

"I'm kidding, Leo. I'm sorry. Just hear me out. Please?"

Leo let out a sigh of frustration and eyed the stone floor of the bedroom. "Fine, but stop making a joke out of everything. This is serious."

"Okay, I'll stop. Promise."

He allowed Lucas to guide him over to the bed where they both sat down and sank into the soft mattress.

"I know I've been a bit off lately," Lucas began.

"A bit off?" Leo said incredulously. "Lucas, you haven't spoken to me for a month. You've done nothing but give me the cold shoulder ever since I found out you were a demon. Yes, I might have been a little prejudiced about your kind in the past but—"

"A little prejudiced?" Lucas interjected.

"Hey, I still kissed you despite the whole demon thing. Give me some credit."

Lucas smiled. "Credit given."

"I accepted it, Lucas. You being a demon doesn't matter to me. I don't understand what the last four weeks have been about. You've been acting normal to everybody else except me. You've only growled at me when I've tried talking to you, and you won't even be in the same room as me. Today is the first time in weeks you've even looked in my direction, and all of a sudden you're hot for me. I'm so confused. Why now?

"And if I'm honest, when I saw you with that girl, it made me jealous. There, I said it. I was jealous, which is ridiculous because I've only known you for a month, and you've practically ignored me for most of that, so I have absolutely no idea how I can feel jealous." He took a huge breath and exhaled slowly while Lucas just sat there, gazing. "Okay, I'm done. You're turn."

"I'm not surprised you're confused," Lucas said at last. "Let me explain everything. I've stayed away from you so you could focus on your training. If you weren't focused solely on developing your magic, you'd never have reached this stage so quickly, and it's so important you're the strongest you can be. We need you ready."

"Yeah, I'm not quite ready though," Leo said.

"Yes, you are."

"But I couldn't beat you."

"Not true. You could have beaten me, and that's why Ela and Cornelius were adamant I stayed away. They knew you were feeling something for me right at the beginning, and it didn't fit in with their plan. They always intended to use me as the final trial. You can't get tougher than a pure demon, right?"

"I guess not, but I still failed."

"You're missing the point. When you smashed my head with the rock, which was genius by the way, you could have easily finished me off then. If that'd been a demon trying to kill you, you'd have incinerated the bastard while they were writhing on the ground, but you didn't because it was me. Why?"

Leo looked sheepish. "I didn't want to hurt you."

"Exactly, so now do you see why it was important for me to drive you away?"

"I get it."

"Good. If it'd been any other pure demon in that trial, you'd have succeeded. I didn't see that rock coming at all. You nearly took my head off," Lucas said with a grin.

"I told you," Leo said with a shrug. "Humans are smarter than demons."

"Don't push your luck," Lucas chuckled, giving Leo a squeeze. "So, we good?"

"Yeah, we're good." Leo said, standing up and walking to the door. "As long as you don't go ignoring me again." He turned his head and smiled at Lucas from over his shoulder.

Lucas shook his head from side to side. "No way, that's not happening again. It killed me to do that to you."

"Really?" Leo laughed. "I thought you'd have enjoyed the reprieve." It was then he noticed Lucas' whole demeanour had changed from comfortable and relaxed to serious and solemn.

The demon cleared his throat and shifted nervously on the bed. "I...I really didn't want to stop talking to you. I hated every second of it. Cornelius and I had some blazing rows over the whole thing. He thought you would take more than two months to reach a stage where you could be tested against a pure demon. He wanted to send me away and everything. I told him that leaving wasn't an option for me, and he called me selfish, said I shouldn't get involved with you, even after the trial."

In the silence that followed, Leo's heart fluttered when Lucas fixed his magnetic eyes on him.

"I've missed you."

Leo shook his head. "You don't know me well enough to have missed me." He didn't dare believe the words coming out of Lucas' mouth. "You can't feel that deeply for a person you've only known for two days. It's not possible."

"Don't tell me what I feel," Lucas snapped, then immediately apologised for his outburst. "I'm sorry, I just—" Lucas ran his hands through his hair, tugging at it in the process.

"It's okay," Leo said, determined to avoid any more drama tonight. "We can chat tomorrow. It's late, and I could really do with some sleep. I'll see you in the morning." He reached for the key to unlock the door. There was a flurry of movement behind him.

"Don't go!"

When warm hands touched the back of his neck, Leo knew he wasn't going anywhere. He soon found himself facing perfect cheekbones and endless blue eyes—eyes that were somehow managing to exude certainty, hope, sorrow, and fear all at once. Gazing up at the demon's beautiful face, it was clear from his expression that there was something he desperately wanted to say.

"You can tell me anything," Leo said, reaching up and cupping the side of Lucas' angelic face. "What is it?"

Lucas exhaled loudly. "Okay, remember the night I broke into your apartment and told you about the angels and how they each have one gift."

"Yeah."

"Even after we became corrupted, we pure demons kept our gifts. I have a gift, but it's also my curse."

The words sounded vaguely familiar to Leo, but he didn't have time to mull it over because Lucas was pouring his heart out.

"I didn't get the gift of strength, or speed, or the gift of creating illusions. I was gifted dreams. In the beginning, I was able to see things not of my reality. I had no idea what they were, so I kept them to myself. I soon discovered they had more significant meanings. They were visions."

"Visions?" Leo asked, eyes wide with wonder.

"Visions that came to be my reality. I have dreamt of many events, events that have come to pass: the great war in heaven, creation, Adam and Eve, the building of the great pyramids, the rise and fall of the Roman Empire, both World Wars, and the election of the first black president. My most recent vision was of a war that would affect the entire world."

Leo's eyes nearly popped out of his head. "A third world war?"

"Relax. Some of my visions never come to pass."

"Let's hope that vision is one of those," Leo said uneasily.

Lucas laughed lightly before carrying on. "Out of the countless visions I've had, I cherish only one. It was one I had over four thousand years ago. In the vision, I'm wrapped in chains. I've been inflicted with wounds that I can't hope to recover from. Pain consumes every part of my mind, body and soul."

Lucas' eyes glazed over and became unblinking. His whole body seized up, and Leo could tell that the demon was somewhere else, on some other plane of existence where he was reliving the vision. To offer some comfort, he took Lucas' hands in his and held them while the demon continued talking.

"I'm being whipped and taunted as I withhold information. They want answers, but I don't give them. I can't see their faces because I'm delirious, and blood blurs my sight, but I know my tormentors; they're my family. I can't tell how long they've beaten me for, it feels like centuries, but I don't beg for them to stop. I know I mustn't give up. They can't break me because they must never know the secret I'm keeping. It's dangerous in their hands. Still, they continue to torture me, tear at my resolve with physical and mental cruelty. It's agonising, and I'm about to break, I can feel them forcing their way through my defences.

"I'm going to tell them everything. The words are on my lips, but suddenly, a dazzling white light rips through the darkness, blinding me. I can't shield my eyes because my hands are manacled behind me. Suddenly, demonic screams of terror ring in my ears. I hear bones snapping, blood spilling, and lives ending all around me. Then silence."

Lucas fell quiet, his glazed eyes narrowing as if they were trying to see through the white light. Leo was totally enthralled, transfixed on every word.

Lucas inhaled sharply. "Something's emerging from the light. It's changing, taking form!"

Leo squeezed the demon's hands. "Come on, Lucas, tell me!"

Lucas blinked and was back in the room. "So...beautiful."

Cerulean eyes penetrated Leo and forced their way into his being, touching his soul. "What was it?" he asked breathlessly.

Lucas' husky voice was barely audible as he continued to touch Leo's soul with his eyes. "Not *what*, but *who*."

In one swift motion, Lucas had pulled him tightly against his chest, leaning down so that their eyes were level. Leo could see the sadness and fear had gone from those intense, pulsating eyes.

"Who was it?" Leo croaked.

"You," Lucas replied, his voice a whisper.

Leo wanted to say something, but he couldn't make a sound. There was a part of him that didn't believe it, couldn't believe it.

"I've been waiting forever," Lucas continued, pressing Leo's hands against his demonic heart, "to see your face emerge from the light, and save me from the darkness."

Leo held his breath as Lucas stroked his face. How could this divine being, this beautiful gift from heaven, have been waiting all this time for him? Even his inner voice had been stunned into silence, offering no smart commentary, no cutting remarks. The feelings he was being exposed to were brand new; they were incredibly empowering and euphoric yet they were also humbling. He had no possible words to describe them. It was like the universe had personally spoken to him and said, *This, Leo Alexander, is what I planned for you.*' Tears formed in his eyes as he grasped this beautiful and sacred concept.

"I love you, Leo."

Leo closed his eyes, the intensity of those three words consuming him. "You can't love me," he whispered.

"Why not?" Lucas demanded.

"Because no one ever has," he replied, closing his eyes while Lucas' thumbs wiped away his tears.

"Leo, look at me!"

At Lucas' command, his eyes fluttered open.

"I have loved you for over four millennia. You just didn't know it until now."

Overcome with emotion, Leo pulled the demon into a passionate kiss. He gasped when Lucas' strong hands gripped his damaged pullover and tore it completely from his body. A growl filled the air, and Leo found himself pressed up against the bedroom door with Lucas' lips on his neck. Their mouths came together once more, tongues tasting and exploring the depths of each other's mouths. He moaned with pleasure and found himself jumping up and wrapping his legs around Lucas' waist. From this position, he felt Lucas' excitement on the back of his thigh, and the feel of the demon's arousal was like an elixir for his own.

"Lucas," he panted through heated kisses.

Lucas grunted in acknowledgement.

"Look at me." The abruptness of his instruction seemed to startle Lucas who stopped immediately and obeyed.

"What is it?"

"I love you too."

Lucas pondered over Leo's declaration briefly before he grinned his all American boy grin. "I know, who wouldn't love this? You're one lucky dude right now."

Leo rolled his eyes but grinned at the same time. "Need I remind you that you've loved me for over four thousand years, and now you finally get to have me? Tell me again who the lucky one is?"

"Hmm, you're right," Lucas' agreed, his eyes twinkling, "Let's see if you're worth the wait."

Lucas carried him to the bed and collapsed into the mattress where they remained until the first light of dawn, lost in each other and surrendering to the unconditional love that had been mapped out for them by the universe.

Outside the bedroom window, a pair of eyes observed the human and the demon as their bodies interlocked. The blackness of the night created a perfect camouflage for the crow's espionage and allowed it to retrieve information that was bound to please its master. Having uncovered a wealth of interesting and valuable information regarding the master's son and the whereabouts of the Power, the crow spread its wings and fluttered into the air before becoming one with the darkness.

Chapter 18
Short Contentment

Beams of sunlight forced their way through the bedroom window, engulfing most of the bed in which Leo lay. He absentmindedly stroked the powerful forearm that was draped over him while watching the dust particles chase each other in and out of the sun's brilliant rays. Lucas slept soundly beside him, his broad chest rising and falling in a steady rhythm. Leo's bones and muscles ached from the exertion of giving into his lustful desires, but he had no regrets.

Lying there, he replayed it all in his head over and over again, smiling and blushing at the same time. Sexually, he'd only ever been with Tyler. When Tyler had flirted with him in the nightclub, Leo thought he'd won the lottery and found a prize worth winning. It had hurt like hell when he learnt Tyler had a serious girlfriend of three years. He lost count the number of times he'd heard Tyler say he was going to end it with Beth, but he was still stupid enough to believe his excuses. Or was it desperation? Loneliness? *'Oh it's not the right time…She's really down…Her cat died…She lost her job…I'll tell her, I promise.'*

He hadn't had time to think about the last time he'd seen Tyler, but as he lay, basking in the warmth of his new lover, he remembered the cruel sting of Tyler's derogatory words, how furious Lucas had been, and how he had to stop the demon from doing the unthinkable. He was surprised at how little he cared about it now. There were no feelings of resentment towards Tyler, merely pity and sadness at how lost the guy was. Leo knew what it felt like to be lost, but he also knew the overwhelming happiness and contentment of being found, and a part of him wished that for Tyler.

Lucas coughed beside him, pulling him out of his thoughts. He cast a glance over his shoulder to see the demon's eyes were still closed. Deciding he'd been lying long enough, he began to slide out of bed, trying his best to be as delicate as possible. He got one foot onto the floor before being tugged back under the duvet.

"Where do you think you're creeping off to?"

The deep husky tone caused Leo to grin. "I was going—"

"I know where you were going," Lucas interrupted, wrapping himself around Leo. "You got what you wanted, and you're sneaking off so you don't have to face the shame of what happened last night."

Leo could hear the smile in Lucas' voice and played along. "I've got no shame about what we did."

"Well, you should. It's probably illegal!"

Musical laughter filled the room, and Leo's heart swelled. He didn't think he'd ever get used to the sound. "Illegal? Oh no! I didn't know. That's it!" Leo exclaimed, springing out of Lucas' arms and the duvet. "We can't do it ever again!"

"That's what you think!" Lucas growled, throwing the covers off and catching him around the middle.

Leo giggled as he was lifted into the air and thrown back down onto the bed. His giggling stopped abruptly when he became trapped beneath a wall of tanned muscle. "We can't...I have to get back to Daniel," he protested weakly as azure eyes rapidly melted his resolve. "He might wonder where I've been all night,"

"It's still very early," Lucas replied with a wicked grin.

Leo looked worried. "What if he had another nightmare and woke up in the middle of the night?"

"When was the last time he had a nightmare?"

"Two weeks ago."

"That would mean that Ela's dream catcher is working, yes?"

"Yes, but—"

"How many times have you been up before him and let him sleep in while you've gone to get breakfast?"

"Loads."

"And when you get back from breakfast, has he ever asked where you've been?"

"Never."

"And what time does he usually wake up?"

"Around nine thirty."

"Exactly," Lucas said, glancing at the clock on the bedside table. "It's only six fifteen."

"Good point," Leo said, letting his hands trail all the way down Lucas' back until they came to rest on his muscular rear. The demon growled again and gave him a look that made him tremble in anticipation.

"I'm so fucking lucky," Lucas declared before crushing his lips against Leo's.

Three hours later, Leo had pulled on his clothes, minus his torn hoodie, and was tiptoeing along the corridor to his bedroom door. Cautiously, he reached for the handle while holding his breath and gritting his teeth, praying Daniel would be asleep. He didn't want to explain where he'd spent the night, and why he was wandering about the Cathedral topless. The door didn't make a sound as he pushed it open and stepped carefully into the room.

He glanced into the corner where Daniel's bed was and saw the duvet moving up and down. He exhaled with relief while closing the door. There'd be no inquisition. He quietly gathered up clean clothing and a towel before locking himself in the bathroom.

Once in the bathroom, he studied his reflection in the full length mirror, marvelling at how well he looked considering he'd hardly slept the night before.

'I've been waiting forever…to see your face emerge from the light, to save me again…I have loved you for over four millennia…You just didn't know it until now.'

He replayed Lucas' words in his head and beamed. He'd never felt more alive. His mind, body, and spirit had been changed forever after the encounter with the pure demon, and the irony wasn't lost on him. Lucas had awoken something in him, and it was something that he swore to embrace. Whatever it was rushed around his body like an electric current carrying feelings of euphoria, lust, calmness, peace, and deep spirituality.

Images of the night's events flashed through his mind as he stood under the water, ensuring the grin never left his face. Even as he dried himself off, he was smiling and revelling in the recollections of the love making session. While pulling on a pair of black jeans and a black hoody, his inner voice spoke to him.

'Right you, don't get too carried away. He's a demon, remember?'

Leo rolled his eyes at his reflection as he styled his hair. There was no way he was going to mess this one up by listening to his subconscious fears and doubts. He thought he'd been in love with Tyler; now he knew he most definitely hadn't. Whatever he'd felt for Tyler was long gone and had been eclipsed by an overwhelming force. It was deep, and it was powerful, and it was real.

"Lucas," he said out loud, slipping his feet into a pair of converse shoes. Saying the name gave him goose bumps. All he wanted to do was go back to the demon's room and spend the entire day tangled up in him, but he knew he had a sacred duty to another young man. With one last fuss over his hair, he shut the light off and left the bathroom.

Standing by Daniel's bedside, he watched the sleeping boy for a moment and felt a different kind of love touch his heart. Since he'd become Daniel's unofficial guardian, their relationship had deepened immensely in the short time they'd spent together, and it was clear to everybody that the boy viewed Leo as a father figure. It made Leo think about the love he felt for the youngster, and he couldn't help wondering if it was the same as a father's love. Did it measure the same even though Daniel wasn't his son? Did it mean the love was purer because Daniel wasn't his own flesh and blood yet he loved him like he was? Leo knew it really didn't matter; love was love.

After a few more moments of watching Daniel, Leo finally roused the sleeping boy.

"Wake up, sleepy head," he said softly. "Breakfast is ready."

A groan escaped from under the duvet as Daniel stirred. "I don't want breakfast. It's too early," he murmured sleepily. "Let me sleep a bit longer."

Leo gave Daniel another nudge. "Not a chance! You know how Mrs Ellen feels about anybody skipping a meal, and who will get a tea towel across the head? Me!"

"Okay, okay! I'm up." Daniel emerged from the thick duvet and sat up. He let out a massive yawn and stretched out his entire body. "Why do I have to get up early if I'm not going to school?" he asked, rubbing the sleep out of his eyes.

"You know why," Leo said with a smile. "I can't let you stay in bed all morning."

"Why not? Lucas does it!"

"You're only eleven and already you're acting like a teenager." Leo shook his head in feigned dismay. "And Lucas does not lie in bed all day."

"Then how come I never see him until the afternoon?" Daniel asked, narrowing his eyes.

Leo shrugged. "He's out of the Cathedral in the mornings."

"Doing what?"

"I don't know, you'll have to ask him."

"Okay, I will," Daniel said with another yawn. "What's for breakfast?"

"I've no idea. Why don't you get yourself showered and dressed, and meet me in the dining room?"

"Cool. What are we doing today anyway?"

"Depends," Leo answered, watching the boy as he collected his clothes for the day. "I haven't checked in with Ela and Cornelius yet. I have to tell them about my final trial last night."

Daniel turned his head, his eyes sparkling with interest. "That was last night? What happened?"

"I fought Lucas."

Daniel blinked twice. "Lucas?"

"Yup."

"Did you win?"

"Of course I did," Leo lied. "Shower first, then I'll tell you."

"You're a terrible liar," Daniel chuckled, wandering around the room in only his boxer shorts. "I won't be long. I can't wait to hear about this fight."

When Daniel walked towards the bathroom, Leo's eyes were drawn to the base of the boy's spine. There was a mark there, three inches long and an inch wide, which could easily have been mistaken for a purple birthmark, but he knew better. It was the mark of the Power: the first and last letters of the Greek alphabet, Alpha and Omega. They'd entwined together in a beautifully intricate symbol that branded this child as divine. His eyes followed it until Daniel entered the bathroom and closed the door.

Picking himself up from the bed, he visited the kitchen where he found Mrs Ellen tipping flour into a large plastic bowl while humming along to the radio.

"Nothing like a bit of Dolly Parton to start the day," he said as a way of announcing himself.

Mrs Ellen glanced up from the bowl. "Ah, good morning to you, Leo. How are you, son?"

"Fine thanks, Mrs E. You?" He walked to the fridge and took out a carton of orange juice.

"I'm grand," Mrs Ellen said, abandoning the bowl and retrieving two tall glasses from the cupboard under the nearest dresser. "You'll be having breakfast, so you will."

"Bring it on, I'm starving," Leo replied, nudging the fridge door closed with his elbow.

"That's what I like to hear! It's pancakes today, so it is," Mrs Ellen said, placing the glasses onto the worktop nearest Leo.

"Nice one. Do you have raspberry jam?" he asked while opening the carton and tipping the orange juice into the glasses.

"I certainly do, homemade and everything," she said proudly, returning to her bowl and picking it up with both hands. "Now, get yourself a comfy seat in the dining room, and I'll bring them through when they're ready." She shuffled over to the cooker where a cast iron girdle was heating on the Aga.

"Thanks, Mrs E."

"You're welcome," she replied, stopping suddenly as if she'd only just noticed him. Cocking her head to one side, she pursed her lips together. "Leo, is everything okay?"

"Yeah, why?" he asked as he returned the carton to the fridge.

"You look...different."

"I didn't get much sleep last night, I probably look like death warmed up," he joked.

"No...no that's not it. You look quite the opposite, so you do, glowing and everything."

"Oh, I don't know about that," he chuckled, walking back to the counter where the two glasses rested. "Maybe it's just the lighting in here."

Mrs Ellen straightened her head and spooned out the pancake batter, dumping it skilfully onto the girdle. It hissed. "Yes, maybe that's it," she said, dropping a second spoonful of batter onto the hot metal plate.

Leo picked up the two glasses and made his way carefully to the kitchen door. He was almost through the threshold when Mrs Ellen piped up from her pancakes.

"Oh, and Leo?"

"Yeah?" he replied, stopping and glancing back.

"It's so nice that you and Lucas are speaking again."

"How did you—"

"Just a hunch," she said with a shrug, a smile playing at the corners of her mouth.

He felt his face flush but laughed all the same. Mrs Ellen went back to her pancakes without another word while he moved through to the dining room. He'd just sat down when the door swung open. Daniel came into the room sporting his trademark blue hat, his damp fringe poking out from underneath.

"That was a quick shower, Dan the Man. You usually take hours."

Daniel pulled out the chair to the right of Leo and climbed into it. "I remembered it was pancakes for breakfast when I was getting into the shower, so I rushed. Mrs E's pancakes are awesome."

"Yup, they certainly are," Leo nodded in agreement. "She has raspberry jam too." He laughed when Daniel's eyes widened with excitement.

"Score!"

Leo handed the boy a glass of orange juice. "Here you go."

"Cheers," Daniel said, taking the glass and putting it to his mouth. "Tell me about your fight with Lucas."

"Not much to tell really," Leo replied with a shrug, smiling when Daniel took a huge gulp of juice. "It was in the courtyard, we fought for a little while, and he beat me."

"Was it close?"

"Nope, little man, it wasn't close. I kicked your teacher's ass."

Lucas came swanning into the room from the lounge and made his way around the table with a dazzling smile on his face. Leo's eyes followed the demon intently, taking in the tight white t-shirt and snug fitting stonewash denim jeans that made the demon's thighs and rear more appealing than usual.

"Hey Lucas," Daniel said brightly before taking another gulp of juice.

"Morning, little man," Lucas replied, hooking a shabby brown boot around the leg of the chair opposite Leo and pulling it out from beneath the table. After sitting down, he reached over to Daniel, and the pair of them bumped their fists together. "So, what's for breakfast?"

"Pancakes."

Lucas punched the air. "Score!"

Daniel giggled while Leo rolled his eyes.

"Isn't it a little early for eye rolling?" Lucas asked, smirking and raising an eyebrow.

"When it comes to over excited Americans, it's *never* too early," Leo teased, using the glass of orange juice to conceal his own smirk. "Sleep well?"

Lucas looked thoroughly amused by the question and fell into a thoughtful silence, his expression gradually becoming more sincere. "The best sleep I've had in four thousand years."

Daniel's mouth fell open. "Four thousand years?"

"Lucas is being dramatic, Daniel. Don't listen to him."

"Yeah, I'm trying to steal Leo's crown as biggest drama queen," Lucas grinned.

"Good luck," Daniel joked, ducking as Leo attempted to swat him.

At that moment, Mrs Ellen came into the room carrying a large silver tray containing two plates of pancakes, a mountain of toast, a jar of homemade raspberry jam, two knives, two forks, and a small pile of napkins.

"Morning, boys," she said to Daniel and Lucas, placing the tray between the two before lifting the plates off and setting them on the table. "Can I get you anything else?"

"No thanks, this is perfect Mrs E," Leo replied and picked up a knife and fork. He handed them to Daniel before taking a set for himself.

"Would you like something to eat, Lucas?" Mrs Ellen asked as she took the napkins off the tray and sat them neatly on the table.

"No thanks, I've eaten already," Lucas replied.

"Right you are. Enjoy your pancakes." Mrs Ellen picked up the empty tray and bustled out of the dining room without another word.

Leo began devouring the pancakes immediately and couldn't help moaning with pleasure when he took the first bite. "Oh my god," he murmured, closing his eyes and savouring the taste. "These are…there are no words!"

"Best pancakes ever!" Daniel exclaimed before cramming in another forkful.

For a brief moment, there was silence except for the scraping noises of knives and forks against plates, and the sounds of chewing.

"What?" Lucas said, looking at Daniel.

As he chewed, Daniel's jaw moved rather slowly as he stared at Lucas in quiet contemplation. "How come I've never seen you eat?"

Lucas' face split into a wide smile. "You've seen me eat before, little man."

"No, I haven't. Not a single thing," Daniel said, stuffing a forkful of pancake into his mouth and looking to Leo for support.

Leo's stomach knotted. They'd agreed to keep Daniel in the dark about Lucas' demon side because they didn't know how he'd react. After all, Lucas was one of the things that had killed the boy's parents, and it would surely be too much for him to take in. The last thing they needed was for Daniel to freak out and run away.

There was also the small matter of Daniel not knowing that the Power of creation was living inside of him, bound to his soul until his heart stopped beating. Leo sensed the time for telling Daniel absolutely everything was close at hand, and it was a feeling he couldn't quite shake. Again he wondered, 'How do you tell a person they are, in essence, God?'

'With great fucking difficulty' his inner voice answered helpfully.

"Have you ever seen him eat?" Daniel asked Leo.

"Lucas doesn't like to eat in front of people," Leo lied, casting an apologetic look in Lucas' direction.

"That's a bit weird," Daniel said matter-of-factly.

"Well, what do you expect? Lucas is a weirdo," Leo chuckled.

"Might I remind both of you that I've saved your asses on more than one occasion?" Lucas huffed. "Next time, I'll not be so quick to save you from the demons or Templars or whatever other nasty is out to get you."

"Ha, we don't need you anymore," Daniel said through a mouthful of pancake. "Leo will annihilate them with his magic, won't you Leo?"

"Damn right I will," Leo agreed, banging his fist off the table. "I'll send them back to hell where they belong." He bit his lip as soon as he'd said the words.

"That's exactly where they belong, and I'll be glad to help you send them there," Lucas said with a smile. "Now, both of you shut up and eat your breakfast."

Leo felt someone nudging his leg under the table. He stole a glance at Lucas who was gazing at him with warm eyes. The nudge was a clear indication that Lucas wasn't offended. Feeling relieved, Leo nudged back in gratitude before continuing to eat his pancakes in silence as instructed.

After eating every bit of his breakfast, Daniel dropped his knife and fork onto the empty plate. "Mrs Ellen is a genius," he announced.

"Remember to thank her," Leo said as he scraped the last morsels of pancake onto his fork and demolished them. He set his fork down and reached for a slice of toast.

"I will." Daniel replied. He drained the last of his orange juice before leaning back in his chair. As he patted his swollen stomach, his face lit up. "Check it out, I'm having a food baby."

Lucas' musical laugh filled the dining room. "Are you sure it's just one?"

Daniel, tickled by the comment, joined in the hilarity. "Maybe it's twins?"

Leo had just brought the freshly buttered slice of toast to his mouth when his hand froze, and he was hit with a barrage of emotion. Here he was sitting at a table and eating breakfast with the two people he cared most for, feeling like nothing else in the world mattered. He'd seen this image many times before but only in his dreams, yet here it was: reality. When had the heavy unbearable weight of impending doom, the one he'd felt for weeks, been lifted from his shoulders? Now that he'd noticed its absence, he didn't care. He let the contentment and the sheer perfection of the moment wash over him.

Was this what it felt like to be normal, to belong to a 'normal' family? He found it hard to remember because he'd never really had the opportunity of knowing what belonging felt like, and it was something he'd hungered for. It had been ripped away from him in early childhood, and most of the memories of his mum and dad had faded away as time had marched relentlessly on. And now, sitting with Lucas and Daniel, he was getting the first taste of what it was like to belong to a family. Images of school runs, homework, shopping trips, birthday parties, swimming, and many Christmases together flashed vividly through his mind.

'Looks great, right? But are you forgetting something? Newsflash: You don't want this!' Leo's inner voice stated coldly. *'Remember how society hates anything remotely out of the norm? You won't be able to handle the potential bullying of your son when the other kids find out he's got two dads. You've been down this path before, and you know there is nothing for you at the end, so snap out of it!'*

"Leo? Are you alright?"

Leo blinked, and the blissful family images were replaced by Lucas' concerned face staring at him from across the table.

"You haven't said anything for five minutes."

"What? Oh...yeah, I'm fine. Just zoned out."

Lucas looked at him with curious eyes. "Where did you go?"

"Nowhere worth mentioning," he answered with a sad smile. Lucas' gaze never wavered, the curiosity still burning brightly in his eyes. The demon, to Leo's relief, didn't press the matter any further.

"I suppose we better get this lot cleared up," Lucas said finally, standing up and gathering the empty plates and glasses. "Poor Mrs Ellen, she never gets a minute to herself these days. She's always cooking or cleaning for the Elect. It's just as well most of them have got their own cooking facilities in the Haven."

"Haven?" The name was completely lost on Leo. "What's the Haven?"

"It's where they all sleep," Daniel chimed in as Lucas clattered plates and cutlery together. "You know the building in the courtyard that's straight across from the Cathedral?"

"Yeah."

"The Haven is hidden underneath it. I've been in loads of times."

"You have?"

"Of course. Where do you think I go when I call on Cameron, Ross and Felicity?" Daniel asked incredulously. "I told you this weeks ago."

"Oh." Leo felt stupid. "You never told me it was a massive underground motel," he said, trying to recapture some dignity. "I thought you were calling on them from the building itself."

Daniel looked very amused. "Did you really think over a thousand people were living and sleeping in that small building?"

Leo shifted sheepishly in his chair.

"It was built over seventy years ago during World War Two," Lucas explained, grinning at Leo's embarrassment. "It's quite vast actually, six floors deep. The floors are identical and each one has twenty five rooms that sleep eight people, four shared kitchens, and four shared bathrooms. It's not the most luxurious, but I've stayed in much worse."

"I can't believe you thought they all stayed in that one small building!" Daniel crowed.

"I can't believe they've let you teach for so long," Lucas teased, picking up the dirty dishes and walking to the door.

"Hey," Leo protested, folding his arms and scowling. "I'm not at my best in the mornings. I take ages to wake up properly." The other two laughed at his weak excuse, and their laughter infected him. He joined in, shaking his head despairingly at his own stupidity.

The demon paused at the door and turned to face Leo. "I've got no complaints about your performance in the mornings," he said with a wink. "I'd say you're pretty much perfect." His eyes twinkled playfully for a second, and then he was gone.

When the door Lucas walked through closed, the one at the opposite side of the room opened. Ela came into the dining room followed by Cornelius and a man who Leo had seen a few times around the Cathedral and knew to be an Elect. They all wore severe expressions, and the vibes they were giving off killed the jubilant mood that had existed moments before. Ela smiled briefly at him as she swept gracefully across the room in a turquoise dress, long and sleeveless, that flowed behind her. She sat down on the chair Lucas had been sitting on while Cornelius hobbled to the seat at the head of the table. He placed his walking stick across his lap and clasped his wrinkled hands together before resting them upon the table top.

Leo took in the heavy bloodshot eyes and the pale complexion of the priest. It was clear he hadn't slept the night before. He remembered the first time they'd met. The vibrant energy Cornelius had back then was gone, and it was obvious the month's events and the pressure of keeping Daniel safe had taken its toll.

The man Leo didn't know, who looked to be in his early forties, stood behind Ela and smiled over at Daniel. With a mop of thick black hair, big hazel eyes and chiselled features, he was conventionally handsome. His red chequered shirt was rolled up at the sleeves, exposing hairy and muscular forearms while his dark blue jeans showed of solid thighs. At that moment, Leo wondered if all the members of the Elect were beautiful because every single one of them so far had been stunning. They might not have reached the standard set by Lucas, but in the league of mere mortals, they ranked high.

Cornelius cleared his throat. "I have news."

"Let me guess, you've won the lottery?" Leo was perhaps more sarcastic than he'd intended to be, but the negativity oozing from Cornelius was making him nervous.

"Daniel, I have arranged for you to visit the Haven," Cornelius told the boy. "Cameron's father is giving some of the children a history lesson, and I think it might be of interest to you. I believe you already know John. He'll escort you to the Haven right now."

"Hang on a minute," Leo said.

"We don't have a minute," the priest interjected. "This is of the utmost urgency. For now, he'll go to the Haven where it's safe. John is one of the strongest members of our order, so Daniel will be well protected."

Leo knew there was no point in arguing with Cornelius; it was clear the old man's mind was made up. "You'd better go dude," he told Daniel. "I'll catch you later."

To everybody's surprise, Daniel slumped back in his chair, folded his arms, and glowered. He responded with a one word answer which he spoke with impressive conviction. "No."

Leo felt every eye in the room land on him, and he knew exactly what they were thinking. He'd had the exact same thoughts himself when other people's children were being unruly in public. He'd glared at those parents who struggled to get their offspring to behave, judging them for failing to control their squealing little brats. He now knew how the flustered parents had felt; karma was a bitch. He kept his own eyes on Daniel who was doing his best to look as defiant as humanly possible.

"Dan, it's only for a little while. I'll come and get you when—"

"I'm not going! I want to stay and listen."

"Out of the question," Cornelius stated emphatically. "There are important matters to be discussed, and it doesn't concern young boys."

"If it's about the demons who murdered my parents then it does concern me!" Daniel retorted fiercely.

Leo's mouth fell open. Cornelius' jaw tightened, and his hands, which were still clasped together, trembled while Ela and John stared at the boy with nothing but sympathy.

Daniel's angry eyes burned into Cornelius. "Well, is it about them?"

At that moment, Lucas re-entered the room and answered Daniel's question. "Yes," he said before walking over to Leo and standing by his side.

"Lucas," Leo warned.

"I want to know!" Daniel cried.

"I agree with you, little man. We have to talk about this now."

Leo jumped to his feet and slammed his hands on the table. "No, we bloody well don't!" he roared, his eyes flashing with anger. Everyone looked at him, shocked by his outburst. "We agreed not to tell him anything until it was the right time."

"I know, but come on," Lucas said, holding out his hands, "will there ever be a right time?"

Leo didn't have an answer to the question and found himself hanging his head and closing his eyes. It was hard to believe that only moments ago, despite the desperate situation surrounding Daniel, he'd been content and happy without a single care in the world. All that had changed in an instant, and now the weight of the world was pressing down on him again, doing its best to smother and suffocate him.

"You're not going to tell that child anything, Lucas, and that's an order!" Cornelius snapped, raising his hands into the air and slamming them on the table like Leo had done moments before.

"I don't take orders from you," Lucas growled.

Cornelius responded with a look of hostility.

"Tell me!" Daniel whined.

"Can you all just shut up for a minute?" Leo shouted. The room fell into a reluctant quiet. "I need to think."

You're going to tell Daniel eventually, so you might as well tell him now. He's waited over a month, and in that time he's only ever asked about it twice. And you promised after all.

His inner voice made sense. Daniel was going to find out everything at some point, so what was the point in putting it off even longer? He found himself nodding slowly.

"Okay," Leo said, opening his eyes and exhaling loudly. He sat down and was immediately ambushed by pleading blue eyes. He knew that he couldn't deny his boy the answers any longer. "What do you want to know?"

"Why did my mum and dad die?" The question sprang from Daniel's mouth like a bird that had been cooped up in a small cage for days and had suddenly been freed.

"They died protecting you from the demons who came to your house that night," Leo answered steadily.

"Why did they come to my house?"

Leo swallowed. "I told you already, remember? They came for you."

"Why?"

Suddenly, Cornelius was on his feet. "This is absurd! He is far too young to know!"

"Cornelius," Ela said, speaking for the first time since entering the room. Her tone was firm yet calming. "Be at peace." The Grandmaster earned herself a contemptuous look from Cornelius, but he didn't argue and returned to his seat. "Thank you. Leo, please continue."

Leo wasn't sure whether to thank Ela or berate her. Now that he'd begun answering Daniel's difficult questions, he'd have welcomed Cornelius' objections. The pressure of having to tell a young boy that his parents were murdered and mutilated because they wanted to kill *him* was making him perspire heavily. A bead of sweat fell from his forehead and hit the table.

"Leo, why did they come for me?" Daniel repeated.

"You have something they want."

Daniel nodded. "Yeah, you told me that. What is it?"

Leo lifted his head and looked at the others. They were all watching him expectantly except Cornelius who refused to meet his eye. There was no turning back now. With a huge sigh, Leo began to explain. "It's you, or rather, something that's *in* you. Inside of you lies something very powerful, and the demons want it. We call it the Power."

"The Power?" The frustration lifted from Daniel's face and was replaced by a mask of intrigue. He unfolded his arms and rested them on the table.

"Yeah, it's like a…" Leo hesitated, struggling to find the right words. He wanted to deliver the news in a way Daniel would understand without being overwhelmed. In the end, he realised it was useless. There was no easy way, so he decided to blurt it out. "Basically you have the Power of G—"

The sound of a chair scraping across the stone floor drowned out Leo's voice, and he whipped his head around to glare at the culprit: Cornelius. The old man was on his feet again, and his eyes were set on Ela.

"Someone approaches, they've passed through the barrier."

Another chair scraped across the stone floor as Ela shot to her feet. Leo had considered the possibility that Cornelius was lying in order to prevent Daniel from knowing the truth, however, Ela and Lucas' faces told a different story.

"Demon?" Lucas asked urgently.

Cornelius closed his eyes and inhaled deeply. "No, it's human…more than one…ten, maybe fifteen…main entrance."

Leo rose from his chair and pulled a fearful looking Daniel to his feet.

"Templars. They know he's here," Ela surmised calmly. "Lucas."

Lucas became a blur as he sped into the lounge, leaving the door swaying gently in his wake.

"Woah!" Daniel exclaimed, staring open mouthed at the door Lucas had vanished through. "How did he do that?"

"Lucas is a demon," Leo said.

Daniel's eyes bulged. "A what?"

"A demon," Ela interrupted. "He used to be evil, but now he's good. It's a long and fascinating story that must wait for another time. John, take Leo and Daniel to the Haven and set up guard. Send the Elite to me at once."

The aura of calmness radiating from her was extraordinary; Leo could feel it. It seeped into his body and soothed, allowing him to clear his mind and focus on protecting Daniel. He balled his hands into fists as he felt the divine magic stirring within.

"Stay close," he told Daniel as they moved beside John.

"Nobody gets in or out until I tell you," Ela told John. "Send all the children down to the sixth floor and lock the d—"

An audible gasp caused Ela to stop in mid-sentence. Cornelius, who was still leaning on the table, had paled even more.

Leo's chest tightened, and he knew beyond any doubt that whatever Cornelius was going to say was not going to be pleasant. His suspicions were confirmed when the old man opened his eyes and focused them on Daniel.

"What is it, Cornelius? Tell us!" Ela urged.

"It's her," Cornelius replied, his voice carrying a myriad of emotions.

Leo didn't need to ask who he meant by 'her'. He felt a tug at his sleeve and glanced down to see Daniel gazing up at him with fearful eyes. He automatically wrapped a protective arm around the boy and drew him close.

"Are you certain?" Ela asked, still sounding calm.

Her tone also conveyed strength and fearlessness which was a massive security for Leo and helped to calm his own rising fear. Cornelius, on the other hand, was a stark contrast to the powerful woman whose title was Grandmaster.

With shaking hands, the priest reached for his walking stick and placed the end on the floor with a resounding clunk. "I'm certain. I can feel her presence. We need to get the boy out of here now," Cornelius said as he stepped away from the table and shuffled towards Daniel.

"John, go and alert the others," Ela commanded. "Send me the Elite at once, and hide the children. May God be with you."

"And you, Grandmaster." John bowed his head and was gone.

"We have to get Daniel to my chambers immediately," Cornelius said hurriedly. "There is a secret passage that leads out of the Cathedral."

"Hang on a minute," Leo demanded. "What about Lucas? Somebody needs to help him fight that bitch!"

"I'll go," Ela said at once, striding over to him and grasping him by the shoulders. "Leo, you must concentrate on protecting Daniel. He's the most important thing, and everyone else is insignificant. Do you understand?"

Leo nodded slowly. "Yes."

"Good. Go now, before she co—"

A blinding flash lit up the room, and Ela crumpled to the floor.

A petite feminine figure stood in the door frame opposite Leo, her right arm extended and a cruel twisted smile on her crimson coloured lips. Thin tendrils of smoke snaked around the china doll hand, the result of the magical blast she'd hit Ela with.

"Too late, Grandmaster," Morgana chuckled, her grey emotionless eyes fixed on Daniel. "She's already here."

Chapter 19
The Return of the Templars

"A ring, a ring o' roses, a pocket full of posies," Morgana sang without emotion, her sinister stare frozen on Daniel who peeked at her from behind Leo. "Atishoo, atishoo, we all fall—"

With stunning speed, she flung her hand forward and unleashed a thin stream of forked lightning. Cornelius didn't even have time to scream before the electrical blue force hit him. He buckled and collapsed to the floor like Ela.

"Down." Morgana finished the nursery rhyme, and a huge grin darkened her porcelain features. "My favourite children's rhyme," she said. "It was about the plague, did you know? It was such a wickedly deserved affliction on humanity." She didn't take her eyes off Daniel who was now staring in horror at Ela and Cornelius' unconscious bodies. "Don't worry, little one, they're not dead yet."

Leo's eyes flickered to the nearest door, the one leading to the corridor where the kitchen lay.

"Don't be stupid," Morgana said, shifting her eyes from Daniel to Leo. "You'd be dead before you could take one step."

"Really?" Leo replied confidently, surprising himself and Morgana. He couldn't show fear; it was a weakness which monsters like Morgana were skilled in exploiting. It was then he realised that he wasn't actually scared, or rather, not as scared as he expected he would be. There was a small bit of fear, but that was only from the thought of what would happen to Daniel if Morgana got her hands on him.

Morgana laughed coldly. "I don't blame you. I'd run from me if I were you."

"Do people normally run from you?" Leo asked in his most arrogant voice.

The humour lines disappeared from Morgana's face instantly, replaced by an expression far scarier than any demonic visage. "Pure demons flee from me," she boasted, her hands twitching by her sides. She took a step forward.

"Is that so?" Leo said with as much indifference as he could muster, his eye drawn to her hands. They had twitched again only this time there had been sparks of blue. "I find that hard to believe. I've seen a pure demon in action, and he was much scarier than you."

"You doubt me?" The humour returned to Morgana's face. "Maybe I'll kill your demon companion after I'm finished with the Power, then you'll see for yourself."

"I'd like to see you try—"

Intuitively, he knew the attack was coming. When the electric blue lightning sizzled through the air towards him, he summoned an energy shield simply by willing it. The lightning struck the invisible barrier causing the air to ripple before it fizzled into nothingness. He kept his face passive as Morgana gave one of her hollow chuckles.

"Impressive. Somebody's been practising," she sang, bowing her head slightly.

"I'd be careful if I were you," Leo warned, while all the time being aware of Daniel cowering behind him.

"And why would that be?"

"You said it yourself. The Seers told you I'd be your equal," he said, reminding her of their very first conversation.

"The thing with Seers is, more times than not, they get it wrong." Morgana raised both hands and released a double stream of lightning.

Before his training, Leo would have expected Morgana's magical onslaught to hit his shield like a sledgehammer and rip his solar plexus to bits, but there was nothing, not even a twinge of pain. Ela and Cornelius had been expert mentors, and he was not afraid.

The electrical bolts struck, and they engulfed his energy barrier, lighting it up like a brilliant blue sun. Watching the erratic pattern of the lightning from behind his shield, he observed the blue forks dancing around the sphere and marvelled at their beauty. It was then he heard a choir of voices in his head. They spoke their words all at once, words that Lucas and Noah had spoken to him, but ones he'd never understood until now.

'She can use Elect magic, but it's tainted...She takes her magic to a dark place where it loses its divinity...You're pure...Yours is the gift to change.'

Slowly, he reached out and pressed his hand against the shield, and the lightning was drawn to his palm like a magnet. He looked at Morgana. She'd stopped the flow of lightning and was surveying him through narrowed eyes.

"You're going to have to do a lot better than that, Elect scum!" she spat venomously.

The green of Leo's eyes began to sparkle. He could feel Morgana's energy mixing with his own, and the longer he held it in his palm, the more he could 'see' it. Her energy was darker than dark. It was tainted, and it burned like acid. It writhed and wrestled against his will like a blue flamed viper, relentlessly sinking its fangs into his energy force. Her once divine energy was angry and full of hate. It despised itself for what it had been forced to do. It hadn't been created to do evil, but it had been defiled and abused, conjured to perform countless atrocities. He knew what he had to do, what he *could* do.

His own pure and celestial magic overpowered the evil within Morgana's corrupted energy. In a split second, the lightning that'd gathered in his palm no longer shone an intense electric blue but glowed a dazzling emerald green. The anger and hate living in Morgana's magic had been transmuted into divine energy, and he was determined to show her the magnitude of God's power.

"Give me your best shot," she said, attempting to sneer but not quite pulling it off.

Leo detected the concern creeping into her voice and smiled inwardly. She'd felt the energy of her own magic being changed, and judging by her reaction, she clearly hadn't experienced such a transmutation before. He knew he had the advantage.

Within Leo's energy shield, which had become invisible again, the streaming tendrils of lightning had formed into a football sized orb in front of his chest. They danced over and under and in between each other in their spherical form, emitting a steady humming noise that was pleasing to his ears.

"Have you thought," he asked softly, "that it's maybe you who should be running away?"

A terrifying resolve swept across Morgana's face. "The time for talking is over," she stated, twisting her hands in circular motions and creating a small cyclone of black energy around each one. "One for you, one for the brat."

"Where's the one for Lucas standing behind you?" Leo asked her calmly. In her panic, Morgana spun around to be confronted with nothing but fresh air giving him the perfect opportunity to make a pushing motion with his hand.

The lightning orb became an enormous green bullet that streaked through the air, slamming into its target's back and exploding like a firework on impact. There was a terrible shriek of fury followed by the sound of snapping wood.

"Holy shit!" Daniel cried, gawping open mouthed at Morgana who lay motionless on top of the shattered remains of a dining room chair.

"Hey! Watch your language young man," Leo scolded.

"Did you kill her?"

"Of course I haven't ki—"

The sound of running footsteps interrupted him. A burly Templar, dressed in biker leathers, came thundering into the room, crossbow in hand. Stopping suddenly, he studied the scene he'd stumbled upon. His eyes flew to Leo and then to Daniel before he noticed the three unconscious bodies on the floor. Recognition set in when he saw Morgana, and his hostile gaze instantly turned to Daniel.

"The Power!" he grunted in a Neanderthal manner, lifting the crossbow in the boy's direction.

The lightning had struck well before the Templar's finger could find the trigger on his weapon. Leo continued to stream the lightning into the Templar's strong body even after he was on the ground convulsing and screaming in agony. Leo was furious that the Templar had dared to point his weapon in Daniel's direction let alone fire it. It was only when he began to smell burning flesh that he stopped. He cast his blazing green eyes at Daniel.

"Are you okay?"

Daniel nodded. "Yes," he whimpered, staring back at Leo with a mixture of awe and uncertainty.

It was only then Leo realised that Daniel had never seen him use magic at this capacity before and wasn't surprised to see the boy looking shell-shocked. Leo's eyes were otherworldly balls of emerald flame, and his voice, although recognisable as his own, sounded as if there were other voices, both masculine and feminine, mixed in with it. The overall effect was both haunting and eerie, and he couldn't blame Daniel for freaking out.

He took the boy's hand in his own. "Dan, it's okay. It's me."

"I know, it's just…your eyes, they're like green fire."

Leo smiled. "I know. I don't even know why or how, they just go like this when I'm using magic." Daniel went to ask another question but Leo cut him off. "Questions later. We need to get you somewhere safe."

"But—"

"No buts! We need to get you out—"

"Morgana!"

When Daniel spoke her name, Leo stood to his full height and looked to where the fallen Templar queen was lying. She was stirring.

'Kill her.'

A coldness shrouded his soul as he heard the words of his inner voice. He wasn't ready to take a human life, not yet. If he killed her, then he'd be changed forever, and that was a path he wasn't prepared to venture down anytime soon.

"What are we going to do?" Daniel asked urgently.

Without hesitation, he gently pulled on the boy's hand and led him to the corridor where the kitchen was.

"What about Ela and Cornelius? Shouldn't we go back for them?" Daniel asked between shallow breaths. "What if she kills them?"

Leo had considered this, but the Grandmaster had told him the most important thing was to protect Daniel. In his heart, he knew Ela and Cornelius would be fine; they were the most powerful members of the Elect, and in spite of their age, he was confident they'd recover. It was fortunate for Morgana that she'd been able to attack without warning or it might have been a very different outcome for the Templar leader. She'd said herself they weren't dead, and he doubted she would waste any time dealing with them when she regained consciousness.

"She won't kill them," he assured Daniel. "That's not why she's here. Lucas will help Ela and Cornelius, so don't worry." Even as he was saying it, he knew he was clutching at straws as nobody could predict what Morgana would or wouldn't do, and he had no idea what state Lucas was in. "Man, that felt good to kick her ass back there!" he added.

Daniel giggled nervously but didn't say anything. His little hand had a cast iron grip on Leo's, and his head and eyes had become fawn like, darting around to scan the surroundings for predators. "Where are we going?" he asked eventually.

"The kitchen. We need to make sure Mrs Ellen is safe."

Grey walls blurred past as Leo hustled Daniel along the chilly corridor. Every ten seconds or so, Leo glanced anxiously behind to ensure danger wasn't following. So far, so good. Although it was mid-morning, an array of medieval looking torches hanging along the walls lit their way. A lot of the corridors were constantly gloomy and dim due to the lack of windows in the building's design, but he didn't think it was a bad thing as it added character and ambience. As they neared the kitchen, a beam of daylight spilled into the corridor from the partially open door and cut through the gloominess.

Leo stopped at the door and peeked into the bright room. Daniel, not thinking of any of the potential dangers, swept in front of him and reached out to push the door open. In an instant, Leo's hand was around the boy's bony wrist and tugging him away. Daniel went to protest, but Leo silenced him by pressing a finger to his lips.

"We don't know who's in there," Leo whispered. "It's probably Mrs E, but it could just as easily be a Templar. I'll go first."

He gently moved Daniel out of the way and stepped up to the door. His ears didn't pick up any noises, and he wondered if the kitchen was occupied at all. Just when he decided he was going to burst in, he picked up the sound of a knife repeatedly hitting a chopping board along with tuneful humming.

"It's Mrs E," he told Daniel and pushed the door open, exposing them completely to the harsh light of day.

Mrs Ellen looked up from the carrots she was busily chopping at the kitchen island, her smile as warm as the cosy kitchen. "Hello boys, did I not feed you enough at breakfast?" she asked with a laugh, placing the knife down beside the mountain of carrots and wiping her hands on her apron. "What are you for?"

Leo bustled Daniel into the kitchen and slammed the door shut. He noticed a key in the lock and promptly turned it, feeling the grinding of the metal mechanism as it sealed them in.

Daniel, with his arms waving wildly, ran over to Mrs Ellen and frantically explained what was going on. "Mrs E, Mrs E! We're being attacked by the Templars!"

Instead of showing any sign of alarm, the old woman simply stepped out from behind the worktop, walked towards Daniel, and wrapped her arms around him in a grandmotherly fashion.

"Alright, alright," she said soothingly, "calm down. Everything's going to be okay, so it is."

"They're here! And *she* knocked out Ela and Cornelius! And we don't know where Lucas is!" he continued in his distress.

"You listen to me. Leo and I are going to take care of it, so we are," Mrs Ellen explained, lightly stroking his hair. "Before we do anything, I need you to help me with something."

"What is it? Daniel asked, peering up at her through floppy black hair. Although he was calmer, traces of panic still lurked in his eyes.

"I need you to go over to the tattie shed and cut chips. Can you do that for me?"

Daniel gave a little nod. "Is it one barrel or two?"

Mrs Ellen smiled. "One will be plenty, my boy." She took his face between her hands and gave it a little squeeze. "Good lad."

When Daniel had wandered over to the partitioned section of the kitchen where the potato cutter was, Mrs Ellen's calm face vanished as she turned to Leo.

"What's going on?" she demanded in a tone he'd never heard her use before.

"Morgana and fifteen of her followers," he replied, suddenly feeling a little intimidated by the woman. "They know Daniel's here."

"Bastards!"

After all the drama of the previous month, Leo didn't think he could ever be shocked again, but Mrs Ellen's expletive proved him wrong. Currently, she was not the homely, warm and gentle lady whom everybody adored with all of their hearts. In a matter of seconds, she'd become a severely pissed off Irish woman who was tearing off her apron and tossing it next to the chopping board.

"Morgana took out Ela and Cornelius," he said.

"Dead?"

"No, just unconscious."

Mrs Ellen sighed with relief. "And Lucas?"

Leo bit his bottom lip. "I don't know."

"Do you have your phone?" Mrs Ellen asked him.

"Yes," he replied, digging into his pocket and fishing it out.

"Call him," she instructed.

Leo's thumb had barely touched the display when there was an almighty crash. Jumping with fright, he dropped his phone and watched it skitter along the floor towards the door, the words 'Calling Lucas...' flashing up on the screen. Its journey ended when it collided against brown worn out boots that were partially covered by sodden stonewash denim material. A large tanned hand scooped the phone off the floor.

"Awful jumpy this morning, aren't we?" Lucas said as he stepped into the kitchen, amusement dancing in his eyes. He held out the phone. "Anyone would think we're being attacked by a bunch of leather clad morons."

The joke was wasted on Leo; his thoughts were elsewhere. He reached out and took the phone from Lucas, his eyes never leaving the place where the door used to be. It was gone. The massive oak door had vanished; the only evidence of it ever being there was the wooden frame partially hanging off the wall that it had once been attached too.

"Lucas," he said, not bothering to conceal his disbelief. "Did you just…rip the kitchen door off its hinges?"

Lucas glanced over his shoulder briefly to admire his handiwork before answering. "Yeah, I did. Pretty cool, huh?" he replied. His broad grin fell when he caught Mrs Ellen's penetrating stare.

"Did nobody teach you how to open a door properly when you were in America?" she asked tartly.

"I…well…I," Lucas stammered. "I was saving time. I'll fix it later."

"You're damn right you'll fix it later, so you will! Bloody Americans!"

Despite the Templar threat surrounding them, Leo couldn't help but laugh. It was incredibly funny to see a six foot five pure demon being rebuked by a tiny old woman and looking utterly ashamed of himself. The amusement didn't last long as his ears picked up the sound of footsteps racing along the corridor outside.

The three of them exchanged knowing looks and got into position. He and Lucas pressed themselves against the wall at either side of the doorway while Mrs Ellen shuffled over to the kitchen island and picked up the knife that lay there. As she stared into the corridor from behind the island, she began humming while the knife continuously sliced through carrots and knocked against the wooden chopping board rhythmically.

Leo's heart battered against his chest and pounded in his ears as the footsteps in the corridor grew louder and faster. Adrenaline raced through his body and heightened each of his senses. A familiar slicing noise coming from the partitioned area of the kitchen filtered through the tension. Leo cast his eyes across the room to see Daniel loading a bucket of tatties into the chipping machine. Daniel had his back to everything and was blissfully unaware of the impending chaos.

The running footsteps grew to a crescendo before stopping abruptly. From the corridor, a strong female voice called into the kitchen.

"In here!"

A biker's boot had barely crossed the threshold when Lucas sprang into action. He rammed his fist into the woman's throat, and she buckled to the ground in a fit of gasps and coughs as she grasped her shattered windpipe. At the sight of their fallen comrade, a trio of armed Templars exploded into the kitchen.

The first one, a tall and slender male, leapt over the body lying in the doorway and stormed towards Mrs Ellen, bellowing war cries that would not be out of place during a Jacobite Highland charge. His two companions attempted to follow, but their journeys and war cries were cut short by Lucas, who grabbed them by the scruff of the neck, lifted them off the ground like they were nothing more than bags of feathers and launched them one at a time into the corridor. Their collision against the solid stone wall was colossal and seemed to rattle the entire Cathedral.

Leo was planning to take out the Templar who had charged into the room ahead of his comrades but his plan was made redundant by Mrs Ellen. One moment she'd been holding the chopping knife, the next there'd been a flash of silver, and the knife was buried deep in the Templar's forehead. As the Templar hit the ground, Leo stood with his mouth hanging open, perplexed.

"Don't look so surprised, Mr Alexander," she chortled while coming out from behind the island. "I was born into the Elect, so I was. I've got years of battle experience behind me."

"And many more in front of you by the look of things," Lucas added with a warm smile. The demon reached out and tenderly squeezed the old woman's shoulder.

While watching the warm exchange between the two, Leo began to understand why Lucas was so fond of humans and wondered if the demon had realised just how human his own behaviour had become.

Mrs Ellen placed a chubby hand against Lucas' cheek. "Don't think your American charm will make me forget about my door," she teased.

Lucas laughed before moving to the body that lay lifelessly at Mrs Ellen's feet. Leo's stomach gave a dreadful lurch when the demon bent down and pulled the knife out of the Templar's forehead. There was a squelching noise coupled with the sound of metal scraping against bone. Blood pitter-pattered across the floor as he handed the knife to Mrs Ellen, leaving an artistic trail of scarlet liquid from the corpse to the kitchen table.

"That's a good knife, so it is," Mrs Ellen commented as she took it from him.

Lucas grinned. "You do love a knife, Mrs E," he chuckled. Without another word, he moved to the entrance and used his foot to roll the Templar woman out of the way before peering into the murky corridor.

While Lucas scouted the corridor, Leo couldn't stop his eyes from studying the bodies on the floor. The Templar who'd suffered the broken windpipe still gripped her throat, her face forever frozen in an expression of pure terror and panic. Mrs Ellen's victim, however, stared up at the ceiling with insolent eyes, his face contorted with rage and fury.

"The corridor is clear," Lucas announced, returning to Mrs Ellen's side. "I've no idea how many Templars are left, but I reckon we'll be okay. John will have rounded up the Elite by now, so they won't stand a chance."

Leo's ears pricked up at the mention of the Elite, and he tore his eyes away from the fallen Templars. "Who are the Elite?" he asked. Although he could have guessed, he didn't rely on assumption these days no matter how probable, and he'd developed the habit of always asking about anything he was remotely unsure about.

"They're the ones who have the strongest connection to the Divine and utilise their gifts to the maximum," Lucas explained. "They're like our nuclear weapons."

"How many make it to Elite status?" Leo probed further.

Lucas shrugged. "Not many."

Mrs Ellen cleared her throat. "Don't you be forgetting about Morgana. You know as well as I do that she's Elite material. The child is still in danger as long as she's here, so we best get to the Haven."

"True," Lucas said, nodding. "Okay, you guys stay here with the little man while I track down Ela and Cornelius. Any idea of what happened to them?"

"Morgana attacked us, and they were knocked unconscious," Leo explained. "There was nothing I could do to help them either. She was too fast, and I had to get Daniel away from her. I couldn't help them." His cheeks flushed.

"She attacked you, and you managed to get the little man away from her?" Lucas queried, his eyebrows rising to the ceiling.

Leo gave a shrug. "I sort of…kicked her ass first." A tiny smirk tugged at the corner of his mouth.

"Nice one!" Lucas beamed. "Seems like you're learning."

"I've had excellent teachers," Leo said modestly.

Lucas gave another heart stopping smile before he became all business like again. "Where did Morgana attack you?"

"The dining room." Leo replied, bracing himself as a shadow crossed the demon's face. Shadows were rarely good.

"I came back through the dining room," Lucas stated. "They weren't there."

"Was Morgana?"

"No," Lucas answered, exchanging a look with Mrs Ellen.

"Oh, shit!" Leo groaned, not missing the silent interaction between Lucas and Mrs Ellen. "She was coming round just as Daniel and I made our way to the kitchen. I thought Ela and Cornelius would be alright because I assumed she'd come straight for us."

What have we discussed about assuming anything?' his inner voice asked when Mrs Ellen and Lucas didn't respond apart from staring at each other with concerned expressions. Leo didn't have the time or desire to engage his inner voice in debating the rules of assumption. Instead, he focused on the fact Ela and Cornelius were missing.

"Okay, you two, what's with the looks? What have I missed?" he asked, looking back and forth between Lucas and Mrs Ellen.

"You've missed nothing," Mrs Ellen assured him. "We're only worried about Ela and Cornelius' safety, that's all."

"She wouldn't kill her own father, would she?" Leo wondered aloud. Their expressions told him the answer, and he was jolted into action. "Hey, Daniel," he yelled over the din of the potato chipper. "Are you done yet?"

Daniel looked over when Leo shouted. He turned the machine off, and the slicing blades came to a gradual stop. "Did someone say something?"

"Yeah," Leo replied. "Are you done?"

The boy looked into the barrel of potatoes and assessed his progress. "Almost."

"Thanks, young man. That'll do for now," Mrs Ellen told him. "I'll fill it with water later. Out you come."

Daniel wiped his hands on his jeans as he walked over. "Where are we going? Are the Templars gone?" Before any of them had a chance to answer, Daniel's eyes were drawn to the corpses lying on the kitchen floor.

"We're going to find a safe place for you and Mrs E to hide, little man," Lucas said, stepping in front of him. "Then Leo and I are going to find Ela and Cornelius."

Leo wrapped a protective arm around Daniel. "I'm not leaving him," he told Lucas. "He stays with me."

"I understand your desire to protect him, but I can't fight Morgana without your help," Lucas said gently.

He knew Lucas had a point, but it didn't make the thought of leaving Daniel any easier. "What if—"

"Mrs Ellen will take Daniel to the Haven where they'll both be as safe as houses with the entire Elect there to protect them," Lucas interrupted. "We can concentrate on finding the others."

"The Elect are family, Leo," Mrs Ellen said, rubbing his arm gently. "We look after our own."

The sincerity woven into the woman's words won Leo over, but he had to make sure that Daniel was happy with the plan too. He gazed down at the boy who was looking up at him with trusting puppy dog eyes. At that moment, a powerful feeling of unconditional love embraced him tightly. A warmth enveloped his mind, body and soul, and he was all of a sudden emphatically thankful to God for placing this boy into his life.

"I'll be okay in the Haven with Mrs E," Daniel said with a small smile. "It'll be good to see Ross, Hattie and John."

"Atta boy!" Lucas said, reaching over and tugging Daniel's hat down over his eyes.

"Hey!" Daniel protested, his small smile now a massive grin.

"You look better with your face covered," Lucas teased.

After he'd pulled his hat back up to its proper position, Daniel gave the demon a playful shove. "Shut up!"

"Boys," Mrs Ellen said firmly, "we need to get moving. Lucas, check the corridor again." Lucas reacted immediately and shot to the door. "Daniel, come with me," she said, holding out her podgy hand which Daniel took. "We'll follow Lucas closely. Leo, you stay behind Daniel and I, okay?"

Leo gave a single nod and moved into position behind Daniel and Mrs Ellen.

Once Lucas had given the all clear, they left the cosiness of the kitchen for the coldness of the corridors. As they passed the two Templars that Lucas had hurled out of the kitchen, Leo could see the chest of one rise and fall; he was still alive. The other hadn't been as lucky. He didn't move at all, and crimson blood had pooled around his head. Averting his eyes, he focused on getting Daniel to safety.

It didn't take them anytime at all to get through the Cathedral, and they were soon huddled in the doorway that led out to the courtyard. Lucas left them there for a brief moment to ensure that it was safe for them to cross.

"There isn't a soul," he said on his return, his voice uneasy.

Leo shared the demon's concern. The lack of Templar activity was deeply unsettling, and he couldn't help but wonder why Morgana wasn't tearing the place apart to find Daniel. The thought still buzzed around in his head as he passed through the door and followed the others across the snowy courtyard. A cold breeze brushed his cheeks, and snow crunched beneath his boots.

When he finally stepped out of the shadow cast by the enormous Cathedral, the sun caressed and warmed the back of his neck. While he walked, he noticed hundreds of little hand and foot prints in the snow, and under one of the apple trees was an enormous snowman that the Elect children had made. In front of the statue of the Virgin and her infant being watched over by Michael, a perfectly smooth igloo, big enough for a child to crawl into, glistened gloriously in the morning sunshine.

It was a beautiful picturesque scene, but he couldn't appreciate it. He needed to know where Ela and Cornelius were in relation to Morgana. If she had them in her wicked talons, there would be severe consequences. He tried not to think about the worst case scenario and scanned ahead, relieved to see they'd reached the Haven door which was closed.

The door itself was stunning, and he was ashamed he'd never taken the time to explore the architecture of any of the smaller buildings before. To appease his shame, he let his eyes roam over the enormous bronze tablet that'd been fixed onto the original door.

The sun's rays were a spotlight that illuminated the tablet brilliantly like it was the star attraction, and he found himself squinting so he could study it. Through his squint, he could make out that the tablet had been divided into four equal sections, each housing an engraving of a magnificent and terrifying beast.

In the top left section, the engraving showed a proud yet ferocious looking lion sitting on its haunches, mouth gaping open in a silent roar. Coming out of the lion's back was an enormous pair of eagle's wings. To the right of the lion was a gigantic bear holding three human ribs in its mouth. The bear stood on its hind legs and had raised itself to its full height. Directly underneath the lion was the third beast. As he marvelled at every intricate detail, he decided this engraving was his favourite. It was a leopard with four heads and the wings of a fowl. Two of the heads looked passively at him whereas the other two seemed to be snarling viciously. The final beast was the most shocking out of the four as it reminded him of the sea creature he'd once seen in a dream. Although there were similarities between the two in terms of shape and size, the beast in the engraving had much bigger teeth and had ten horns protruding from its head.

"It's so cool," Daniel commented. "Even though I see it every day, I still think it's awesome."

Leo watched as the boy traced his hands over the lion with the eagle's wings.

"Yeah, it's beautiful," Lucas commented. "Do you know where these beasts come from?"

"I don't know...the Bible?" Daniel asked with a shrug.

Lucas nodded. "Yup, that's right. There was once a man who lived a very long time ago who could interpret the dreams and visions of powerful kings. He was a member of the Elect, like Leo, and was one of the most devoted and faithful servants of God that ever lived.

"One time, he was thrown into a den of lions by a King called Darius because he refused to stop praying. Everyone thought the lions would kill him, but an angel of the Lord intervened and stopped the lions from harming him. During this time, God sent the man a vision while he slept, and it was to do with these four beasts and the end of the world. He recorded it all in the Bible. Remind me to show you it sometime. We could read it together if you want."

Daniel, who had now moved on to stroking the leopard with the four heads, was clearly intrigued by the story. "What was the man's name?"

"Daniel," Leo said.

""What?" Daniel asked, looking up him with a puzzled expression.

Leo smiled. "No, silly. That was his name—Daniel."

The Haven door was suddenly flung open, and John stood in the threshold. "Quickly, come in," he said urgently, stepping aside and gesturing widely.

Lucas ushered Daniel and Mrs Ellen through the door before signalling to Leo to do the same. Leo entered the Haven and found himself in a small barren alcove where John and eleven Elect members were waiting. They were all dressed in plain white robes and were standing in front of another door which had been painted blue. Once Lucas had joined them in the alcove and sealed them all inside, John began his interrogation.

"Where's the Grandmaster? Did the Templars see you coming here? Have you killed Morgana?"

Lucas raised his hand. John fell silent. "The Grandmaster and Cornelius are unaccounted for, Morgana is still alive as far as we know, and the Templars didn't see us coming here."

John looked troubled. "When did you last see the Grandmaster?"

"I saw her about ten minutes ago in the dining room," Leo said. "Right after you left, Morgana attacked both her and Cornelius. I managed to knock the bitch out and run to the kitchen where we found Mrs Ellen. When Lucas came to find us, he came back through the lounge, but Ela and Cornelius were gone, right?" He glanced over at Lucas for confirmation.

"Right," the demon said. "The lounge was completely empty."

"Where was Ela when you ran to the kitchen?" John quizzed.

"She was lying on the floor by the table, Cornelius—"

"I don't care about Cornelius!" John snapped. "I want to know about the Grandmaster! Why didn't you assist her after you'd taken care of Morgana?"

Leo held up his hands. "Whoa, wait a minute! The last thing Ela said to me was to protect Daniel no matter what. I would have helped her, but a Templar came into the dining room and attacked us, so I had no choice but to run."

"You always have a choice!" John fired back. "Your poor choice may bring about Armageddon! How could you be so fucking stupid?"

Leo's mouth fell open.

"Mrs Ellen, take Daniel downstairs to his friends," Lucas instructed while glaring at John. "Stay there until Leo and I come back."

"Stay safe, both of you," Mrs Ellen said, hugging them both with tears in her eyes. "May God be with you."

"You do as Mrs Ellen says, okay?" Leo told Daniel as he pulled him into a tight hug. "I'll be back as soon as I can."

Daniel nodded. "I will. Hurry back," he said while bumping fists with Lucas. Mrs Ellen wrapped an arm around the boy's shoulders and guided him towards the blue door which opened at her touch.

"I don't understand why you're angry, John, I really don't," Leo said the moment the blue door was closed. "Ela gave me strict instructions—"

"Grandmaster."

Leo turned to where the female voice had come from and was met with a familiar face: Lucas' blonde haired friend. He couldn't deny it—she was stunning. With piercing blue eyes, full pouting lips and blonde hair, she was the definition of beauty. She was the same height as Leo and had a tiny frame. Physically, she looked as if she would break, however, her aura told a completely different story. There was strength and purity there. And it wasn't just *her* aura. The aura of the other ten felt exactly the same, and he understood immediately who these people were: the Elite.

Elite or not, the woman's condescending tone bugged Leo to no end. "Excuse me?" he said.

The woman smirked. "We refer to her always as Grandmaster, and never Ela."

"How nice for you," Leo said acidly. "I'll call her whatever the fuck I want, and I'll call her by her name which is Ela."

"Leo—"

"As I was saying," Leo continued, completely cutting off a bemused Lucas. "I don't get why you're angry. Daniel is safe, just like Ela wanted. How does that create an apocalypse?"

John's eyes flashed with anger. "Oh my god, you don't know."

"Don't know what?"

"He doesn't know, does he?" John said heatedly, turning his fierce stare onto Lucas.

"No, he doesn't," Lucas said with a stare that rivalled John's.

John let out an exasperated sigh and began pacing in front of the other Elite members. "I can't believe he doesn't know!"

Leo threw his hands up into the air in his usual dramatic fashion. "Oh, for fuck sake! What the hell haven't you told me this time?" he yelled at Lucas.

"Okay, calm down," Lucas told him. "You can't blame me for this one. It was Ela's choice."

John stopped pacing at once. "Her choice? The Grandmaster didn't want him to know? Why?"

"She didn't want it to cloud his judgement," Lucas said, talking directly to John but pointing at Leo. "If he knew what her role in all of this is, he might make decisions based on that and lose sight of the mission."

"Uh hello! *He* is right here!" Leo yelled again. He stepped towards the demon and held out his hands in a strangling motion. "I swear to God, Lucas, if you don't tell me what the hell is going on right now I'll strangle you with my bare hands!"

"Really? *This* is going to be our next Grandmaster?" the blonde woman sneered. "Are the High Council kidding us with this?"

Leo spun around. "Will you just shut the fu—" As he processed her words, he was stunned into silence and could do nothing but stare open mouthed. Eventually, he swallowed the shock and found his voice. "What did you say?"

The woman shuffled uncomfortably on the spot as every single member of the Elite glared at her. "I said—"

"Silence, Cerys!" John ordered. "She doesn't know what she's talking about. Impudent girl!"

Leo watched as Cerys shrank back and bowed her head.

"My apologies, John," she said meekly.

"And I should think so too!" he replied curtly before turning to Lucas. "We have to tell him."

Lucas sighed. "Fine, but be prepared for an emotional outburst of epic proportions," he warned, and folded his arms.

"There will not be an emotional outburst!" Leo hissed. "Just tell me about Ela!"

John cleared his throat. "What do you know about Baal?"

"Just what Lucas told me, but that might not be worth much," Leo responded, giving Lucas a pointed look to which the demon rolled his eyes. "He helped Lucifer throughout the war in heaven, escaped the abyss, can open portals and yada, yada, yada. Your lot trapped him underground in some big cavern hundreds of years ago, right?"

"That's correct," John said, "but what you don't know is that he was sealed in the cavern by a potent binding ritual involving blood. The Grandmaster who performed the ritual sacrificed his own life to imprison Baal, and when—"

"I don't mean to be rude, John, but shorthand it."

"As you wish," John said reproachfully. "Basically, the binding was done through blood, and as long as the Grandmaster's bloodline lives on, Baal will always be trapped."

Leo's heart grew heavy, and his insides began to twist. He already knew what was coming.

"That Grandmaster's name was Frederick St Clair. Ela St Clair is the last living descendant of Frederick and is the key to Baal's release. There are no others." John paused, his hazel eyes never leaving Leo's. "When she dies, the binding will break, and Baal will be released."

"And then what?" Leo asked, his voice small and tired.

John grimaced. "And then...we die."

Chapter 20
Hopeless

Nobody spoke or moved for a long time after John had finished speaking. Leo felt every eye on him, waiting for the emotional outburst that Lucas had promised.

'Give them what they're waiting for,' came the sound of his inner voice. Despite the tense situation, his inner voice appeared to be thoroughly amused by the whole thing. *'Make a scene!'*

"No," he said to both John and his inner voice. "There's no point in getting ahead of ourselves. We don't even know if the Templars have Ela," he pointed out. He began pacing. "Maybe they got away? Is there anyway of contacting her?" His hopeful green eyes darted between Lucas and John.

"I'll try her cell," Lucas said, pulling out his phone.

"Wait!" John ordered, placing his hand on Lucas' arm. "What if she's hiding somewhere and her phone alerts the Templars to the hiding spot?"

"John's right," Leo agreed, his pacing coming to an end. "We can't risk it if she's hiding. What if we try and find her using magic, like the time I found Daniel at the stadium?"

Lucas nodded. "Yeah, that's probably our best bet. Why don't you create a power circle and—"

A buzzing noise followed by a jaunty ringtone cut Lucas off, and the demon looked down at his phone. As his cerulean eyes scanned the screen, a troubled expression crept across his beautiful face. "It's Ela," he announced, swiping the screen and holding the phone to his ear. "Hello? Ela! Are you...No, we're all okay."

Leo stepped towards Lucas as the demon fell silent for a moment.

"Yeah, he's here, hold on," Lucas said finally and lowered the phone. "She wants to talk to you."

Leo took the phone, noting that Lucas had suddenly become withdrawn. "Ela, are you okay?" he asked immediately.

"I'm fine," she rasped, her voice raw.

"You don't sound fine."

"I'll be okay," she assured him before succumbing to a fit of coughing and spluttering. "Leo," she said, after managing to compose herself. "Listen to me. The Templars have me—"

"Where?" Leo interjected. "Where are you?"

"That doesn't matter. I'm with Morgana right now. She wanted me to call you so she could tell you something."

"Has she hurt you?" he almost shouted down the phone.

"No, not yet," Ela said bravely even though she sounded worse after her coughing fit. "The Templars are going to try and offer you a trade for my safety, but you must refuse! You must never leave Dan—"

There was an uproar of angry voices and a sickening thud from the other end of the phone. A long moment later, a cruel voice slithered through the phone and into his ear.

"Sorry, Leo," Morgana said, "Ela had to go."

"You fucking bitch!" Leo cursed, causing shocked looks from Lucas and the Elite. He quickly pulled the phone away from his ear, swiped the device onto speakerphone and held it out so everyone could hear. "If you hurt her, I'll kill you!"

Morgana's familiar hollow chuckle echoed out of the phone. "Don't worry, I'm not going to kill her yet. I'm taking her somewhere lovely."

"That's nice of you," Leo replied drily.

"If you head north, about twenty five miles outside of the city, you'll find a woodland walk leading to the Fyrish monument. I'm sure a local such as yourself will know it well. If the boy isn't delivered to me at exactly seven thirty tonight, she dies."

"You know as well as I do that Ela would give her life to stop the Power falling into the wrong hands. There's no way you're getting him."

"Then your Grandmaster dies," Morgana stated.

"If she dies, you'll release a terrible evil on us all," Leo explained.

"And what might that be?" she queried with an astounding lack of interest.

"Ela's ancestor is Frederick St Clair," Leo informed her, doing his best to keep his voice even. "She's the last remaining St Clair of his bloodline." He heard Morgana breathing, and it was clear she was mulling over this new information, however, the entire alcove soon sank into despair when she began to speak again.

"The great Frederick St Clair would have spawned a far superior specimen than this pitiful excuse for a Grandmaster," Morgana jeered. "Nice try, Elect filth. I'm not so easily fooled."

"You're making a huge mistake! You have to believe me. Ask Ela." Leo's words fell on deaf ears.

"How stupid do you think I am?" she asked.

"Very fucking stupid," Lucas responded coarsely.

"If she is who you say she is," Morgana continued, "why has she never reproduced to ensure the ritual held strong? Why is she not in hiding? I know how the Elect operate, and if what you're telling me is true, the High Council wouldn't have let her out of their sight. I'm afraid you underestimate my intelligence."

Leo and the entire Elite jerked in fright as Lucas exploded.

"You don't have any fucking intelligence!" he roared. "It's fucking true, alright! If you kill her, Baal will be freed and we're all fucked!"

Lucas' thunderous voice bounced around the alcove, fading bit by bit until it was no more. Every eye was locked onto the phone that Leo held in his hand, anxiously awaiting the Templar Queen's response.

"Fyrish Monument, seven thirty. Bring the boy."

The line went dead, and Lucas exploded again. "Son of a bitch!"

"Call her back," John instructed.

"What for?" Lucas yelled in frustration. "She doesn't believe us."

"Lucas, calm down," Leo said gently.

"Calm down?" Lucas snapped, snatching the phone from Leo. Did you not hear what that psycho bitch just said?"

"Yes, I did, and getting pissed off and aggressive isn't going to help. It's not the end of the world."

"Jesus Christ," the demon seethed, throwing his hands up to the ceiling and stomping towards the door that led to the courtyard. "Not yet it isn't, but if she kills Ela, it will be!"

"Oh, come on, Lucas!" Leo said hotly. "There's one thousand three hundred and ninety four of us, and only one of him."

Lucas burst out laughing; there was nothing angelic or musical about the sound. "Wow. All your new found power has gone to your head. There could be a million of you, and it still wouldn't be enough. Baal will crush each and every one of you and use your bones to decorate his throne." Lucas paused and took a calming breath. He ran a hand through his cropped blond hair.

When the demon turned to look at him, Leo could see his usually azure coloured eyes had dulled to an indigo blue. He could sense real fear radiating off Lucas in great big waves and wanted nothing more than to embrace him and tell him everything was going to be okay.

"Apart from Lucifer," Lucas said softly, slumping against the door of the Haven and lowering his head, "Baal is the strongest demon in existence, and the most insane. If he's released, the only one who can save us is God."

While the Elect contemplated Lucas' calamitous scenario, Leo gawped at them all in disbelief, shaking his head as he scanned all of their dejected faces. They'd accepted the worst so easily, and it infuriated him. When he realised there wasn't a single person in the alcove who was prepared to act, he took matters into his own hands and began marching towards the door where Lucas was moping.

"Where are you going?" John called after him.

"I'm going to my room to change," he replied sharply.

Lucas raised his head. "What for?"

"For fighting Morgana and her Templars," Leo answered. "Get out of my way."

"Don't be ridiculous," Lucas said, getting to his feet and blocking the door. "You'll get yourself killed."

"What do you think will happen if we stand around here like idiots and wait for Morgana to kill Ela?" Leo asked as he stopped right in front of his lover. "You all need to get a grip and realise that Baal hasn't been freed yet. Jesus Christ! How you lot have survived persecution is beyond me."

"And what exactly do you mean by that?" an irritated female voice snapped.

Leo silently prayed that it was Lucas' mystery woman asking the question. He wasn't disappointed when he turned to find her glaring at him. She took a few steps forward and broke away from the rest of the Elite, her white robes swaying delicately behind her as she sashayed forward.

"I don't get how you've lasted this long against the demons and Templars when none of you have any balls. You're all supposed to be the Elite, for fuck sake, and look at you! It's pathetic!"

The woman looked him up and down, her lip curling slightly. "You're lucky I have to adhere to the Elite code of conduct or else I'd put you in your place, boy."

"Listen, bitch, don't let some bullshit code of conduct stop you trying," Leo goaded. He cast a glance to the Elite who were standing in stunned silence. John had fixed his wrathful gaze onto the woman, his face pink with fury. Lucas remained at the door, looking uncomfortable and awkward.

"Like I said, if it wasn't for the code—"

"Cerys!" John shouted. "Hold your tongue!"

"Cerys?" Leo repeated, trying out the name on his tongue and making a face. "Nice name, it's…pretty."

"Leo, that's enough," Lucas scolded. "We don't have time for this."

"He's right, stop this nonsense at once! We have to come up with a plan. What do we do now?" John demanded of the room. "Any ideas?"

"I suggest we rally all the Elect members we can spare, and bring Ela home. Or maybe you'd all rather stay in here and wait for Baal to come and collect your bones," Leo replied abrasively.

"That's all very well, but we don't know how many Templars she'll have with her. She could have hundreds of thousands for all we know, and we can't fight that many," John pointed out. "I know we have our magic, but so do a lot of the Templars, and they're lethal in close combat."

"John's right," a female with a heavy Irish accent said.

Leo looked over his shoulder and took in the Irish woman's appearance. She was late thirties, svelte and tall with white freckly skin and sage green eyes. She had a slim face with high dramatic cheekbones and a narrow, well-defined jaw. An air of grace and elegance surrounded her, and she reminded him of the elves from Tolkien's works. The whiteness of the robes made her thick flaming locks even more striking as they rested on her shoulders.

"John's right," she repeated with a sly smile. "We don't know how many Templars there'll be. So what? Who cares? The more the merrier. We'll have a field day taking them out, so we will!"

Leo raised his eyebrows. "Are you…"

"Of course I am. Can you not tell?" Her eyes twinkled as she gave him a warm and genuine smile that she'd obviously inherited from her mother. "My name's Cathy, Cathy Ellen. It's finally nice to meet the famous Leo Alexander, so it is. I've heard lots about you."

"All good things, I hope," he quipped, instantly warming to her.

"Aye, mostly. I thought you'd be taller though," she teased.

Leo grinned. "Good things come in small packages."

"So does poison."

"I like you," he told her. "Want to come and kick some Templar ass?"

"It would be my pleasure," Cathy said with a smile. She took a step forward and stood beside John. "John," she said softly, adopting a more solemn expression. "We have to do this. We can't let her kill our Grandmaster. Even if there wasn't the question of Baal, we'd still owe it to her, so we would."

John's brow furrowed as he considered Cathy's words. It didn't take him long to reach his decision. He let out a prolonged sigh before turning to the rest of the Elite. "We take three hundred Elect plus all of us—"

"You'll need more," Lucas interrupted. "You'll need the strength of the entire Elect if you want to stand against the Templar army, and even then…it might not be enough."

"We don't know what size of army Morgana has at Fyrish," John countered. "She may only have a couple of thousand for all we know."

"Exactly. We don't know jack shit. What if the entire Templar army is waiting for us?"

"Lucas, I can't see how nearly a million Templars could pass through the Highlands without detection, it would be impossible."

Lucas shook his head defiantly. "There are ways."

"You know as well as I do," John argued, "that the Templars are a highly secretive and private order that wouldn't risk exposing themselves to the world. I firmly believe we'll not be met with their full might. They'll have an army waiting for us, but I think it'll be one we can handle. Now, are you with us?"

While Lucas gave John an intense stare, Leo reached out and placed his hand on the demon's chest. "We can't do this without you," he whispered. "I need your help to get her back."

Lucas' eyes softened, and he let out a long sigh. "Fine, I'll help. Please continue with your plan on how to get us all massacred."

John nodded. "We'll be accompanied by three hundred Elect including the Elite," he said in a business-like manner. "The rest will remain here and cast every protective enchantment they know upon the Haven to ensure Daniel's safety. Trust me, with that amount of Elect magic, Lucifer himself would struggle to break through."

"That's good enough for me," Leo said.

"I'll organise the Elect from in here," John continued while looking at his watch. "It's almost one. I need time to brief everybody on what's happening, so let's say we meet in the main hall in twenty five minutes. Go and get ready, do what you have to. I'll see you then." John and the Elite moved to the blue door where they disappeared one by one until only John remained. "Twenty five minutes," he reminded them before he too vanished.

The door emitted a soft blue glow that steadily increased until it illuminated the entire alcove with its intense brightness. It continued to dazzle until he could barely look at it. Then, as if someone had flicked a switch, the light snapped off, and the door was gone.

"Neat," he commented. Although he couldn't see the door, he sensed it was there, and he knew exactly where it was, assuming it had something to do with his Elect powers. He turned to Lucas. "I suppose we better get ready."

"Wait a minute," Lucas said, giving his best puppy dog eyes.

Leo sighed and looked up at him. "What for?"

"I think you should stay here with Daniel."

"Get out of the way, Lucas," he said irritably, reaching around the demon's torso for the door handle.

"Hear me out," Lucas pleaded.

"You have ten seconds."

"What if this is a trap? What if the whole Templar army is at Fyrish waiting for us?"

"Then there'll be a lot of dead Templars," Leo said matter-of-factly.

"You might be juiced up on your new found power and feeling invincible, but a Templar army of *any* size is dangerous."

"And so is an Elect army backed up by a pure demon."

"It won't be enough—not if they have thousands more than us."

"Lucas, we have to do this or Baal will be—"

"I know that!" Lucas snapped, his eyes turning into shiny onyxes. His expression softened immediately when he saw the flash of fear on Leo's face. "I think you should stay here, look after Daniel. That way you'll know he's safe."

"Do you know how strong a thousand protective Elect enchantments are going to be? Daniel will be safe here, you said so yourself. Now, get away from the door and let's go."

Lucas' hands shot to Leo's shoulders and gripped firmly. "I can't let you go, you have to stay here."

The demon's indigo eyes expressed a fear and desperation that stopped Leo dead. He could feel the hands that gripped his shoulders tremble, and it was only then that he got it. He felt his irritation towards the demon melt away as he reached up and cupped the demon's face with both hands, his thumbs lightly stroking the impossibly perfect cheek bones.

"What is it?" he asked softly. "Five minutes ago, you were more than happy for me to tag along to save Ela and Cornelius, and now you want me to hide. I don't get it."

Lucas pulled him into a cast iron hug. "That was before I knew there could potentially be tens of thousands of Templars. It's too dangerous."

Leo nestled into the muscular chest and inhaled the intoxicating masculine scent. "You always said there'll come a time when I'll have to face the danger and fight the darkness. That time has come."

Lucas sighed and peered down at him. "You're right. I just don't want anything bad to happen to you."

Leo smiled and gazed into smouldering eyes. "As long as I have you, nothing bad can happen to me," he whispered before standing on his tiptoes and placing the gentlest of kisses onto Lucas' warm lips. He felt the demon reciprocate, and the gentle kiss became heated and passionate. After minutes of frenzied kissing, Lucas growled, and Leo found himself being spun around and pressed up against the door. "Lucas," he protested weakly, gasping in delight and running his hands through soft blond hair. The kisses came faster and harder now, landing all over his face and neck. One of Lucas' hands tugged the zipper on his hoody and exposed his chest.

"I've got to have you right here, right now," Lucas panted.

Driven by the lust bubbling through every vein in his body, Leo suspended every thought in his head and grabbed Lucas' jaw roughly, forcing the demon's eyes to his. The indigo was gone, replaced by an intense pulsating azure that was both hypnotic and shocking. Words weren't necessary; the want in his hungry emerald eyes was enough, and Lucas got the message.

*　　　　　　　*　　　　　　　*

"We've got three minutes left."

"Fuck!" Leo cursed, pushing his feet through the legs of ripped black jeans. They were back in his dormitory. "I can't believe we wasted so much time!"

Lucas grinned broadly. "I wouldn't say the time was wasted. I found it useful actually. De-stressed me."

"Shut up!" Leo replied while frantically buttoning up his jeans. He threw himself onto the bed and reached for his favourite pair of black boots. "How was it de-stressing? The Elite almost caught us!"

"They might have learnt something if they did. Uptight bastards."

"Lucas!" Leo exclaimed with a chuckle. "They believe being gay is a terrible sin, and they hate demons. What would they think about the two together? They'd have us burnt at the stake."

"I don't give a flying fuck," Lucas responded, his grin stretching even wider.

"Save that flying fuck for me," Leo quipped as he finished lacing up his boots. He got to his feet and tucked in his tight black t-shirt. "Okay, I'm good to go."

Lucas frowned as he scanned Leo's attire. "You'll need something warmer than that," he said. "You'll freeze to death."

"I don't want to be restricted with jackets and coats when I'm fighting. I'll be fine."

"Hang on, I think I might have something in my closet. Wait here."

Less than a minute later, Lucas returned with a small leather jacket. Beams of wintery sunshine streamed through the window and illuminated the red leather like a spotlight. "Try it on," he said, tossing it across the room.

Before Leo had zipped it up, he already knew it was perfect for him. It was tight where it needed to be without being binding, and once it was tied, he stretched out his arms and moved them vigorously in wide circular motions. The leather scrunched and creaked, but he could move freely.

"Hmmm, fits perfect" Lucas commented, taking a step forward, his eyes narrowing in a feral fashion.

Leo held up his hand. "Whoa! No you don't! We don't have time." He swallowed when Lucas took his outstretched hand and kissed the back of it.

"I know, just saying."

"Yeah, yeah," Leo said, rolling his eyes and pulling Lucas out into the dormitory corridor. "Come on, they'll be waiting for us."

When Leo entered the hall, he saw that most of the Elect were sat in the pews and chattering excitedly while a minority stood in small groups saying nothing. Lucas guided him to stand by one of the pillars where he leant his shoulder against the cold stone and folded his arms, waiting for the meeting to start. Lucas stood protectively behind him.

From amongst the crowds, John finally emerged and made his way to the pulpit. As he ascended the small wooden steps, the noise in the hall gradually faded until there was nothing but silence.

"Elect brothers, Elect sisters," he bellowed, his voice bouncing off the walls. "Our Grandmaster has been taken by our enemies and is being held to ransom. We refuse to meet their demands, and the course of action decided by the Elite is war."

An excited murmur spread through the hall but stopped when John raised his hand. Leo found it quite strange that God's chosen people would be so happy at the prospect of war and what it entailed.

"We leave immediately and will travel on the Sunday school coaches," John continued. "The monument lies at the top of a hill and is only accessible by foot. I'm told it takes about an hour to get to the top. The path is flanked by trees most of the way up which will provide us with cover as we ascend. The last six hundred metres up to the monument has no trees to shelter us, so we'll be exposed to whatever Templar army there is, including their archers. The top of the hill is flat moorland with the monument in the middle. The plan is to stop a little before the trees end, recuperate from the trek, and then send scouts ahead to see how many Templars we're dealing with. Any questions?"

Leo raised his hand.

"Yes, Leo?"

"What happens after we've found out how many Templars there are?" he asked, his cheeks reddening when all eyes turned to him. Lucas placed a supportive hand on the small of his back.

"Depending on their numbers, we'll have to devise the best possible plan of attack. Whatever the number, there'll be bloodshed."

A loud collective whooping noise made Leo jump, and once again he felt uncomfortable at the apparent jubilation the Elect were displaying at the prospect of killing other humans. He scanned the sea of faces housed in the Cathedral's main hall to see most of the Elect were either smiling, patting each other on the back or gripping each other in eager anticipation. Just as John started talking again, he felt something brush against his ear.

"Shocking, isn't it?" Lucas whispered. "Even God's chosen ones get pumped up and buzzed at the thought they might get to end a life, and yet they look down on demons for doing exactly the same thing. You must hold on to the discomfort and disapproval you're feeling right now, it's what sets you apart from them. It's what makes you better."

Leo shook his head sadly. "I'll be no better than them in the next hour after I've killed my first human."

"Yes, you will."

"You can't know that."

"Yes, I can. You'll kill out of necessity, but you won't celebrate the deed. You'll mourn because *you* are a being of light."

Leo scoffed. "Yeah, right." He heard Lucas laughing, and it made the hairs on the back of his neck stand on end.

"You can be so fucking stupid, Leo Alexander."

Before he could fire of a quick witted comeback, he was distracted by a sudden burst of activity. The Elect were on their feet and moving towards the main doors.

"Show time," Lucas said as they began following the crowd of war ready Elect out of the Cathedral and down to the car park.

Before stepping onto the coach, Leo glanced skywards. The sun had disappeared, and the sky was spattered with blackening clouds that seemed to be growing bigger with each passing second.

With a shiver, he climbed aboard and made his way to the back. "I'm smoking on this bus," he announced as he squeezed into the back seat.

"You might upset someone," Lucas smirked.

"Don't care."

"Rebel," Lucas teased while sparking up a cigarette. "Open that window," he added with a nod of his head.

Leo reached up and opened the window that was above him before he lit his own cigarette. He noted that none of the Elect batted an eyelid. They obviously had murder on their minds. He stole a glance at the Cathedral as the coach drove carefully alongside the bank of the river. It was then that something began to burrow in the pit of his stomach, twisting and squeezing ruthlessly until he had to tear his eyes away. He took a couple of quick drags on his cigarette.

"You okay?" Lucas asked, snaking around in his seat to inspect the Cathedral.

"Hmm?"

"Did you see something back there?"

"No...no, I didn't," Leo replied.

"Then why are you trying to break the Olympic record for the fastest smoke?"

Leo blew a cloud of smoke towards the open window before responding. "I have a bad feeling about leaving Daniel."

"You were right before," Lucas said reassuringly, placing a hand on Leo's knee. "Over a thousand Elect members are there to protect him including a crazy Irish woman. He'll be perfectly safe." The demon flashed a small smile.

"I know. I just feel bad for leaving him."

"Typical paternal feelings."

"How would you know?"

"I've read about it."

"You read?"

"Ela bought me a Kindle last year when I came to Inverness. I *love* it!"

Leo flicked his finished cigarette out of the window. "E-reader or Fire?"

Lucas exhaled sharply in mock disgust as he handed Leo his cigarette end. "Uh, Fire. No contest."

"Cool," Leo said, shutting the window after discarding the cigarette end, highly amused by the thought of Lucas lying in bed with a Kindle Fire for company. "You're full of surprises."

"You have no idea," Lucas grinned, pulling out his phone and swiping the screen. "It's almost two."

"Whoa! You can tell time too? You really *are* full of surprises!" Leo teased despite the feeling of unease in his belly. He grinned when Lucas gave one of his hearty laughs.

"You know, I might let those Templar folk kick your ass if you're not careful," Lucas threatened.

"Yeah, yeah," Leo said with a camp wave of his hand. "I've heard all these threats before. If you wanted me dead, you'd have done it by now."

"Fair point," Lucas agreed with a smile. "There are for more advantages keeping you alive."

"Like my super wit and intellect?"

"I was gonna say your smoking hot body and sexual prowess, but if you want to go with super wit and intellect, that's fine by me."

"Hot body and sexual prowess? Why thank you," Leo chuckled, fixing his eyes on the sky. It had grown even darker, much like his mood.

After a short silence, Lucas launched into an amusing story about Mrs Ellen, a Halloween party and thirty pumpkins, which distracted him from the heavy feeling of dread in his stomach that was growing more intense as they drew nearer to Fyrish. He was grateful for the humour and banter that Lucas had provided throughout the journey; it prevented him from having to address the feeling in his gut that something was terribly wrong.

Fyrish car park was a lot smaller than the Cathedral's and had a wooden fence marking its square perimeter. Opposite the car park's entrance was a single path that led to the monument. The three coaches parked parallel to each other, and the Elect clambered off. Leo went to stand up when a warm hand enveloped his.

"You sure you want to do this?" Lucas asked, his bright eyes burning.

"Lucas, we've been through this—"

"I know. I just wanted to make sure."

"I'm sure," Leo said, squeezing the demon's hand.

Lucas smiled and kissed him. "Okay, let's go."

The moment Leo stepped off the bus and onto frozen ground, his heart became a jackhammer that pounded against his chest. His ears were ringing, his head felt like it was full of cotton wool, and his throat had become dry. As he wondered about how mad his life had become, a sharp wind shook the giant evergreens that surrounded the car park, causing some of the snow to fall from their leaves. He wrapped his arms around himself to evade the coldness of the wind, but it did little to help.

He walked away from the coaches, and the feeling he'd been trying so hard to contain since he'd become embroiled in the Daniel saga hit him like a snow plough. It sprung up from his solar plexus like a crazed animal and thundered through every fibre of his being. He shivered violently, and it had nothing to do with the cold. In the background, he could hear John organising his soldiers of light. Leo didn't hear what he was saying, nor did he care. He was thinking about Daniel, and the boy's curse.

'A curse?'

'Yes, a curse!' he told his inner voice bitterly. 'The affliction bestowed upon him means that he'll always be in danger.'

'But what if you save Ela? Daniel lives to see another day,' his inner voice persisted.

'Yeah, but for how much longer? The whole thing is cruel and unjust! There will always be something coming after him, won't there? He'll have no peace until he's...' Leo couldn't say it.

'Until he's dead.'

Those words were the catalyst he needed. His muscles flexed, and his fingers twitched as divine energy bubbled beneath his skin. 'The Templars and demons can keep on trying,' he told himself, 'but they won't get near my boy.' In his gut, the twisting and squeezing had relented and began to retreat. He became calmer as resolve and determination set in.

"Hopeless," Leo said aloud, causing Lucas to turn his cerulean gaze on him.

"What?" the demon asked, slipping an arm over Leo's shoulders.

Leo cracked his knuckles and shrugged the demon's arm off before walking with purpose to stand at the front of the deathly silent Elect army where John was waiting impatiently. Cathy and the rest of the Elite stood beside him.

"Leo," Lucas called after him, his feet crunching in the snow. "What did you say?"

"The Templars' quest," Leo answered coolly. "It's hopeless."

"How so?" the demon asked, falling into step beside the energised Leo.

"Because as of this afternoon," Leo said, green sparks igniting in his irises, "the Templars will have a new quest."

"And what might that be?" John asked upon hearing Leo's words.

Leo stopped in front of him, his eyes blazing with emerald fire. "Their new quest," he said loudly, turning on his heel and striding towards the monument path which was nestled in between a thick growth of trees, "will be to fear me."

From behind him, the bloodthirsty Elect roared their approval.

Chapter 21
A Fatal Deception

The scots pine trees shrouded the Elect like a vast green and white cloak as they trudged up the slippery path leading to the monument. Occasionally, the wind would blow chunks of snow off the trees and send them falling to the ground where they would land with a muffled thump. Compared to Inverness, Fyrish had been hit with higher levels of snowfall that had turned everything a serene white. The woodland path, which had been relatively sheltered from the snow by the giant evergreen trees, was terribly winding and grew steeper and steeper with every step. The only point the incline changed was when it descended and levelled off at a small, fast flowing river. On either side of the wooden bridge that crossed the river, the natural forest floor disappeared and was replaced with large stone steps that had been pounded into the earth. The steps proved treacherous to climb, and a few of the Elect found themselves slipping and falling down them. With the support and encouragement of their comrades, the fallen were soon helped back to their feet and continued their march up Fyrish. Apart from trees, stone steps, and the bridge, there was nothing to see on the ascent up to the monument except a thick blanket of snow that smothered the entire forest.

Leo walked alongside John and Lucas while the rest of the Elect marched behind. After thirty minutes of trudging up the path, his breathing grew heavy and beads of perspiration began to form on his forehead which he wiped away with the back of his hand.

"Smoke?" Lucas offered for the tenth time.

"Are you crazy?" Leo wheezed. "I'll die if I have one of those."

When they had clocked up an hour of intense walking, he was surprised to find he was breathing much more easily, and the muscles in his legs no longer ached. There had been a point in the harsh journey when he was going to complain about being cold and tired from climbing the never ending hill, but he wasn't about to lose face in front of the others. Sometimes. he would glance back to check how everyone else was doing, and his spirits would lift a little when he saw how fresh and energised the Elect army looked. They had not tired since beginning the climb, and this filled him with hope.

They're only three hundred plus the Elite,' his inner voice chirped. 'The Templars could have hundreds of thousands waiting at the top of this monument for us.'

'Yeah...thanks for reminding me,' Leo thought sarcastically.

After what seemed like another hour of dragging his feet up the slippery path, he was elated when the incline came to a gradual end. He noticed the dense forest was beginning to thin out as they continued their expedition on level ground which allowed for some sunlight to peek through. The peeking sunlight became a glare when the trees in the forest grew sparser still. He looked ahead and groaned when he saw the incline was set to grow steeper once again. It was at the foot of the incline that John gave the command to stop.

"We're close," he said, narrowing his eyes and scrutinising his surroundings. When he was satisfied there was no immediate danger, he raised his hand. "Cerys, Cadence, Christopher."

Three members of the Elite stepped forward on John's command and stood in front of him, bowing their heads slightly. A strong wind swept through the forest, pulling at Cerys' hair and the majestic red hooded cloak she wore over her white robes.

Leo attempted to discreetly check out the other two, but his glance became a prolonged stare. Cadence and Christopher were almost exact copies of Cerys; the only differences were that Cadence had brown hair, and Christopher was a man with a shaved head that had rune symbols tattooed all over it. They also wore hooded cloaks but of a different colour; Cadence's was a burnt orange, and Christopher's a sapphire blue. When they stood side by side, the girls were the same height, but Christopher dwarfed them considerably. Leo had never seen triplets in real life, and a myriad of thoughts and questions that he'd quite like to ask them flooded his brain.

"It's time," John announced. "Remember, scouting only. Do not kill any of them, it'll only alert them to our presence. Find out where they're keeping our Grandmaster, and how many Templars we're dealing with. Are we clear?"

"Clear."

The answer came as one, the three voices blending harmoniously together. Each triplet then reached behind their heads and pulled up their hoods in perfect sync before vanishing completely. Leo stared where the triplets once stood, shaking his head lightly as fresh footprints were formed in the snow by invisible feet.

"I actually don't know why I'm surprised," he muttered with a rolling of his eyes. "Of course invisibility cloaks exist, why wouldn't they?"

"They sure do," said Lucas cheerily. "However, they're the only three in existence. The triplets are descendants from—"

"Stop!" Leo interrupted. "Not the time for a history lesson."

Lucas smirked. "Suit yourself. I'm going to check the back of the group to make sure everyone is okay. I won't be long," he called as he disappeared behind the crowd of stony faced Elect.

Heavy charcoal coloured clouds had rolled in from the east and were looming menacingly. Leo dropped his gaze from the sky and turned to John. "What now?"

"We wait here. My scouts move quickly, they'll be back shortly."

"Isn't it a little cold to just wait around?" Leo moaned.

John smiled patiently. "So heat yourself up then," he said with a wink.

Leo was about to ask John how he was supposed to go about heating himself up when he felt a sudden warmth on the back of his neck. Upon turning around, he discovered some of the Elect had pulled their magical resources together and had created a gigantic rainbow coloured bonfire.

"Oh," was all Leo could say as he walked over to get a better look. Drawing nearer to the fire, he marvelled at the way it was burning without any wood or foliage to feed it. He held out his hands to the flickering flames which, at this side, were a fuchsia colour. A tingling sensation started in his finger-tips when he made contact. It spread to his palms and arms before continuing to the rest of his body. Soon, a glorious heat enveloped him from within. As the last of the sunshine disappeared behind a curtain of gloomy grey, the heat was exactly what he needed.

Ten minutes later, he was sat by the fire and enjoying the heat along with the rest of the Elect, casually observing the remaining Elite. They stood guard and watched for any signs of the enemy, their heads constantly turning and swivelling like anxious does protecting their young.

"Are you ready for a smoke yet?"

Leo jumped. There had been no warning or sound of footsteps to indicate Lucas' arrival. When he looked, the demon was holding out an almost empty packet of cigarettes, so he reached out and took one, lighting it off the magical flames that danced merrily before him.

"Thanks," Leo said gratefully.

"No worries. How you holding up?" Lucas asked as he lit a cigarette of his own.

"Better now that I'm warm."

"I did tell you to wrap up."

Leo gave a flippant wave of his hand. "Yeah, yeah. I know. How long do you think Team Triplet will be?"

Lucas shrugged. "They're quick and efficient. It'll depend on what they find up…they're back."

Leo followed Lucas' gaze to see the triplets in their brightly coloured cloaks striding through the snow towards John. He swallowed the lump of anxiety that had formed in his throat before rising off the ground to meet them.

"Report," John demanded.

"The Grandmaster is chained to the monument and is surrounded by ten Templars armed with spears and shields. Morgana is there too. That is all."

There was a grave silence as John shared a dark look with Lucas before turning to the triplets.

"Where's the army?" he asked Cerys.

"There's no army," she said. "I thought it was odd too…"

John suddenly looked deeply troubled as he turned to exchange yet another dark look with Lucas. "Something's very wrong."

"Could they have cast some sort of cloaking spell to hide the rest of their army?" Leo suggested quickly. From the skies above, the first few droplets of sleet fell and landed on his head. The droplet trickled down to his forehead, and then slid to the bridge of his nose. "I mean, they might have set a trap, right?"

Lucas shook his head. "Nah, no way. That's not their style."

"They're definitely up to something," John said, bringing his hand up to stroke his chin as he faced the triplets once more. "Did you get any vibes while you were up there? Did you sense magic?"

Christopher spoke up for the first time. "There was nothing, John. I couldn't sense any magic apart from Ela's." He swallowed and started to kick the snow at his feet apprehensively. "She's really weak. They've…" Christopher hesitated. "There's no time for details. We need to hurry."

Leo had heard enough. He flicked his cigarette to the side and started stamping his way up the hill towards the monument. The wind howled wildly turning the sleet drops into tiny projectile needles of ice that pricked and stabbed at his face.

Without warning, shouts and cries split the air. He spun around to investigate the source of the commotion and felt a surge of panic wash over him when he saw a significantly larger Templar army advancing on the Elect from the rear.

"Holy shit!" he whispered to himself as the Templars let loose a whistling volley of arrows and bolts. Leo winced as the arrows and bolts hit their targets; impaling chests, arms, legs, and any other body parts they could pierce. A number of the Elect crumpled and fell, many dying before they even hit the ground. The Templars fired off a second round, but their arrows and bolts bounced of an array of powerful protective energy shields. The Elect army unleashed their divine powers upon their enemies, and it wasn't long until the air was alive with magical energy. Screams of anguish and pain shook the snow covered hills of Fyrish as the bitter rivals clashed in a dance of magic and medieval weaponry.

"Leo, go! Save Ela!" John bellowed while incinerating a deadly ball of ice in mid-air. "We'll deal with these bastards!"

Leo was about to yell a reply when a fireball came tearing straight at him. He dropped to the ground, and it went whizzing harmlessly overhead before exploding into the trunk of a nearby tree. The giant evergreen swayed and creaked dangerously in the wind until finally losing its balance and falling towards the earth. It headed straight for the unsuspecting triplets who were doing their best to battle a never ending onslaught of Templars. With his emerald eyes ablaze, he cast a glowing white energy shield around the triplets. Heavy sleet lashed off the shield momentarily until the falling tree collided into it and bounced off. He exhaled noisily as it rolled harmlessly down the hill, taking out some Templars along the way.

Cerys caught his eye and gave him a curt nod before launching herself back into the fray. He watched as she extended one of her elegant legs with extraordinary force and rammed her foot into the stomach of an oncoming Templar. With her foe doubled over, she clamped her hands on the sides of his head and twisted savagely. There was a loud snapping sound as the Templar spiralled into the air and landed hard on the blood stained snow.

"Leo!"

Leo jumped and tore his eyes away from Cerys. Lucas was inches away from him, his cropped blond hair wet and tousled.

"Come on! We've to get to the monument!" he exclaimed pulling on Leo's hand and taking off like a bullet.

It didn't take long until Leo's legs grew tired from being hauled up the hill. He was soon stumbling and slipping in his efforts to keep up with Lucas' demonic super speed. "Lucas," he gasped. Lucas stopped instantly, and Leo doubled over, taking huge breaths of freezing air which he could feel burning the inside of his lungs. "I can't—" In one smooth move, Lucas scooped him into his arms and began to power up the slope as if he weighed nothing.

"Hold on tight," Lucas advised before increasing his speed even more.

Leo had barely locked his arms around Lucas' neck when flashes of white and green flew past his eyes. The bitter wind shrieked incessantly in his ears like a banshee while he tried to establish where they were in relation to the monument. He grew nauseous as he attempted to focus on the blurry surroundings, and in the end, he had to close his eyes. He had no idea how long Lucas had been running up the hill for or how far they were from the monument until the demon alerted him with a whisper.

"We're here."

Leo forced his eyelids apart and unlocked his arms from around Lucas' neck. He shuffled down the demon's body and planted both feet securely into the snow, his eyes scanning the new environment carefully. The giant monument lay only two hundred metres in front of him and was an impressive stone structure made up of four single pillars that stood side by side, their tops curving and joining together to create three identical arches reminding him of the five pillars of Islam. In the centre arch of the monument, Ela was suspended in chains while nine leather clad Templars surrounded her, equipped with spears and shields, their faces hidden behind black balaclavas. The Grandmaster was shivering, clothed only in her turquoise dress and flip flops. Scattered around the monument, Leo noticed, were large boulders roughly the same size as those lying in the Cathedral courtyard. A plan began forming in his head.

A hooded figure stood directly in front of Ela, spear in hand, and appeared to be goading the battered and bloodied Grandmaster. Though the face was obscured, the feminine frame and long raven hair flowing out from under the hood let him know exactly who it was.

"Morgana," he hissed. "Okay, what's the pla—"

Leo stopped speaking when he saw Morgana driving the bottom end of her spear into Ela's jaw. The Grandmaster's head recoiled from the blow, and then lolled to the side where it hung limp and lifeless. He balled his hands into fists as a terrible rage brewed deep inside him. The air became statically charged, crackling and sparking as he summoned mystical energies to do his bidding. Beside him, Lucas let out a low, spine chilling growl. Nine Templars cheered their leader on as she struck Ela for a second time…a third…a fourth. The rage moved up to Leo's chest where it bubbled away like hot magma waiting to erupt in an explosive display of volcanic vengeance.

"Leo?"

Lucas' voice trembled, and Leo, sensing the demon's fury, set his gaze upon him.

"I need to be a demon for this, can you handle that?"

"Yes," he replied at once, letting magic flow freely through his entire being. "Do what you have to." He blinked once, and Lucas was in demon form.

The red flecks in the middle of Lucas' black eyes had grown bigger and were pulsing. "It's kill or be killed," he said, his voice demonic. "Don't hesitate, they won't."

Leo's eyes dazzled brightly as the magic turned them into flaming emeralds. "I've got this," he assured Lucas. "What do you want me to do?"

Lucas fixed a death stare on Morgana who was still pummelling the Grandmaster. "We have to be careful, we're too far away. If we get this wrong, even at my top speed, I'd never reach her in time. Morgana will kill her instantly if she sees me coming."

Leo fell silent for a moment as various plans formed in his head. "Run full speed towards Ela," he instructed.

"What?"

"Do you trust me?"

For a split second, Lucas' eyes shifted from deathly black to shimmering cerulean as he crippled Leo with an intense stare. "Until the end of time." Although in demon form, Lucas' voice sounded human.

Leo's heart fluttered, but he knew there wasn't time to dwell on sentiment. "Go. Now!" he commanded as he released a small translucent orb of energy into the air where it zipped off towards Morgana.

The demon shot off like a rocket, his shoulder and back muscles rippling beneath the sleet soaked white t-shirt as he worked his arms to get more speed. The denim material of his jeans stretched over the bulging muscles in his thighs every time he lifted his legs and pounded his feet into the snow; Leo had never seen a more magnificent creature.

Lucas had taken ten long strides when the nearest Templar saw him. "DEMON!" the Templar roared, raising his spear.

The other Templars, including Morgana, whipped their heads around when they heard their comrade's cry but had no time to react. The glowing orb that Leo had released found its way to Morgana's side where it hovered patiently, unnoticed. Leo gave his hands one thunderous clap, and the orb exploded with a whooshing sound. It expanded rapidly and pushed all of the Templars off their feet, scattering them several metres away from the monument.

While the Templars gathered their senses and struggled to their feet, Lucas had already snapped the chains off Ela's ankles and was just about to break the ones binding her wrists when a large fireball, conjured by one of the Templars, missed the demon's head by mere millimetres and whizzed through the archway. Lucas responded by rising to his full height and snarling at the advancing enemy.

"Tell your Templars to back off, Morgana, or I'll rip their fucking heads off!" he spat, glowering at the hooded figure.

With the Templars preoccupied by Lucas, Leo was able to get closer to the monument and assist his lover without detection. He watched Morgana as she raised a hand, commanding nine warriors to draw back their spears. She swiped her arm down and nine spears hurtled towards Lucas. The deadly missiles came to an unexpected stop inches from the demon as they thudded against Leo's energy barrier and fell harmlessly onto the snowy floor. The furious Templars continued their assault by arming themselves with smaller blades, which they pulled from beneath their leather jackets, and rushing Lucas. The demon settled back on his haunches, roared like a ferocious lion and leapt into the middle of the mob who were hell bent on carving him into little pieces.

As Lucas disappeared from sight, Leo's eyes followed the hooded Morgana who hung back from the rest of her attacking Templars and looked like she was readying a magical attack. In his anger, he let his mystical energy consume the nearest boulder and magically propelled it through the air directly towards Morgana's head. Her legs buckled, and she crumpled to the floor in an unconscious heap. He quickly turned his attention back to Lucas and Ela, the blood in his veins running cold when his brain processed the gruesome scene laid out before him.

In the short time it had taken Leo to knock out Morgana, five bodies lay slaughtered on the ground and were all missing at least two limbs and a head. He could do nothing but watch as his demon lover took great pleasure in ripping apart two more Templars with his bare hands before unceremoniously dumping their bodies on the ground.

The two remaining men stepped forward causing Lucas to turn his feral eyes on them. His lips were pulled back, his teeth were bared, and bloodied saliva trickled from his mouth as he snarled at them. Leo was impressed that the men weren't fleeing in terror at the sight of the savage beast before them. Lucas was truly terrifying in his current guise yet the Templars stood their ground and circled the demon slowly, waiting for the opportunity to strike. Unfortunately for them, it was Lucas who struck first, and he did so at lightning speed, closing his hand around the neck of the nearest Templar and tearing his throat out. The last man standing dropped his blade and held up his hands in surrender. Lucas roughly yanked off the Templar's balaclava to reveal a young boy, no more than seventeen years old.

Leo held his breath as Lucas touched noses with the boy and growled menacingly. The boy trembled uncontrollably but did not look away, choosing to hold the demon's stare instead while muttering under his breath.

"Lord's Prayer?" Lucas jeered through gritted teeth. "Do you think that'll stop me from ripping your heart out and feeding it to you?"

"Lucas, wait!" Leo cried. "Let him go."

Lucas twisted his head around and glowered. "Why?" he snapped, lifting the boy into the air by his head and presenting him to Leo. "This is the enemy! He wants to kill Daniel!"

"I know that," Leo said, sounding calmer. "Look at him. He's just a boy."

"They all look the same to me!" Lucas snarled, turning his eyes back to the quivering Templar and studying him.

"Please, Lucas. Don't kill him."

After an intense moment, Leo sighed with relief when the young Templar landed on the ground at Lucas' feet. The demon delivered a swift kick to the boy's face, knocking him out.

"Thank you," Leo said, placing a hand on Lucas' shoulder and squeezing. He could have smiled when Lucas rolled his eyes at him; the action was too human and looked foreign on his demonic face.

"Don't mention it," Lucas grumbled as he reverted back to his human form. "Let's get Ela, and get out of here."

When they reached Ela, Lucas broke the chains around her wrists. Leo was there and caught her when she slumped forward.

"Ela!" Leo exclaimed, lying her gently down on the ground. He took her hand in his. "Lucas, she's freezing!"

"We need a fire," Lucas said.

Leo's eyes flashed with emerald flames, and a ring of fire sprouted up from the ground and encircled the three of them. The fire was a metre tall and radiated an astonishing heat. He pulled off his jacket and placed it over her. "Why isn't she waking up?"

"She will. Give her five minutes."

Five minutes passed, and Ela was still unconscious and freezing. Leo tried rousing her by shaking her gently but to no avail. "We have to get her to a hospital. What if she's got hypothermia?"

Lucas nodded in agreement. "You're right," he said, taking Ela in his arms and lifting her like she was a bag of feathers. "We'll have to run."

"Run? I'll never be able to keep up with you!"

"You won't have to. Get onto my back."

"Are you serious?" Leo asked incredulously, waving his hands over the wall of fire and extinguishing it.

"Deadly," Lucas replied. "Get on."

"Fine. What about Morgana?"

"Fuck! I forgot about her. Where is she?"

"I took her out, over there," Leo said, pointing to where she lay face down in the snow. She was still breathing which he wasn't sure if he was entirely happy about.

"She's still alive. Take one of the spears, and stab it through her heart," Lucas ordered.

Leo's expression told the demon just how horrified he was by his request. "I can't do that," he protested. "Can't we just leave her here? The cold will kill her."

Lucas shook his head. "She's gonna wake up, and when she does, she'll be mightily pissed off and will bring down the full wrath of the Templars on us all. Get it?"

Leo knew that he was right; Morgana's revenge would be terrible. He had to kill her. Trudging over to where the spears were, he picked one up and carried it over to the fallen Morgana. When he reached her, he slipped his foot underneath her shoulder and rolled her onto her back. He carefully lined up the spear with her heart, and then lifted it into the air, preparing to strike. Seconds before he was about to drive the blade into her chest, he happened to glance at her face and something purple caught his eye. It was a purple fringe. The realisation hit him like a sledgehammer, and he was on his knees in a heartbeat, sweeping Morgana's hair away from her face.

"Holy fuck!"

"What is it?"

"This isn't Morgana."

"Are you sure?" Lucas asked, placing Ela on the ground and sprinting over to inspect the body.

"I'm sure," Leo said, getting to his feet. "I know what that psycho bitch looks like, and this isn't her."

"Fuck!" Lucas cursed, peering down at the false Morgana.

"If she isn't here, where the fuck is she?" Leo's chest tightened. He knew exactly where she was.

Lucas' eyes darkened. "The bitch has played us."

"Oh my god…Daniel," Leo whispered, his hand covering his mouth.

"We have to go," Lucas said urgently.

Leo didn't need to be told twice. He turned away from the false Morgana, at exactly the same time as Lucas, to witness the young Templar boy plunging a spear through Ela's chest. Time stood still as the biting wind whipped Leo's face and hauled at his clothes. The sleet continued to bounce of his face, but he didn't feel any of it. He heard nothing except the beating of his shattered heart, and the whistling of the piercing wind. His wide eyes flitted between the boy and the spear that he had so skilfully impaled into the heart of his dear friend and mentor.

The implications of the Templar's actions finally overrode his shock, and something inside him snapped. Lightning flew from his hands, and a fork of brilliant electric blue struck the boy in the middle of the chest, blasting him off his feet and slamming him against one of the monument's pillars. He streamed the lightning continuously, holding the Templar in place until his murderous body was smoking, and the life was fading from his eyes. When he stopped the flow of lightning, the dead boy slid down the pillar, staring at Leo with vacant eyes. Guilt and remorse attacked his conscience simultaneously, and he suddenly felt like vomiting.

"Leo, quickly!"

Lucas' voice saved him from dealing with his emotions, and he rushed over to the demon who was doing his best to stem the flow of blood pumping from Ela's chest.

"Jesus Christ! There's blood everywhere!"

"We need to stop the bleeding, get me the jacket! Quick!"

Leo looked to where Lucas was pointing and realised the Templar must have discarded the jacket they'd covered Ela with before carrying out his grisly deed. That thought made him even angrier. He scrambled over to the jacket and retrieved it for Lucas who pressed it against the wound.

"She's still breathing…there might be a chance…" Lucas tried to sound hopeful, but his eyes gave him away. "You have to try and heal her!"

Leo closed his eyes and took one of Ela's hands, sandwiching it in between both of his and gently trying to rub some warmth into it. It was like holding a block of ice. As he began to channel every ounce of energy he had into healing Ela's wounds, the wind carried loud and angry voices to his ears. He opened an eye, scanning to see where the noise was coming from.

"It's just the Elect. Keep going," Lucas told him over the rabble of voices which were growing louder very quickly.

Leo shut his eye and merged his divine energy with Ela's. As the two powerful energies came into contact, the sounds of the Elect's voices and stampeding feet started to fade. Suddenly, his entire body juddered as a foreign energy invaded his system. His head flung backwards, his eyes snapped open, and a rush of overwhelming power took hold of him and propelled him upwards. Clouds flew past as he soared into the brightest parts of the sky, continuing on through the atmosphere and into the unknown depths of the cosmos.

Chapter 22
Between Realms

Leo had no idea how long he'd been travelling through the cosmos for, but the journey, which had been a blur of stars, planets and asteroids, came to a sudden end when he found himself being hauled into what appeared to be a black hole. The moment he entered the black anomaly, a white light appeared that steadily grew in intensity until he was blinded by it. He wanted to close his eyes, shield them from the dazzling light, but he didn't have any eyelids to perform such an action. It should have worried him that he was either dead or had been hit with a spell, but worrying was hard to do when you didn't have a physical body riddled with hormones and pain receptors to process and feel such things. There was only one way to describe how he felt: peaceful. The perils and worries of the real world didn't seem to matter here, and wherever here was, the rules didn't apply.

He soon realised that he didn't care if he ever went back to his body. In his conscious mind, he knew Ela had been brutally murdered, and that he, or his body at least, was at the top of Fyrish hill in the Highlands of Scotland. He knew exactly how he *should* be feeling, but he was experiencing real difficulty in actually *feeling*. He was experiencing a tremendous sense of weightlessness, and he felt like all the negativity and problems of human life had been taken away. He was completely unburdened. Nothing mattered here; here was love, happiness, contentment, tranquillity and peace in their purest form.

As he basked in the glory and awe of overwhelming love, he felt a presence approaching him. The blinding white light dimmed gradually, and he blinked before bringing his right hand up to eye level, turning it around and inspecting it closely. It looked and felt like a normal hand, but he knew it was all an illusion. He touched his face; the skin was warm and smooth.

"Hello, Leo."

He lowered his hand slowly to his side, his eyes focusing on the shining white orb that hovered before him. He suspected the voice had come from the orb, but he didn't respond, just waited. A few seconds later, the orb began to change shape, stretching and twisting into a humanoid shaped silhouette. Radiant rays of white exploded from the silhouette like giant laser beams, twisting through the air like a kaleidoscope and drawing his attention to the fact there was now a sky above him, an ocean in front of him, and a sandy beach beneath him.

The view above his head was a stargazer's dream: a night time sky speckled with millions of glittering stars that were laid out in fascinating clusters and constellations around a magnificent full moon. Beneath his feet, the moon cast her silvery light on the dry cool sand, illuminating the shards of crystal within its grains. The ocean in front of him acted like an enormous mirror, reflecting the picturesque sky off its perfectly still surface. The faintest of breezes tickled his nose and ruffled his hair as the rays of light were drawn back inside the silhouette. The rays completely vanished leaving Ela St Clair in their place.

"Ela!" he exclaimed.

S.R. FRASER

She smiled sadly, folding her arms around her midsection before turning her back on him and gazing out into the depthless ocean. "Yes, it's me," she confirmed.

"What's happening?"

The gentle breeze grew slightly stronger and tugged on Ela's clothes. "I brought you here," she said, her eyes fixed on the water.

"Where are we?"

"We're between the spiritual and physical world."

"Are we dead?"

Ela laughed softly. "You're not. I am."

Leo gasped. "Oh, Ela."

"It's okay, really. It was only a matter of time before it happened, although, I didn't think it would've been a Templar. I'm sure Lucas told you about my ancestry."

"He did," Leo said, taking a few steps forward until he was standing beside her. "Ela, I don't get it. If you were the last living descendent of Frederick St Clair, why didn't you continue the bloodline?"

Ela sighed and finally pulled her gaze away from the ocean. Her eyes, with their peculiar shade of pale blue, were full of regret. As she spoke, melancholy laced every word. "When I was in my late teens, I decided the Elect way of life wasn't for me. I did everything in my power to rebel against my parents. They taught me from a young age that my sole purpose on this earth was to protect the Power and to create life, ensuring that our bloodline survived, and that Baal would remain forever imprisoned. I, like most teenagers, had other plans for my life. I wasn't going to have a baby because my parents demanded it of me. I was going to travel the globe and see as much of this beautiful world as I could. And I did, Leo. I have seen more of this planet than the majority of the human population, and it is breath taking." She smiled. It was genuine and warm.

"What was your favourite part?"

She gazed out into the still ocean once more as she pondered over his question. "All of it," she finally said.

"Our world is wonderfully majestic. I can't believe I used to deny the existence of a creator."

Leo raised his eyebrows. "You did?"

Ela nodded solemnly. "I did."

"What changed your mind?"

"The more I saw of this world, the more wonders I unlocked. With each new wonder, I became enlightened. For this world to exist, everything, and I mean absolutely everything, has to be in perfect harmony with everything else. Have you ever looked at our world and thought to yourself—how? How is it that this planet is the perfect distance from the sun so that we're neither too close that we'd burn, nor too far away that we'd freeze? How did the moon come to be the correct distance away from the earth so the tides are perfectly controlled? How is this planet perfect in every single way possible for human life to exist?"

Leo shrugged. "I've no idea, I'm not a scientist."

"We're the most advanced we've ever been in the field of science, and they boast about their achievements, their research and experiments, and how great science is. And yet, despite their unnerving levels of intelligence, they belittle the idea of God, denying He exists because there is no evidence. I wonder, seeing as they're so adamant He doesn't exist, why they persist in trying to unlock the secrets of the universe with the motive to disprove His very existence? Always busy trying to explain the universe through theories that are highly probable but never exact." Ela shook her head despondently. "The truth is, Leo, their theories will never be exact, and they'll never unlock the secrets of the universe. Do you know why?"

Leo found himself shrugging again. "I don't know. I'd like to think that it's not their secrets to unlock, that it's not for any of us to know."

Ela turned and beamed at him. "You'll make a fine Grandmaster." Just then, the breeze became a gust, unsettling the ocean and sending loose grains of sand rolling along the beach. The sudden change in weather seemed to instil a sense of urgency in Ela.

"Sorry, I seem to have gotten a little side tracked and haven't answered your original question. In the early days of my rebellion, I found myself in Madrid where I fell in love with a man called Carlos Rodriguez. We hit it off straight away, and I soon found out he was an Elect too. An Elect who was also rebelling was my perfect match. His rebellion was a lot darker than mine which I soon discovered. He was into demons in a big way although nothing with pure demons or your average demon. It began with lesser demons. The experience of being seduced by a demon is intoxicating and completely mind blowing. We became hooked and moved onto incubi and succubi, conjuring them whenever we could. We let ourselves slip into orgasmic states of unconsciousness for days…you don't seem shocked by this."

"I'm not. Let's just say I would be the last person to make judgements about sleeping with a demon." He knew exactly what it was like to be seduced by a demon, and he couldn't wait to have sex with Lucas again.

Ela raised her brows. "You and Lucas have—?"

"Yeah. It was great. Best sex ever. Like I said, no judgements here."

The Grandmaster smiled before continuing. "With years of demon orgies under my belt, I thought I was well versed in using contraception, even with Carlos. But accidents do happen. I fell pregnant. Long story short, I had an abortion. I didn't want a baby at the time, and I was determined not to let my parents win. Days after the abortion, I experienced severe haemorrhaging and was rushed into hospital. I fell unconscious in the ambulance and woke up three days later to find myself in a hospital bed recovering from an emergency hysterectomy."

"Oh, Ela," Leo said sympathetically, his hand reaching over and resting on her shoulder.

"I didn't get over it for years, decades even. As you would expect, my parent's blamed me. They hated me for a long time, but we reconciled shortly before they left this world." Ela closed her eyes and smiled. "I can feel them close by. They're calling to me." After a few moments, her eyes fluttered open and the smile was gone. "I don't have much time left. I brought you here to tell you something I should have told you a long time ago."

"What is it?" Leo questioned. "And please don't talk in riddles. I'm sick of solving them." he added grumpily.

Ela flashed another smile. "I don't do riddles," she assured him before getting serious again. "It's about Eden's Gift and the ally of the Elect. I have reason to believe Noah was the last Grandmaster to possess Eden's Gift. Once Baal has been destroyed, you must channel all of your energies into finding it."

"Destroy Baal? How am I meant to—"

"You will. Baal is strong, but you're stronger. Lucas saw you killing him in a vision."

"Lucas said his visions don't always come—"

"Leo, please! No more interruptions. I have to cross over soon, and our time here will end. There is one other thing. The Elect's ally is here in Inverness."

"Where?"

"I only know it resides in Inverness. I don't know the exact location, but you have to find it." Ela delicately cupped the side of Leo's face. "Our time is up for now."

"Wait, what about Daniel?"

"I'm not worried about Daniel. He has you to protect him."

"Then he's royally fucked." Leo said bluntly.

Ela chuckled. "Not at all. You must go to him now."

"What if Baal is already there?"

"Baal is trapped until I cross over. There isn't much time. We must say goodbye."

Leo swallowed hard. He didn't think he'd be able to cry in Ela's illusion, but it turned out he could.

"I know," Ela said soothingly, pulling him into a tight hug. "It's not forever, sweetie. It's just for a little while. We'll see each other again."

"I know that," he sniffed, "It's just that…I can't do this without you."

Ela released him from her hug and took a step back, smiling down at his tear stained face. "You can, and you will. Believe in yourself. I do, and so does Lucas. And most importantly, so does Daniel. You're his father now, and he needs you." Ela began walking backwards onto the water. The rising wind tugged at her clothes. "Go to him now. Remember, once Baal is gone, look for Eden's Gift. You'll need it." She turned on her heel and continued her journey across the water.

"What if I can't find it?" he shouted after her.

"You will," she replied, coming to a stop in the middle of the ocean.

"I love you!"

"I love you too," Ela called over her shoulder. "Now, be brave. The lions are coming." With those words, she raised her arms into the air and became the blazing white silhouette again. She shone so brightly that everything else started to blur.

The sandy beach under his feet disappeared, and he had the sensation he was falling rapidly through space and time. He'd have thrown his arms out to try and grab onto something, but whatever illusion Ela had created was gone, leaving him in what he assumed was a spirit like form. As he sped through the void, the brightness faded to black, and he heard a low droning sound. The longer he fell, the louder and clearer the sound became. It was a voice, a very familiar male voice, and it was calling his name.

"Leo! Can you hear me? Leo! Wake up."

On a Highland hilltop, lying before the Fyrish monument, Leo Alexander's body jerked violently as his spirit returned home.

Chapter 23
War

"He's awake!"

The first thing Leo became aware of was how heavy his body felt. He prised his eyes open before dragging his head off Lucas' lap.

"Don't get up!" Lucas instructed, placing a hand on Leo's shoulder.

"I'm fine," Leo replied groggily, ignoring the demon's concern and sitting up. Ela's body was beside him, lying in the snow, and getting soaked by the sleet. John and Cathy were crouched beside her with their heads bowed low, tears spilling from their eyes, both consumed with grief. He shuffled across the snow and knelt by Ela's head, placing a hand on her cheek. He stroked it gently for a minute and studied the peaceful expression on the former Grandmaster's face. She wasn't in there; it was a shell. A useless shell that looked beautiful and sophisticated, even in death. He leant forward and kissed her on the forehead.

"Until we meet again," he whispered. After paying his final respects to his fallen friend, he stood up on shaky legs.

"Are you okay?" Lucas asked, getting to his feet and watching Leo's every move.

Leo shook his head. "Not really, but my pain doesn't matter right now. We need to get to the Cathedral, and we need to get there fast."

"By the time we get to the Cathedral," John said quietly, looking up from his kneeling position, "Baal will have begun Armageddon."

Feelings of defeat and despair hovered around Leo, waiting to ensnare him in their cold calculating jaws as he looked at the Elect members gathered around Ela's corpse. At a quick glance, he estimated there were seventy left and was thankful to see the triplets were amongst the survivors. "There has to be a way!" he said desperately, holding his hands out, "The world hasn't ended yet."

John lowered his eyes back to Ela. "We're too far away, and we can't just leave our deceased friends and family up here. By the time we bury our dead and return to the buses, it'll be too late."

Leo nodded his head. "I understand, John, but I have to get to Daniel before Baal does."

"I know." There was a short silence before the Elite leader continued. "You and Lucas return to the Cathedral. Do what you can while we bury our dead. If the world hasn't ended, we'll meet you there."

"The world won't end today," Lucas said confidently. "We'll see you guys at the Cathedral. Come on, Leo." The demon turned on his heel and started striding through the snow.

"I'm sorry for your losses," Leo said to John and the severely depleted Elect army. After taking one last look at Ela, he jogged across the hilltop towards Lucas who waited at the top of the path that would lead them down to the car park.

"Leo, are you sure you're—"

"Don't," Leo interrupted, his eyes pleading. "I can't talk about it right now. I have to stay focused on Daniel." The demon didn't say anything for which he was glad. After a moment, Leo spoke again. "Let's go."

The demon gave a little nod. "Sure," he said before turning, bending his knees, and arching his back forward. "Climb on, and make sure you keep your legs above my waist."

Leo clambered onto the demon's back and fastened his arms securely around his strong neck and broad shoulders while keeping his legs above his waist.

"You need to take a tighter grip," Lucas instructed.

Leo complied and squeezed his arms as hard as he could.

"That's good. Now, just to warn you, I'm going into demon mode, okay?"

"Do what you have to. Let's just get out of here." Leo saw the back of Lucas' neck go from smooth and tanned, to papery and pale. Crimson veins poked through the rough skin confirming the transformation was complete.

"Ready?"

"Yeah, I'm ready."

The wind whipped Leo's face and whistled in his ears signalling that Lucas had begun flying down the hill. His stomach flipped and lurched with every stride the demon took, so he closed his eyes and concentrated solely on not falling off. His knuckles were white as he clung on, desperately trying to ignore the growing strain in his muscles from gripping so tightly. Every now and then, he'd open an eye and try to take in the view, but he'd only last five seconds before feeling nauseous and have to close it. It didn't seem like any time had passed at all when Leo felt Lucas gradually slowing down.

"We're almost there," he told Leo. "We're nearly at the river."

Leo was hit with a rush of adrenaline. His mouth became dry, and he felt light headed and dizzy. His guts curdled with anxiety at the prospect of what they were walking into.

'You're probably going to die, you do know that, right?' his inner voice asked reproachfully.

He was saved the hassle of engaging in an argument with himself when the sound of wailing sirens erupted in the distance. He opened his eyes to find they were standing outside the entrance to his flat. A handful of Invernesians scoured the city in boisterous groups looking for evening entertainment. Ahead of him was a Police car which had just finished racing across the bridge, its tyres squealing as it swung violently into the street running parallel to the River Ness. That particular street led to the Cathedral.

"That's not a good sign," Lucas said dolefully.

"Move!" Leo commanded, squeezing his aching arms and legs against the demon like he would a horse.

Everything went blurry as Lucas bolted across the bridge and overtook the squealing police car. Seconds later, they'd stopped abruptly. Leo's eyes took a moment to adjust, and when they did, he realised they were standing in the Cathedral car park at the bottom of the steps leading up to the giant building. Looking down at them from the top of the steps and blocking the main doorway, was a large crowd of armed Templars.

He unwrapped himself immediately from Lucas and found his footing on the snowy ground. From inside the Cathedral, he could hear that a fierce battle was taking place; screaming, shouting, and the sounds of magical explosions rang through the night, and there was no second guessing where the fight was taking place.

"The courtyard," Lucas said, still sporting his demon look. "We need to get to the courtyard."

"How are we going to get past the welcoming committee?" Leo asked.

"They won't be a problem," Lucas replied.

"Lucas, there's like a hundred of them! How the hell will they not be a problem?"

"Because we have back up."

"Really? I don't see any back up!" Leo said irately. Lucas nodded his head backwards in a brisk motion. Leo glanced back to find the car park littered with several police cars and five black Range Rovers. A squad of forty or so poker faced policemen stood behind the vehicles. A man in a beige trench coat emerged from the sea of uniforms and marched in their direction, his bearded face steely and focused.

"Senor Lucas," the man said in a thick Spanish accent. "What's happened?"

"They've come for the Power, Carlos," Lucas answered without looking at the man. "How long have you been here?"

Leo searched his memories and remembered that Lucas had called this man to report the murder of the Macintoshes. Carlos was an Elect which meant the men behind him were also Elect.

The Spanish man's honey coloured eyes flitted between Lucas and Leo. He ran a hand through his long brown hair while responding to the question. "Twenty minutes ago. We intercepted a call to the Police informing them of a disturbance at the Cathedral. We didn't want to act until we knew what was happening."

Lucas nodded, his black eyes devouring his potential victims. "Good."

"We need to get in there. Can your men help?" Leo asked, looking hopeful.

"Of course. My men are prepared to attack. Just tell me when to give the order."

"What kind of attack have you got planned?" Lucas asked.

Carlos stroked his well-groomed beard. "One that will annihilate every one of those bastards."

Lucas finally pulled his feasting stare away from the enemy to look at Carlos. "You never disappoint, Senor." The demon grinned exposing almost perfect teeth, his incisors now razor sharp fangs.

"Ready when you are, friend," Carlos said with a grin of his own.

Lucas let the grin disappear from his face and returned his soulless gaze to his imminent prey. He curled his lips back over his teeth. "Carlos, when your men launch their attack, Leo and I will run to the main door. You and your men guard the main entrance after we've gone in, and keep any civilians away from the building until this is over. Anything trying to get in or out of the Cathedral that isn't Elect, kill them. Entiendes?"

"Si, Senor. I understand perfectly."

"Good. Leo, stay close to me. Cast to kill. Okay?"

Leo nodded and fixed a hostile gaze on the Templars as the air around him became magically charged.

"Give the command," Lucas told Carlos.

As Carlos marched back to his men, Leo turned to look at Lucas. The demon was quivering with anticipation, and his forked tongue swiped off the excessive saliva that ran out from the sides of his mouth. It had just occurred to Leo that once they went into the Cathedral there was no guarantee that they'd both come out alive. With that sickening thought, he reached over and took Lucas' rough, veiny hand and squeezed tenderly. Lucas didn't turn his head, and he showed no reaction to Leo's touch except for a gentle squeeze of his own.

Carlos shouted and several beach ball sized orbs of varying colours streaked through the air towards the Cathedral. Around half of the Templars lifted their arms above their heads and summoned one enormous energy shield. The orbs rained down and exploded against it in a chorus of deafening bangs.

"Shit," Lucas cursed.

"Again!" bellowed Carlos.

"Bastards," Lucas snarled when the Elect's orbs failed to penetrate the Templars' defence for a second time. "They're too strong."

"We're getting into that Cathedral," Leo stated, the air around him beginning to crackle incessantly. "Elect!" he shouted. "Prepare to attack again."

"Leo, it's useless," Lucas told him.

"Get ready to run," Leo ordered, his eyes flashing with emerald fire. He threw his hand skywards, and a massive bolt of forked lightning rained down on the Templars. The holy men let out a collective scream of outrage as their defence was completely obliterated. Carlos' men let loose a fresh wave of deadly Elect magic. It exploded among their enemies, scattering them in different directions. When the dust settled, around half of the Templars were either dead or unconscious.

Leo's legs felt like lead as he chased Lucas up the stone steps. By the time he reached the top, the enemy had rounded on Lucas and were using their swords, axes and maces to drive him back. Despite the pure demon's speed, they managed to spill his blood. Enraged, Leo unleashed a tirade of magical attacks in the form of fire, setting several of the Templars ablaze before sprinting towards the Cathedral door.

As he approached the thick wooden doors, he threw a powerful blast of energy at them, blowing them from their hinges and sending them crashing into some nearby pews. His eyes swept vigilantly from wall to wall and floor to ceiling as he ran to the door leading to the dormitories. He hugged the wall next to the door and reached out to it, slowly pushing it open and expecting an array of arrows to come flitting through. When nothing deadly came through the door, he poked his head around and discovered a lonely dormitory corridor.

"Empty."

Leo jumped when Lucas' voice came out of nowhere.

"Stop doing that!" Leo hissed.

"Doing what?"

"Scaring the shit out of me! Make noise so I know you're there!"

"Oh, sorry."

"It's okay," Leo replied, his tone more neutral, and turned his attention to the deserted corridor before them. "You want to lead the way?"

The demon nodded. "Sure."

He followed Lucas into the lounge, a room which had always been warm, inviting and homely with beautiful comfy furniture and a roaring fire. Now it lay in ruin, with the furniture overturned and broken, the fireplace black and empty. The Templar's cruel hand had touched the very heart of the Cathedral, tarnishing it forever. Leo found himself moving to the couch which had been tipped on its side, its white innards spilling out from the gashes in its red velvety fabric. Crouching down, he placed a hand on one of the cushions, pressing into it and feeling its softness. Lucas squeezed his shoulder.

"Everything alright?"

Leo shook his head softly. "No, no it's not. This room...I...I sat on this couch countless times with Daniel...reading, laughing, messing around, talking about...well, everything really. I remember the times we'd sit around the fire with Ela, and she'd tell us about her life and the things she'd seen. We'd all listen, captivated and enthralled as she whisked us off to Turkey or America or Egypt. We felt safe here—loved. Look at what they've done to it. They've tainted our sanctuary."

"I know."

"I've never hated anybody before, Lucas, but I hate *them*. I hate that they want to kill Daniel. I hate that they think they're doing God's work. But most of all, I hate them for making me feel hatred."

"Wanna go kill some Templars?"

Leo stood to his full height. "This ends tonight."

They swept out of the lounge and entered the dining room to find that it had also been smashed up. The sight of the broken chairs and chopped up dining table fed Leo's rising fury. He followed Lucas into the corridor beyond the dining room door.

As expected, the corridor was dimly lit by the Cathedral's wall mounted torches. Not all of the torches had been ignited, so the corridor was gloomier than usual. Directly opposite where Leo stood was Mrs Ellen's kitchen. It was in total blackness. The kitchen door still lay on the floor from where Lucas had kicked it off its hinges hours before.

"Wait while I check in here," Lucas instructed, moving into the kitchen and being swallowed up by the darkness.

Leo waited in the corridor, straining his ears in an attempt to hear the sounds of the fight, but he could hear nothing, a testament to the thickness of the Cathedral's old stone walls. He heard a creaking noise and spun round.

"It's only me," Lucas whispered, emerging like a phantom from the darkness of the kitchen. "Nothing in there."

"Everyone must be in the courtyard," Leo said, turning on his heel and running down the corridor. Lucas caught up with ease.

"The courtyard is enclosed, so there is nowhere for the Templars to run. Use a chain lightning spell," Lucas advised as he ran with perfect grace alongside Leo.

"Got it," Leo replied as they came to a blind corner in the corridor. Lucas signalled for him to stop by holding up a veiny hand. He blinked, and Lucas was gone. Even though he was used to Lucas' abilities, he was still mightily impressed every time he witnessed them.

"Clear," Lucas announced seconds later.

Leo broke into another run and rounded the corner. One hundred metres down this particular corridor lay the double doors leading to the courtyard. As he ran towards them, he couldn't help wondering what they were going to find when they arrived at their destination. How many Templars were they dealing with? Had they broken into the Haven? What would the death toll be?

"They'll be going for the Haven," Lucas said as if he'd just read Leo's mind. "We're almost there. Remember, summon chain lightning and take out as many as you can, then get yourself inside the Haven, find Daniel, and get the hell out of here."

"What about Morgana?" Leo asked. The distance between them and the courtyard doors were closing rapidly.

Lucas let out a blood curdling growl. "I'll take care of her. You concentrate on getting into the Haven and finding our boy."

"Got it," Leo said as they came to a stop in front of the courtyard doors.

"Okay, you ready?"

"Almost," Leo replied, reaching over and wrapping his hand around the back of Lucas' head and pulling him into a lingering kiss. With his eyes closed, it felt every bit like Lucas. When he broke the kiss and peered up at the demon, he couldn't help but grin.

"What was that for?" Lucas asked a little breathlessly.

Leo shrugged. "I just wanted you to know, in case one of us dies, that I love you."

Lucas reached over with one hand and placed it against Leo's cheek. "I love you too, but we're not dying today. Are you ready to show those Templars that they made the biggest mistake of their lives coming here tonight?"

Leo's eyes blazed with dazzling emerald light as white sparks of energy crackled around his hands. "I'm ready."

Lucas kicked the doors open and charged through them. The sound of war ripped through the corridor like a tidal wave, stirring up a fresh surge of adrenaline inside Leo which drove him through the double doors and into the heart of the fight.

It was carnage. The Templars were like a colony of attacking ants; they were everywhere. Bodies littered the bloodstained ground of the courtyard, both Elect and Templar. Arrows, fire, spears, ice, crossbow bolts and lightning whizzed through the air. Swords, axes and maces clashed and scraped together as each weapon tried to claim a life. The dull thudding of freshly killed bodies hitting the frozen floor was almost rhythmic while the pools and rivers of blood created artistic patterns in the snow. Over by the Haven, a large group of Templars were trying to fight their way inside.

As Leo stepped into the fray, his eyes were drawn to several Templar soldiers who were wildly swinging their medieval weaponry at three Elect women. It was clear by looking at their young heart shaped faces, their gentle brown eyes, and their long auburn hair that they were sisters. They had been backed against the square base of the frozen marble fountain and were frantically summoning energy shields to their defence. Their shields fizzled into nothingness under the might of the Templar attacks, and the women, realising they were about to be defeated, had joined hands, preparing themselves for death. The eldest sister stepped forward and acted as a human shield for her younger siblings while staring at her foes with fierce defiance. Her two sisters wept silently behind her, awaiting their fates. Evil laughs and taunts spilled from the Templars' mouths like poisonous bile as they raised their weapons to land the fatal blows. Red hot anger erupted within Leo, and there was nothing he could do to stop himself from releasing it.

He thrust his hands violently outwards, and the air around him exploded with mystical energy. The frozen waters of the fountain became a blazing inferno that rose high into the air where it twisted and coiled together until it became the shape of a unicorn. Wide eyed with fear, the Templars slowly backed away from the flaming mythical beast that reared up on its hind legs before leaping forward. The Templars disappeared under a blanket of fire as the unicorn landed on top of them, reducing them to nothing more than ash and dust. Once he saw that the sisters were safe, he lifted his burning emerald eyes to the heavens and commanded the element of lightning. A blue and white bolt streaked down through the sky and struck him on the chest where it then travelled to his fingertips.

"Elect filth!"

Upon hearing the words, Leo snapped his head forward and set his eyes upon the foreboding Templar standing before him. The brute's blood stained axe glinted as he twirled it around in his hand. He had a bald head which was splattered with blood and laden with scars. It was clear his pudgy nose had been broken more than once, and he was missing his left ear. His eyes were like Morgana's, grey and devoid of humanity. When he spoke, it sounded like he smoked a hundred cigarettes a day.

"Come on then, faggot, let's dan—" The lightning struck before the Templar troll could react, and his whole body convulsed as the electricity flew through him, shocking him to the core and annihilating his central nervous system.

When Leo shut off the lightning, the troll's lifeless body hit the ground hard. He didn't have a second to dwell on the kill as a large group of Templars, who had witnessed the flaming unicorn and the lightning attack, were thundering towards him to avenge their fallen comrades. A flash of blue and white lit up the courtyard momentarily as Leo threw a bolt of lightning and struck the closest Templar in the face. The bolt split into tendrils on impact and each tendril struck the others in the same place. Their collective screams of agony pierced the air and caught many of the Templars' attention.

Like a stampede of sleek black bison, the Templars surged forward as one. Leo took a deep calming breath and closed his eyes. Everything in the physical world slowed down as he reached deep into his solar plexus and touched the divine power residing within his soul. The tendrils of lightning which carried out his bidding withdrew and were sucked back into the palm of his hand where they began to form into an electrical orb of energy. The orb pulsated and grew bigger and brighter as he drew on his own divinity. When he'd powered the orb sufficiently, his eyes fluttered open to see more than fifty Templars just metres away. He tossed the charged orb above their heads where it rapidly spun and hovered in the air, releasing a chain of lightning that struck the entire group. Some Templars turned their eyes to look at the beautiful orb; most never. Those who'd dared to look saw a flash of blue and white before their lives were snuffed out.

After the mass electrocution, Leo stood still for a moment, gazing at the enormity of his destruction. He'd killed more than fifty people in less than thirty seconds yet felt no remorse. He felt no pleasure from the killings either, but he'd expected to feel some form of guilt; it never came.

'They'll kill you without question. Their sole purpose is to end Daniel's life. Don't question your lack of guilt. Embrace it.'

Leo, spurred on by his inner voice, turned his attention to the large group of Templars congregated around the Haven. It was clear they weren't letting anyone in or out, but he couldn't figure out why. He assumed the Templars would have used all of their resources to storm the Haven and destroy the Power; it didn't make sense.

"They can't get the door unlocked," Lucas said, appearing beside him. Blood dripped from his hands and mouth, and he was topless. "It's sealed magically, and only a true Elect can open it. Morgana won't be able to open it without one of your kind."

"She's a smart girl," Leo said, eyeing up the Templars who guarded the Haven, "she'll figure it out. We need to draw them away so I can get in."

Lucas was about to speak when a female Templar came out of nowhere and swung a mace at his head. In the blink of an eye, the demon grabbed her wrist in mid-swing and crushed it. She let out an agonising scream that was cut short when Lucas took her head in his hands and viciously snapped her neck. He let her body fall to the ground before crouching in front of Leo.

"Get on my back," he instructed, "I have an idea."

Leo climbed on without question and held onto the demon's broad shoulders, marvelling at how hot the skin was. "What's your idea?"

"We're going in. Clear a path like you did at Fyrish."

"There's too many of them. I can't."

"Yes, you can!"

"Lucas, there was only ten of them at the monument," Leo pointed out. "There's five times that amount!"

"You just fried fifty people and didn't break a sweat."

Leo opened his mouth to protest further but closed it when he realised Lucas was right; he could do it. Holding his hand flat out, a transparent orb formed in his palm and slowly grew to the size of a football. He was amazed at being able to concentrate so well with a mini war being fought all around him. When the orb had accumulated enough energy, he sent it whizzing over to the Haven where it stopped right in the middle of the Templar guards.

"Go!" Leo yelled as he locking his arms around Lucas' neck. An explosion was followed by a whooshing sound as the orb expanded with great speed. Every Templar was hurled backwards as the energy swept them off the ground. The courtyard blurred as Lucas seized the opportunity to race across the battlefield, and the next thing Leo saw was the familiar bronze tablet depicting the beasts from the biblical book of Daniel.

"And that's how it's done," Lucas said smugly.

"That was easier than I thought," Leo commented as he scrabbled down from Lucas' back. He observed the fallen Templars who were all doubled over, squirming on the frozen ground and gasping for air.

"Good job," Lucas grinned. "Maybe next time you'll—"

The bolt was lodged in Lucas' shoulder before either of them could react. The demon snarled ferociously and whipped his head around to find his attacker perched on the marbled shoulder of Michael. The Templar had reloaded his crossbow and was once again taking aim at Lucas.

Leo raised his hand to cast a fireball.

"No." Lucas pushed Leo's hand down. "Let the little fucker try it a second time."

The crossbow recoiled in the Templar's arms as he released the bolt. When the bolt was almost upon him, Lucas reached out a hand and swiped it out of the air. He grinned toothily at the shocked Templar before pulling his arm back and hurling the bolt back at him. The Templar fell from the statue with the bolt protruding from his forehead.

"Fucker!" Lucas repeated while yanking the bolt from his shoulder. There was a squishing noise as the wound closed over, and Lucas' demonic body healed itself.

"That would be so cool if the noises weren't so gross," Leo said, his expression one of revulsion.

"Demonist," Lucas joked before pushing the Haven door open. "After you, sir."

The door swung open to reveal a severely pissed off Morgana, wearing a gold horned helm and a gold plated suit of armour. Both were dented and stained with blood.

"Lucas, look out!" Leo shouted, but it was too late.

Lucas went completely rigid when the axe embedded itself into his skull. He stared blankly at Morgana for a moment before muttering, "Son of a bitch." Morgana wasted no time in conjuring an energy blast which projected Lucas into the air and through the statue of the Virgin.

"Alone at last," Morgana sneered, swinging another of her throwing axes at Leo.

Leo dropped to the ground like a stone and kicked out as hard as he could. His foot collided with her knee, and she crumpled to the ground. She attempted another strike with her axe, but he struck out again and kicked her across the face, sending her sprawling along the floor and back into the alcove. He pulled himself off the ground and stepped into the alcove to see her struggling to her feet. When she finally stood, she limped to the wall and leant against it for support. To her left, the blue door that led to the Haven was visible, an indication she had penetrated the powerful magic that concealed it.

"You're not going in there," Leo told her.

"Fool!" Morgana spat, putting weight on her injured knee and twisting it so that it cracked loudly. "I've already been in. Where is he?"

Leo's mind raced; she obviously meant Daniel. If he wasn't in there, then where the hell was he?

"I'm going to ask you one more time," Morgana hissed, her armour scraping against the wall as she pushed her body off it. She took a step forward, limp now gone, and pointed a throwing axe at him. "Where is the Power?"

"I don't know," Leo answered honestly.

"Liar!"

"He was supposed to be here. We left him while we went to save Ela."

Morgana smiled wickedly. "Oh, and how did that work out for the old dear?"

"About the same as it did for the Templars who were stupid enough to get in Lucas' way," Leo fired back, his anger stirring. The fireball came at a frightful speed, but he had been prepared, sending an ice spell to freeze it in mid-flight. It fell to the ground and smashed into shards of ice at his feet.

"They trained you well," Morgana said, her tone indicating it was a fact rather than a compliment. "This is your last chance—where is he?"

"For the last time, I don't fucking know! All I know is that he and the world are in even more danger because you fuckwits have set Baal free!"

Morgana let out a high pitched sound that could have been a laugh. "If you think that fantasy story will distract me from killing you then you are sorely mistaken."

"He's telling the truth."

Morgana's eyes shifted from Leo to Lucas who'd just entered the alcove. The axe was gone from his head, and his demon healing abilities had eradicated all traces of the wound.

"Your actions have freed Baal, you stupid little bitch," Lucas sneered while coming to stand at Leo's side. "And like always, myself and the Elect are going to have to clean up your mess."

"If Baal has been freed, why isn't he here?"

"He'll be here," Lucas replied arrogantly. "Just be thankful you'll be dead long before he does."

Morgana's eyes narrowed. "I won't be the one dying, demon."

Leo held Lucas back as the demon made a move to attack. "Help the Elect to clear up the courtyard. Give any Templar left standing the chance to surrender," Leo instructed. "I'll take care of this one."

"Are you sure about this?" Lucas asked, his brow furrowed.

Leo nodded. "I owe it to Ela."

"How pathetically noble of you," Morgana jeered, anticipation and excitement dancing in her eyes.

Lucas gave Leo's shoulder a squeeze. "Be careful. I'll see you outside when you're done," he said before leaving the alcove.

Morgana ran her tongue over her bottom lip. "I thought he'd never leave," she purred. "I'm really going to enjoy this."

Leo raised an eyebrow. "You're going to enjoy dying?"

"I never told you what I did to the seer who prophesised your coming, did I?" Morgana asked with a smirk, slowly pacing around Leo like a hungry lioness.

Leo turned on the spot, following Morgana as she stalked him. He did his best to look bored. "No, you didn't, but if it's going to be a long story, save it. Your girly voice kinda grates on me." He enjoyed watching the smirk fall from her face.

"You need to learn to respect your elders, little boy!"

"Respect is earned, not gained."

"You sound like that pacifying, shrivelled up old crone that my followers butchered at the monument."

Her words stung, but he didn't let it show. "So, are you going to tell me about the seer already, or are you just going to bore me to death?" He could tell Morgana wasn't used to people talking to her in such a disrespectful manner; she couldn't hide the fury from her face.

"I plucked her eyes out!"

"Wow. Did the truth about me being your equal upset you that much?" Leo had adopted the arrogant and pig-headed tone he used whenever he was trying to piss somebody off. The twitch in Morgana's lip told him it was working.

"You're not my equal!" she screamed, her face twisting into something far more frightening than any demonic visage.

"Jeez, calm down. I know I'm not your equal—I'm your superior."

"I'm going to rip out your spine, you little bastard!"

Leo looked at her with mock outrage. "Well, there is absolutely no need for that. Violence never solved anything." Morgana's twitching had gotten out of control, and he couldn't contain his grin.

"Once I'm done with you," she continued, "I'm going to find that little boy you're so fond of, and I'm going to kill him."

Morgana's words cast a shadow over Leo's face, and he knew it was time to stop talking. "You'll not lay a hand on him," he vowed, readying his mystical energies. It was then that he noticed the air behind Morgana begin to ripple. At first he thought it was his imagination, but when the rippling grew larger, there was no doubt something unusual was happening.

The Templar Queen, blissfully unaware of the strange phenomenon occurring behind her, cackled and proceeded with berating Leo. "And tell me…"

While Morgana spoke, the rippling in the air became a swirling oval shaped mass of black mist. The mist cleared, and Leo's whole body froze as he stared into what could only be described as an oval shaped television. On the screen, he could see an enormous demon peering back at him with the most terrifying expression he'd ever seen. The demon wore a shabby brown cloak, was bare footed and had a large black crow perched on his shoulder. Everything from the blade grasped in his right hand, to the black, red flecked eyes, reminded him of Lucas. It could have been Lucas, he thought, only there were two stark differences. The first was the height and build; this demon was far bigger.

The second was the aura. Even in his demon form, and when acting evil for training purposes, Lucas never 'felt' evil. The creature he was looking at was evil in its purest form. As their eyes met, he knew this was Baal.

"…who's going to stop me?"

As Morgana finished her question, oblivious to the monstrous terror behind her, Baal stepped through the screen and into the alcove. Leo was too stunned to do anything other than watch as Baal thrust his blade through Morgana's armour and into her back. The only noise she made was a gasp, and the only movement was that of her head which she lowered to look at the huge blade poking out of her stomach. Baal rested his chin on Morgana's shoulder, turned his black, cracked lips to her ear and gave her an answer to the question she'd posed to Leo.

"That would be me."

Chapter 24
Baal

When Baal spoke, Leo had the overpowering urge to rip his own ears off. His spine tingled unpleasantly, and the hairs on his arms stood on end. The voice was insidious, designed solely to eradicate any essence of goodness that existed in the world. Lucas' demonic tones were angelic in comparison. Despite its wickedness, Baal's voice was deeply attractive, hypnotic, and enticing.

Leo forced his eyes away from the pure demon and settled them on Morgana who was clutching the end of Baal's blade, whimpering and petrified.

Baal, still resting his chin upon her shoulder, smiled broadly. Leo cringed at the mouthful of twisted teeth, all pointed and lethal looking.

"You want to kill my poor, defenceless little Power," Baal crooned in Morgana's ear. He tutted twice, turning his hand slightly so the blade bit into even more of her flesh. "You Templars should have learned by now that you shouldn't touch things that aren't yours, especially when those things belong to me."

The demon retracted his blade with such speed that Leo never saw it leave Morgana's stomach. Blood gushed through her fingers as she desperately pressed her hands against her wound in order to stem the crimson flow. The battle armour she wore prevented her from getting to the wound, and she fell to her knees, her eyes locked on Leo's.

"Help…me," she pleaded, her voice trembling and weak.

Baal, taking hold of one of the horns on Morgana's golden helm, lifted his demonic blade into the air and decapitated her with one swift swing. The crow that was perched so contentedly on the demon's shoulder began to hop up and down, squawking relentlessly at the sight of the headless corpse. Finally, Baal settled his foul gaze upon Leo.

"Good evening," he said pleasantly, tossing Morgana's head behind him. It sailed through the portal and bounced against a stone floor before eventually coming to rest at the foot of a giant throne.

The throne, to Leo's disgust, had been constructed entirely from human bones and had two magnificent wings, gigantic in size and gloriously white in colour, attached to the sides. He instantly knew who the wings belonged to. Once he'd gotten over the initial shock of the death chair, Leo noticed that it was sitting upon a large platform of grey rock with nothing but blackness surrounding it.

He opened his mouth to speak but was distracted by something moving from inside the portal. A bald hulking demon with huge black feathered wings stepped through the mystical gateway and joined them in the alcove wearing only a pair of black jeans. Every muscle in his veiny body rippled as he stalked to Baal's side, his black eyes roaming across Leo like he was something tasty. It took Leo a minute to notice that a red headed woman had also come through the portal. She was tiny in comparison to Baal and the other demonic brute, but she carried herself as if she were superior to everything and everyone around her. Although she wasn't in demon form she wore demonic energy like it was a cloak, shamelessly flaunting her feral nature in a scarlet coloured backless dress. Her red stiletto heels clicked noisily against the stone floor of the Haven alcove as she too came to stand at Baal's side. Despite being mortally terrified, Leo did wonder why she had opted for her human visage when her demon counterparts had their game faces on. The wonder of such things quickly disappeared when Baal turned his head and gazed almost lovingly into the eyes of the crow sitting on his shoulder.

The demon raised his hand, and the big black bird hopped onto it. "My beautiful Izeel," Baal murmured, planting soft kisses on the bird's breast. "Go and find it for me."

The crow cawed twice before spreading its wings and taking off into the air, swooping at Leo on its way past. Leo knew what the crow was going to search for, or rather, who.

"Forgive us for being rude and not introducing ourselves," Baal said with a little bow of his head. "We're several centuries behind schedule, but who's counting?" The smile he gave Leo was plagued with ominous intent.

"Father, this one reeks of—"

Baal raised his hand, and the bald headed demon fell silent immediately. "I know, Motaris," he responded softly. "I know."

Leo wanted to run, but he knew he'd be dead long before he took a single step. Various plans of action were running through his head when all of a sudden Baal was no longer standing in front of him.

"So," the demon whispered in Leo's ear, his voice sweet poison.

Leo gasped, and his whole body shuddered at the close proximity of the pure demon. He was smothered by a coldness unlike anything he'd ever felt before, and it chilled him all the way to his soul.

"I believe you know my son," Baal said, placing his hand delicately around Leo's neck.

When he felt the frozen hand of the demon, he trembled and let out a terrified whimper. Lucas had been right about pure demons; their energy and power were in a completely different league, and even after four weeks of intensive training, he felt completely out of his depth.

"Ssshhh, it's okay, it's okay," Baal said soothingly.

Leo took a deep breath when Baal's other arm snaked around his waist, pulling him closer. He shuddered as he felt long twisted nails trailing back and forth across his neck.

"There we go, nice and relaxed. Now, I wonder if you could tell me something—"

"Just kill him already and be done with it!" Motaris yelled impatiently, glaring at Leo.

"SILENCE YOU IMBECILE!"

The walls of the alcove quaked and quivered at Baal's outburst, and Leo almost lost control of his bladder. The bald demon followed his master's orders and fell silent.

"Motaris, you made me frighten our new friend." Baal's tone was sickly sweet. "That won't do at all. I'm so very sorry, sometimes Motaris forgets himself. I hope you can forgive me."

"Yes, totally forgiven," Leo croaked immediately, hoping to appease the demon.

"How very kind of you," Baal said with a grin, turning Leo's chin so he could peer down into his eyes. "Now, tell me something. How do you know my Lucas?"

Leo was thrown by the question. He was expecting Baal to ask after Daniel. As he stared into the abyss that was Baal's eyes, he opted for honesty. "We're just good friends."

The demonic grin was replaced by a menacing expression. "*Just* good friends?"

Leo nodded.

"Is that so? Well, I have it on good authority that you two are something much more than friends, Leo Alexander."

"I don't know what you're—"

"His scent is all over you," Baal hissed. "I can smell it. You're his."

Leo swallowed the lump that had formed at the back of his throat when he felt Baal's hand dropping to his chest. It slithered across his body and came to rest above his heart. The demon closed his eyes, deep concentration etched upon his face.

"Ah!" Baal exclaimed after moments of quiet contemplation, his dark eyes snapping open. "There...there it is. Oh my..."

"What is it, master?"

Leo glanced at the female demon who had spoken for the first time. She stood with her hands on her hips, head held high.

"Natalya, come!" Baal clicked his fingers, and the red head was over in an instant. "Read him," he ordered, his face a picture of disbelief.

"As you wish, master." Natalya placed her hands on the sides of Leo's head, her violet eyes honing in on his.

"What are you—" he started to say but was promptly stopped when a bright violet light blinded him.

A high pitched buzzing filled his ears as moving images flashed in his mind's eye. It soon dawned on him that the images were actually a movie of his most recent memories. Fyrish, the Cathedral, Daniel, Cornelius, Ela, Wendy; every memory he had was there for her to view and feel. As she continued to invade his mind, she finally found what she was looking for: Lucas. Natalya became privy to it all, shamelessly watching the love making scenes with particular interest. There was another flash of violet light, and he found himself back in the alcove. Natalya was staring at him with the same expression of disbelief that Baal wore.

"I...it's not possible. This has never happened before," she said, pulling her hands away from Leo and shaking her head slowly from side to side as if it would somehow change whatever truth she'd discovered.

"Does he know what Lucas is?" Baal demanded.

Natalya slowly turned her head to look at her master. "Yes. Even after he found out what Lucas was...he still...it made him love Lucas more," she said, moving to Baal's side. "They've even—"

"I know what they've done! Izeel told me everything. Lucas was purely acting out of lust and his natural animalistic desires. It wasn't anything other than lust. Lucas is a pure demon, and we are not made to be loved, especially by humans."

Natalya looked into Baal's eyes before setting her gaze upon Leo. "I know master, but this one loves Lucas with everything he has and everything he is. And from what I witnessed moments ago, it's clear that Lucas… he…"

"What? What about Lucas? Speak, Natalya!"

"Lucas loves this human in return."

For a long time, nobody moved. An icy breeze blew in from the door leading to the courtyard and pulled Leo's attention away from the demons for just a second. He could hear shouts, cries, and the occasional explosion which let him know the fight was still going on outside. Evidently, so could Baal. The monstrous beast closed his eyes and inhaled the air deeply.

"Death…it's everywhere. The smell of bodies already starting to decay, the sound of souls being dragged into hell…all so nourishing." He appeared to bask in this knowledge before his eyelids shot up to expose a bloodthirsty hunger in his eyes. "Natalya, Motaris—it's time."

Motaris moved towards his father, and Leo's whole body tightened immediately.

"Oh, don't worry my dear boy, they aren't going to kill you," Baal reassured him in a friendly manner as his two minions flanked him, one on either side. "That pleasure will be mine."

"Father, your orders?" Motaris asked.

Baal's head swivelled around so he could look into Motaris' equally black eyes. He took his son's hands and squeezed them tenderly, his expression one of childish glee and anticipation. "Kill them, my son! Kill them all."

"It will be my pleasure," Motaris replied.

Just as Motaris finished speaking, movement from inside the portal caught Leo's eye. Carried on wings that were black and silent like the darkest of nights, five demons emerged from the shadows that shrouded the platform of rock, landing side by side in perfect sync at the edge of the portal. The gruesome five were followed by another group, and then another. The demons kept coming in hordes of five until there were seven rows of them standing at attention and staring through the portal.

Baal raised his hand in the air, sending the demons into a frenzy. They growled, snarled and pawed at the ground with their dirty unkempt human like feet. Baal dropped his hand, and the demons exploded through their master's portal.

"Holy fuck," Leo said disbelievingly, his voice no more than a whisper.

"Fly, my children! Fly!" Baal crowed, clapping his hands and stamping in ecstasy as they flew overhead. "Make Daddy proud!"

Leo covered his face and cowered as thirty five pairs of black wings rushed past him and swept with terrible grace into the courtyard. Motaris and Natalya sprouted similar black wings and leapt into the air behind the small army of demons. The tormented screams came instantly.

It was then that Baal lifted his blade and pointed it at Leo. "What. Are. You?" He stabbed the air on every word. "You don't feel any different to other humans…but you can't be…human." The demon made a face after saying the word 'human' like it left a bad taste in his mouth.

Leo, after realising that the only way to stay alive was to keep Baal talking, found his voice. "I'm only human," he said with a little shrug.

"I don't believe you!" Baal growled, blade pointing menacingly. "Pure demons are not capable of love. You did something to him. A spell! It has to be a spell because my son would never fall in love with a human, especially one that's so displeasing to the eye!"

Despite the fact his fear, up until this point, had compelled him to do nothing except tremble and cower before Baal, the demon's words more than stung. It was like Baal had come right up and slapped him across the face, and Leo didn't appreciate it one tiny bit. "Excuse me?" he said, moving his hands to his hips. "I'm displeasing to the eye? Do you own a mirror?"

Baal's eyes lit up, and he looked thoroughly amused. "I shall teach you some manners in due course, but first I would like to point something out to you," the demon said, lowering his blade to the ground and scraping it against the stone floor. "My son Lucas, pure demon and grandson of Lucifer, does not love any human, of that I'm certain."

Leo could sense his time was running out, so he knew he had to ready his divine magic while the demon talked. He'd be lucky to get one shot at Baal, and it would have to be one hell of a shot. "You wouldn't know love if it smacked you on your pasty leather face," he said acidly. The demon's eyes, if it were possible, darkened even more.

'Oh yeah, that's a fucking marvellous idea, isn't it?' his inner voice ranted, *'Play Russian roulette with your life by angering the psychotic, terrifyingly powerful, and human hating pure demon.'*

"This is like déjà vu," Baal continued as if Leo hadn't spoken. "I distinctly remember telling Lucas the exact same thing several hundred years ago. Funny how everything comes full circle, isn't it?" The demon leant on the hilt of his blade and engaged Leo as if they were old friends rather than bitter enemies. "Some millennia ago, Lucas had this…delusion, if you will, that the Lord was going to accept him back into heaven and offer His unconditional love if he would betray me, his own father. Now, I ask you, what kind of benevolent God would ask such a thing? Oh, I know, it was probably the same benevolent God who asked Abraham to sacrifice his only son." Baal laughed coldly and shook his head. "But I'm digressing, aren't I? Anyway, I obviously found out what Lucas was up to and allowed him to carry on acting the double agent until the day he confessed his treachery to me. As you can imagine, I was heartbroken….and I was hurt. And when I hurt, my dear boy, *I* hurt. I took his wings."

The picture of the horrific scars on Lucas' back flashed in Leo's mind. "I know it was you," he stated, his words dripping with hate and accusation. "You gave him those scars."

"The first time he lost his wings was to that sanctimonious, self-righteous, holier than thou imbecile, Archangel Michael. Angelic magic, of course, made it very painless. But when he stood before me boasting about his new found love for God and flashing his brand new white feathered wings—" Baal paused, took a breath and composed himself. "I guess you could say I was upset."

"What kind of father could do that to their own—"

"A father who takes betrayal very personally!" Baal roared, the red flecks in his eyes pulsating wildly. "And I, Baal, Lord of the Eastern dominions of Hell, and commander of sixty six legions of demons, ripped that little traitor's wings off with my bare hands, and I took euphoric pleasure in doing so! As you can see, they now make an excellent addition to my throne."

"You bastard!" Leo shouted as red hot rage possessed him. He launched the fireball before he knew what he was doing, but Baal, using his blade as a shield, deflected it with ease.

The demon's evil laugh rampaged through the alcove and out into the courtyard as he danced on the spot, clapping his hands and stamping once again. "You're a feisty one! I love it! But we're not going yet! I haven't finished making my point."

"Could you make it sometime today please?" Leo said sharply.

"No need for rudeness!" Baal retorted with his hands on his hips and leaning forward like a parent scolding a naughty child. "I want you to know all the details so you can hate Lucas just as much as I do." He went back to leaning on the hilt of his blade as he spoke. "Like I was saying, I punished him like any responsible and doting father would do, and he loved every moment of it. You see, I understand Lucas and why he betrayed me. He seeks redemption for his...colourful past. He likes pain. It appeases some of the guilt he feels for the appalling atrocities he carried out in the name of his father and his grandfather."

Leo would have been lying if he said he wasn't intrigued. The mystical energies he'd conjured were at full strength; he could feel their potency as they bubbled under his skin. He was ready to fight for his life, but his curiosity about Lucas' past got the better of him, so he kept his magic at bay and listened.

"I assume you know about the visions."

Leo gave a nod.

"I bet he never told you the truth about the very special vision he had, did he?" Baal sneered scathingly. "Of course he never. It's the source of the great shame and self-loathing he feels. It would change the way you Elect fools look at him if you knew the sordid truth."

"I highly doubt that, but do go on," Leo said snidely.

"Lucas was the one who told Lucifer and me about the Power's existence. The other three Archangels kept Lucifer in the dark as far as the Power was concerned because he was already showing signs of his true nature. They distrusted him immensely. But then something truly wonderful happened. Lucas had a crystal clear vision of this beautiful creative force that would finally rid us higher beings of God's unholy creation—the creation of mankind. And guess what? He couldn't wait to tell his grandfather."

Leo suddenly felt sick as he grasped the full and terrible meaning of Baal's words.

"And when the Power was hidden by the cheap magic tricks of your order, Lucas was the one who discovered what the sneaky Grandmaster had accomplished. It came to him in a vision, and he wasted no time in letting the whole demon world know about it. So you see, this business with the Power is technically all his fault. He was the one who sold his soul to the Devil—not once but twice—and he is the sole reason this war started in the first place. And here comes the point."

Baal straightened up to his full height, lifting the blade off the ground and letting it rest against his leg. "That little boy, the one you love and adore more than anything else in this world, is going to die a most horrid and painful death at my hand. When I have that magnificent Power, I'm going to suck this miserable and disgusting world into oblivion, and it's all Lucas' fault."

In Leo's mind, a fog had lifted. Everything made perfect sense as far as Lucas' issues were concerned, and Leo got it. All those times he felt the anger, the disappointment, the guilt and the shame radiating off Lucas, and now he finally understood why.

Baal took three gigantic strides and put his face right up to Leo's, his wide evil smile stretching from ear to ear. "You still think Lucas loves you? If he didn't have you and the Elect to help him stop this war, could he really find redemption? He's using you to end this war. You're his ticket back home. He doesn't love you, and he never has. He loves what you can do for him."

"That's not true," Leo whispered, tears forming in his eyes.

"You know I'm right, sweet boy. And here is a final revelation for you, a crucial one that I feel I have to impart before I cut you into teeny tiny pieces. If Lucas loved you like you think he does, where is he now? Hmmm? Pure demons don't love anything but themselves, and he's no different. Did it ever occur to you that he's seen these events unfolding in a vision and has deserted you? That perhaps he saw this happening and has left you here to die? Think about that while you're shedding your last tears of sorrow and grief."

Baal whipped a skeletal fist towards him with the speed of an angry striking viper. There was nothing but shock in the demon's face when Leo's strong hand clamped over his fist and halted it mid-flow.

The emotions coursing through him were raw and undiluted, but they weren't sorrow and grief like Baal had assumed. His tears were for the overwhelming love, compassion and pride he was feeling for his lover. Lucas had committed the worst crimes in the history of the world yet was doing everything in his power to atone despite the fact the odds of him finding any kind of peace were stacked against him. He'd already been on the gruelling journey of redemption for such a long time and was still fighting, still hopeful in trying to right his wrongs. Lucas, the pure demon, had more humanity inside of him than most humans, and it was Leo who had unlocked it. Those humbling and empowering feelings he'd experienced when Lucas had confessed he'd been waiting for him for over four millennia surged through every fibre of his being, making him feel connected to the universe. Even in the desperately hopeless and terrifying situation he was in, he heard the infinite divine whisper to him, echoing the words *It* had spoken to him once before.

'This, Leo Alexander, is what I planned for you.'

It made him feel invincible, and when he caught Baal's fist, he knew the demon didn't stand a chance. "Maybe you can think about this while I'm kicking your demonic ass all the way back to hell," he said fearlessly, staring into Baal's eyes with a burning intensity that confounded the demon. He steadily increased his grip on the demon's fist. "You're wrong. Lucas loves me, and I love him, so keep your poisonous mouth shut about things you can't even begin to comprehend." He felt the bones in Baal's hand start to shatter under his iron grip. The demon tried to break free, but Leo was too strong. "And here is a final revelation for you, a crucial one that I feel I have to impart before I blast you into teeny tiny little pieces. You were right. I'm not *just* a human. I'm *Elected*, you fucking moron!"

Leo's eyeballs ignited into dazzling emerald flames as he released Baal's fist and slammed both of his hands, palms first, into the demon's chest. A radiant green light burst from his hands, and a deafening explosion rocked the walls and foundations of the alcove. Baal was blown backwards through his own portal where he hurtled, unconscious, into his prized ivory throne, smashing it into smithereens as he crashed through it before disappearing over the edge of the platform.

As Leo watched Baal being consumed by the monstrous jaws of darkness, a strong hand grabbed his shoulder, spun him around and pulled him into a tight hug. His face was pressed against bare flesh, and his favourite musky scent invaded his sense of smell.

"I thought they'd killed you!" Lucas' voice was hoarse.

Leo let himself get lost in the hug. "I'm fine, I'm okay."

"Where's Baal?" Lucas asked, holding Leo at arm's length and inspecting every inch of him. "Did he hurt you? What did he say? Do you know where Daniel is? Where's Morgana? Did that bastard hurt you?"

Leo couldn't help but laugh. He pressed his index finger to Lucas' soft supple lips. "Hey, I thought I was the one who asked all the questions?"

"I was worried," Lucas said with a shrug, smiling coyly and gently pulling Leo's finger away from his mouth after kissing it tenderly. "When I saw the demons flying out of the Haven door, I thought the worst."

"I'm fine, Luc, don't worry," Leo said reassuringly.

"Luc?"

"Oh, you don't like that?"

Lucas looked at him thoughtfully. "Luc sounds good, baby," he replied with a grin before pulling Leo into a kiss. "Fuck," Lucas cursed. He pulled back quickly. "I'm sorry."

"For what?"

"I'm still in demon mode, and I know you don't like—"

"Shhh," Leo interrupted, smiling and shaking his head lightly. "I don't care."

The demon raised his eyebrows, an expression of both surprise and adoration on his face. "I fucking love you." Lucas shifted into a more human appearance before kissing Leo. "Okay, so seriously. Where's Baal?" he asked after pulling back.

"Oh, yeah…Baal. I blasted him through there," Leo replied, pointing to the portal. "He went over the edge, so I don't think we'll be seeing him anytime soon."

"Don't be so sure," Lucas said, releasing Leo and striding over to the portal. "He'll be back soon."

"Thanks for killing my buzz," Leo said drily.

Lucas knelt down on one knee and held out his arms, his palms facing the gateway. The demon started to draw his hands together but did so at a painfully slow speed. It was as if a strong force was living between his hands and was preventing him from closing them. However strong the force was, Lucas battled on and was soon more than halfway to making his hands meet.

"What are you doing?"

"I'm…trying…to close…portal," Lucas said through gritted teeth.

Leo's eyes were immediately drawn to the portal and sure enough, it had gotten smaller.

"It's working! Keep going."

With every muscle in his upper body vibrating and rippling with the effort, Lucas finally managed to clasp his hands together before falling onto all fours. Leo ran over and knelt beside him, placing a hand on his back and rubbing gently.

"So that's how you got into my flat before."

"Yeah," Lucas said after catching his breath. "A gift I inherited from my dad. I rarely use it. It hurts like hell, and it completely wipes me out for like five minutes after. I'm pretty much useless until I've recovered."

"I can see that," Leo said, helping Lucas to the nearest wall and propping him against it. "Maybe we should save this gift for special occasions?"

"Great idea. We'll wait here for a few more minutes until my strength comes back."

"Wait a second, Luc…you said the angels only got one gift. How come yours is plural?"

Lucas grinned. "I'm special, remember?"

"Lucas," Leo said, giving him a stern look.

"Hey, what happened to Luc?"

"I'll save it for those rare moments when I'm not mad at you."

"No worries, I'll remember that," Lucas said, giving a little chuckle before turning serious. "I don't know why I got two. All I know is I got the portal thing from my dad and the visions from my mom. My dad had two gifts too, must be a male thing passed down through his line."

"What else can he do?"

"Sounds ridiculously shit, but he can enchant animals on the earth. He has a fondness for ravens and crows. He can communicate with them, see through their eyes, that kind of thing."

Leo's face fell.

"What?"

"Baal had a crow! He sent it to look for Daniel."

"Izeel! Someone should wring his scrawny little neck." Lucas threw an arm around Leo's shoulder. "Help me up."

Leo complied instantly and got the demon to his feet. He attempted to move forward, but Lucas stayed put.

"Almost there, another minute."

"We might not have a minute," Leo said, turning on his heel while Lucas grabbed his arm. It wasn't with his usual strength, but it was enough to stop Leo.

"No!" the demon said firmly. "You're not going without me. It's a bloodbath out there, and you don't even know where Daniel is."

"I have to!" Leo exclaimed, his eyes wide and fearful. "If that bird finds Daniel, Baal is only a portal away from starting the apocalypse."

"Tune in…just like you did in your apartment, with the football stadium."

"There's no time for that," Leo protested.

"We have time, trust me—" Lucas suddenly ceased up and slid down the wall. He clutched at his head, and his glowing cerulean eyes moved rapidly from side to side.

"Lucas!" Leo was on his knees, gripping him by the shoulders. "What is it?"

"A vision," he gasped. "It's Daniel."

Leo's heart juddered.

"He's alive...I see him. He's fighting off Izeel!"

"Where?"

"In the...someone's helping him...I can't see who."

"Where is he? Is this happening now?"

"Yeah, happening now...They've caught Izeel...they're putting him in a metal container...no, wait! It's the..." Lucas snorted with laughter. "Daniel's just stuffed Izeel into the potato peeler and switched it on." Lucas made a face. "Man, that's not pretty!"

"Lucas, who's with him? Is it Mrs Ellen?"

Lucas' eyes swivelled around in their sockets while he watched his vision unfold. "I can't see yet. It's from Daniel's perspective, he's looking at his handiwork. Whoever is with him is filling up the fry...sorry, the chip barrel, with water from the hose. Come on, little man, lift your head...let me see who's helping you. It's Cornelius!"

Leo's body sagged with relief. "We need to help them. Let's go!" Leo tugged on Lucas' arm while casting an anxious glance at the door to the courtyard.

"Hang on, I can't just shut the visions off. I have to let them run their course. It's okay, Cornelius has bought us some time. I think he told Daniel to shut off the hose."

Leo grew agitated, a horrible feeing rising from the pits of his stomach. "What's he doing with the hose?"

"I told you, he's filling the chip barrel with water. Daniel has just shut the hose off and is now peeking into the potato peeler...I don't know what they're planning. Maybe it's for the bird?"

"What's Cornelius wasting time with that for?" Leo exploded. "The bird has been shredded for fuck sake! He needs to get Daniel as far away from here as possible!"

"Oh."

"Oh?" Leo repeated, verging on hysterical. "What is it?"

Lucas' eyes snapped sharply back into focus and went straight to Leo's, his expression one of pure and utter horror. The instant their eyes connected, Leo knew.

"The water...it's not for Izeel," Lucas said, a shadow falling over his face. "It's for Daniel."

Chapter 25
Prophecy Fulfilled

'And you will fail to protect it in its current guise…He will foresee it…He can't stop what he did not create, Leo…His gift is his curse.'

Noah's words of warning came flooding back to Leo, and the truth hit him like it was a speeding double decker bus. They were going to lose Daniel. Lucas began climbing to his feet, but Leo wasn't waiting.

"Leo!" Lucas bellowed.

Leo took a single step out into the courtyard but was hauled back inside the alcove just as an arrow struck the spot where his foot had been. "Get off me!" he yelled while trying to shrug Lucas off. "I have to get to him!"

"You'll be no use to him if you get yourself killed," Lucas shouted back furiously and spun Leo around to face him. "You were nearly skewered! Calm the fuck down, and listen to me. You're gonna get onto my back. I'll take us to the kitchen. There's a gauntlet of Templars and demons out there, and I need you to keep them off us while I concentrate on running. Got it?"

Leo nodded.

"Good," Lucas said, turning abruptly and exposing his bare back for Leo to mount.

The second he was securely fastened to Lucas, the demon bolted into the courtyard. Leo wished he could have closed his eyes as Lucas sped through the carnage, but he knew he couldn't. Dead bodies; Elected, Templar and demon, lay everywhere and white coloured snow was sparse. The ground had become a shocking carpet of scarlet slush with a collection of severed limbs, decapitated heads, and entrails littering the once beautiful courtyard. If his heart hadn't been pumping the adrenaline through his body so fast, and if he hadn't been so fearful for Daniel's life, he'd have probably gagged at the sight and smell.

As Lucas raced through the courtyard, Leo was able to summon the elements to protect them both from the demons. He discovered that he didn't have to watch out for any Templar attacks because the demon enemies posed a far bigger threat to the zealots than he did. Templar and Elect were fighting side by side to overcome a more fearsome and dangerous adversary.

The double doors leading into the Cathedral were drawing closer and closer. "Almost there," Leo said, squeezing Lucas' shoulders to encourage him.

They were metres away from the door when the tackle came. Lucas took the brunt of the attack and hit the ground hard while Leo rolled off the demon and onto his feet instantly. He turned his head sharply to the double doors where the mountainous Motaris stood, smiling unpleasantly and blocking the way in. He had a huge double headed axe in one hand and a claymore to rival Excalibur in the other.

"Deceiver!" Motaris sneered, his eyes wild and animated. "You came to join the party."

"Motaris," Lucas replied, getting to his feet and pulling his samurai style blade out of the air. "It's been awhile, brother."

"You're no brother of mine!" the gigantic demon spat. "Weak, pathetic, disloyal traitor. Look at how low you've fallen. Helping the enemy and fucking mortal men at the same time. You disgust me!"

"Hey, bruiser! Get out of the fucking way!" Leo snapped, his eyes full of emerald fire.

Motaris gave Leo an ugly grin. "Why don't you make me with your magic, you little fairy."

"Gladly!" Leo fired back, launching a flurry of fireballs.

As Motaris deflected the fireballs, Lucas sprang into action and charged at his brother. Leo was impressed when Lucas leapt ten feet into the air. He was stunned, however, when Lucas planted both feet firmly into the chest of Motaris and dropkicked him not only through the double doors, but through the thick stone wall of the corridor that lay beyond. Lucas landed gracefully and turned to Leo.

"He'll follow us to Daniel. I'll take care of him."

Leo didn't want to leave Lucas alone to fight Motaris, but he had no choice. "Be careful."

"You too. Go get the little man," Lucas replied, before disappearing into the thick cloud of dust that had formed as a result of the wall's decimation.

Leo didn't hesitate and burst into a sprint, zipping through the double doors and into the corridor. From beyond the dust cloud and wall debris, he could hear the clash of swords and axes and Motaris' roars of fury.

He motored through the corridors, his mind going full throttle. What was Cornelius playing at? Had the old man been a double agent for the Templars all along? Or was he merely panicking at the fact Baal was now free and forsaking his sacred duty as protector of the Power? It didn't matter, he would make Cornelius pay. His thoughts were dark with vengeance as he ran; his hammering heart stone cold. With various ideas of revenge circulating wildly in his head, his brain was a second too late to process the blur of red that whizzed overhead. In an instant, he was staring into the violet eyes of Natalya who caught him by the throat with one hand and brought his journey to a rapid halt.

"Sweetie, what's your hurry?" Natalya asked, lifting Leo up by the neck. "Don't you want to have a little chat? You know—just us girls." She gave Leo a charming little smile before dumping him onto the hard floor. "You're obviously the girl out of you and Lucas. I mean, come on, he's so masculine and rugged compared to you."

"Fuck you!" Leo snapped while getting to his feet.

Natalya backhanded him into the corridor wall, sniggering as he hit it face first. "Excuse me? Rude!" she berated, the clicking of her heels echoing down the corridor. "I only wanted to have some girl talk about Lucas. I thought we could compare notes, if you know what I mean. He's a Trojan in the sack, isn't he?"

As the metallic taste of blood filled his mouth, Leo grasped the wall and used it to prop himself up. "I don't have time for girl talk," he replied, keeping his back to her and spitting out a mouthful of blood.

When the clacking of heels indicated Natalya was right behind him, he pushed off the wall and used the momentum to swing his hand through the air. Her nose shattered under his fist, and her piercing scream of fury filled the entire corridor. He quickly capitalised on his attack by throwing the demon backwards with a powerful energy blast that carried her to the blind corner of the corridor and pinned her against the wall. He cast another spell as he ran towards her, noting the expression of pure fury on her now demonic visage.

"Sorry, Lady in Red," he quipped, sending a large blue frosty orb in her direction. "You'll need to cool off before the girl talk commences." The orb struck her chest and expanded rapidly.

"You little sh—" Natalya screeched, her last word cut off when the orb began engulfing her in a blanket of transparent blue. In seconds, every last part of her, including her enormous wings, were covered. The blanket solidified and encased her in a prison of dense ice. He didn't stop to gloat and continued his sprint to the kitchen, trying not to think the worst as he rounded the blind corner and past Natalya's icy incarceration. He wasn't sure how long it would hold her, but it really didn't matter. Only Daniel mattered.

A beam of artificial light poured out of the gaping hole that used to house the kitchen door. His legs powered on as he got closer and closer to the light, never slowing despite their aching tiredness.

Diving into the kitchen, he immediately found Mrs Ellen's body lying on the floor. His insides froze. He knelt down and pressed his index and middle fingers to her neck. Underneath the aging skin, he felt the consistent beating of Mrs Ellen's pulse. Relieved, he stood up quickly and moved deeper into the room towards the partitioned section.

Four steps and he'd be there. He held his breath, listening carefully for any sounds. Three steps. He could see the top of the potato peeler, the machine that had ended Izeel's wretched life. He strained his ears. There was nothing at first, just the squeaking of his boots and the thumping of his heart, but then, as the chip barrel came into view, he heard the soft sloshing of water. Two more steps.

"Daniel?" he called out, his voice shallow and ghostlike. He took the final step.

The blood in his veins turned to ice when he saw Daniel slumped over the chip barrel with gnarled hands forcing his head under freezing cold water. Leo's bottom lip trembled when he looked at the boy's little arms hanging by his sides, limp and lifeless.

"Leo, I had no ch—" Cornelius began but was silenced when Leo's energy blast sent him spinning through the air.

Daniel's head slid out of the water as his body, no longer being held in place by Cornelius, slumped to the sodden floor. Leo was over at Daniel's side in a flash and fell to his knees, the glacial water soaking his jeans. He grabbed the boy by the shoulders and shook him aggressively.

"Daniel! It's Leo! Daniel, can you hear me?" He was trying his best to keep calm, but he couldn't stop the tremors of panic that rocked his body from head to toe. He put his ear to the boy's mouth and listened for signs of breathing. "No! Daniel! No!" he shouted as he started pumping the boy's chest. After a few pumps, he pinched the boy's nose and breathed into his mouth before continuing the chest compressions. "Come on, Daniel! Breathe!" Just as he brought his mouth to Daniel's for the second time, a flash of red lit up the kitchen, and he was hurled across the room. He landed heavily on his back and skidded along the oak flooring until friction ended his journey. By the time he'd clambered to his feet, Cornelius was standing over Daniel with red energy dancing in the palm of his hand.

"Get the fuck away from him!" Leo growled, sending another energy blast at the old man. Cornelius raised a hand and deflected the energy before sending a blast of his own. Leo dived out of the way, and it sailed past him, smashing into one of the kitchen units and reducing it to kindling.

"Leo, please," Cornelius begged. "It's the only way—"

"Bastard!" Leo roared as he hurled a fireball. His anger and rage aided the power of the fireball causing it to tear through the room, leaving a trail of orange and yellow in its wake. The fireball burnt a hole through the energy shield Cornelius had conjured before continuing on its trajectory and exploding against the old man's chest. Cornelius flew back into the potato peeler, knocked it over and sent the lid scuttling along the floor. A mass of black feathers and ear splitting caws came tumbling out of the machine. The injured crow fell silent when it realised it was free and shook its head a couple of times before taking in its surroundings. When its eyes fell on Daniel, it hopped up and down and started cawing incessantly.

Leo ran over and kicked the bird savagely. It hit the partition wall with a resounding thud before it dropped to the floor in a flapping frenzy of wings. The air above the crow became distorted; Baal was coming. Leo stumbled towards Daniel and fell to his knees once again. He brought his hands together and was about to press down on Daniel's chest when the boy's little body was unexpectedly hauled off the kitchen floor. Leo was pushed onto his backside and could do nothing but stare open mouthed at what was happening.

"It's begun!" Cornelius gasped from beside the chip machine.

Leo shuffled backwards as Daniel, still unconscious and unbreathing, was suspended in mid-air by an unseen force while his aura radiated a pure white light. He slowly stood up, never once taking his eyes off Daniel despite being aware that Baal's portal was almost fully formed.

"What's happening?" Leo asked, his voice hoarse from all his shouting.

"It's the Power," the old man wheezed as he slumped against the chip machine. "Three...minutes until...bind itself to new...soul."

From Daniel's solar plexus, a sphere of dazzling golden light emerged and floated serenely above him, spinning slowly and reminding Leo of the way the planets rotated silently and majestically through space. The sphere was mesmerising in every way as it hovered and spun, casting many shades of golden light upon everything it touched. All of the negativity he'd been feeling melted away as he gazed into the core of the sphere. Perfect contentment swathed him in a shroud of gold; the warmth and splendour of the divine power caressed his face and made him forget everything.

"So...beautiful," Leo whispered, reaching out to it. "I can feel...the power of God...I hear...the universe." His fingers were inches away from touching the Power when a hand of iron gripped his wrist.

"I don't think so," Baal said, his grin wide and terrifying. "That shiny bundle of creation belongs to me."

Before Leo could think about casting a spell, Baal twisted his wrist and snapped it like a twig. His stomach gave a great lurch as his pain receptors went into overdrive. Baal's other hand gripped him by the throat and picked him up off the ground.

"I'd kill you right here, right now, but I don't want you to miss my end of the world party," the demon chuckled.

Leo braced himself as he was tossed like a ragdoll towards one of Mrs Ellen's cabinets. There wasn't a plate, saucer or cup left in one piece when he picked his battered body out of the wreckage. With his broken wrist clutched to his chest, he gritted his teeth and charged at Baal who had just extended a veiny hand in the direction of the golden sphere. Summoning every last ounce of strength in his mind, body and soul, he tore across the kitchen. Sparks, which were electric blue in colour, crackled noisily in the palm of his good hand. When he was close enough, he jumped into the air and latched onto Baal's back by wrapping his legs around the demon's waist. His lungs burned in protest as he let out a primal scream before slamming his lightning enchanted hand down on Baal's neck and digging his fingers into papery skin.

The kitchen was filled with a spectacular strobe light effect as vast levels of volts surged through Baal causing him to fall down onto a trembling knee. Just when he thought he'd bested the demon, he felt every muscle in Baal's body coil beneath him and sensed whatever was about to happen was going to hurt a lot.

With a hellish howl, Baal sprang off the floor. Leo's vision blurred as he was crushed between the demon and the plasterboard ceiling, the latter crumbling and falling about him in big chunks. He began his descent, no longer stuck to Baal, and landed hard on the soaking wet floor. A fresh wave of pain shot across his broken wrist causing him to grit his teeth. He used his healthy hand to push himself up onto all fours, but he didn't see the papery white foot that sailed into his ribs, shattering several of them at once, before it was far too late. The force of the kick sent him on a vertical path back up to the ceiling where he displaced some more plaster before hurtling to the ground again.

"Pathetic!" Baal hissed. "And to think my Lucas has been fornicating with you!"

A hot sticky glob of demon saliva hit Leo's face as he lay writhing on the ground, retching up blood.

"Weak little fool! I'm going to enjoy the rest of eternity torturing you."

Leo's consciousness was desperately trying to slip away, but he was focused on fighting off the darkness that was closing in on him. He shook his head vigorously and fought every ache and pain as he struggled to his feet. Through hazy eyes, he could make out Baal's sizeable frame leering over the brightly shining Power and Daniel's floating body. For the second time, Baal reached out.

"Get…the fuck…away from him."

The demon's hand stopped instantly. "You're determination is admirable yet annoying," he said, trying to hide the disbelief in his voice that Leo was still standing. "I wanted to torture you at my apocalypse party, but it seems you're in a hurry to die. Any last words?"

Leo cleared his throat and tried to stand as tall as he could. "Fuck y—"

A scarlet red whip was wrapped around his neck before he could finish his sentence. Baal pulled on the whip, and Leo sank to his knees, fighting for precious oxygen and trying to squeeze his fingers between his throat and the rope. He dug his feet into the smooth wooden floor, but his wet boots prevented him from getting any grip. It wasn't long until he was kneeling before Baal who had pulled his deadly looking blade from the ether with his whip free hand. His gaze darted to Cornelius who had remained huddled behind the chip cutter for the entire time. Their eyes met, and he silently pleaded with the old man for help. Cornelius looked away.

"The problem with you Elect filth," Baal sneered, resting the sharp tip of his blade between Leo's eyes, "Is that you never know when to give up. In the end, it's what always gets you killed."

Leo stared straight into Baal's eyes as the demon retracted his arm and drew his demonic blade backwards. The muscle in Baal's forearm twitched, and the blade came speeding towards him. A split second later, there was a scrape of metal, and Leo was blinking at the blade which had come to an unexpected halt inches from his face. When he realised he was still alive, he saw that a familiar samurai blade had prevented Baal's from stabbing his brains out.

"The problem with you, Father," Lucas said, his voice quaking with rage, "is that you talk too much. In the end, it's going to get you killed." Lucas swung his blade and cut the whip in half, freeing Leo from its strangling hold. He swung again and hit Baal's blade upwards. The demon's arm was knocked into the air, exposing his torso which Lucas kicked forcefully, sending him crashing through the partition walls.

"Lucas!" Leo croaked, using his remaining energy to stand up. "Get Daniel! He's not breathing!"

Upon hearing his name, Lucas turned to Leo which was the distraction Baal needed. The demon was behind Lucas in the blink of an eye.

"Lucas!" Leo screamed, but it was too late. Baal drove his blade through Lucas' back like it was butter. Lucas looked down at the silver blade poking through his chest before he lifted his head and set his cerulean eyes upon Leo.

"Take one last look, lover," Baal mocked, "and say goodbye to your—"

The demon stopped talking and promptly withdrew his blade from Lucas' back when rays of golden light erupted all around the room. Baal shoved Lucas to the floor before fixing his onyx eyes onto the Power.

"You're too late, Baal!" Cornelius yelled triumphantly from his position behind the chip cutter, "you're too late!"

"Noooooo!" Baal bellowed, launching himself at the golden ball of light, his flailing hands trying to ensnare it in their evil grasp.

There was a blinding light and a deafening explosion. For Leo, everything that followed seemed to happen in slow motion. The Power exploded in a spectacular display of gold and white. He saw the shockwaves rippling towards him and expanding as they drew closer. When they hit him, they dragged him off his feet and hauled him backwards. As he travelled through the air, he saw the shockwaves knock Baal into the nearest stone wall. He saw them knock the chip cutter over onto Cornelius, trapping the old man beneath it. He saw Lucas being swept across the floor and into Mrs Ellen's unconscious body. He saw Daniel fall to the ground, a soulless shell, a lifeless corpse.

And then, he saw only darkness.

Epilogue

The sterile smell of disinfectant irritated her nostrils as she walked through the narrow corridors of the hospital. Her Jimmy Choos clicked efficiently against the hard floor causing heads to turn and looks to linger. She despised this place. It was everything that she hated in the world: disease, desperation and death. She'd been coming here for ten months, but it hadn't gotten any easier. An obese nurse, who was pushing a patient in a wheelchair, approached. She stepped to the side so the nurse could pass easily, giving a small smile and a nod of her head.

"Thank you, love," the nurse said as she waddled past.

"No problem."

Reaching the end of the corridor, she turned left and stepped through the doors to the Intensive Care Unit. She stopped at the hand sanitising station and pumped a wad of disinfectant gel into her palm. She rubbed the cold gel into her hands as she walked, stealing glances into the wards that flitted past. It wasn't visiting hours, but that was okay; she had an insider. As she approached the reception desk of the ICU department, her husband was waiting.

"Hello there, Mrs Cameron," Alex beamed, looking over his glasses and studying his beautiful wife intently. "If it's possible, you get more beautiful every time I see you."

"Mr Cameron," she replied, a coy smile forming on her luscious red lips. "Ever the charmer."

"I love this coat on you," he said, pulling her into his arms and kissing her on the forehead. "The purple really suits you."

"It's my favourite winter coat, darling. I bring it out every year," she said, wrapping her arms around his muscular frame. "I can't believe Christmas is only a month away."

"I know. Our first one as a family."

His words made her feel warm inside. "I know, I'm so excited." The moment the words left her mouth, her stomach knotted, and she was overcome with a heavy burden of guilt.

"What? What is it sweetheart?" Alex asked, his voice full of concern.

She sighed. "How can I be excited when he's—"

"Hey, that's enough of that," Alex said firmly. "You're entitled to feel excited. You have to stop feeling guilty about living. You know he'd say the same. He wouldn't want you wallowing and wasting your life."

"I know, I just…I hate that I can't help him."

"You help him every day by coming here. Don't forget that."

"He has nobody."

"He has you."

She wanted to ask Alex if he'd ever wake up but there was no point. She knew the answer. He'd told her a million times that it was possible, but with each passing day it would be less likely. They fell into silence, wrapped up tightly in each other's embrace. Her head rested on his chest, and for a long time all she could hear was the sound of his heartbeat.

"I hate not knowing what happened to him," she said at last, lifting her head and gazing into her husband's warm brown eyes. "He just disappeared from the face of the earth. It's not like him. I mean, when he text to say he was sick and would be off work for a month, I knew there was something wrong. And then he wouldn't return my calls or reply to my messages."

"I know honey. It's the not knowing that drives people crazy."

"Lying on the Cathedral steps, an anonymous phone call to the ambulance services. I don't get it."

A pager on Alex's belt beeped, and an alarm sounded in the distance. "Shit!" he cursed, reading the pager display. "Emergency. I have to go. Let yourself into his room, babe. I'm finished in a few hours, so I'll be home to help with bedtime. I love you."

She closed her eyes as he kissed her quickly on the lips.

"Love you too," she replied, watching him run down the corridor and disappearing through a set of double doors. Her gaze lingered on the swinging doors momentarily, her thoughts buzzing with theories about what had happened to her best friend. Snapping out of her mini daze, she made her way to his room.

She closed the door after entering, her ears picking up on the various beeps and whirs of the machines attached to the man she'd come to visit. As she took her usual seat on the left hand side of the bed, she took his sallow and moist hand in hers and squeezed gently. The bruises and cuts had long gone from his face, and his wrist had healed as well as expected, but the purple circles beneath his eyes remained. His chest rose and fell in a steady rhythm as he lay in his coma. Every day she came, and every day her heart broke.

"Oh, Leo. What happened to you?" she whispered. "Why didn't you come to me for help?" Her eyes filled up, and she caught herself before the first tear fell. She wouldn't cry; she had to be strong.

"You've missed so much," she said, forcing her voice to sound normal. "My wedding was beautiful, you'd have loved it. There were hot guys in kilts, one of them single and very much gay. Your type too. And the honeymoon! My god! Venice for a fortnight. Stunning. You need to see it before it sinks." She laughed at her own joke. "And, of course, you've been an uncle for a month now. Remember when I got sick at the restaurant? Well, funny story! Turns out I was pregnant. Thank god I wasn't showing during my wedding. Could you imagine my mother? We had to take the dress out a little bit, but it was all good in the end. They're with my parents at the moment. Yeah, you heard me right the first time. *They.* Only I could end up falling pregnant accidentally and having twins! I can't wait for you to meet little Caleb and Lydia. Lydia is feisty like her mum, and Caleb smiles and giggles all the time. Both blonde hair and big bright blue eyes. You'll fall in love with both of them, and I know they're going to adore their uncle Leo. They're going to need him."

A fresh wave of emotion hit her, and she couldn't stem the flow of tears.

"*I* need you, Leo. You have to wake up," she sniffed. "I need you. Who else is going to tell me that I'm doing everything wrong?"

She closed her eyes and pressed his hand to her lips, kissing it tenderly before holding it against her forehead. She stayed like this for a long time, the only activity in the room coming from the machines that beeped and whirred noisily. Time flew by, and she eventually found herself glancing down at her watch. She was sad to see her time was up, but the twins had to be collected. With a heavy heart, she stood up and kissed him on the forehead and stroked his face gently.

"I'll see you tomorrow, my dear friend."

And with those words, she turned and walked out of the room.

Printed in Great Britain
by Amazon